Edward Everett Hale

Ups and Downs

An Eveyday Novel

Edward Everett Hale

Ups and Downs
An Eveyday Novel

ISBN/EAN: 9783744661263

Printed in Europe, USA, Canada, Australia, Japan

Cover: Foto ©Andreas Hilbeck / pixelio.de

More available books at **www.hansebooks.com**

An Every-Day Novel.

BY

EDWARD E. HALE,

AUTHOR OF "THE MAN WITHOUT A COUNTRY," "TEN TIMES ONE IS TEN," "HOW TO DO IT," ETC.

BOSTON:

ROBERTS BROTHERS.

1873.

STEREOTYPED BY JOHN C. REGAN,
19 SPRING LANE, BOSTON.

CONTENTS.

(iii)

UPS AND DOWNS.

CHAPTER I.

THE LAST DAY.

IT was the day before Commencement at Cambridge; and they sat together in Massachusetts Twenty-seven, the pleasantest room in the oldest building then inhabited by students in Harvard College.

It was the pleasantest room then. I think it probably is now. It overlooks both the " yard," that is the College yard, and the " Common," that is the Common of the town. Jasper had lived in Massachusetts Twenty-seven for two years. In summer he had a spy-glass hanging by a cord from the open window, ready to be trained on any passer, near or distant. He said, that, though a wayfarer were passing a quarter-mile away, a shrill shriek for an instant would make him turn an unsuspicious look directly to the spy-glass. Nay! It would make her turn, if the object of the reconnoissance were a she.

Here they sat in Massachusetts Twenty-seven. The work, and even the play, of the four college years were over, — the next day was to graduate them, to give them their guide in life ; and the next day they were to be men, to instruct and astonish a waiting world.

Preparatory to which they were sitting, most of them on the two hinder legs of their chairs, some of them smoking, and all of them occasionally sipping, — not

(1)

juleps, not cocktails, not smashes of any form, but iced lemonade. Such was the daily entertainment in Massachusetts Twenty-seven. Jasper was the great unrequited discoverer of the scientific fact, that, if the ice-man come late, you can keep ice for six hours in the pail in the wash-stand. For these six hours the hospitable entertainment above described endured for all comers, — generally indeed protracted till the six o'clock bell for evening prayers, which were then one of the institutions of the University.

—"The best education our country can afford!" said Horace, laughing.

"Top-notch and nothing less!"

"And, at the end of four years, we are here smoking and laughing, with no more idea what we will do with the best education our country can afford, than we had the day we first saw each other, in our freshman round jackets and swallow-tails."

"St. Leger, what have you done with that olive-green frock?"

"Don't laugh at the olive-green! I will wear it on the stage to-morrow if you make fun of it. How queer it was that day! Those two examination days were the hardest days I have ever spent here!"

"Of course they were. Is that perhaps one of the dodges of what they call Life, — that the gates are made narrow so that one shall be more at ease when he gets in?"

"I believe I knew the multiplication table better then than I do now. Jasper, what is nine times eight?"

"Dear old Watrous!" said Jasper, to whom the question recalled some sophomore story, "he is probably now on the topmast of his beloved 'Marie Antoinette,' and she is tossed on the top wave of the highest curved meridian of the Pacific Ocean; and Watrous, with his weak eyes, is looking for fish and cursed by an exuberant captain below, because he does not cry 'There she blows!'"

"Stuff!" said St. Leger, between the curls of his cigar. "Watrous is lying on the turf in the Friendly

Islands, and two lovely Tahitian girls are fanning him with palm-leaves."

"I hope so," said Horace; "but, in the Friendly Islands, they eat white people alive, and there are no Tahitian girls within two thousand miles."

"How can you be so statistical? Do you remember how we all deaded when George Simmons asked us whether London or Amsterdam were the more northerly?"

"I remember we deaded. I forget what he asked us. That is the curse of such questions. For, if he asked me to-day, I should not know any better than I knew then. Yet that afternoon I must have known, after he told me."

"And you are the man who has the best education his country can afford!"

"Yes: you see unfortunately my country could not afford a Malte-Brun professor of Geography. I know as much of Amsterdam — and as little — as I did the day I came here!"

"I mean to go to Amsterdam," said Jasper. "Dr. Palfrey told me he spent a day there. Then I shall know where it is. That is the only way. I don't wonder so many fellows go to Europe."

"No, nor I, when they have a maternal relative to pay the bills, as you have. When shall I make you understand, Jasper, that that carnal advantage which you enjoy, unimportant, indeed, to the philosopher, materially changes the character of some people's aspirations and projects, Here am I, wondering how I am to pay Madam Hyde for the patches on the trousers I wear, the strap-buttons on those I don't wear, and the silk gown I am to wear to-morrow, — and I am invited to go to Holland with a gentleman whose friends fear to trust him on the other side of the ocean alone; who has a wild desire to ascertain the position of Amsterdam. Yet no man explains to me first how Mrs. Hyde is to be paid, — second, how my state-room is to be provided."

"Ma'am Hyde is not married: she is an ancient virgin, vulgarly called an old maid."

"She is a nice old soul anyway, and has been very kind to me. But I wish you would not turn the conversation from this subject of finance. I do not suppose we all mean to go through the world the beggars, or putative beggars, that we are."

"What does putative mean?"

"What does beggar mean? I have begged for nothing. I have only said that I have the best education my country can afford, and I have meekly inquired what I am to do with it. Can any man inform me? Where is a market for abscissas and ordinates? Who will give me my living in return for an adequate explanation of the meaning of the word asymptote?"

"I would have given five dollars to anybody who would have provided me with it one day when I had the blackboard before me and Pierce behind me."

"Had you only had the five dollars to give! I find those most willing to recompense me for my wares who have nothing but good wishes to give."

"We are in the prime of life now; we may forget about these asymptotes and paroxytons. I am shaky myself; and what can I hope for from the rest of you? Is there, then, no method by which we can store away what we now have and enjoy, for the blessing of after days?"

"When we are on the shady side of thirty, like that fellow with the manilla-stick that came into Commons yesterday."

"Yes, think of it; the days will come when we are no longer in the graduating class; when ten graduating classes are behind us; when eager statesmen, looking for young life to recruit the treasury benches in Congress, will no longer send us private despatches, such as Jasper expects to receive to-morrow; when careful papas, desirous to find safe tutors who shall escort two brave boys and one lovely blonde, — oh, lovely ! — through Europe, will no longer address themselves to Horace, as he expects to be addressed to-morrow ; when a new-founded university at the West, represented at our annual games by a committee of ten trustees seeking a president, will no longer wait upon me impressively, as I expect them to do to-morrow. More briefly spoken, the days will come when we are aged men, when we are past thirty. What shall we have laid up in provision for those years?"

" What indeed, seeing we have nothing to lay?"

" There must be something that improves by age, which, perhaps, by borrowing from Jasper a little capital, we could store up now, which at thirty will be so valuable that we shall in that dotage be able to sell it for enough to pay him, and to provide for the decline of life. What is there which grows more valuable as it grows older?"

" Is that a conundrum?"

" Conundrum? no! It is a most serious question, bearing on the whole future of life."

" What grows better as it grows older? I thought everybody knew. Wine does."

" Yes," said Horace, pensively; " but it is very hard to keep it. Is there nothing but wine?"

" Trees," said Jasper. " Soap," said Gilman " Paper," said Ferguson. " There is a note my father sent me yesterday, on paper ten years old: see how hard and firm that is!"

" Wine, soap, paper, trees. Can that be all? And none of us have any wine or trees or paper; and we have only five half-cakes of soap between us. Jasper will have to lend us a good deal."

" Perhaps Jasper will save us the other half of the trouble by buying the wine, the soap, the paper, and the trees, and keeping them for us. Is not there at the Grange some cluster of tight old barns, which could be locked up, and marked St. Leger, or Ferguson, Gilman, and Haliburton, in which from time to time, as good wine, soap, paper, and trees turned up, you could store them away for us? Or the trees might stay out doors."

" Plenty of them," said Jasper, laughing, " without buying. Come and see the Grange, and you shall all make your own arrangements. I have told them, Horace, that you will arrive with me ; and, if the rest of you fellows would come before August, it would be jolly."

Jasper Rising, the host in this interview, and the centre indeed of the circle wherever they were, had fairly earned the thorough love and thorough respect with which the others regarded him, in the well-worked and well-crowded and well-amused college-life which was ended on this day. He had been sent to college by the relative of whom the boys had spoken as his "maternal uncle," one of Nature's noblemen, who, having early struck off westward, self-reliant and enduring, had, before twenty years, established on Lake Michigan an immense lumber business, receiving timber from every stream in a principality, cutting it in his own mills, and delivering it where most needed in the then new region of the north-west. All this work left him none the less the chance and the time to do what was a thousand times better, — to build up "the Grange," which was the most comfortable and home-like of homes. Since Jasper was a child, he had lived here with his widowed mother so long as she lived, who was not the sister of John Hughitt, but a cousin of some distant remove. But he was fond of her, and she of him; and when his wife fell ill, and dragged along a wretched career of invalidism, Mrs. Rising, who went there first as a guest, and then staid because she could not be spared, became gradually installed as the domestic head of the immense establishment. Jasper always called John Hughitt "uncle"; and John Hughitt loved him and treated him as if he had been the son who in truth died in his cradle. When the time came, he sent the boy to college, — he had taken infinite pride in his success, — and now Jasper was to go back with "the best education his country could afford" to work his way as he could into the management of the mills, and the immense mercantile and financial interests connected with them. He was, indeed, virtually John Hughitt's son, and was so regarded by his friends. Of the five young friends who sat finishing his ice, or looking out through his spy-glass, or in otherwise awaiting evening prayers, he was the only one whose future seemed to be definitely determined.

" I say, Jasper," said Horace Kenney, after they had finished the plan for the storehouses, " did you see old Bernhardt? "

" Of course I did," said Jasper. Bernhardt was the leader of the band which was to play at Commencement.

" Did you ask him about the Adelaïde? "

" Adelaïde! Jove, no! What possessed me! I forgot it clean and clear. I must have been crazy. But, — I don't know, — he was full of some stuff about two trombones. Is it too late now? "

" Too late! of course it is, you good soul; and it does not make the least matter. Who cares whether the Adelaïde is played or not? Like enough Miss Marshall will never think of it again. If she does, of course she will not care."

" But I care," said Jasper. " I don't see how I forgot it. I mean to go in now and see Bernhardt. I told you she should have the Adelaïde, and she shall; besides, I want to see that fellow about my uncle's shot-bag. Who of you fellows wants to go in? I can be back to chapel."

But they all tried to persuade him not to go. Horace cursed himself for having said anything about the Adelaïde. But the truth simply was, that Miss Marshall had spoken pleasantly of the air, and Horace had said it should be played at Commencement, and Jasper had undertaken to see to it. This being so, they might as well have turned to heaving the half-finished Bunker Hill Monument over, as to stop him. He bade them make themselves comfortable, and crossed alone to Stearns's, to drive a little mare into Boston, give his order about the march, inquire about his uncle's shot-bag, do one other errand if there were time, and be back for their last meeting at chapel and tea.

" What a good fellow he is! " said Horace, as he ran down stairs. " There is not a fellow in the class who deserves Jasper's luck as Jasper does."

" Born with a silver spoon, and has always known how to use it."

CHAPTER II.

PUSS — AND BERTHA.

HOBSON'S choice," as we are taught by John Milton, was the choice which was given to the Cambridge undergraduates of his day, by the man to whom they went to hire horses. "You must have the beast who is next the door or none," said Hobson then.

But Stearns, of our New Cambridge stable, in these days of which I write, knew no such arbitrary law; and the pretty, glossy little Morgan mare, which was led out and harnessed into a "buggy" at Jasper's order, knew his hand and touch and voice as well as did the favorite in his uncle's stable at the Grange. Jasper had driven her, whenever he drove at all, now for three years. Stearns always managed to have her ready at Jasper's order, — having, perhaps, a fine instinct which taught him when Jasper would come to use her. "She is mine, pretty creature, to the extent of sixpence," Jasper used to say, quoting what was one of the latest Carlylisms of the time. But the sixpence was a large one. For had anybody footed up the three "term-bills" which Stearns sent to Jasper every year, and which Mr. Hughitt punctually paid, he would have seen that the mare was his to an extent much larger by that count than was his horse at home. In the three years that he used her, those "term-bills" would have paid for her three times over.

"I shall be back before prayers," said Jasper to the hostler; and, as he looked at his watch, he saw that he had an hour and fifty minutes for his three errands.

Let it be observed to distant readers, that, as the bird flies, the farthest point he was to go to was not four miles away. But, in those primeval days, the only public conveyance at Jasper's command was a long four-horse omnibus, such as is now unknown in all parts of the world, unless they use them in Alaska, which once an hour would have carried Jasper to Boston. Under the agreement which the young men had made to meet at evening prayers, the omnibus was useless to Jasper.

"Is it the last time, Puss, that you and I shall go over the causeway together?" said Jasper, almost aloud, as the little creature rushed toward town with him. "How little while it is since I learned your merits, pretty one, — that day of the Watertown picnic, when Alice Cohoes and I were all too late, when she would have been mortified if we had reported long after the rest of the party, and when my pretty Puss took that long upper road with us, did four miles in seventeen minutes, and then paced into the village ahead of all the rest of them, as slow and demure as any of the old Quakers on the road." Thus his soliloquy went on, — and one and another memory of Alice Cohoes came into it, and of Pauline and the Leslies, and wonders that all the people of his sophomore year should have scattered so, — wonders whether Alice liked her new husband as well as the husband liked her, — wonders what women found to like in such veterans. The new husband was, in fact, twenty-seven years old, — six years Jasper's senior. Ah! it was a short ride before Puss brought him to the toll-house, and stopped of her own accord that he might pay his toll.

After the bridge was crossed, no more such two-forty trotting. - Perhaps Jasper really loved the little mare most for what he called the divine instinct, by which she accommodated herself to relations, as different from those of the Arabian deserts, as are the entanglements of the narrow streets of Boston. Never did he need this instinct more than he did to-day. For, when he rendered himself at the office where the Boston Brigade Band received its orders, it dawned on him for the first time, that the band did not sit at the office all day

and all night, tuning their horns or practising marches.
The office, on the contrary, proved to be a snuffy little
room up two flights of stairs, the door of which no one
had even taken the precaution to lock, seeing there was
nothing to steal there but a rusty stove, two arm-chairs,
and a "Times" seven days old, — a room in which
you could not play a trombone, and in which, at this
moment, there was not so much as one weary arpeggio
note still resounding from the forgotten end of the finest
twiddle of the last quickstep of the month's practice.

Jasper stamped round, — knocked on the door, —
knocked at all the doors, — went down stairs and
knocked, — went up stairs and knocked, — and disin-
terred at last a frightened copying-girl, who was making a transcript of a long mortgage deed to be ready
in the morning.

No, — she knew nothing about the Brigade Band, —
believed their office was down stairs, did not know when
they came, did not know when they went away, did not
know if they had any secretary, far less knew who he
was, — did not know anything, in short.

And, as Jasper retired, he was just "mad" enough
to say to himself, she did not want to know anything.
But she did, — that girl did, — she wanted at that moment very much to know how she could get the grease
out of the front breadth of her new merino. I believe
she also wanted to know the significance of the myth of
Ceres. Most Boston girls of her time did whom I
knew. But of this I am not certain.

The Directory served Jasper better. The Directory
showed that the secretary of the band was Mr. Shrapnel,
and that Mr. Shrapnel lived in Berlin Court. The Directory also showed that Berlin Court opened from
Menotomy Street, that Menotomy Street ran from Sun-
moon Street across to Merrimac Street. With the last
name Jasper was familiar; and so, after long delay in
these tentations into which he had been led, he began
an experiment in Boston geography.

He was rapidly threading Sudbury Street where it
runs down hill, — when he met his destiny. Under the

edge of the quaint old house where still stands there, a crowd had assembled so dense that he had to check the mare again, and in a moment, being part of the crowd now, to ask what was the matter. A teamster — not drunk, — no, sorry — had made a botch in turning the corner, his wheels had slipped, so that, in spite of him, he had backed with his heavy load upon the sidewalk, — a frightened little German boy had been thrown down and badly jammed. This was the story.

Puss again, the little Morgan mare, understood her part, — to possess her soul in patience, and stand harmless and unharmed. Jasper was on the sidewalk in a moment, — in a minute he understood the trouble. The little boy was in the lap of a motherly woman who sat on the doorsteps. The medical student who had been improvised, pronounced, what everybody knew, that the poor little leg was broken. All this time the child was screaming, the teamster protesting sorrow, the crowd maledicting, and most persons advising. But Jasper, in a moment, discerned that the child was not friendless, — the girl with a loaf of bread was the child's sister. Only the girl could not speak English. Nor, for that matter, could Jasper speak much German. But thanks to five or six terms of Follen's German Reader and Hermann and Dorothea, — thanks to dear Roelker, whom so many men since and before have thanked, — thanks to a warm heart and determined resolution, — Jasper made out, through the girl's repressed sobs, what her agonized words meant; and he made her understand, that, if she would sit in the buggy, he would lift the little one upon her lap on the seat, and would lead Puss to the home, — wherever the home might prove to be. It was bad German which said all this; but the poor child understood enough. She climbed to the seat; the motherly woman lifted the screaming boy there, with help from the teamster, and hindrance from twenty others; Jasper took the little mare by the head, and, guided by two capless and hatless boys, who were delighted to be of importance, led her from corner to corner, not far, to the two German children's home.

Here he rang loudly. In a moment the excited and wondering mother appeared; and, in a minute more again, Jasper and she had carried the poor little fellow to a bed. Jasper made offers about going for a doctor; but there was no need. A bigger boy, who knew where to go, was sent, and Jasper saw that he was not needed. The house was comfortable enough, — a little two-story brick house, in which, had he only known it, these people occupied four rooms on different floors. They thanked him civilly for his attention. He promised to call before the week was over, and see how the little Wilhelm was. He found Puss the admired centre of all the boys of the neighborhood, took his seat again, and again started for the discovery of Berlin Court. This time no accident intervened. What was more, Mr. Shrapnel was at home. "Would he bid the band bring the Adelaïde?" Would he? Of course he would. They had selected it to bring. If the gentleman would look he would see. Here it was, in the trombone's music. Adelaïde! Of course they would bring that! In fact, it seemed as if they had never thought of bringing anything beside! Jasper left, with that cheap feeling to which boys of twenty are too often reduced by pretenders who have a little more brass than they, — that he was simply a fool, — at least, he thought he had given two hours, more or less, to a fool's errand.

He looked at his watch to see he had thirty-five minutes. Five minutes finished the message for the shot-bag, — two minutes more bought four cakes of brown Windsor soap for a joke on the fellows, — five minutes creeping brought him to the Boston toll-house, — and then, "Now's your time, Puss," — and by the middle road to Stearns's, eleven minutes and a half took him to Dr. Webster's house. There Puss and he assumed a gait more sedate; and just as Paddy Kiernan, the "janitor," was beginning to ring the first bell for evening prayers, Jasper walked into Massachusetts Twenty-seven.

The adventure was nothing in itself. But it seemed worth while to tell it here in the beginning of this story.

Because, so far as I know, it was in this adventure, that, for the first time, Jasper met his destiny. This tearful, brown-faced Bertha, who had hardly made out his German, and hardly make him understand hers, — this girl of the heavy shoes, the loaf of bread, the freckled face, and the wounded brother, was to be the woman to whom Jasper was one day to give the whole treasure of a man's love, and who was to give him the whole treasure of a woman's. Neither of them dreamed of this, this evening, nor thought of the other for a moment. But, after many ups and downs, this was to come. And to tell the progress of those ups and downs is the business of this story.

CHAPTER III.

COMMENCEMENT DAY.

A BRIGHT morning, presaging a hot day. But no
danger of rain! The class, that year, breakfasted
with the President, in a comfortable, rambling old
wooden house, which still stands, — which was, in those
days, the abode of a hearty and noble hospitality.
Then, by gatherings and marshallings and calls of the
classes, well known to Harvard men, the procession of
graduates was formed, to move to the church under the
escort of the seniors. He whom they had nicknamed
St. Leger, whose real name was Asaph Ferguson, was
one of the marshals, chosen by the class for good address, handsome face and figure, and ready tact. He
and Follett were here and there and everywhere, making old gentlemen fall in, respectfully notifying professors and other dons that all was ready, — waving batons
forward to Mr. Bernhardt and his band, and backward
to loiterers who had not found their places in time, —
and at last the class, radiant in shiny new round hats,
headed by the band, who were playing the march in
Der Freischutz, moved along the front of University
and Holworthy, followed by what, in their young enthusiasm, they really thought was one half of the wisdom, science, eloquence, and wit of America. For
these boys, let us confess it, had not yet learned much
of their own country or its greatness.

The class numbered about seventy. Of the seventy,
some thirty, or less, marched in silk gowns, mostly of
the most flimsy and perilous material, but still unques-
tionably silken. The academical customs had almost
faded out. It was only on two or three state occasions

that these robes were worn. And no man dreamed of adding to his permanent wardrobe such a garment, for the improbable chance or the infrequent ceremony when it might be used. But, to prepare for such exigencies, their loyal friend, of whom Jasper's comrades in Massachusetts spoke so gratefully, — who repaired the rents of the cricket-ground and the Delta, restored buttons which had vanished, and, in general, cared for decaying broadcloth, kept a narrow store of silk gowns, sufficient for Exhibition purposes; and for a wretched half-dollar the boys might hire one. These were the flimsier of the flying robes of the procession. Their number was eked out by those which other boys had borrowed from their friends among the neighboring clergy, — so that, by hook and crook, the procession assumed the semblance of academic dignity.

Arrived at the church, the seniors opened to the right and left; and the procession passed through, followed then by their young escort, who gathered in the front pews. The president, the venerable Josiah Quincy, took his place in the pulpit of the church; which was surrounded, for the occasion, by a large temporary platform, through which, here and there, appeared some mysterious pinnacles of painted wood, — a part of the architecture never very intelligible, and wholly inexplicable now that their basis was concealed.

The fact that near thirty of the young men wore silk gowns, was sufficient evidence that there were to be the same number of addresses, longer or shorter. One's rank might then be measured by the length of his address. If it were four minutes long, it was the minimum of honor; if it were fifteen minutes, it was what they now call *summa cum laude*. Thus, as in most things, do academical authorities reverse the judgments of an active world. There was one result of this multitude of speakers, which later authorities at Cambridge have forgotten. To hear each of the speakers came a certain clientèle of his friends or relatives. The church, therefore, though of considerable size, was in those days crowded with an audience, in which, tired though it soon was, there was one sympathetic corner for each speaker. In latter days, they have reduced the length of the exercises two-thirds, by diminishing the number of the speakers in a larger proportion. The audience diminishes in precisely the same ratio with the speakers.

Of our five friends of Massachusetts Twenty-seven, Horace did the salutatory Latin. He *salved* the old men and the old women, the professors and the tutors, the sophomores and the freshmen, and drew the annual laugh as he looked at the galleries on both sides, blazing with thin muslins and pink ribbons, — pink was in that year, — and *salveted* " *vos quoque* the pretty girls who have done us the honor to take a part in our annual solemnity." All our friends had something or other to say upon the stage, in colloquy, dissertation, or oration. Probably not one of them would have crossed the street to change his college-rank by one or two grades ; but all of them were glad to be among the " first twenty." And all this speaking, and the music of the band which came in for relief sometimes, lasted, hour after hour, — hear this, degenerate moderns, — from nine in the morning till after two in the afternoon ! " The fellows " went out, and they came in ; they lounged in the bookstore, they swung on certain chains in the yard ; they gave the last orders to the men who were arranging for them entertainments for their friends, — not then called " spreads," as now ; they hurried back to the church, to hear one favorite of the class or another. But there was one close rally of them and of all the audience, as the game drew near its conclusion, as everybody else had been bowled out by the unwearied president, and Jasper stepped forward, a little pale, but with almost a smile on his face, to deliver the closing oration, — the first honor of the day.

No : it makes little difference what were the words in which his subject was printed on the bill, "Modern Conservatism," "The Demand of our Time," "New Light and More," "The Lesson of To-day," — they call it one thing or another : that matters little. These timid but courageous young fellows, anxious and confident at once, who have spent four years in studying antiquity, but have spent the latter part of those four years in forecasting their own future, if they are true to themselves, always hit on substantially the same line of emotion, — it is scarcely thought, — and, by whatever name they call their essay, they try to show us in the same moment the caution of their retrospect, and the cheerfulness of their outlook. Jasper's "oration" was moulded chiefly around certain things which had impressed him in the history of the Greek democracies. He knew next to nothing about them, as how should he? Nobody had told him! But in the I. O. II. Library he had found "Thirlwall's History of Greece," which had not long been printed; and he was in fresh amazement over what he thought its revelations. Of some of the things he had learned there, he spoke now, — spoke, be it remembered, in words which he had written down; then copied, then revised under the careful eye of Prof. Edward Channing, (blessing and honor be on his name!) which then he had committed word by word to memory, and had repeated in one or two "rehearsals" before an instructor in elocution. Think of the eloquence likely to follow such a process!

But Jasper was handsome, graceful, and confident. Whatever else he knew, he knew that he could repeat the words of this oration, though he were burning at the stake. He looked, only too carelessly, round upon the assembly, and began. His eye fell on one and another of the favorite belles in the gallery: he even noticed Miss Marshall, and was pleased to see that she was there. And as he went mechanically on with Bœotia and Epaminondas, he was thinking of the Adelaïde, and wondering if she had noticed it. His eye ranged out at the open door; and he could see a lobster-man weighing a lobster in the street; was even amused with the dumb-show, as the purchaser counted out his pence, Jasper's lips going steadily on with the thirty tyrants of Athens and their fall, till he was fairly startled when he detected himself in this odious parrot's talk, and

2

compelled himself, by an effort of which he was conscious, to return to some thought of what he was saying, and to renew the interest which its idea had for him when he began. He compelled himself with some success. His eye lighted, fortunately for him, on two fine boys, who, in a favorable seat, were leaning forward, their arms just supported by the top of a pew, and drinking in his words as if he were an oracle. Jasper's eyes ceased wandering, and fixed on the eyes of one of these boys. He even forgot the rest of his audience, as he spoke to him, and, with a revulsion, of which he was himself aware, spoke with a tone now wholly real and natural, as if the words were new to him, when at the end of a paragraph he came upon the epigram, —

"Never did Senate of Greeks rise to the sacrifices of Christian patriotism. Separate men were unselfish; but never did an assembly act as one. We must come later down, into another civilization, before we find a unanimous Senate, of one heart and one soul, pledge to a country just born in throes of agony, their lives, their fortunes, and their sacred honor."

There was a freshness in the tone which struck on the jaded audience like water-drops on the dry desert.

From the seniors before him, from old men behind them, even from women in the galleries, there came a hearty round of hand applause; not a noisy manufacture of a sympathetic *claque*, but the genuine sympathy of an assembly which believed. Jasper waited till it seemed over, tried to begin then with, —

"The lesson which Athens teaches," — as it was writ down on the manuscript which the good old President held behind him, but was interrupted by a second and by a third wave of the same applause, which then died unwillingly away. When it was hushed, Jasper stepped forward again to say, —

"The lesson which Athens teaches," — and in the instant felt that he had forgotten this catch-word, and had no idea where he was to begin. He had been wholly absorbed, as the applause spent itself, in watching the eagerness of the two boys who were his audience.

It was a trifle in itself, that slip of memory: it was probably to Jasper one of the prime blessings of his early life. For by a divine instinct, by a rapidity of perception for which words have no name, he knew that he had lost the catch-word; and he did not care that he had lost it. He did not sacrifice the infinitesimal differential of the millionth part of a second in seeking for it. What he was there for, as he now felt, though it had never crossed his mind before, was that those two eager boys, who would be freshmen to-morrow night, should take true views and manly, of the place of men in a republic. He saw that they believed in him, whoever they were. He saw that he had a golden opportunity with them. Perfectly careless, therefore, for the loss of the catch-word, perfectly careless of what he had written down, perfectly careless of himself, he went on speaking across the audience to those two.

"You see, do you not? I am sure you see, or I can make you see, that so long as those men thought of themselves, — of their own eating and drinking, their own clothes and houses, their jealousies and quarrels, — they were thinking of things so small that they could not be great men. You see, or I am sure I can make you see, that it is only when men have an object nobler than such trash as that, that they come into the line of what we call greatness, or that the plans they make, are worth even their own remembering." This was the idea which was on his paper, in words more like fustian. Fortunately for Jasper, he had now cut wholly loose from the paper; and the intense earnestness with which he spoke in these sentences to the two boys was his salvation. He saw, more than ever, that they believed in him, that they comprehended him. For the first time in his life, he drank in the delicious inspiration which is for the moment the divine life of the speaker who is at one with his audience, no matter whether that audience is large or small. Jasper's thus far was two. But, in this inspiration, he went on. The house was hushed as death in presence of his earnestness. The still calm did not frighten him, however; nothing fright-

ened him. Of course there was no danger now. It
was divine power by which Jasper was carried on, —
the divine power of a human soul in complete accord
with one, two, or three other souls, doing its infinite
best to move or to persuade them. Step by step of his
appeal he pressed forward much as he had meant to do ;
for his thought had been serious in the preparation of
the whole. And for five minutes of absolute self-for-
getfulness to him, — five minutes of eager, breathless,
confident and excited attention of his audience, — he
told the two boys, and others around them, whom he
began to notice now, what was the sway over the world
which in our time men would win, when for the world
they were ready to live, and for the world to die. Of
course he said a word then on the magnificent prospect
which the world of to-day offers to such devotion.
And, as he said this, his mind acting as all along it
did, a hundred times as fast as his lips, he said to himself as he spoke, " Why, this is just what Tennyson
says in ' Locksley Hall ! ' — why, yes ! that was what I
copied out, to finish my oration with, — why, yes ! this
is my oration ! I must finish it now ; " and so he came
to the words again, which of all this outburst were the
only words upon the manuscript, —

" Not in vain the future beacons : onward, forward, let us
    range, —
  Let the peoples spin forever down the ringing grooves of
    change.
  Through the shadow of the world, we sweep into the wider
    day :
  Better fifty years of Europe, than a cycle of Cathay."

And then, with a smile of the real triumph which he
felt, he was done. He made his bow to his audience,
of course ; that etiquette reminded him that he must
turn and bow to Mr. Quincy. Then, he hardly knew
how, he stepped down the steps to where the fellows
were now clapping and stamping, hardly held in from
cheering, and staggered into the seat which Horace
kept open for him ; and, pale and frightened, for the

first time nestled back into it, to wonder with an infinite wonder, as he reflected on what he had been doing.

And the assembly had waited dumb while he bowed to them, waited till they saw his back as he bowed to the President, had roused then to some consciousness that this appeal was over, when he stepped, almost staggered forward, across the platform; and then it burst into that rapture of applause which sounds so seldom, which is perhaps only due to youth, simplicity, intense conviction and emotion together, when they all appeal to us as one.

It is strange to say, the words from Tennyson were new to ninety-nine out of a hundred in that assembly. They had been published in London only a few months before; and Jasper's quotation was probably the first of ten thousand repetitions of them before such audiences in the generation which has since gone by.

Wave after wave of applause swept over the assembly. Horace found some means to slip his hand into Jasper's. That was a comfort; and, by the time stillness came, he was as ready as any man for his part in the closing ceremonies.

It is not necessary to detail the course of those solemnities. An hour or less closed them all. And then, relieved at last from escort duty, these young men, each with a parchment diploma tied with a light blue ribbon, ran joyfully, and with the sense of complete freedom, to the room or suite of rooms where the party of his friends — ladies and gentlemen, flames and teachers, father's friends and mother's friends — were assembled. These people had earned their appetites, and were to refresh themselves, as they could, with salmon, lobster salad, sandwiches, raspberries and cream, and the other luxuries of a summer collation. In those days, such parties were at every exhibition, at " Class Day," and at Commencement. Never is hospitality more charming, nowhere are hosts more sedulous, nowhere are women more lovely, never is sympathy more genuine, or talk more witty or more true. Jasper was supported by Horace and George. He was happy. He was a freeman; he had pleased his friends; he was not himself disappointed. No one could flatter him. The truth itself as to what he had done that day was the best possible compliment. No one tried to flatter him. His friends were proud of him. His teachers were more than satisfied with him. Everybody admired him. "Dear boy," said Dr. Liston, as he pressed his hand fondly, "I am so glad for you. If only she could have been here."

And Jasper bowed; he knew the good doctor meant his mother.

"Kenney," said Dr. Webber, — if he was the divinity professor of those days, — "I have heard nothing so fine as your friend's oration, in the Commencements of thirty years, No! fine is not the word; I have heard nothing so strong, so manly, and so true."

"You use just the right words, sir," said Horace, delighted. "When you know him as we do, you will know he is himself true, manly, and strong."

"He is going back to Michigan?"

"Yes sir! He has a splendid opening, almost in the line he describes. His uncle is rich; and his enterprises cover half that country. And Jasper will be needed in them all."

"So the President told me. I remember no young man who has so auspicious a beginning."

So sped the afternoon. At last it was over. They all went to the President's to tea; and at last that was over. As Jasper went up at ten o'clock at night, he met Horace on his way to his room.

"Good-night, old fellow! There is a letter for you on your table. I brought it from the office."

And Jasper ran up two stairs at a time, struck a match, and found it. The hand was awkward and not familiar; but he knew the name.

DEAR MR. JASPER, — I rite these lines to beg you to come home imediately. We have had a horid fire, wich is not indeed out, at this riting. It is with distress that I inform you that Mr. Hughitt stept off the roof of the lenetoo as he was carrying a hose, and never spoke another word. We have been working all night; and I hope still we shall save the north warf: but the others are all gone. The Sarah is burnt to the water, and the Thetis and the Jasper; indeed, The Mary Ann wich is at Green Bay, is the only vessel left. Come as soon as you can, and excuse haste.

Yours to command,

ANDREW HAZLITT.

Andrew Hazlitt was the oldest of the fresh-water skippers, — a favorite of Mr. Hughitt's and of Jasper.

Jasper read his letter twice, and then lighted a cigar. Then he reached far out of his window, and cried, " St. Leger ! St. Leger ! "

A head appeared from the other entry of Massachusetts.

" Are you undressed, St. Leger ? "

" No ! what's up ? "

" I wish you would come round." And Ferguson, whom they called St. Leger for fun, came, — came quickly. As he ran into the room, he found Jasper making rings of cigar-smoke. Jasper gave him a cigar, but, before he lighted it, handed him the letter, which he read.

" What does all this mean, Jasper ? "

" It means, my dear boy, that I am a beggar."

CHAPTER IV.

HOT AND TIRED.

IF any one have supposed that Jasper's blunt announcement to Ferguson of the great misfortune that was on him, showed want of affection for John Hughitt, his uncle, or in any way a hardness of heart in the midst of catastrophe, it is because he does not know young men well, and, which may be pardoned, because he does not know Jasper Rising. The truth is, that with young fellows like these in their closest intimacy, a great deal is taken for granted ; and there is what to cynics seems an affected reticence, when they have to deal with matters of affection, of sentiment, or other phases of the inner life. In this case the whole electricity of the day's thunder-cloud had flashed out in an instant. In the midst of praise and congratulation and flattery, Jasper had caught intimations not unlike what Dr. Webber had expressed to Horace ; and, fairly or not, he had the notion that people thought it was easier for him to speak bravely because he was a rich man, or next to a rich man. There was not a feeling of envy of his companions, for Jasper was not a fool, but an impression that he could not be rated for his own merits, because he had the luxury of fortune. And therefore it was, that, when he saw Asaph's honest face all struggling with sympathy which Asaph was powerless to speak, his eyes filling with tears which Asaph had no wish to check, — when Asaph blundered out his question, " What does this mean?" Jasper replied by an ejaculation quite as far from the deepest grief of the moment, an ejaculation, which, if you opened it out to the full extent of words, would mean exactly this :

" There is only this comfort in it all, the four fellows and I are all equals in the world. If you have to
start on the world without favors, why, just so have I."

There was no prayer-bell the next morning; but Jasper woke, of course, at six minutes before six, just as
regularly as if Kiernan were beginning again on the
" tap, tap, tap," of the " second bell; " woke from a
sleep as steady and sound as if he had not been the
hero of the day before, and had not learned at night
the saddest news he had heard, with one great and infinite exception, since he was born; first of all, to the
thought that the day had come at last for which he had
been hoping in most of the mornings for four years past,
the day when he should not have to rise at the tap of
the bell, but might turn over and take one nap more;
woke, alas! to have the second thought come in a moment, that there was something else before him than
another nap, and to the consciousness, alas! that there
was no comfort in the bed, and little comfort anywhere that day.

After breakfast, the four came up again to Jasper's
room, quietly enough this time, and very thoughtfully.
All of them had the memory of that Tuesday afternoon,
with its nonsense about the way in which their fortunes
should be made, and its certainty that everybody, if he
chose, might lean on Jasper in the making. And now
all of his friends, with the carefulness of young men,
which is a very different thing from that of men who
are used to care, were wondering what they could do to
relieve Jasper's anxiety, and, almost by a law of Nature, drifted together here to make such offer and such
suggestion as each man could, and to relieve him, as
far as they could, at the least, of petty annoyance.

Ferguson had told the others, and Ferguson's advice
was substantially best worth their taking. Horace was
to stay in Cambridge three or four weeks to work over
a boy who was behind-hand in his mathematics for the
freshman examination. He therefore undertook the
clearing Jasper's rooms, the sale of his furniture, the
packing of his books, and the forwarding of the boxes

to Jasper wherever he might be. "Hard to tell that," said poor Jasper. Horace was also to pay Jasper's bills, of which he made a list, not doubtful as to amount, nor fearful, indeed. His uncle had just made him a remittance, quite large enough to clear everything; and though the fellows all begged him to take money from them, to pay them when he should "have a chance, you know," Jasper said no! He would keep a hundred and fifty dollars, and would leave the rest in Asaph's care and Horace's. "Hard on old Harvard," said he, "if with 'the best education my country can afford,' a hundred and fifty dollars will not start me somewhere"; not that he had any real expectation of any resurrection of the lumber affairs. But Jasper, better than any of them, knew the country, knew the West, and knew himself. I am not sure but the experience of the Commencement platform, of the presence of mind with which he had plucked safety and victory there, out of the failure of his preconcerted plans, had a good deal to do with his confidence as to himself of to-day.

So they talked, so they decided, not saying much of the great grief of personal loss, but feeling it all the same, while Jasper, with George's help, filled up one and another trunk with clothes, packed one smaller valise for immediate purposes, sat down, every now and then, to write a note of farewell and apology to Mrs. Quincy, to Mrs. Channing, to Judge Story, or to others who had been kind to him; remembered one and another forgotten commission, which he dictated to the faithful and accurate Ferguson; and so at noon, looking up for the moment the chaos of the room, but yesterday so pretty and comfortable, they went with him to the omnibus at Willard's, and bade him good-by.

Five in the afternoon saw Jasper in the Norwich train on his way to New York. He had made his state farewell calls in Boston on the old family friends, and others who had been kind to him there. He had had a long and thoroughly discouraging talk with Edmeston & Co., his uncle's business friends in Boston, to whom he had sometimes had occasion to go before, with one or

another commission about money or affairs. The
Edmeston he liked was in Maine. From the other
Edmeston, if indeed he were not the partner named
Lavingstone, Jasper got no comfort. The truth was,
that the country was just on the eve of a convulsion;
and men of real intelligence and foresight knew it was.
Every ship was running before the wind, with all its
flying kites out. No one dared take in an inch of sail;
and yet there were a hundred reasons for being sure
that a complete cyclone would be on them soon.
When, at such an instant, you see from your own deck
one of the outside cruisers of the fleet flap over on her
beam-ends,—when you see her rise for an instant, only
because all her top-hamper is gone, and one, two, or
three of her masts are snapped and trailing in ruin
from their stumps,—you are in no condition, while
wondering at what moment the storm may strike you,
to say much to anybody in the way of encouragement.
All the great typhoons which have swept away credit
and commerce in England and America have been pre-
ceded by special accidents, which seemed wholly separate or independent, in which one or another strong
firm went under. Separate or sporadic such accidents
seem. But each one of them is enough to give one
more hint of the shakiness of all foundations. And so
each one does vastly more than it would do at any
other time to abate and chill that mutual confidence
which is the foundation of all our enterprises of to-day.

Jasper came to the station, therefore, hot, tired, and
discouraged. The day was one of those dragging sultry
days of middle July. Half the people he had tried to
see were not at home,—an experience which is one of
the most depressing ones on days when you are so cast
down or jaded, that you would be glad of shade and a
chair, even if it were in an ogre's cave that they were
offered you. The people he had found were not those
he wanted to find,—another misfortune; and the only
one to whom he went for counsel or suggestion had
offered him none.

So Jasper was hot, tired, and discouraged.

Hot, tired, and discouraged, he rode to Framingham, which is the first station for express-trains west of Boston.

It was a little thing that roused him there, but it was enough to give a different color to his afternoon and evening. He had a pretty habit, which I only knew in one other man, of filling a mug at the station water-tap in the five minutes' stop of a train for wood and water, of carrying it along the side of the train, and offering it to tired and hot-looking women sitting within, who were afraid to go out and seek it for themselves. After years have introduced the water-boys in cars, or the travelling water-butt and faucet. But, in the earlier days I write of, Jasper found eager welcome for his cup of cold water, and never travelled in hot weather without trying the experiment, almost as of course. As he passed along with his second mugfull, and looked up at the open windows, his eye caught on a face which seemed not strange ; and in a moment, when the girl he looked upon said prettily, " Ich danke," Jasper saw that she was the German girl whom only on Tuesday he had picked up in Sudbury Street, and carried with her little brother to their home. He ran back with his empty mug, then came at once into that car to join her, — and of course was free now from this wondering and brooding, — the suspense and questioning which had been the curse of the last twelve hours.

Sure enough the little lame boy was there also. His leg was nicely done up in splints, and he sitting, not very sorry to be the hero of the occasion, at full length on the seat he occupied. Bertha's mother, careful, anxious, thoroughly respectable, and greatly frightened, and Bertha herself, made all the rest of the party. Jasper's first words, in poor enough German, were to excuse himself for leaving Boston without coming to inquire after his little charge. Then, by hook and by crook, he made out the detail of their story and plans.

The doctor had set the little boy's broken leg, as he saw. Nor was the fracture a very bad one. But it would need time for the healing ; and the time would

have been tedious in so hot and confined a region as
that which Jasper had found them in in Boston. So as
Mrs. Schwarz had a brother, a lieber theurer Bruder,
who had a pleasant house in the highlands of New Jersey, not far out of New York, they had, with the doctor's permission and connivance, started to take the
little fellow there, evidently sure of a hospitable welcome. Indeed, as Jasper made out, Bertha had already.
been invited for a visit in her vacation, and would have
gone alone. Jasper pleased himself with the notion
that he could be of some service to them in the transfer
to and from the Norwich boat; and, in the amusements
and difficulties of talking German with them, was well
kept from brooding over his own position, in the ride,
which is not a long one, for the rest of the way to Norwich. Arrived there, it was true enough that his presence was a real advantage. How they expected to
transfer poor little Wil. I hardly know. The transfer
was made by Jasper's bodily taking the child in his
arms, after the great mass of travel had gone by. Then
when two women stopped on the gang-way to wonder
if they must go, and inquire where their trunks were, —
or when an orange-seller selected the middle of a flight
of stairs for his trade, — or when a stout gentleman set
down two valises and a band-box in the door-way of a
cabin, while he counted his money and hunted up the
baggage-checks which he would need the next morning,
Jasper's cheery loud voice, " Please make way for this
boy, — will you let this boy pass, — will you step aside
for this boy, — this boy is lame if you please," —
cleared the track once and again, till the little fellow
was comfortably disposed of in a state-room, and the
women had him again in their especial care.

At the landing in New York the same scene was renewed. They were not to go at once to the country home,
but were to report at the store, — as it was vaguely
called, —which proved to be the counting-room of a great
wholesale basket establishment in which Mr. Kaufmann
Baum was a junior partner. " Will you have a carriage,
sir,"— " Here's your nice comfortable carriage," and

the rest of the war-cries of the Six Nations, who still assemble in barbaric pomp at the New-York landing as five of them did when Hendrick Hudson first stepped ashore, would have been to poor Bertha's mother as unintelligible as the classical Onondaga itself was to the English seaman then. But Jasper had kept his forces well in hand. You always arrive in New York on these Eastern boats an hour or two before the great city is itself awake, always excepting that guard, which, as above, by night and day patrols its shores. With difficulty untold, however, Jasper made his friends understand that Mr. Baum would certainly not be at the counting-room before nine o'clock ; and so, as I say, he held them in hand, nor let them rush on too soon to Richmond. At nine he liberated them. He had used his skill in physiognomy well, in selecting an amiable chief from the men of the war-whoops, — I think a Scot of the clan of McDougal. Again he lifted little Wil. to a seat. They found without mistake the counting-room, behind more baby-wagons and market-baskets and baskets without a name, than Jasper had before known there were in the world. Although Mr. Baum would not be there for an hour, he would be there then ; and Jasper was able to leave them, confident that they were comfortable, and that, as far as they were concerned, all was well.

So much had the little German girl done for him on what would else have been the hardest day of his life. She had kept him from himself, — no slight protection.

CHAPTER V.

AUNT MARY.

NONE of the social contrasts of our modern life are more curious than some of those which show themselves in the condition of emigrants from the same family, who meet in America after long separation. It was certainly no want of natural affection which had kept Bertha's mother and her uncle parted in the few months since Mr. Schwarz and his family had arrived in Boston. So soon as they had arrived Mrs. Schwarz had written to her brother, and had received from him that cordial invitation to join him on as long a visit as she would care to make, which she was now accepting. From week to week almost, she had proposed to make the visit, and from week to week it had been deferred. From week to week, for the same reason, the prosperous, active, New York merchant, to whom every hour was precious, had dismissed from his mind any wish to go to Boston to find his sister. He knew perfectly well, that he was more prosperous in external affairs than her husband was, and, in whatever way was courteous, he had offered such facilities and helps as he could, to aid in their establishment in their new home. But his brother-in-law Schwarz was not in need. He was as proud a man as was Kaufmann Baum, and not in the habit of asking help of any man, unless he needed it. It was more than twenty years since Baum had crossed the Atlantic, leaving his sister a little child, the youngest of the immense family, which was but just beginning to swarm.

Kaufmann Baum had in that time thriven in his worldly affairs; and when our little Bertha and her lame brother and her mother found him in New York, he was, not a rich man, but a successful merchant of fifty years old, who had in his hands the management of the business of a large firm, and had the thorough respect and confidence of all men with whom he had to do. It was thirty years since he first left Germany, — his youngest sister, Margaret, the Mrs. Schwarz whom he now met, then little more than a baby. In the earlier part of that time he had made one or two visits to Hamburg; but for the last twenty years, the inducements to cross the ocean had been less, and an occasional letter on each side had kept up the friendly intercourse between the divided parts of the family. Just who Schwarz was, whom his sister Margaret had married, he did not know. When he remembered his father's little house and shop, some ten miles from Altona, distance lent enchantment to the view, and it did not occur to him to measure their economies and simplicity squarely and distinctly against the comforts of his present life. Meanwhile, as the thirty years crept by, the comforts of the Baum establishment in Germany grew less and less. When at last Margaret did marry this Mr. Schwarz, who was half book-dealer and half music-master of a neighboring town, she knew that she went to life rather less easy than her father's; but she loved her husband, and she did not care. On Kaufmann's side, in New York, there had been no great sense of enlarging grandeur; on Margaret's side, in Germany, there had been no distinct sense of decay. When she found herself living in four rooms, in a narrow street in Boston, she did not think herself in hard or narrow circumstances; and when Kaufmann Baum drove up to his pretty house in Orange, from the station, and stopped to enjoy the opening of the rhododendrons in his avenue, he did not often reflect that he was not used to avenues or rhododendrons in his boyhood. But when in his own counting-room he saw her, with her characteristic best dress, looking just as his own mother looked when he went to the village church with her in Lauenburg, he was partly amazed and partly

amused. He was amazed that he himself had not been
conscious that she was not changed as much as he. He
was amused to see how in the complete change of his
condition hers was still precisely the same. When he
turned from the kissing his sister and holding her at
arms' length, to make sure of her and to praise her, —
when he turned to look at the shy, freckled, silent Bertha who stood by, — then ▬▬▬▬ indeed that he was but
nineteen years old again, ▬▬▬▬ his was his own sister
Thekla, whom since then he had not seen, and in this
world would never see. He called her Thekla once,
twice, three times, with his eyes running over. From
that time forth he seldom called her anything but
Thekla ; and the poor shy child was sure of the very
fullest and sweetest of his love.

And so, after eager talking and wondering in the
counting-room, the prosperous brother fitted off sister,
niece, and little lame nephew, under the careful escort
of a spruce clerk, who was not to leave them till he
had delivered them safely at the home in Orange. For
Kaufmann Baum there was, of course, no holiday ; no,
not if fifty sisters and a hundred nieces had come.
Attentive clerk — amused to find himself in charge of
these quaint German people — did his duty well ; his
patent leathers and other elegancies not actually refusing to serve him in such commonplace exigency. And,
a little after noon, the emigrant party found themselves
safely in the airy hall of the pretty house in Orange ;
so that Margaret the mother, and the frightened Bertha,
and poor tired little Wil. went through their next welcome. Elegant clerk of the patent leathers bade good-
by, and returned to the copying-book.

Mrs. Baum was probably more amused than her husband by the apparition ; nay, I am afraid, that, when
she wrote a jubilant letter to her sister about it the next
week, she owned to being "tickled." She had never
been in Germany. A spirited, wide-awake Yankee girl,
whom Kaufmann had fallen in with at Brattleboro', I
believe, — energetic, affectionate, and true, she had
learned in fifty ways to adapt herself to his German

3

habits, knowing that in five hundred, he was adapting
himself to hers. But though she had seen many German
gentlemen, and a few German ladies, she had
never till now seen a simple Lauenburger and the Lauenburger's children, in their own manner as they lived.
She had learned to talk German freely enough, with a
pretty distinct Vermont accent. It was enough better
German than Jasper's, however. And it needed no
correctness of genders to make dear little Wilhelm comfortable, nor anything after the first hand-grip and
hearty kiss, and the sight of her brimming eyes, to
make all the wanderers feel sure that in the palace
around them they were to be perfectly welcome, and at
ease.

Palace it seemed to them. What it was, — was simply that perfection of comfort, and shall one not say
beauty, — the generous wooden house, with a hall running through the middle ; square rooms in each corner,
large and high, with additional rooms gained behind by
a wing thrown out there ; the house in which hundreds
of thousands of people live, — one day we will say
millions, — in the villages round our cities ; in which,
if there be a little breathing space reserved, a little
garden for beauty and fragrance, the highest possibility
of human happiness yet, so far as externals of comfort
and pleasure go, may be said to have been gained.
Mary took Margaret and the lame boy to the regular
" spare chamber " of her pretty house, where she had
arranged a little cot for him, and then led Bertha to
what she told her had been called " Bertha's room "
ever since in the winter they heard that her father and
his family were coming over. How nice that was, that
the room really had her name ! Poor little Bertha was
not so sadly frightened after all ; and when she fairly
saw how pretty the little room was, — and when big
Patrick fairly brought in her travel-worn trunk and un-
strapped it for her, — and she really felt that she was
mistress here, the dear child fairly flung herself into
Aunt Mary's arms. I need not describe the room. It
was pretty enough : you have just such a room in your

house when you try to make it look nice. It was not
the room which upset Bertha. It was that they had
named it "Bertha's room," and that with her American cousins she was not to be a bit homesick, but was
from the first at home.

From that moment there was no danger for our poor,
shy, freckled, heavy-shoed Bertha. In the first place,
she was not always heavy-shoed. When she had put
off her travel-dress, and came down for dinner, she was
in exquisite German neatness of toilette, — as different,
yes, from Aunt Mary in costume, as if she had come
from the planet Hebe ; but in dress as pretty in its way
as if she had been a prima donna assoluta in a German
opera company, and were going to sing the music of
" Leonora." Aunt Mary would have been loyal and
true, — *treue und feste,* — had she come down in hob-
nail shoes and the cap of Cinderella's godmother. But
Bertha had no occasion to ; she was at ease with her
aunt, and her aunt was delighted with her. Little Wil.
had dropped to sleep, and it was clear the bandages
had not been displaced ; and so everybody was thankful, and satisfied with the day. At 5.30 the sound of
wheels on the gravel called everybody to the door, —
Bertha's little cousins, whose older brothers and sisters
were at college and school, Aunt Mary, Mrs. Schwarz,
Bertha, and all, — and in a minute there was another
genuine welcome as Kaufmann Baum, fresh and cheery
after the shipping of ten million or more baskets to
fourteen hundred thousand consignees or less, found
himself at home.

Friday evening, the custom was, that such of the
neighbors as chose, came in to the Baums' house for a
little amateur music ; and to Bertha's terror, not to say
Margaret's, this custom was announced after their coffee had been served. Bertha was, indeed, too much
frightened to dare to ask to go up into her own room, as
she would have been glad to do, though she would have
liked the music. All she could do was to shelter herself behind Aunt Mary or at her side, as well as she
could, and to be thankful, so thankful, that everybody

knew she could speak no English. As if anybody
would have questioned the poor child if she had. By
and by she came to be more at ease. Her uncle's grand
piano was the finest she had ever seen; her uncle's
violin, though by no means what her father's was in his
hands, was the instrument of a man who felt music in
his heart, and attempted nothing he could not do. Two
or three of the ladies who came in, and one of the gentlemen, sang well together. But Bertha's real delight
came, when one of these ladies sat down to the piano,
and accompanied her uncle's violin in a duet from Mozart, of which the theme was very dear to her, but
which she had never heard in this arrangement before.
She fairly came out from her little nest, and, before she
knew it, was thanking her uncle, and, with eyes full of
tears, trying to make him know how much pleasure he
had given her. Kaufmann Baum had been all the evening watching the little frightened bird, while she
thought everybody had forgotten her. He knew perfectly well that she inherited his mother's passion for
music, and her own father's quickness and facility in
execution. But he knew, as well, that she was ill at
ease in his parlor, and that she must not be startled.
Curious as he was, therefore, to hear her play, there
had been no word spoken to her of playing. And now,
in answer to her enthusiasm, Kaufmann only nodded,
and with his bow drew from the violin a few notes of
an air from "The Apollo," which is one of Mozart's
earlier works, least remembered, and asked her if she
played it. He had caught her with guile. It was an
old home favorite, and he knew it. The eager girl,
hardly knowing what she did, turned to the piano,
struck into the air at once in an arrangement which
amazed even Kaufmann Baum, so curiously did it recall even the orchestral harmonies of the piece, as Mozart himself adapted it for the stage. Bertha was perfectly happy. She had never had the command of such
an instrument; but, under her father's careful training,
she was wholly at ease in the control of the piano. No
lesser word describes her power over it. And now that

it did what she wanted it to do as it had never done before, now that it returned the melody and the harmony of her dear Mozart in a fashion not all unworthy of his conception, Bertha was conscious of a new element in her life. With absolute unconsciousness she finished the air, and then was beside herself with terror to find what she had done.

But they soothed her. They did not praise her too much for her comfort. They simply made her understand that she could play accompaniments for them a good deal better than they could play them for themselves. In a word, they made the dear child feel that she was of use, and so they made her comfortable. And when her comfort was thus once secured, why, her place at the piano was fixed for almost all the evening. Child though she was, she had brought into Kaufmann Baum's Friday soirée the element of genius ; and they all knew perfectly well, that, excepting as genius can be copied by talent, this element had never been there before.

CHAPTER VI.

JASPER RISING TO ASAPH FERGUSON.

DUQUESNE, MICHIGAN, July 26.

DEAR OLD BOY,—Here I am at last. I have been here twenty-four hours and more. I answer your first question first, and tell you that everything is as bad as it can be.

My poor aunt was in bed when the fire broke out; had been for weeks, as I told you. She struggled up, of course, when they brought him in; but he spoke no word,—if indeed he were alive. If anything could have broken her more, it was of course that. She almost killed herself by the efforts she made that night, and in the days between till the funeral, and since the funeral till I came, has not left her bed again.

But I am before my story. You see I have taken one of our large Western sheets, that I may tell you the whole of it, to do my best to give you the full worth of your quarter.

I had a tough day the day I left you,—you remember how muggy and hot it was,—till I was fairly on the train. Then I had quite an adventure, which will make you laugh if we ever see each other again. No matter what it was now; but that in my poor way I did the duty in New York, Friday morning, of the father of an interesting family, till I left them in better care than mine. For an hour or two at least, I forgot this wretchedness; and that does not happen to me often. There came a day not to be got rid of so easily. You do not know what a business-day in New York in the end of July is, and I hope you never may. But after it, there was the boat up the river at night,—and such

a night! if you remember it,—which made some compensation. Once for all, let me relieve you by saying
that I have not any night carried my troubles to bed
with me.

You know my tastes so well, that you know I would
gladly have taken the packet-boat on the canal at Albany. Such times as I have had ever since I can remember anything, on these boats and the Ohio boats
with dear Uncle John! But now, of course, time is
everything to me,—and, to my relief, I found we were
just early enough for the first Schenectady train. That
in its turn arrives just in time for the passengers to
change cars at Schenectady for Utica. No! If a
snake-head had come through the bottom of that car
and spitted me from the toe of my foot to the longest
hair in my scalp, I had not been here. You may tell
Fergus, therefore, of my happy escape. You know
how afraid he is of railway riding. Tell him that I do
not think, among all my fellow-passengers, more than
seven were spitted by snake-heads, and that, in the
week of my travelling, I certainly did not see ten col-
lisions, all told. That will satisfy his taste for the
horrible, and will be quite safe for you and me. You
need not tell him that my eyes were put out by cinders,
and that I was three strata deep in Mohawk valley dirt
when the day ended. I satisfied myself at Utica that
I should gain nothing by lying over Sunday at Syra-
cuse; and I stopped there, therefore, and took the day
at our dear Trenton Falls. Ah well! It is as lovely
as when you and I were there. People talk of angry
waters. This water is not angry. It is calm, delib-
erate, dignified forethought that sends it on. It was
a good thing to do,—taking the Sunday there. And,
Ferguson. I tell you that I believe I have been more set
on my feet by something a man named Buckingham
said in his sermon at the village, and by lying in the
drawing-room in the evening, while Moore the hotel-
keeper was playing on a parlor organ he has there,
than by any that has happened to me in the week beside.

The next morning, as day broke, we were off for
Utica, two of us in a buggy.

"Few streaks announced the coming day,
How slow, alas, he came!"

Then came my longest pull, — a very hard ride; but
everything has its end, and at night we were in Buffalo.
I inquired instantly about boats, but my luck had left
me. The "Clinton" was gone, which is the boat I like;
and I had to put up with the "Indiana," which I do
not like. However, that is all over now. At Detroit I
spent the whole of one day and part of the next. At
all these places the misery was, that I was meeting
dear Uncle John's friends, and everywhere I had my
sad story to tell. You see, dear old Hazlitt sent his
letter across to be mailed at Kent, struck the mail here,
and it was the only news from here which had got out
at all. Nobody at Detroit had a suspicion of it, and I
had to go through the horror of telling it forty times
over.

But I have used half my paper, and I do not get on.
Generally we come round here by steam from Detroit;
but I could not wait after I had seen and talked with
the Ellises, and tried coming across, which I have never
done before. I probably chose my route wrong, as it
proved, but it is all guess-work. I took the rail to
Dexter, and then came across country, over, under,
through mud and corduroy such as you cannot dream
of. Really I could have walked as fast as we came;
but, after forty-five miles of such walking one day, I
should not have cared to take forty-five the next. Nor
did I care to take so much riding in the "mail," — the
mail a canvas-top wagon with one seat behind the driver, — changing horses when it listed. But I had to.
And then, St. Leger, when the ninety miles were over,
did not I wish for you? I struck the river at Petit Pré,
and there the mail-carrier's labors ceased. Our mail, in
a state of nature, would have waited there for eleven
days. It did not have to wait so long this time. I saw

my old friend Dundas at once, the first man I had seen who knew anything of what had passed here. You can guess if I pumped him for news. I borrowed his canoe, and floated and paddled down the long lovely reaches which make the twenty miles from Petit Pré here. I have done it a hundred times, taking or bringing the mail, but it never seemed so beautiful. How I wished I had you or Horace in the boat! I think it would have knocked you. The sun went down when I had been on the water an hour. Then such a sunset, moonrise, and starlight! and the water and the woods so still! It was eleven o'clock Saturday night when I got in. I was only nine whole days from Boston, including my necessary stops at New York and Detroit. My uncle never did it in so short time. It shows what a science travelling is reduced to.

Now you want to know what I find and how I feel. Dear St. Leger, I find nothing; and I do not know how I feel. As I tell you, my poor aunt is wholly prostrated. All the people in the house are well-nigh panic-struck. They have had nearly three weeks of uncertainty and depression since the fire; and though Hazlitt and John Water have done their best in putting a good front on things, and have kept the different hands here at work in trying to reduce the wreck to some order, there is, after all, but little front to put; and the wreck is of no great account to one who has known the place in its growing activity. There was absolutely nothing here but my uncle's wharves, — which are gone; his warehouse, which is gone; his own house, and a few frame-houses and log-cabins that the work-people lived in. These last are still standing, but poor Andrew did not save his "north warf." Everything that would burn, burned to the water's edge. When I reflect that at eight and twenty my uncle came here and struck the first tree which white man struck here, with his own axe, — that he saw all that was here grow up under his own eye, — I ask myself why, at one and twenty, I hesitate about starting on this ruin to rebuild what my own eyes have seen here. But to this the answer is, first, that the wilderness was his, and the ruin is not mine; second, that my first duty is to care for my aunt, for whom it is very difficult to care in such a corner of the world; third, that at twenty-one, with the "best education, etc.," I am not what he was at eight and twenty. That is a hard confession to make, but I have to make it. At Detroit I spent the day with his counsel, talking about administration on his estate, and all that. I went so far as to ask whether the people interested would possibly appoint me administrator, or ask for my appointment. But it was quite clear that Mr. Ellis thought that a Harvard graduate was not the man to know about these lumber-men and logging rights; he was civil enough, but I saw that I must drop that dream, for which I am sorry, for I know that nobody really understands Uncle John's plans as I do. I have not the slightest fear that the estate will not pay every demand. He was too far-sighted and too honest to die a bankrupt. I hope my aunt may have something. At all events, whatever I have, she has. And with this I must close, well aware that I have told you nothing. Tell the fellows they must all write; and do not think I am down-hearted. Always yours,

J. R.

CHAPTER VII.

BEGIN AGAIN.

IS there anything quite so depressing to look upon as what the smart "man of business" calls the "winding up of a concern"? Imagine Mr. Dennis Maccarty, who moves families into the country at the shortest notice, or removes sea-shore visitors to the city in the fall, — imagine him turned into Raffaele D'Urbino's studio the day after his death, with directions to clear the rooms, and get them ready by to-morrow morning to move in the furniture and fixtures of Dr. T. U. Villalobo, first dentist in ordinary to His Holiness Leo the Tenth, and told to carry what he finds in the studio to the public stores. Imagine Dennis, as he squeezes into a flour-barrel a lovely Madonna, smiling with a divine affection, even when man looks his last upon her face, — crowding after her three or four studies for cupids,— the first conception of a fresco, — and the keepsake best beloved which Michel Angelo left when he was last here. All these are jammed together into the "rubbage-barrel," because they happen to have no frames on them at the moment when Dennis sets his eyes on them. Such is the method by which the "smart man of business" winds up a concern which is intrusted to him, — if by chance he have been trained to the twisting of hemp, and the business in question, like John Hughitt's, were the cutting and shipping of lumber. "We must get the accounts closed, anyway," says the smart man of business.

Jasper had the agony of seeing an administrator smash round, in such fashion, in the midst of his uncle's broken affairs ; had the poor satisfaction of interfering once or twice for the rescue of some correspondent who would else have been compromised in the ruin wrought by the smart man of business; had some moments of success when the smart man of business withdrew for a few weeks from Duquesne to demoralize and disorder something else which he was administering on: but after six or eight months the man of business had made a solitude of the thriving village which was, and called it peace. Jasper at the last took poor Mrs. Hughitt by the easiest stages down to Dexter, found for her as comfortable a home as he could contrive with an old school-friend of hers, and for himself repaired to Detroit to seek his fortune. As for Duquesne, which John Hughitt had built up out of nothing, it all went to ruin again, thanks to the smart man of business; you will find no such place in the present county registers of Michigan; and if you are tempted to paddle your canoe down there, you may pick blackberries on what was the causeway to the wharf, should you be in season.

And so in the spring-time after his brilliant commencement, Jasper found himself in the bustling city of Detroit, — with a little more than seventeen dollars in his pocket, seeking his fortune. He was not in the least downcast. Rather was he elated, because he had at last cut loose from the entanglements, and had some reason to hope that he might never see the smart man of business again. What he was to do, he did not know. But he knew he should find himself at some honest work before he had spent all his money. He must indeed. His aunt's little property, left after the adjustment of affairs, was not enough even to pay her modest charges at Dexter. And Jasper had therefore the thought of her as well as himself, as he looked out on his future.

Detroit was at that moment the most active city of the North-west. Chicago was just starting into being; and Detroit was the great dépôt of the trade of that new region, which was beginning to be one of the gardens and one of the granaries of the world. Jasper had passed through the city, back and forth, once and again. Till now he had never made as long a stay as on the sad day when he had to tell every one the news of disaster. Still he had no lack of personal acquaintance among the lawyers and the men of business of the town; and, on his first morning, confident enough of success, only curious as to what form it was to take, he set himself to visiting in succession the men with whom his uncle had had most to do.

"No? Yes: ah, well! There can be no sort of difficulty." This was the average speech that these gentlemen made to him, when they were twice his age. "No difficulty at all. Young men is what we want, Mr. Rising. The West is to be built up by young men; and young men of education like yourself, why, of course they have the best chance! If I had only had your education when I was of your age. Why,—if you had written to me last fall, I would have asked you to take a desk in our office here; just now we are rather overcrowded. Business you know,—well; perhaps a little dull. But then, you will have no difficulty. Have you had any talk with the mayor?"

No: Jasper had had no talk with the mayor.

"Well, now, that is a good thought. Suppose I give you a line of introduction to the mayor. He knows every thing about the public works, you know, —and they need men, you know,—honest and intelligent men, in every line. He is a very good friend of mine, and I am very glad to introduce you" ("writing with assiduity," would be the stage-direction). "A very good friend of mine,—a very good friend of mine. You know where the City Hall is? Yes; three blocks up,—ten blocks west; Mr, Smith, what is the mayor's given name? Oh, yes! I thought it was John. There, Mr. Rising, there is your note to the mayor. I would go with you myself, but here is Mr. Umbein waiting for me. Good-morning. Come in again."

That is about an average of one class of such interviews. This is the other form.

Mayor, sitting behind a desk, which serves in some

sort as a rampart or barricade. In front, on settees which seem a good deal worn, two emigrant women keeping their children quiet with difficulty; a very suspicious, shiny-hatted gentleman of Bohemian birth and features; a little woman with a black veil down, and a large black bag in her hand; two business men with lithographic plans and other papers. Standing between settee and barricade, two constables, waiting to get in a word. Mayor looks jaded, not to say perplexed, receives Jasper's card and note with a bow, and points to a vacant place on one of the settees. He also writes with insane alacrity, folds and directs his letter (envelopes still unknown), beckons the constables, and whispers to them in an aside, dismisses them, and then takes up the settees in order. Different smart men of business, travellers with letters, steamboat clerks and others, come up and interrupt. But the mayor is steel, and holds to "first come first served." So in an hour it is Jasper's turn.

"Yes, Mr. Ring, I am glad to see you, — I am very glad to see you, only we are so hurried this morning; indeed, we are always hurried. Mr. Hughitt's nephew, I see. Yes; I met him at the convention, in — no; yes, — a year ago last fall. I heard, — yes, — no; I did hear of his death. I was very much distressed. Mr. Fordhammer says you are looking for employment. I wish I could give you any encouragement; not that we ever have anything to offer, but temporarily perhaps, while you are looking round."

Jasper takes heart, and assures the poor mayor that some temporary position, while he is looking round, is all he needs, or would think of.

"Yes, well: but you cannot conceive, Mr. Ring, of the number of people I have here. You see Detroit is the great thoroughfare, — or on the great thoroughfare; our geographical position you know, — and every one who lands here comes to this office." At this moment, by way of illustration, an enraged Norwegian with two dogs, three children, a wife, and a gun, comes in, and is with difficulty made to subside upon the only vacant settee. "There is really nothing, Mr. Ring, that is in the least in my gift. But I will most gladly make a minute of your name, and you would tell me where I might write to you." And then, with a guilty and uneasy look, the mayor draws out an immense address-book, turns up page R, by the alphabet annexed, and Jasper has the pleasure of seeing his name entered at the bottom of the second column of office-seekers whose names begin with that letter. As the mayor copies his card, he observes that the name has two syllables. "Oh, Rising is the name! indeed, I beg your pardon, Mr. Rising; Mr. Fordhammer wrote so hastily! I am afraid I called you Ring. Good-morning, Mr. Ring; good-morning. If anything occurs you shall hear from us. Now, sir," — to the shiny-hatted Bohemian, — "what can I do for you?"

These two interviews, taking a good deal more time in fact than they take either to describe or to read of, may be taken as exhibiting the type of a series of visits which Jasper made on his two first days in Detroit, Tuesday and Wednesday. The plucky, prompt "No!" came in sometimes, and was an exquisite relief when it did come. Jasper says he has always remembered with thankfulness the men who gave it to him, from that day to this. But more often, despite himself, he was bejuggled and pushed along by ill-timed good-nature; sent from pillar to post, and from post to pillar, follow-ing a will-o'-wisp, which, however, always showed dif-ferent colors from those of the last jack-o'-lantern, and led to some marsh of a different-colored mud from that which he grovelled in before.

Jasper went home Wednesday night, meditative as to the "best education his country could afford." That it had done him good he knew. But how droll it seemed that nobody in the North-west seemed to want him any the more because he had such training! No: he would not offer himself as a teacher! That seemed rational, and enough people had proposed that to him. But, first of all, Jasper utterly distrusted his ability in that line; second, he could see that the newspapers, and streets even, of Detroit, were crowded with the announcements of professors, who seemed to have little to do but to profess. Jasper could not believe, yet, that his university training gave him no advantage over the Norwegian emigrants, who had hard muscle, a poor gun, and could live on black bread. "Comes to that," said Jasper to himself, "I can have them or do that." He could not believe that he must go out and take up a quarter-section of land. But, worst come to worst, that is, thank God, what every man or woman in America can do. Before he tried that. however, Jasper meant to test Detroit by some other channel than that which his uncle's acquaintances opened to him.

On Wednesday evening, — conscious that he had paid two days of life, and certain dollars to match; and had only a little experience in return, — he paid his bill at the hotel, took his valise to an emigrant boarding-house, sent a wagon for his trunks, and went to bed, resolved to start on life the next morning without further application to his friends.

What has Jasper Rising to recommend him as a man, pure and simple?

So the next day found him at the various steamboat wharves, inquiring whether this passenger-line, or that freight-boat, needed a clerk. And much shorter measure he had awarded to him here than in the places to which he had carried letters of introduction. Nobody wanted any clerk; and Jasper, in his soul, was quite sure that he liked their way of saying so better than he did the more long-winded way. One rather talkative accomplice, or companion, of the man he spoke to in one of the Mackinaw offices, roused up so far as to take a general paternal interest in Jasper, and ask a good many questions about his plans and accomplishments, ending by his suggesting, that, at, at the freighting-house of Dibbs & Fortescue, on the Windsor side, they had wanted an invoice-clerk the last time he was there; they had asked him about a certain Jem Clavers, who had once invoiced in the Mackinaw employ, and the unknown knew that they did not engage Jem Clavers.

Had Jasper any communication with them? No: Jasper had not. But Jasper was perfectly willing. The only arrangement Divine Providence or human Destiny had thus far suggested was this; and Jasper eagerly took the address of Dibbs & Fortescue, waited for the ferry-boat, and, with some hopefulness this time, pursued his way to the dominions of 'Er Majesty, and without much difficulty found the warehouse which answered to the name.

The manners, not to say the language and the cut of the whiskers, were different from those of the western side of the Strait. But the result was the same. They wanted no invoice-clerk, had wanted none, should want none. Nay, they did not know who could have told Mr. Rising that they wanted one. Nor could Jasper indeed, the unknown having had no visiting card perhaps, certainly having given him none. An allusion to Jem Clavers, however, did bring to light the recollection that they had had a letter for Jem Clavers's mother, and they had asked where he was to be found. Probably it was from this circumstance that the unknown had made his mistake about the invoice-clerk. And so they wished Jasper a very good evening; for the day had now well passed the meridian.

"In pure delights like these,"

Jasper spent the two first days of his life at the emigrant lodging-house; and on Friday night found himself no nearer the object of his quest than on what his friends at Windsor call "the Tuesday morning."

Nor was he nearer, to all appearance, on Saturday noon. Silently he ate his dinner, not of the most savory description, among the Norwegians, Germans, and Frenchmen who had been for these days his boon companions at the three revels of the day. Puzzled more than sad, puzzled because he could not get hold of time's forelock; certain that he was making some mistake, and not yet chiding the selfishness of the world, which would not let him "go shares" with it,

4

he left the table, and stood on the stoop to see the laboring men with whom he had feasted drift off, to the right and left, to their affairs.

" It is not that that man is stronger than I," said Jasper to himself, as a clumsy Wurtemburg lout went lumbering down the street, hardly knowing enough to keep on the sidewalk. " I could pull him round and round in any boat on the river, and walk him to death in the woods or on the prairie. And yet, if I went down with him now, and offered my service to the man on the pier where he has earned his two dollars a day since last Monday, I should be told there was nothing for me to do. Is there a disadvantage in speaking English?

" There goes that hulking Irishman from his shanty, boys following as yesterday ; that man has found some-body who wants him. Yet he is no bigger than I am. He is not half so good-natured. And, if we got into a fight, I could knock him down before he knew we had begun." And Jasper chuckled, even in his desolation, at the satisfaction with which he should give the Kelt No. 6 if it were all in friendly play.

" A hole for every peg except me," said the poor boy. " A hole for a Norwegian runaway ; a hole for a German boor ; a hole for an Irish bog-trotter : only no hole for this poor gentleman."

" Poor gentleman," he said again, cutting off the end of his last cigar and taking out his match-box, a little gold-mounted toy which Alice Cohoes had given him for a philopœna. " A poor gentleman," he repeated aloud, " who still smokes Manuel Amore's cigars, and then wonders why he is not hired as a long-shore man."

And with this he went up to his den under the roof ; put up a little parcel for his aunt, of some trifles which he had promised to buy for her in Detroit. When he came down stairs, he was another man. The new epoch of his life really began, when, in place of the French boots he had been wearing, he put on a pair of brogans, re-served from his last trout-brook ; when in place of his

linen shirt, he put on one of gray flannel when for the
beaver hat he had touched only that when
he met Mr. Fordhammer, he put on a Scotch-plaid coat,
and instead of Huntington's tight-fitting frock, for such
were cut and worn in those days, he put on a well-worn
velveteen coat, left from a hunting expedition in Wisconsin. Jasper had not walked fifty yards with his
parcel when he met Miss Mary Chandler, one of the Detroit belles at that time, with whom he waltzed the last
winter at a party at the Shaws'. He was on the point
of touching his hat; but it was clear that the pretty
lady no more recognized him than she did the awning-
post, though she passed that also every day.

Jasper went to the station of what has since become
the Central Road, and gave his aunt's parcel to the
conductor. He stood to see the train leave, having,
indeed, no call elsewhere; and was then slowly leaving
the dépôt, as the station was in those days called, when
he met his destiny.

His attention was arrested by a sharp, angry call,
" Where is Mr. Keyl? Send Mr. Keyl to me."

Mr. Keyl appeared. He was the " dépôt-master."

" Mr. Keyl, why have these cars not been cleaned
to-day? I spoke of it to George yesterday, and no
one has touched them. Here's prairie-mud which
might have come from Battle Creek."

Mr. Keyl was in no wise dashed by the anger of his
chief. With perfectly imperturbable expression, he informed that officer that it was John's business to clean
the car, and that John had not been seen all day.
" Off on a spree, I guess. He has not had one since
Fast Day."

" What do I care for John? " said the superintendent,
not in the least soothed by Mr. Keyl's indifference.
" Make up John's pay, and ship him as soon as you set
eyes on him; and have these cars fit to be seen before
the train is made up." So storming, he went on his
way.

" Where in hell am I to find any one to clean his

cars for him?" said Mr. Keyl, half under his breath, to a baggage-master who stood by. But, before the baggage-master answered, Jasper stepped forward and said, "Do you want some one to clean the cars? Try me."

Mr. Keyl squirted a little tobacco-juice between the rails, surveyed Jasper from top to toe, and said, "Have you ever worked for the road?"

"No," said Jasper; "but I have cleaned carriages, plenty of them."

"Then clean them cars before it's dark; and, if you like, come round here again at seven, Monday morning, and I'll talk with you. Jefferson, show him John's closet, and where the things are, and tell him where he must fill his pails." So the imperturbable Mr. Keyl, who was at bottom much more perturbable than he wanted Mr. Superintendent to know, went his way with an extra oath or two. Jefferson explained to Jasper the mysteries of long brushes and short brushes; the "dépôt" soon sank into its usual quiet; and as Jasper, infinitely amused with the adventure, brought to light the hideous arabesques of the car-paint from beneath the charcoal dust and mud which a smart shower had plastered on them, he knew indeed that his lowest descent was over, and that he was beginning to rise again.

It is not very unpleasant business when you have good tools, and do it for the first time, with nobody to watch you. And by sunset the three cars were clean, the closet was locked, and the favorite of Commencement day went home.

The fair reader need not be distressed by thinking that Jasper had to spend thirteen hours out of every twenty-four in washing prairie-mud off the sides of cars. Perhaps the fair reader never before reflected that anybody had to do this disagreeable duty, — perhaps she believed the platform, when it informed her that all the disagreeable things in life are done by women, and all the agreeable ones by men. In point of fact, the career of car-scrubbing was only the gateway by which Jasper broke into the magic circle. From this time he was in the game with the others,— was recognized as a co-worker,— and was no longer shoved from pillar to post, as he had been when he seemed an outsider. No: the little one-track road, which has since grown into the Michigan Central, had not, in those days, cars enough to employ any man for his whole time in keeping them clean. And Jasper soon found that his new vocation had at least all the elements of interest which variety can give. Now it was to lend a hand to the baggage-smashers, in handling trunks on arrival. Once and again he was detailed to be an extra-conductor when a special train was sent to an academy examination or a county convention. He was the person who collected forgotten parasols and right-hand gloves, after people had left the trains, and kept them sorted against the owners should apply. When the morose ticket-master had occasion to retire occasionally from duty, either for repentance that he had been so cross to people who had never injured him, or for other religious or personal duties to me unknown, he liked to put Jasper on the service of selling at the window in his stead. At this time, the morose ticket-master was more morose than ever, because, in an access of prosperity, the company had enlarged the building, and given him a more spacious office. The only view he took of this improvement was that it cost him so many more steps daily in crossing from the gentlemen's to the ladies' window. Think of it, gentle reader, and you may understand why the average ticket-seller is low-toned and morose; you may reflect that, if you had his trials in life, you would not be gentle; and you will be all the more disposed to give credit to those ticket-sellers you and I could name, who, in face of such temptations in other directions, keep cheerful still,— look up and not down, look out and not in,— and, caged though they be in their little houses of glass, throw no stones, but lend a hand to thousands of unprotected females, such as you, or such scatter-brained impulsives as your male companion in travel.

For Jasper himself, the new life was not a frolic merely, as you may have thought it, but an experiment. As the heroine of the old novel wanted so much to be loved for herself alone, Jasper was by this time dead resolved to work his own way forward in the world, without troubling its mayors, its college authorities, or its Mr. Fordhammers more. There was, undoubtedly, disagreeable life in this association with baggage-smashers, and in the physical labor it involved. But the men learned to respect him in an hour. They learned to love him in a day. Their tobacco was poor; but Jasper could get used to that. They were very simple people; he had never imagined that any people in the world could be so simple. They talked but little; and what they did talk about was their pay, their food, their rent, and what the company was doing. Jasper had not been in this little circle a week, before his habits of generalization, the ease with which he took the wider view of things, the absolute good temper which grew out of this, and, indeed, his general information regarding things in which they were but specialists, made him of real use to everybody in the station-house; and he was respected accordingly. His great conquest was made one day when he went out as fireman, by sudden substitution for a poor fellow who had cut his hand. Purdy, the engineman with whom he went, was known behind his back, among the workmen, as "old Meat-axe"; and so virulent and unintelligible was the heat of his temper, that no man who could get an exchange ever worked with him a week. But Jasper, who, indeed, knew nothing of these peculiarities, went and came, went and came, two trips out and two in, — and conquered "old Meat-axe." He did it by mere force of intelligent questioning and wise acknowledgment of ignorance. Meat-axe himself was not insensible to this most delicate form of unconscious flattery.

At the boarding-house, where he still staid because

he would not be rolling from spot to spot, and because it was dirt-cheap if it had some dirt in its other attributes also, Jasper was hardly less a favorite. But this mattered the less. He was at the head of the table in a week; for the inmates were here to-day, and gone to-morrow. The "boarding-mistress" was amazed at Jasper's ease in talking French and German with the "Europeans." There were, however, Swedes and Norwegians, not to say Welch and occasional Portingallers on the lake, who were quite beyond him. And he found some home amusement in teaching himself phrases of their language.

Not long after this new life had opened for him, he was waked one night, in the midst of his usual sound sleep, by heavy tramping in the passages, and, in a minute more, was conscious of the tang-tang-tang of what he supposed was the bell of a fire-engine house, which must be somewhere near him. Jasper roused himself enough to observe all this, reflected that it was no business of his, and tried to go to sleep again. But sleep was not easy. It was clear enough that every one else in the boarding-house thought the fire was his own business, whatever Jasper thought; and, at last, he dragged himself to his window and looked out,— to find that a furniture store in the next street was all aflame, and to begin to understand that a new city, like Detroit, had other laws than the old places he was used to, and that it might be his own business to attend to his neighbor's in this extremity. He locked his trunk, dressed as rapidly as he might, and ran down to the fire.

It is an amazing sight, a fire in a new town at midnight,— the discipline and obedience, on the one hand; the amount of spontaneous and unpurchased work, on the other. Here was this furnace, three times heated, of a warehouse, packed full of the most combustible matter. Dark on either side, protected only by brick walls, were other warehouses, in which moving lights showed you that men were working hard to pack and save books and valuables while there was yet time. In the street where Jasper was were two fire-engines, and a hose-carriage or two, and a few men with speaking-trumpets giving intelligent and cheery directions, as if pretending that their wholly inadequate machinery was all that could be asked for in the exigency, and loyally obeyed by every man in the throng with the same affected confidence. On the roofs of the two side buildings, sometimes on the central roof, which had not yet fallen, appeared, in the midst of smoke and steam, other men with trumpets, who conversed, even consulted, with those below. A pipe here, a hose carried there, showed the result of such colloquies. Then came the cheery, "Play away, Hero," "Play away, Tecumseh," and the thud, thud, thud of the most wasteful way of using human power, answered with a will, as if to say that men are always ready to sacrifice themselves, even to the last fibre, if only there be intelligent command and an unselfish motive. "Now then; let her have it! What are you afraid of? Good, once more! Put in, Hero! Play away, Tecumseh! One, two; one, two; one, two. Well done, boys, well done!" and every other word of encouragement, as one or another phase of the unequal war took turn. The brakes of the engines were crowded full, with men in every dress, driving the little machines to the very edge of their possible performance. The dense throng of men looking on, only waited their turn at the exhausting labor, and so understood their position.

"Now, gentlemen, walk up; spell these men; you don't mean to have them work all night, do you? Take hold, with a will! What are you afraid of? You won't empty the lake, I guess." And so Jasper and the men around him rushed forward to take the places of those exhausted; and he found himself with his hands on the large round bar, at the eternal up and down, wondering whether indeed he did anything, or whether he were pulled to and fro himself, in this jerking movement, by a power to which he did not seem to lend the worth or weight of a straw.

He could not even see the stream he was trying to

drive. He could only see the letters "ER," of the word "Hero." But he could hear that hoarse foreman, "Now, then! what are you afraid of?" He almost felt ashamed that he did so little. He was conscious of a new *esprit de corps*, in the mad determination that Tecumseh, which was pumping into Hero, should not over-fill her water-tank, as there were rumors she once had done. Then came the terrible doubt, "How long can I stand this? Can I hold on at this till we are spelled? What a disgrace to let go! Could I let go, if I tried?" And, at that instant, the man next him gave a choking cry, lost his hold, and went down, like a log, on the wet stones.

Jasper and his new next neighbor dragged the poor fellow out, one of them, at least, inwardly grateful for this change of duty. They carried the senseless body out of the crowd, hearing, as they retired, the tireless foreman. "See, gentlemen, do you mean to stand and see men die before your eyes? Walk up and spell us. That's right. One, two; one, two; one, two. How's your water, John? One, two: that's well, Hero; let 'em have it." And so Jasper and his companion laid their burden out on the counter of an open and empty shop, and, by the light of the conflagration, stripped him of his heavy clothing, and applied such restoratives as brought him to.

He sat up, rather wildly, on the counter; hardly more than a boy, though he was so tall; smiled shyly, rubbed his eyes; dropped his head again, as if faint; took a little brandy from Jasper's companion; looked down with surprise to see that he had on no coat, and that his shirt was open; and then made an effort to jump down and leave them. But this they would not yet permit. They did their best to find where the handsome fellow belonged; but so soon as his real consciousness returned, it proved that he did not understand a word they said to him, more than they understood a word of his. He was a Norwegian.

CHAPTER VIII.

OSCAR.

JASPER RISING had certainly never before dragged a Norwegian boy, faint from over-effort, from under the wheels of a gasping and throbbing fire-engine. He was therefore sufficiently excited by the adventure, when at last, perhaps an hour before day-break, he put off his wet clothes, and tumbled into bed for that hour's rest before his day's work began. He had, in the mean while, interested the "boarding-mistress" in his poor waif, and had received her promise to watch by him till morning, and make sure that he should not escape. But Jasper himself, as he thought the thing over, while in the sound of the final noises of the expiring fire, did not forsee the weeks, not to say months, of curious care, and insight into life all strange to him, which this accident opened before him. Jasper was yet too young to know, that we are all of us always sitting before the curtain which screens a tragedy, a comedy, or a farce, and that any whistle or any bell may be the signal for that curtain to rise, that a new drama, which may be a life-long drama, may begin.

What followed in this case was simple enough, — such things are happening all the time. The boy was more clear-headed in the morning; and an interpreter was found at the breakfast-table, by whose help it appeared that the poor creature's agony had come from his fear that his father, who was sick somewhere in the city, would need him. The whole sympathy of the house was enlisted, and the father was found. The story, which is acted out before our eyes whenever we choose to open them, was that of the worn-out emigrant, who has not found his place in the New Continent more than he found it in the Old. He was not really an old man ; but even Jasper, inexperienced as he was, saw that he had played his game through, and that his eager joy, when they brought him his lost boy again, was only a flicker of the light in the socket. Physically he was comfortable enough, in much such a house as Jasper was living in himself. But, excepting for his boy, he was hopelessly lonely. The poor old fellow showed, too, all the signs of wearing homesickness and of heart-broken disappointment. Everything had gone wrong. He had been cheated by his countrymen, he had been cheated by strangers. He had tried trade in New York, and had failed. He had taken up new land in Illinois, and had seen his daughter wilt away and die, and then had seen his wife wilt away and die. At last, in a moment which he chose to call deluded, he had sent out to Norway for the boy he left behind when he came over. This was Jasper's waif. The boy had found his father, and had joined his father's fortunes. But the tide had already turned, — and, at last, dis-couraged, he was giving up the battle. And it was at that time, that the accident of the fire brought Jasper into the little tragedy.

It was almost ended. The doctors can do little when life itself has so long been made to do ten times the duty it should do. Everything was the matter with the poor man, — or nothing was the matter with him, as you chose to say. All was, he was dying. The earthly hull was done with, and the old engine was to work a new one. All there was for Jasper and his friendly boarding-mistress to do, was to make the poor fellow believe that his boy was not left to sharpers, and to see that the closing hours of earth were not painful for him to remember.

So he died and was buried by strangers' hands. And Jasper found that he had now the gratitude and passionate allegiance of this orphaned Oscar, — found that, with all his inexperience, he was to advise as to the boy's future, — found that he had the duty, not difficult, of administering on the poor old father's estate. To think that he, himself just starting on manhood, should be the only child of Vinland who had succeeded in rendering any kindness, or giving any welcome, to this stranded Viking!

Administration was easy enough. The emigrant chest contained all the property, and a hopeless mess it was : some old account-books of the miserable shop he kept for Danes and Swedes and Norwegians in New York; some files of the processes by which he there went into bankruptcy; the land-office documents by which he acquired his title to his farm in Illinois; a lithographic plan of a city, most likely in a swamp, where he had been cajoled into buying a share, and even the deeds of lots, — alternate numbers from eleven to thirty-one. Tied with a blue ribbon, carefully wrapped in parchment, were the letters which Christine sent him before they were married, — tied in with the ribbon was a gold ring. Then a memorandum book, carefully kept, showed that he had sold his farm for less than the improvements cost him, after Christine had died. It showed, had one chosen to untangle it, how everything had gone wrong. Mixed in with these more essential things were a few Norwegian books, which had survived the wreck, because, perhaps, no one would buy them, some magazines and newspapers; and this was all the inventory.

Jasper wrote twice to an attorney in Michigan City about the swamp-lots, and got no answer. It was clear enough that Oscar, like Jasper, was to begin life without a fortune.

But not without a friend; and I have been the more willing to tell the story of the beginning of this friendship in this detail, because the boy Oscar and his poor dying father really rendered to Jasper, as it proved, the service that no Mr. Fordhammer or no Miss Mary Chandler of them all, from the very nature of the case, could render. They saved my poor hero from himself. Jasper was proud, quite too proud to put himself on the society of people who did not seem to want to see

him very much, or whom he suspected of that indifference. He had been compelled, for a time quite too
long indeed, to think solely of· himself and his own affairs. A note once a week to his aunt, and another
from her, the purchase perhaps of a yard of blue barège
that she could not find at Dexter, or some little present
of a pound of better tea than he thought she would
have there, was but a little counter-check in the current
of a week's lonely life. His correspondence with "the
fellows," his old classmates, was running dry. He had
not much to tell them, and they had not much to tell
him. The college pleasantries became a little tame
when they were put on paper; when put on paper a
second time they seemed to reader and writer like
stale tobacco-smoke, and so they never appeared a third
time. With the other workmen and clerks at the station Jasper had a pleasant daily acquaintance, but it
had not anywhere ripened into intimacy. And it may
well have been that pride, dress, poverty, and stranger-
hood may have kept poor Jasper wholly and even fatally
to himself, had not one stroke too many on the brakes
of the Hero engine literally thrown Oscar into his
arms.

So soon as he found how completely dependent Oscar was upon him, Jasper was not the man to let him
go. No! They saw the grave filled above the old
Norseman. Jasper with his own hand smoothed the
gravel and adjusted the sod, and for this act of sympathy the boy thanked him his life long. When they
came home, Jasper explained to him that they were to
sleep in the same room: he had driven Mistress Margaret up to that arrangement. And when, that evening, the grateful fellow forgot himself for half an
hour, in working with Jasper on a Danish or Norwegian exercise which Jasper insisted on writing, Jasper
felt his victory indeed. They used a French "Ollendorff" for the phrases' sake. And Oscar was fairly
amused to see the number of conditions in which they
could place the "gardener," and the "wife of the gardener," and the "friend of the gardener's son." He,

too, forgot exile, forgot tears, forgot everything for the moment, when Jasper had the wit to show him that he, too, was good for something.

And Jasper, of course, had to teach him English too. Not so hard, for these Norsemen are, after all, our cousins. Into one great kettle was plunged a dipperful of Keltic roots, a dipperful of German, a smattering of Latin, and a flavor of Norman-French; and, when we sip the soup from that kettle, we call the delicious compound English. Into another kettle, not quite so large, were poured smaller cupfuls of German roots and Keltic, with a smattering of Latin, and a flavor of French. The flavor of the soup is delicious, only we call it Swedish. These two soups are not very unlike each other: though one is a little dashed when he reads his Swedish Testament to find that a ¡"disciple" is a "lärjunge." * Oscar's language was yet a third of these mixtures of the eternal elements of European speech. It was Danish, as Danish is modified in Norwegian conversation; Teutonic roots more plenty than with us, perhaps; Latin roots, French intermixtures even; and an occasional racy *tang* of the good old Icelandic itself. Oscar knew something of the Swedish also; and while he taught these dialects he learned as well, and while he learned he taught, — only eager to do what would please Jasper, and delighted if, at the same moment, he could serve him. So they both got something which is a million times better than that questionable good, "self-culture."

And now it was Jasper's turn to play Mr. Fordhammer and Mr. Keyl — to find "a place" for Oscar. "A place!" how much satire there is in the word! He had this time his own experience to profit by. He took care that the boy should begin at the bottom, and poor Oscar made no difficulty about that. Bottom indeed! He would have begun at the bottom of a well, or of a lead-shaft at Galena, had Jasper bidden. Jasper had no thought that Oscar was his servant, scarcely ·

* Which is to say, "Learn youngster."

thought that he was his pupil. But from morning
to night, and from Sunday to Saturday, Oscar's feeling, deeper than thought, was simple gratitude that
Jasper was his master. Every day when Jasper went
to his work, Oscar went with him, until Jasper could
make some excuse to send him away. It was astonishing to see how soon he learned the names of streets,
the names of people, and by what a divine instinct he
learned how to do an errand, when he could not understand one word in twenty of those that gave the order.
It was not long, therefore, before Jasper, growing himself in authority now, found a vacant laborer's " place "
that he could push Oscar into as a " substitute." The
" substitute," in this finite world of ours, soon finds
himself a " regular," if he does not drink, if he tells
the truth, and is punctual to his duty ; so little, indeed, does a hard-pressed world demand of its servants. And so, as the summer passed on, the day
that Jasper noted as the Commencement at Cambridge, twelve months after his own triumph there,
he was himself regularly installed in a post of some
little authority in the freight-station, and Oscar was
that day on duty cleaning cars from mud, in the vocation in which his master began.

Oscar was paid his wages week by week, and regularly brought the money to Jasper. Neither of these
gentlemen had attained the dignity and the inconvenience of salaries and quarter-days. Jasper had thought
over, with some anxiety, the business of Oscar's money,
as a part of the guardianship, which seemed, without
any authority from surrogate, or chancery, or probate court, to have alighted upon him. So long as the
poor boy was an expense to him, the problem was
simple enough. But when Oscar's father died, after
all charges were paid, there was a hundred dollars or
more left of what had been the poor fellow's all ; and
now Oscar was earning twice what his living cost, and
all Jasper's little advances on his account were repaid.
All this brought before Jasper the pros and cons of the

case. Was he this boy's guardian, or not? If the
boy wanted to make ducks and drakes of his little patrimony, could he hinder him, and, if so, how? And
was there somewhere in Norway some uncle or aunt
who had a better claim to the rights and responsibil-
ities of guardianship than Jasper had? Poor fellow!
it brought up curiously enough all the memories of his
own orphanhood; and he drew a long breath as he remembered how unconscious and indifferent he then was
to all such thought or care.

But now he was the care-taker, not the cared-for,—
guardian, not guarded. And so, after breakfast one
Sunday morning, he bade Oscar walk down with him
to one of the more secluded lumber-yards by the side
of the lake, found a shady place on a pile of boards,
where they had a back as they sat, and, as soon he saw
Oscar was well engaged with a lath which he was cutting, began pumping him about relatives and home.

"Were you happy at your uncle's, at Molna, Oscar?"

"What is happy?" said the unconscious ward.

"Did you like it? Were they kind? Did you like
them? Did you have a good time?" said Jasper,
finally falling back on the dialect of the Yengeese.

"Did I like it? I did not like it. Were they kind?
They not kind. Did I love them? I hate them. A
good time? I haved a dam bad time."

The answer was at least definite, and its resemblance
to Ollendorff's exercises on the tenses of verbs amused
Jasper, even while he was struggling to maintain the
gravity of a self-appointed judge of probate. He told
Oscar for the hundredth time that he must not say
"dam," that fragment of an English syllable seeming
to be the part of the language which he had first acquired, and, in consequence, to be the last which, with
his dying breath, he would lay down. The poor child
was pure as purity, and had, as yet, no real idea of the
profanity of the expression.

The judge of probate tried again. "But your uncle
had a good house. You had enough to eat. You had
clothes to wear."

"No good house," persisted the ward in chancery. Then came a volley of Danish. Then he explained, " I say house no good, where uncle fight and swear, she-uncle fight and swear, big Michael swear and drink, big Christine swear and drink, all swear and drink; all tell Oscar go carry fetch, go fetch carry; you come here Oscar, you go there Oscar, up stairs Oscar, down stairs Oscar, in-door Oscar, out-door Oscar. I say no good house; I say dam bad house. No, no, no! not dam bad; I say bad, bad, bad house. What for I care good clothes to wear, if Christine drink, if big Michael lie, if mine uncle swear, if mine she-uncle scold? No good house; no good uncle."

This was by far the longest speech Oscar had ever made in the English language, and it reflected immense credit on his teacher and the Ollendorff.

It did not appear to Jasper that his case in chancery was getting on particularly well. He tried on another tack.

"Let us see: how many weeks since you wrote to your uncle to tell him your father died?"

The boy started up at the words, walked sharply to the end of the pier, threw into the water the stick which he had been cutting, and looked as if he would be glad to go in after it. Then, in his impulsive way, he rushed back to Jasper, his eyes streaming with tears; he fell on his own knees in the chips before him, and hid his head between Jasper's knees. He sobbed there passionately, and looked up to say:

"I no tell you lie, my master!" The poor boy, having chosen from the beginning to call Jasper master, could not be prevented when he was in the least excited. To say "Jasper" seemed to be a forced piece of etiquette or decorum; and Jasper never heard him say "Mr. Rising," though behind Jasper's back no one ever heard him say anything else. "I no tell you lie, my master; you say to me, 'Write letter to your uncle;' I write him. You write him name and place. You give me money, and show me, tell me carry him to office, post-office. I no say yes; I no say nothing. I

5

take that dam letter, and I no go to that dam post-office....I go down to ferry. I wait till boat just fore being come in,—all water boil, bubble, boil; I throw that dam letter in water; I throw in that quarter dollar you give me. Boat come in : all boil water, no letter there ; I go home, I no say I take letter to that post-office."

And having relieved his conscience thus, he fell to sobbing again on Jasper's knees.

"So," said the judge of probate to himself, "we have not so much as given notice of the death of the intestate." He let the poor boy sob on a minute ; and Oscar first broke silence.

"O my master, I bad boy, I bad boy! but certain true, my master, I no say dam again."

The feeling that he had displeased Jasper, in anything he had asked or bidden, was much stronger than any feeling that he had wronged his uncle.

"No matter, no matter, dear Oscar. But what for you do this? Why not tell your uncle that his brother is dead?"

"Not he brother ; not he brother !" Here another volley of Danish, ending by an explanation, in very broken English, that this beer-guzzling, gin-drinking Viking of fire-water was brother of Oscar's mother and not of his father, — as if that had made any difference. And then to Jasper's persistent "why," the boy at last looked him squarely in the face, with his great black eyes :

"Letter go Norway, go to mine uncle. Mine uncle read him. Uncle say, 'Catch Oscar again ! Oscar big boy now ; Oscar cut wood, row boat, catch fish, go fetch carry. Oscar come home.' Mine uncle send what you call sheriff, president, governor, some little sort of king, catch poor Oscar, put those iron things on him hands, tumble him down, carry him home." Oscar had been terribly impressed by seeing a Cleveland house-breaker arrested and carried off one day by an Ohio officer with a warrant. " Poor Oscar leave him master ; go to him uncle. No, no, no !"

Jasper meanwhile had been going over the natural notions of probate law, and trying to adjust the eternal rights and wrongs. What reason, divine or human, was there, why he should undertake to send this boy home? All that God or man wanted was, that the boy should be cared for, should be kept from temptation, as far as might be, should be kept from swindlers and thieves.* Any decent probate court in the world would bid a young man of this age choose his own guardian; and Jasper saw no reason why he should attempt to press the matter of a return to Norway farther. He had sounded Oscar pretty thoroughly, and had found out his wishes. So he tried to turn the talk to some indifferent subject, a passing steamboat, a flight of ducks on the lake, and then on one or another occurrence in the street as they walked home. But Oscar was silent; not sulky nor moody, but thoughtful, and would scarcely reply. When they had come up into their own room together, and Jasper had sat down to some writing, Oscar crossed the room, opened the drawer of the bureau, drew from it a pistol which Jasper kept there, and, with the simplicity of a child, carried it to him.

" Kill me, my master; kill your boy."

" My poor Oscar, what do you mean?"

" I mean kill Oscar; no send him away."

" But my poor child," said Jasper, in tears himself this time, " who wants to send you away? What are you afraid of? I will never send you away."

" O my master! what for you ask about letter? What for you ask about mine uncle? and what for you tell me to write letter? What for you tired teach poor Oscar, take care poor Oscar, make poor Oscar home?"

Jasper was fairly upset: he promised the boy, by all that was holy, that he should never be parted from him but with his own consent. He tried to explain that all the uncles in Norway could not take him against his will. He soothed his wounded love as best he knew how. He fondled him and caressed him. He told him that he loved him too well to do anything which would

not be for his best good. In all of which Oscar caught
the spirit, if he did not make out the words. Once and
again he made Jasper repeat those which said they
should not be parted; and then his handsome face
cleared almost as suddenly as it had clouded, and he
seemed perfectly happy.

Jasper took him to church with him; and the boy,
who did not understand ten words of sermon, prayer,
or hymn, regarded the whole service as a sacrament
binding him and "his master" together for weal or for
woe. Jasper tried as he came home to explain to him
about the disposition of his wages. But the boy did
not care, and could not be made to care. Once assured
that he would be no burden on Jasper's purse, that was
enough. For the rest: "You take my dollar. My
dollar you dollar, all one; I your Oscar, you my master.
That's all."

It was not long before this contract of wages brought
out a result for both of them which neither had imagined. The winter which followed these events was
one still remembered through the North-west, and indeed
through the Atlantic States, for the sudden contraction
in all credits, — which resulted, rightly or not, from the
New-York panic which sprung from the London panic,
when the great houses of Westerholm, and of Alters and
Alters went under so suddenly. With a sudden jerk all
loosened credits were twitched up. Many a rein
broke with the twitch. Many a horse balked, shied, or
started and ran. For months upon months chaos reigned
among men who borrow, and among men who lend.
And in the midst of this chaos, Jasper Rising found, to
his amazement, that he was a capitalist.

He went in one day to a little carriage-factory, where
he knew the people, to inquire about the best way to
purchase some varnish, which the station-master needed
in some miserable car-repairs. He saw at once that
the place was in confusion; and, as he looked round,
satisfied himself that some "smart man of business"
had got in there by way of setting to rights some matter of which he knew nothing. He got his information,

however, from Buffum, the principal, and left the shop,
to find that this gentleman followed him into the street.
" You know we are all broken up here," Mr. Rising.
No: Jasper had not known anything of the kind. Such
things happen very quickly; and he was in no circle
where they talked of them. So poor Mr. Buffum had
to explain: an every-day story. The little carriage-
factory had always been run very much on credit. Buffum's partner, a showy, unreliable fellow, of the satin
waistcoat and heavy gold-chain type, who always cared
more about horses than he did about carriages, had
taken occasion, a month before, to run away with somebody's else wife, and all the ready money of the concern which he could lay hands upon. This had been
an ugly thing enough: then the panic had come; no
bank in Detroit would renew a penny of their paper,
and so the modest little establishment was knocked
higher than a kite, as Mr. Buffum put in, before he
could turn round. Every carriage they had, finished or
unfinished, was attached, " grabbed," in the elegant
phrase of the streets, by one creditor or another. All
the material that could be removed was seized in the
same way. And the creditors who had not succeeded
in "grabbing" what they thought sufficient had got
some sort of proceedings in bankruptcy a-going, by
which such rights as there were in the shop itself and
any other property there, were to be sold at auction for
whom it might concern. The workmen were hanging
round to secure, as they might, their back pay. The
foreman, an honest fellow, was there, keeping an eye
on the wreck. But the snug little factory of Buffum
& Woods, which a month ago was as promising an establishment for its size as there was in the street, would
very soon be nowhere.

Jasper was interested in all this story of ruin, but he
did wonder why Mr. Buffum told it to him. How
should Mr. Buffum know that he had seen like ruin on
a much larger scale, only a year ago, at Duquesne?
He was entirely surprised, when Mr. Buffum closed his
story by saying, " Really, Mr. Rising, we owe very lit-

tle. I have got orders in my pocket now from Ann
Arbor, from Marshall, from Dexter, why, even from
Cleveland, Mr. Rising, on which we would make profit
enough to clear every cent of this debt, if they would
only give us time. And is it not a shame for an honest
man to see the work of ten years swept away and his
family left begging, to see as good men as my workmen
there sent out on the streets in the middle of winter,
for want of a miserable discount of five hundred dollars?"

Jasper was disgusted. This was exactly like Duquesne. He showed his sympathy by some kind question; and Buffum explained, that the men to whom he
owed money were, with scarcely an exception, his
friends, even his companions, — that there was hardly
one of them who wanted to be hard on him. But the
squeeze in the money-market affected them all alike;
no one of them alone could afford to lose his claim,
even though it seemed a trifle. There were one or two
strangers, and of course the workmen, who must have
cash; and, if anybody was to have cash, all must have
it. Buffum supposed that it was too late to save the old
firm from bankruptcy. But here was the shop, here
were the men; in especial, here was the foreman, on
whom Buffum could not help passing an eulogy, finding
to his joy that he had in Jasper a listener. Up till this
moment, Jasper had felt that Buffum knew of his own
misfortunes, and was telling his story for mere weari-
ness of spirit, because he must tell it, or die. But now
Jasper found, that all this narrative was an introduction before Mr. Buffum asked him, if he, Jasper Rising,
did not want to step into the breach, poor Mr. Buffum
being only eager to show him what resources and what
securities were still left to him, though now rendered
unavailable.

Jasper was on the point of laughing in his face.
His one feeling was that of pure fun, that he should
have been mistaken for a capitalist. But to laugh
would have been unkind. And Jasper walked on, gulp-
ing down that temptation; and still showing so much

of a fellow-sufferer's sympathy that Buffum in his turn went on with what he had hoped, and what he wished, and what he could propose.

The upshot of it all was, that at this projected auction-sale, which would scatter the whole concern to the winds, nobody expected to realize a thousand dollars cash from everything there was, not "grabbed" or "grabbable." With that result nobody would get any dividend of any value, the shop would be destroyed, Buffum ruined, the workmen scattered. "But if, Mr. Rising, anybody liked to take an interest in the concern to the amount of a thousand dollars; if, — I thought it possible some friend of yours would, — or perhaps you yourself might think of it ; why, I do assure you, sir, if you will only look at our contracts any man would be wholly safe ; and if, twelve months hence, he wanted to withdraw, he could take out twice the money he put in."

Drowning men catch at straws, or Mr. Buffum would never have made this proposal to a man he knew so little as young Rising. But he made it ; and, seeing that he said nothing, he went on, "There need not be a thousand dollars in cash, Mr. Rising. Five hundred dollars in cash would pay the workmen, and pay these New York bills for iron and for fringes ; and I can make every other creditor give us three months' time, till we can deliver these dearborns in Peoria, if I only have your name in the firm, or the name of any other man who has people's confidence. If Woods had not run away, though he did nothing but drink and swagger, I would not have been here."

Jasper did not permit himself to be melted by the poor man's eagerness ; but as he talked, he thought perhaps he did see the chance for the boy Oscar which he should not have dared to look for. He had no wish to start Oscar in life without a handicraft. "Either a handicraft, or a liberal profession," John Hughitt used to say ; "though you never work a day in either." It had only been as a temporary thing that he let Oscar scrub the sides of cars ; and, for himself, it was only

as a temporary thing that he was keeping books in the
freight-house. He had found out, from the beginning,
that Oscar had the divine tact with tools, — that he
was deft and successful in handling them ; and it had
been to him merely a question of time and opportunity
how and when he should place Oscar in some form of
apprenticeship which might make him master of a craft,
and so, to all intents, master of the world. Perhaps
that time had come. Jasper would not encourage Mr.
Buffum ; but asked him if he could bring round all the
papers to the freight-dépôt after business was closed, —
" and, Mr. Buffum, ask your foreman to come too."

For Jasper Rising had read history enough, and seen
business enough, and watched enough failure and success, to believe in men, more than he did in plans or
compacts, or anything else on paper. And yet further, he guessed, and he guessed rightly, that the crisis
of the Buffum carriage-factory depended not on Mr.
Buffum, so sensitive and nervous, nor on the ideal
capitalist yet to be discovered, but that it depended on
this Dundas, the foreman, who had or had not given a
reputation to their work, and who would or would not
give reputation to it in the future. So he asked for
Mr. Dundas, as well as the Peoria orders, and the
Cleveland contracts, and the other pieces of paper.

Dundas came. Jasper liked him, and he liked Jasper. Piece by piece, they all went over every bit of the
tangled history of the firm. Piece by piece, they went
over the work still possible. The hours went by in the
dark freight-station, and Jasper sent out Oscar for
some biscuit and a jug of water for their supper. Eating as they worked, they unravelled the tangle. Then
Dundas and Jasper went down into the dark by themselves, and he gave to Jasper his version of the successes and failures of the shop ; and Jasper, with perfect frankness, told both of them why he dealt with
them at all. He saw with pleasure that Dundas took
in his motive and plan for Oscar ; and, at the least,
they understood each other, when, at midnight, he took
such papers as he needed, and said he would be pre-

pared before the week was up to make them a proposition.

He spent the week in inquiry and consultation with different parties concerned. And all this talk and counter-talk ended in the establishment of a new carriage-building firm, of

BUFFUM, RISING & DUNDAS.

Not that they had any sign painted. They had no money for signs. But they drew up the papers. They agreed with the creditors of the old firm; they turned the old books bottom up, and began at the end of them; they had the old bill-heads altered in red ink by Oscar. The agreement, in brief, was this:

1. Dundas pledged himself personally that Oscar should learn all of the wheelwright's and coach-builder's craft that a man who cared to know could learn between the ages of seventeen and twenty-one.

2. On this understanding, Jasper lent two hundred and eleven dollars and seventeen cents of Oscar's property to the new firm, — securing it in such ways as he could, but considering that he had a right to invest it thus as the premium for the boy's apprenticeship.

3. On the same understanding, he paid himself into the new firm three hundred and fifty dollars, being very much the major part of his own earnings during the year.

4. All three principals bound themselves not to draw a penny for personal expenses from the new firm for six months. They would live by their wits, or on their relations, rather than on the business.

5. The new firm was thus able to buy the good will of the old firm and its stock in trade, with the right of redemption of the heavily mortgaged store, and to redeem some of the most essential articles seized by creditors. It paid four or five hundred dollars in money, and it gave its new notes at four, five, six, and seven months. Dundas was sure, and Rising satisfied

himself, that these notes could be met, and more than met, by the contracts they now had on hand.

I suppose the transaction was one which no probate court in the world would have authorized. But Jasper had to be his own probate court. He explained it to Oscar as well as he could, who simply said, "No my money; all your money." And when he found that he was to smooth spokes with a draw-shave, instead of washing mud off cars, Oscar was delighted. Jasper kept at his desk in the freight-depôt. Only he spent three hours of the evening at the counting-room of the new firm, writing up the books, acquainting himself with the correspondents, making out the men's accounts, and, in general, learning and supervising the new business. Oscar always sat, with some book or some whittling, at his side.

Six months run by fast when every one is so busy. At the end of six months the new firm was on its feet. It had money at its bank; it had credit; it was in favor with the best people in Eastern Michigan for its thorough work and neat and new devices. The banking and business world had forgotten the existence of the defunct houses of Alters & Alters, and of Westerholm. Buffum, Rising, & Dundas had paid the notes with which they bought their establishment; had even taken up some of them before they were due. Credit is a plant which grows rankly and fast, by the same tokens and by the same laws as those under which it is so easily withered and destroyed.

What pleased Jasper most in the success was the daily development of Oscar. Oscar was in the right place at last. He was not in the least above filing iron, or drilling rivet-holes, — not he. But he punched and filed not as a slave, but as a man of genius compelling metal to obey his higher purpose. Did you never notice the difference between the way in which a sculptor chisels marble in his studio, and the way in which a stone-cutter, with tools precisely like the other's, cuts a grave-stone in a stone-yard? There is that difference between the way in which a child of God, born to inven-

tion and the control of matter, handles his wood and
his iron, and the drudgery in which another child of
God, who was never made for this service, lets the iron
and the wood master him.

And after some months' trial, Jasper left his friendly
railroad-station to give his whole time to the correspondence, accounts, travelling, and other business of
the new firm. Queer enough, his last service in the station, after he had bidden them all good-by, was to a
person he had seen in old days, if he had remembered
her. The afternoon train was leaving, and an Eastern
party, a little late, hurried into it. One of the party, a
young lady encumbered with her hand-baggage, dropped
a parasol as she stepped up, and did not observe it.
Jasper saw it fall, sprang forward, tapped at the window, and handed it to her. She opened the window,
took it, and shyly said, "Ich Danke!" But Jasper
saw so many German travellers, that even this did not
help him. "Where in the world have I seen her?" he
said, as he turned away.

But she remembered him. This was Bertha, on her
way to Milwaukie with some German friends of a friend
of her uncle.

CHAPTER IX.

HOW BERTHA BEGAN.

THE most astonishing marvel in human life is, I suppose, the sudden change from a girl to a woman. Boys change to men slowly. The change with them requires from five to ten years. And colleges were instituted for the wise oversight and conduct of the human being in that transition. In our times they prefer to wait and receive young men, to send them out a few years older. But a girl changes into a woman of a sudden. You leave her, for your vacation journey, cutting out paper dolls, and mending those very weak spots where their dresses meet their necks. You come home, and you mistake her for her mother, so cautious and thoughtful is she; nay, if you saw a gray hair or two, you might mistake her for her grandmother. I will not say but I have seen this change from girl to woman come on in twenty-four hours.

When Jasper Rising bade Bertha Schwarz good-by, at the warehouse of her uncle the basket-dealer, she was a German girl, who spoke English very badly, and was frightened to death whatever happened or did not happen. Not two years after, when he handed her parasol into the open window of the railway carriage, and said to himself, "Where have I seen her before?" she was a woman as completely as she is to-day, — in thought, in feeling, in bearing, and in appearance. There is no reason to wonder that Jasper did not know her, while she did know him. If dress goes for much, I am by no means certain, that, in bidding farewell to his short railway duties, Jasper was not wearing, to the last thread and button, the same travelling-suit with

which he went, with Bertha, from Boston to New York
two years before. But, on the other hand, I am quite
certain that Bertha had long since doffed the quaint
German dress which the fifteen-year-old child wore
that day, and that the most brilliant costume of the
most fashionable promenade of Detroit was not more
distinguished than the travelling-dresses in which she
and all the ladies of the party were arrayed. And in
those days there was not a place in the world which
ran more madly into the matters of distinguished costume than Detroit did.

For, I am sorry to say it, our poor little Bertha had
fallen into the hands of some people who had plenty of
spending-money, and did not know how to spend it.
Such people infallibly take to gambling or showy dress,
or both ; perhaps both are the same disease, with only
a change in the symptoms or the name. I say Bertha
had fallen into their hands. Not that they had sent
out strong ruffians into the streets of New York, who
had seized her behind, put a sponge of chloroform to
her nose, and carried her into the Astor House, where
two other stout men with pistols and three glaring
women with diamonds made her promise to serve them
for forty-seven years without lifting her voice above a
whisper. I observe in the weekly newspapers long stories founded on such transactions, generally with a
large picture on the first page. But I have never met
such events in my life, — nor did Bertha in her life.
And at the time of which I write chloroform had not
been invented. Nor were the properties of sulphuric
ether known, unless by Dr. Jackson, and he had not
yet mentioned them. What I mean when I say that
Bertha had fallen into their hands is, that she had
agreed to go to the West with these people to be a sort
of home governess to their children for a year at least,
and to render such other services as might be expected
of a young lady in their family. Mrs. Rosenstein, the
head of the clan, chose to regard her, in externals, as a
sort of adopted niece ; and although she did not absolutely buy all her frocks and bonnets, she did supervise

such purchases, made such additions as she chose, and
kept Bertha looking very much like the rest of her train,
— with such rebellions on Bertha's part as I shall try to
describe.

All this had come about, not unnaturally, in the time
which had passed since we left little Bertha, as she was
then, playing Mozart at the musical party at Kaufmann Baum's in Orange. That visit at Orange, of her
mother and brother and herself, proved to be a long
one. And it was wholly satisfactory all round. The
lame boy got quite well. Mrs. Schwarz and Mrs.
Baum ceased to be afraid of each other, — and at no
period despised each other. This is a great point to
gain, when two women, by no agency of their own, are
brought into very close personal relationships. Mrs.
Baum was not in the least "stuck up," as our expres-
sive local phrase has it, by the prettiness of her house,
or the prosperity of her husband. Mrs. Schwarz was
as simply and sweetly herself, in the unwonted circumstances of life at Orange, as she would have been were
she singing in the village church in Lauenburg. And
thus it came about, to the great delight of Kaufmann
Baum, that as the two sisters sat together in the long
mornings of that summer visit in the pretty house at
Orange, and as they rode together in the afternoons,
and as they sat on the piazza in the evenings, they
came to rely on each other very thoroughly, and to
love each other with a very genuine love. It was by
no means manufactured as a sort of duty-love by a
certain law, for persons who in that law were sisters.
As for Bertha, or Thekla as Baum still called her nine
times out of ten, her place had been sure next his
heart, and his wife's heart, and everybody's heart from
the beginning.

Of course that visit ended. As I say, the lame boy
got thoroughly well, his broken leg hardly a perceptible
shade shorter than the other. With real grief on both
sides they parted. But Bertha was to come back at
Christmas, — and she did come. And she came again
at Easter. And if Kaufmann and his wife could have

brought it about, by keeping up all the festivals of Luther's calendar, or of anybody's calendar, they would have had a new visit from Bertha at Whit-Sunday, and at Martinmas and Michaelmas, and on St. Bertha's day and St. Wilhelm's day and St. Kaufmann's day. Whenever a decent excuse could be made, they had a long visit from Bertha. And Bertha grew to feel herself quite as much at home in Orange as she was in Boston.

It was while she was on one of these visits in Orange that Bertha the child became Bertha the woman, by that sudden marvel of which I have spoken. The novelists talk of the slow unfolding of the bud of a rose when they describe this phase. I have seen rose-buds unfold very slowly, when they were trying to open themselves in late October. On the other hand, I have left a morning-glory bud tight twisted when I went to bed at eleven o'clock, and when I was on my piazza at five the next morning I have found it in the fullest glory and beauty of its life. I do not mean to say that Bertha looked like a morning-glory, but I do mean to say that her change from girlhood to womanhood was almost as sudden. And so it happened — of course, for these people lived in America — that Bertha began to occupy herself with thoughts as to what she could do to earn her own bread and butter, her cotton, woollen and linen, and withal her shelter over her head. That is to say, she began to think that she must not live at her father's charge any longer, nor at her uncle's, and to look with an inquiring look upon the shop-girls who sold her tape and needles, and to wonder how they got their places, and who hired them. She looked with a supreme admiration upon the school-mistresses, called "teachers," in the public school where her brothers went. But she did not aspire to a destiny so ennobled as theirs. To her father and mother she knew she should never dare to speak or to write of these day-dreams. But none the less did she dream them; and she was soon resolved that they should not be always dreams, but should become realities.

So she opened her mind one day to her Aunt Mary, as they were taking a brisk walk together. She could speak to her Aunt Mary a great deal easier than to her mother about such things. She made rather a botch of it; but it amounted to this, that she knew her father and mother had a hard time of it, and that she felt that she ought to help them; and though her father had never said a word to her about it, and never would, she could not but feel it was quite time that a great girl like her should be earning something. " I am sure, Aunt Mary, that I see plenty of girls here, who are no bigger than I am, and who do not know any more, alas! than I do, who must earn their living, for they have no one else to earn it for them."

By this time Bertha spoke English very accurately, though she had, of course, a well defined Lauenburg accent.

Aunt Mary heard her all through, without interrupting her; nay, perhaps not helping her as much as Bertha would have wished her to help. But when Bertha worked through, occasionally breaking into some exclamations in German, her aunt said:

"Oh, dear! my poor little Thekla. I knew you would come to this some day, but I did not think it would come so soon!".

" Why, what do you mean, dear auntie?"

" Mean, darling; I mean that I went through all this when I was sixteen, — and I suppose dear Margaret went through it when she was sixteen, — and that I knew, of course, that you must go through it too; but I did not think it was quite time, I hoped it would not worry you quite yet. How old are you, darling?"

Bertha said stoutly that she was seventeen. Aunt Mary laughed:

" As if I did not know all about it. As if we did not hear all about the birthday party, the week after Thanksgiving, — that must be now four months ago. My little Theklein is sixteen years old plus four months, and that she calls ' almost seventeen.'"

" Well, my dear auntie, I am as big as most of the

girls of seventeen whom I know. I am really too tall to have it decent for me to dance where other people are dancing. I am ashamed of myself, I am so tall."

"And so we must go to work, because we are too big to dance; — what a hard world it is, to be sure, in its demands on us."

"Oh! please do not laugh, — pray do not laugh, — dear Aunt Mary ; if I were not so stupid, I could make you understand how I feel, and what I think I could do. Of course I know I cannot teach geometry and trigonometry, and all those grand things, as Miss Birdsall does ; but I know I can teach little children things they have to know, — I can teach quite as well as Sarah Stone can. Or, if it seemed best, if the way opened, I can keep accounts, just as well as Mary Billings can."

"Darling, dear, do you not suppose that I knew all that, — and that you sing better than anybody within ten miles, and play better, and, for that matter, do everything better ; and best of all, that you love your auntie as nobody does within ten miles, and that she loves you as she loves nobody but her children?"

Of course Bertha knew that every word of this was minted from God's own truth, and she just turned half round, and looked her full-eyed thankfulness ; but she would not be bribed even by tenderness from her purpose, only this time she went on speaking in German.

"My dear little aunt," she said, in the pretty phrase in that language which Aunt Mary loved so well to hear, "do I not know this last better than you can tell me? But you shall not lure me and coax me from what I have resolved upon, — and you love me too well not to give me counsel, now I ask you for it. I do not ask you whether I ought to help my dear father and my dear mother. For I know I ought to. And also, dear little aunt, whatever you think, I know I can. What I ask you, then, is not about either of these two things, for you see they are all settled. I ask you how I am to do it. That is all!"

"Yes, darling, yes," said Aunt Mary, almost in a dream, — for in truth her own girlhood there in Hins-

6

dale was all coming back to her as the eager child spoke,
—"yes, darling, yes; and I will come to that pres-
ently. But my little love,"—for they were still speaking
in German,—"have you thought of this,—which is
what most girls forget,—have you thought of how
much help you are now to your father and your mother,
and Wil. and my dear Fritz, and all? Do not forget
that it is a great deal for your father to be free from
every bit of responsibility about the accounts, about his
bills and other people's bills, and a great deal for dear
Margaret to be free from all thought about the children's bibs and tuckers. And what my little Rosebud
is ever to do without you, I am sure I do not know."

"Do not break my heart, dear auntie;—all this I
have thought of, yes, even of Rosebud I have thought,
and how I should ever live without the little darling.
But you see it all. I am here to-day, and Rosebud
lives, though I know she is counting the days till I return. As for the accounts, and all that, my dear father
brags of it and makes much of it. The truth is, that
it is not much in reality anyway, and Wil. can do
it all, as well as I; and it would be good for him to
do it too. For the bibs and tuckers, auntie,—see here."
And Bertha really opened her little Hamburg leather
memorandum-book as they walked, and showed Aunt
Mary the careful account where she had recorded all
the family sewing which she had done in six months.
It footed up one hundred and seventy hours, all told.
"See, dear auntie," said the eager girl, who had, as
it was clear, gone over her whole ground before she
spoke a word, "only see; here are not twenty days'
work of a hired seamstress. My mother could hire a
girl for fifteen dollars to do all the sewing I have done
in six months. Surely my work might be worth more
than fifteen dollars." Clearly enough, Bertha had
thought the whole matter through, and so Aunt Mary
plainly saw.

She did not in the least discourage her. She told
her she would herself write to Bertha's father and
mother, by way of giving her countenance to the plan.

She told her that she must accustom herself to the idea
of work that was hard, — and worse than that, work
which was lonely; but she found that Bertha had
thought all that over ; and could tell her, by a spirit of
prophecy, a good deal which Aunt Mary was talking of
as only learned by experience. Aunt Mary knew a
great many things which Bertha did not know. But
Bertha had had one experience of which Aunt Mary
knew nothing. She had changed her country. In that
experience, even while she was a girl, she had gained a
curious double view of the world. As the astronomers
would say, she had got a second observation, with a
considerable parallax. So there were many things
which Aunt Mary had only learned as a woman, which
were familiar to Bertha as a child.

And so that visit was the end of the vacation visits
of childhood, — unconscious, and without count of
time. From this time forward Bertha also is a person
of plans, of engagements even, who counts her days
and weeks, and must husband time. From this moment
her Ups and Downs begin.

She went back to Boston, fortified by Aunt Mary's
letter, and saw her uncle had written a few lines with
his views. To tell truth, Uncle Kaufmann, who had
long since tried to transfer her wholly to his larger
and more prosperous home, and had failed in that, saw
certain advantages for Bertha's training and for her future in the new and wider life which she proposed,
which he could not expect, if she always remained under his brother Schwarz's roof-tree. Schwarz was a
kind father and an honest man. But he was one of the
kind, who, at Lauenburg or in Boston, would be much
the same man, — and in a new world, as in the old, he
was wholly satisfied with his little house, his little
trade, his little round of pupils in music, and as Kaufmann would have said, his little life. Now Kaufmann
knew reverently, as has been already said, that in Bertha's life there was the divine genius which might be an
eternal joy to her and all around her, or which might
be so thwarted, hemmed in and pestered, so long

as th[...]fc lasted, that she should grind through life in
grief and misery. And without looking far into the future, Kaufmann Baum believed, that, for the scope and
power of this divine genius, it were better that Bertha
should not live always in the restrictions of her father's
habits and home. So, when he was consulted, he gave
his cordial assent to the scheme of her "working for
her living," to take the phrase which the new-fledged
" work-woman" herself employed.

So it was, that, not very long after Bertha's return,
when one day a friend of Baum's came into his counting-room, and asked him if he could recommend to a
friend of his at the West a good girl who could teach
his little children the rudiments of music, Bertha's
uncle of course thought of her and named her. The
fitting correspondence passed on both sides. The Western "friend" was Mr. Rosenstein. Mr. and Mrs. were
to be at Saratoga before long, and it was agreed that
Bertha should be sent up to them to meet them at the
United States Hotel there. Do not let us do Mrs.
Baum injustice ; let us acknowledge that in the correspondence she saw the vulgar purse-pride which we have
since learned to designate by the word shoddy, — a
word, by the way, which originally denotes a very useful material, which may be applied in a perfectly legit-
imate way. Mrs. Baum probably knew, from the mere
choice of Mrs. Rosenstein's note-paper, and the method
in which she used sealing-wax, just what type of person
she was, as well as she knew it ten years afterward. I
have no doubt she told Kaufmann. And I have no
doubt that he said that that was the fortune of war, —
that if Bertha meant to be a teacher she must take her
chance, — that there were worse things than mere vul-
garity in the world, — and that, in a republic, the children even of vulgar people had a right to an education.
And so it was that poor Bertha made her *début* in the
new part of the " maid who earns her living," as she
was welcomed by the exuberant and overacted tenderness of Mrs. Rosenstein in her own " private parlor "
at the great United States Hotel.

The Rosensteins made a long business of their journey West. They had to make a long stay at Niagara.
Mr. Rosenstein made rather mysterious visits thence
into one and another region of Upper Canada, as it
was then called. Let me hope he was not making arrangements for smuggling. They came to Detroit by
steamboat; and Mrs. Rosenstein had a very terrible
time on the lake, and her health was such that she had
to lie by at Detroit at the best hotel for two or three
days to repair damages. You would have said that the
shopping of Detroit could have had but little attraction
for a lady, who, within a month, had exhausted the
novelties of Broadway. But that is because you are a
reader too gentle to know what are the temptations of
shopping, as shopping, to people who do not know what
money is for. And, for that matter, there were things
in those days, in which the ladies and gentlemen of
Detroit showed quite as much extravagance as even
New York or Paris showed. So, in spite of Mrs. Rosenstein's prostration of nerves, she had to have a carriage every day, and go to Tom's or Dick's or Harry's
to make good the necessary stores in some article of
prime utility before they were banished to that "dreadful Milwaukie."

So was it, in fact, that they came late to the railway
station, and had to hurry to the train. Then was it
that Bertha dropped her parasol, and that Jasper
picked it up and returned it to her, as has been already
said and sung.

The chapter cannot end better than by an illustration from the ride which followed, of what the Rosensteins were, and their children, and of Bertha's success
in her new *rôle.*

The very moment after Bertha thanked Jasper for
the parasol, the little train began to move, — how unlike the giant serpents, as one is tempted to call them,
— the long convoys which move out so often now on
the Michigan Central or the Michigan Southern. Shrill
and loud in the first clatter of motion rose the voice of
Mrs. Rosenstein, not yet seated.

"I told you we should be late, Franz; I knew the driver did not know the way. I was sure he should have turned down by the distillery." Then without waiting for an answer, "Set down that basket anywhere, Ferdinand, and come back to me. No,—not on that seat,—put it where we can see it. I cannot sit there, I must have two seats together. Perhaps these people will move to the other side. Why, is this where the sun comes in? I can never ride on the sunny side. It is a shame the car should be so jammed up with people. Go and tell them, Franz, that they must put on another car!"

Franz was not a hired servant, as the reader may suppose, but the husband of Mrs. Rosenstein; and was capable, in his own way, of displays quite equal to hers of his own very cheap and worthless personality.

At last, by infinite negotiations, two sets of double seats were secured, one on the shady side, one on the sunny side. The shady side was occupied by Mrs. Rosenstein and her daughter Adelaide; a little dog was in front, also a tall wicker-basket from which a fuchsia-bud appeared, two travelling-bags, a large lunch basket from which a black glass bottle-neck protruded, a camp-stool, two parasols, an umbrella, and Franz's fishing-rods. The sunny side was occupied by Bertha and her charge, Master Ferdinand Rosenstein, Theresa and Charlotte. They had under their feet a good deal of portable luggage, and each of them some piece of the day's spoils in shopping in hand.

After the train was well in motion, so that the excitement of the entrance was a little subsided, it appeared on an inquiry for papa that he had gone forward to smoke. Mrs. Rosenstein and Adelaide refreshed themselves, with a good deal of parade, from some sherry that was in the black bottle, and, with a good deal of fuss, each ate an orange. This physical duty done, Mrs. Rosenstein felt that it was time for her to display to the travellers,—most of whom were stock-raisers returning from a great sale of cattle,—the true elegance of her breeding and her indifference to expense. So she swayed forward to the other party, and said, serenely this time, "Where is that little jewelry parcel, — who took that? Is it possible that we left it on the counter? Oh, no! dear Lotty; not that one, those are only some little articles of *vertu*. I mean the jewelry, not from Black's, — he is at New York, — but from this man's. For such a place as Detroit, they were astonishingly pretty."

"Dear mamma, you took them yourself; they are in your gray bag."

"Did I, my love? I think not. I could not have taken them, you know."

But it proved that she could and did. A thorough excavation conducted in the gray bag, under the direction of Bertha and Charlotte, exhumed from various parcels of ribbons, confectionery, patterns, and trash generally, two neat jewellers' boxes, on which Mrs. Rosenstein descended. Of course she opened the wrong one first, that it might produce its full effect on the drowsy grazier opposite. Of course she found it was wrong, and she said, "Oh, no! not that of course — amethysts are not what we want now, of course. That is not what I am thinking of, my sweet. Cannot you guess what I am thinking of? Such an unconscious, simple little toad as you are!"

Bertha was undoubtedly flattered that she was called a toad so loudly and affectionately. She must have felt much more pleased when Mrs. Rosenstein, with a jerk, opened the other box, and disclosed a pretty enough simple bracelet — gold — or gilt, as the case may have been. She lifted it out with due ejaculations, and said, "I am sure my sweet child knew who it was bought for. Such a pretty circle belongs only on a pretty arm. Slip up that sleeve my, dear;" and so, to poor Bertha's dismay, not to say disgust, the bracelet was clasped with an audible snap on her arm. "Sweets to the sweet, my child, — and prettys to the pretty; that is what I say. No! not a word, — nothing could be more pretty or becoming. The moment I

saw it in the case, I said, ' That bracelet only belongs
on our dear Bertha's arm.' "

Dear ·Bertha could not help remembering that the
sweet bracelet had been the cause of a most disgraceful
fight, or haggle, between Mrs. Rosenstein and the jew-
eller.   But this, Mrs. Rosenstein herself had fortunately forgotten.   She sailed back to her own seat in the
pride of a brilliant *début* before the graziers and other
herdsmen.   There was no part in which she cast herself so often as that of the " Affectionate Patron."

The effect of the *début* was a little dashed, however,
by her finding that Adelaide had taken advantage of
her temporary absence to arrange the shawls for a nap,
and had even lost herself in sleep already.   Mrs Rosenstein missed the chance of serenely commanding that
another seat should be cleared for her, by saying before
she knew it :

" What! are you asleep again?   You sleep all
the time.   If you choose to go to sleep, don't muss up
my Canton crape, — and do have some mercy on your
own bonnet.   A hat that cost fifty dollars mashed like
that !   Get up, you lazy girl ; get up, and sit up, if you
can ; and do give some thought sometime to your
mother ! "

The high comedy of " The Affectionate Patron " was
followed, without drop-scene, by this little selection
from the farce of " Mamma in a Rage."

CHAPTER X.

HONEST WORK.

THE new carriage-building firm of Buffum, Rising, & Dundas, worked its way into notice and success, not too rapidly, but very certainly. A good combination is honest, well-informed determination, which was here represented by Jasper; sensitive idealism, which was represented by Buffum; and practical, shifty common-sense, with experience in the handling of things, which was represented by Dundas. In truth, the partners in a firm, or in other partnership, as, for instance, the matrimonial alliance, succeed best when they are not much like each other. Jasper was constantly teaching certain lessons to his hands, to his customers, and to those from whom he bought material, which did the firm good, and, in the end, raised its reputation. Old Edgar, a real frontiers'-man, almost of the Natty Bumpo type, was in the habit of paying his taxes, and buying his powder, salt, and nails, by getting out every winter, when the snow was deep, a load or two of wagon-spokes, which he then hauled into Detroit, for sale to the wheelwrights, as his annual sacrifice on the altar of civilization. He appeared one day and asked for Dundas, who was in general his ally.

"Mr. Dundas is out, — out of town. Can I do anything for you?"

The old man was a little lost at having a new face to study, and a new hand to deal with. Indeed, he did not like it, more than the Georgia boy liked to be "put out to a strange gal." But he did not want to haul the load back to Clear Rapids, and he was used to leaving most of his spokes at this place. So with a great effort he stated his business.

"Oh, it is Mr. Edgar!" said Jasper. "I am very glad to see you, Mr. Edgar; we know all about you here."

This encouraged the old man; and in a remarkably short time he got through with the necessary introductory preface, about the freshets and the drift-wood, and the deep snow, and his wife's sore throat, and the general news of Clear Rapids, — intelligence all of which in an indefinite way was to justify him in asking one dollar and a half a hundred more for his spokes than Buffum & Woods had ever paid, or, indeed, than anybody in Michigan had paid for spokes till that hour.

To his surprise, he found that Jasper, instead of beating him down, even rose on the price which he proposed.

"The price is well enough, Mr. Edgar, if the spokes are good; and you never sold us any unsound wood yet."

"Come and look at them," was all the old man said, with a modest pride which was in itself dignified.

"No," said Jasper, "I don't want to see them. You are a better judge of spokes than I am; and, if I did not trust you, I would not deal with you at all. I will tell you what I will do. How many spokes have you?"

The old man said that in the two loads there might be a matter of twenty-seven hundred. The truth was, he knew there were exactly twenty-seven hundred.

"Then," said Jasper, "we will take five hundred spokes; but you shall pick them out yourself; you shall give me the five hundred best spokes in your wagon, and I will give you thirty dollars for the lot; that is more than the rate you have fixed for them."

The old man started, and said he was not used to trading in that way.

"No," said Jasper, "I know you are not; and I know it will take some time to unload and load the wagon, and to pick the spokes over. For that I rely upon you, and for that I pay you. You shall have one of these men help you unload and load."

The old man thought it over and agreed; and for the next three hours the loafers of Detroit who passed that way had the satisfaction of seeing the process of the sorting out the best spokes from those which were not absolutely of the first quality, and of hearing his explanations of the principles which guided his selection. Whether, with his diminished load, the old man went to all the other wheelwrights in town, and sold out to them at the price he originally demanded, it is not our part to inquire. Jasper had taught all his men that none but the very best material was to come into that shop; and this was one important step towards teaching them that none but the very best work was to go out of it.

There was no lack of occasions for the repetition of the same lesson. Slack work is, alas! so common in a country which is not even half begun, far less half finished, that a man who sets himself to thorough work, whether it be in finishing wagons or in collecting taxes, will find he is every hour arousing the surprise of those he works with. Not many days after the spoke business with Edgar, a wide-awake, jaunty young fellow stepped into the new counting-room, looked round with the air of one who was a good deal more at home than the owners of the establishment, and said in a condescending way, "Where's Woods?"

Now, Woods was the defaulting partner of poor Buffum, whose sudden departure for parts unknown had so nearly reduced the infant carriage-factory to "everlasting smash." Buffum could not bear the name. If a young man, handsome in exterior, perfect in education, faultless in morals, of attractive demeanor, the descendant of a long line of noble ancestors, and authorized to draw on the Bank of England indefinitely at sight, had come to Buffum and had asked permission to pay his addresses to Rebecca Buffum, had that young man's name been Woods, Buffum would have bidden him go perish. When, therefore, the affable and condescending New-Yorker asked "Where's Woods?" Buffum would not even be civil to the man, — he only growled out, " Don't know."

But Jasper, who took the man's measure in a moment, and saw the patent-leather bag in his hand, — who also would have been civil to Woods himself, or to the great author of Woods's misfortunes perhaps, had he come into the counting-room, — Jasper looked up and said, " Mr. Woods has left this firm. The last we heard of him he was on his way to Botany Bay. He is probably there by this time, if he has not yet been hanged."

The stranger, who was quite indifferent to Woods's existence, — and was, as the books say, already weary of the subject, — affably said, " Then he has left the firm. I only called on the firm, — had no acquaintance with Mr. Woods." This was a lie. The last time he had been in Detroit, Woods had taken him out in his own buggy to a miserable drinking-house where they affected to have a trotting-park, — had talked big about Fashion and Boston, and the other celebrities of the day, — from such careful study as he made of " The Spirit of the Times " every Sunday; and the stranger who was now dealing with Jasper had, then and there, played euchre with him and some companions they picked up there, till daybreak the next morning.

" I only called on the firm," said he. " I represent Tubalcain Sons, — travel for their New-York house. Looked in to see what you want in our line this spring. Looks of your shop, you will want to give us some large orders."

" No," Mr. Fortinbras," said Jasper, quietly, " we shall not have any orders for you." Buffum went on writing. Buffum knew what was coming ; but they had had Tubalcain's hardware so long that he knew he should never have had the nerve to break the thread. He would have said they would take just a small order this time, with a hope that Tubalcain Sons would die, or the runner would die, or that possibly he, Buffum, would die before another visit came on. But Jasper had no intention of dying, or of having any question about Tubalcain Sons' hardware.

"No, Mr. Fortinbras, we shall not have any orders for you," he said simply, without the slightest tone or accent from which the agent could guess why the accustomed yearly order was withdrawn.

But Mr. Fortinbras was not timid, nor easily snubbed. Had he, indeed, been a man of Mr. Buffum's nervous make, he would not so long have held to the career of a travelling salesman for the New-York branch-house aforesaid.

"But you have not seen our new styles, Mr. ——," said he. And he rapidly opened a marvellous permutation, double-combination, triple-bolting lock, which fastened the patent-leather bag. "I want to show you — just to show you — the patterns which our Mr. Sella got up after his last visit to America. You know, sir, that those English makers never do understand our styles till they have seen what sort of a country this is, — great country, — fast country, and their old John-Bull ways will not quite answer, not quite." All this very volubly, as he was disinterring from the bag the card on which were sewed the patterns in question. "Now look at that, sir. See how neat that turn is. Tubalcain Sons have taken out patents for that curved button in England and France, and have applied in Washington. But for all that, we make no change in our price to our old customers. We can put you these buttons, with the nuts and screws, at eleven sixty-two the gross; they cost us, without saying one cent of the duty, — they cost us nineteen shillings six in Lamech's Cross. Lamech's Cross, you know, is where our works are."

Here, in despite of good lungs, Mr. Fortinbras had to stop for breath; and Jasper, nothing loth, had his turn.

"If they cost the firm nineteen shillings six, the firm was cheated," said he; "that's all." And he opened a wicked little drawer in his desk, and began taking from it old, dirty, rusty bits of iron. "There's one of Tu-

balcain Sons' last style of buttons. It broke in the
shank there, without the strain of a pound on it. Bad
stuff. There's one of Tubalcain Sons' screws. The
cutting is so irregular, that you can see it is wrong
without a gauge. There is one of their nuts,— it will
not turn on the screw nor on any screw. There is
a side spring — or what they called so — of their make.
It broke in the workman's hands before ever the carriage went out of our shop. Lucky that for us. No,
Mr. Fortinbras, I don't suppose your house cares much
for our trade; but, if they do, you can tell them that
they had better go back to the traditions of old English
work, — pay less attention to styles, and more to the
stuff behind them."

"But, Mr. Buffum!"—

"My name is Rising, sir,— this is Mr. Buffum."

"I beg you pardon, Mr. Rising; of course we have
just what you want. We know our market, I think,
and we know what a shop needs which turns out first-
class work. Those styles, — well, at the price we put
them at, of course you do not expect actually first-
class iron or work, Mr. Rising; but if you want, why
— you know we supply the very tip-top city-makers.
Goddards, Tolman & Russell, Flint & Fergus, the
best Philadelphia men, all have their fancy irons from
us. Just let me bring you some cards which I have in
my lodgings; and I can show you work that your best
Michigan thorough-breds cannot jerk in two."

But Jasper was pitiless. His business then was
something far beyond getting good iron fancies into
the shop. And he said dryly, "No, sir; we will not
deal with your house. You have sold us bad iron. Of
course I know that you could have sold us good iron.
I have sent my own orders to Ibbotson Brothers, and
my own goods are in the New-York Custom-house to-
day. I knew I was dealing there with men whom I
could trust; and I told them so, paid a good price, and
I did not ask for samples."

Mr. Fortinbras tried to get in a word edgewise, but
it would not answer. Jasper bowed him out, and he

withdrew, crestfallen. Doubly crestfallen; for he had lost his order, and, more than this, he had lost the expected invitation from his friend Woods, to see the Bantam Mare trot against Gen. Cass and Old Hickory. And though Mr. Fortinbras had not expected much amusement from this spectacle, he had looked forward to a satisfactory night at poker, euchre, or whatever might be the favorite play with the Red-Creek fashionables that year. All these hopes were disappointed as Jasper bowed him out of the counting-room.

"Now, Fergus," said Jasper, turning to a bare-armed, paper-capped Scotchman who was waiting for him, — "now I can talk to you. But did you hear what I said to that fellow?"

"Why, yes; I did, sir," said the Scot, not quite certain whether he should have listened to a counting-room conversation.

"I am glad you did, and I wish every man in the shop could have heard it. For what it means, Fergus, is this: that we will not have any poor work go out of this shop. Cheap work may go out of it, very often; and I hope it will. I hope we shall make such wagons that old Edgar himself will be glad to buy one to take his wife to meeting in. They shall be cheap, because they shall be the best he can get for his money. But they shall not be cheap because they have bad iron in, nor bad leather, nor bad work. And so you see, Fergus," — and here Jasper's voice took on a more kindly tone, — "so you see, that is the answer I must make to you about taking your poor countryman into the shop. He is not a good workman. You know he is not. You had to tell me he was not. Now, we are all in one boat. You and Oscar and Smith and Walter have just as much reason for wishing this shop to have a first-class name as Dundas, or Mr. Buffum here, or I have. None of us can afford to take on one poor workman, — more than we can afford to buy that poor cockney's slag because he paints it and patents it, and calls it iron. To tell you the truth, I do not dare take on MacDonald.

"But I'll tell you what I have done. Edgar's neighbor at Clear Rapids was here yesterday, trying to sell me some stuff. I told him that I had a man I wanted him to take at his saw-mills. You know I was brought up to lumbering, and he likes to talk with me. I told him of MacDonald, and his family; and he says if we will wait three weeks, he will put up a house for them, and Mac shall be put on the mill as one of the night-gang. And then if he is good for anything, he shall work his way up. He's good pay, and honest as Bass Rock. And then, Fergus, if you like, we will take that boy of his — Andrew, do you call him? — into the shop, on the same terms Oscar is working at. You shall see to him yourself, and you shall make him, before you are done, as good a finisher as you are. We can get along with boys who are learning; but I will not risk the record of the shop on men who have never learned. I think you understand."

Fergus was a Scotchman, as I have said; and he did understand. What is more, he was really grateful. Mr. Rising had done a great deal more and better for his poor friend than he had proposed, and Fergus had got a lesson which filtered into the comprehension of all the hands.

Such a determination, once started by Jasper, had been taken up in a spirit perfectly kindly by both his partners. Buffum, whom one is always tempted to call poor Buffum, — so frail was, in his case, the wicker-work around the glass vessel, if one may borrow the convenient image of a demijohn, or damajan, to denote the make-up of his life, — poor Buffum was an idealist, who, but for such friendly stay and help as Jasper was giving to him, would have wholly gone to the wall. Because he was an idealist, he simply exulted in the theory of perfect work, and perfect work alone. Dundas was no idealist. He was simply a good mechanic, well trained. He, therefore, simply hated bad work. He hated it as a gentleman hates to hear a nasty story. He hated it as a good sewer hates to see bad stitches, even in a piece of work where bad stitches will never be seen again, and where they hold the cloth together. He hated it as a Latin teacher hates to hear a boy say : " *Tres partes*, three parts ; *divisa est*, divide ; *omnis Gallia*, all Gaul ; " that is, he hated to see a thing badly done, or wrongly done, even if a superficial world, looking on, said that the result was all the same. Dundas hated bad work because it was bad. The three partners, therefore, were wholly in assent about the new departure of the firm ; but it must be owned that they needed all Jasper's determination, and his firm way of putting things, to start the firm in its new career, and to teach the little world inside the shop, and the large world outside, what the new departure was.

Nor was that lesson very quickly taught. The world is slow to believe in improvements. A clever French writer says of advertisements, that the first time an advertisement is printed you do not see it, the second time you see it and do not read it, the third you read it and forget it, the fourth you read it and resolve to ask your wife, the fifth you read it and do ask her, and on the sixth reading you go and buy. This statement expresses, without the least exaggeration, the world's slowness to learn of real improvements in its condition. That is the reason why the most eager and plaintive wish of any real reformer is still, what it always was, that people who have ears may learn to hear. But the general impression is, that people who have ears need not trouble themselves to hear, but, instead of that, that they should turn to and talk about themselves.

If Buffum, Rising & Dundas had issued any number of handbills stating that all their work was thorough work, no human being would have believed them because they said so. Nor did anybody to whom old Edgar told his story of the spokes remember it a minute after he told it ; nor did the loafers who stopped to inquire as to the unloading of his cart. Nor did the loafers at the Cass House bar, to whom Fortinbras, a little drunk, told, with many oaths, how he had been snubbed by a man whose name he did not know, who

7

was nothing but a —— carriage-builder, remember his story an hour. But when, at the end of the autumn, Hubbell, the cashier of the Bank of Confidence, came into the bank-parlor a little late, and a little dusty, and had said that his wagon had broken down, and he had had to walk, Mr. Anstey, the President, put down his paper and said, "Let me tell you whom to send it to. Send it to those men at Buffum's. You know I bought my new buggy of them, — it was last December, — and, by Jove! we have not had to tighten a screw on it, and it runs like oil." This being the longest speech Mr. Anstey had made for many years in the bank-parlor, and Mr. Anstey being respected in the inverse ratio of his loquacity, — and no wonder, — Hubbell did send the wagon to the new men at Buffum's, when, under jury rig, it made its way into the regions of the bank. And, when this sort of thing happened twenty times over, people began to recollect, what they had never taken the trouble to remember, the parables which at the moment they could not understand, of Rising's dealings with Edgar, and of his harshness to the cockney runner.

The idealist firm, although they dealt in material things, had, as all men have, the eternal questions presented to them, and had to make their answers accordingly.

It was at the time of the outbreak of the Mexican War. All three of these men had voted against that war as steadily as they knew how. Jasper had spoken against it in one and another ward-meeting, and sometimes on stumping expeditions in the country. Dundas, in his quiet way, had talked down one and another braggadocio declaiming in favor of manifest destiny; and Buffum, in his sensitive way, hated any war, most of all a war with a weak nation from which a strong one had stolen a ewe lamb. So they had all said, as individuals, that the war was wrong; and whatever honors it might bring to individuals, it would never bring any credit to the country. Mr. Polk, however, had not had occasion to consult Buffum, Rising & Dundas, and the war had gone on. I suppose Jasper himself thought that he had done his duty in the premises, and that he had as little to do with it as with the Wars of the Roses, when one day he was invited to go into partnership with Mr. Polk as one of the principals.

A tall, gray-haired, gentlemanly man of military bearing, and with a gold button on his cap, came into the counting-room, said his name was Croghan, that he was Col. Croghan of the Engineers, and that he had come West from Washington on the Government's affair in regard to its contract for army-wagons. Jasper bowed and said nothing. "We have published an advertisement, Mr. Rising, explaining what we want; and I have at the fort some wagons which I could show you, with the modifications which Gen. Scott and Gen. Jessup propose."

Jasper bowed again, and said nothing.

"To be perfectly frank with you, we have not had exactly the bids we liked in answer to our advertisements. The order is a large one, and we know the time is very short. The large Eastern houses are full of other work; and, though we have given some large orders there, we shall not be supplied. I happened to be in Detroit on business; and I heard of your firm, and I thought I would come and see you. The West has some great advantages in the selection of lumber for wagons."

Jasper bowed again, but still said nothing.

"I think I can make you understand what we want," said the colonel, a little surprised. "We know our time is short, and we are disposed to be liberal. What we should like would be to engage the whole service of some men who understood their business, some men like yourself, who would be willing to make a large contract with us. Of course they need not do the work in their own shops, — we want the first of these wagons in five weeks from to-day, — but such men could command the services of all the small shops in this part of the country. The Government is very liberal about advances; and really, Mr. Rising, your own work here would be rather that of inspection than of manufacture. So you sent us good wagons, we should pay well for them, and pay promptly."

It was in this way that conscientious officials dealt with conscientious workmen before contracts, also, when reduced to one of the meanest sciences of social life.

This time Jasper had to speak. "We saw your advertisements," he said, "and we determined not to bid."

"I know you did not bid," said the colonel, a little dashed by Jasper's reticency, "and I can very well understand why you do not want to bid. It is all a demagoguing pretence, the whole theory of advertising for bids. I told the quastermaster-general so when he began. Now he has lost a month, perhaps he knows it. I should not think you would bid. It is we who bid now. In short, we must have the wagons."

Jasper bowed again.

"You will not, of course put an unfair price on your work. But the country wants good work, and the Government has no time to spare. So we are willing, as I said, to pay well, to pay the highest price, if you will only enlist for us the best service of the men who can do these things."

"Yes," said Jasper, "I understand what you want; but we do not want to build these wagons."

"Does your work press you so?"

"Not at all," said Jasper, laughing; "I wish we had ten times as much as we have. I should sleep better for one."

"Then, why not take our offer? or why not make us one? Name your terms, say for two hundred of these wagons, and see if I cannot come to them."

"I have named my terms, — they are, that we do not want to build them at all."

"I do not understand you. You say you would be glad of work, and you will not take it when I offer it."

"I said I should be glad of ten times as much as we are doing; and I should. But I did not say that I wanted to do work for this war."

"Let me be as frank as you have been, Col. Croghan, and do not let me offend you. You believe in the administration, and you believe in the war. You are doing your duty, therefore, in building these wagons as best you can. I do not believe in the administration, and I do not believe in the war. What I could do to prevent it I have done, and now I cannot help it. I do not choose to make money out of what I think a public wrong."

This time the colonel was puzzled.

"The responsibility is not yours," said he.

"No. But it would be if I made a profit out of wagon-building which the war made necessary. I wish the war had not been begun."

"Perhaps I do," said the colonel, "but I did not make it."

"No," said Jasper; "nor I, thank God. Nor will I make money out of it."

"And your partners?" said the colonel, looking round.

"Have talked with me of this, and we agree."

The colonel rose, and gave Jasper his hand with great cordiality. "Pardon me," said he, "are you Quakers?"

"So far as this goes you can call us so," said Jasper, laughing. And they parted.

So the new firm lost a connection, out of which they could have easily made twenty thousand dollars before twelve months were over. But they saved their self-respect; and really that was worth — something — more.

CHAPTER XI.

THE GOVERNESS.

BERTHA SCHWARZ had just entered what was called the school-room, at Mrs. Rosenstein's house in Milwaukie.

"O Bertha, I am so glad you have come! Mayn't I string beads while I say my verb?"

"You must not say Bertha to Miss Schwarz."

"Who are *you?* I will say Bertha if I choose. Mayn't I say Bertha?"

"You sha'n't say Bertha. If you do, I'll tell ma. Ma said we must say Miss Schwarz. Did not she, Miss Schwarz? Ma! ma!" this last an octave higher, and ten fortissimos louder, "Ma! ma! *Shall* Charlotte say Bertha?"

Such was the hopeful and agreeable beginning of one morning's skirmish or running fight, in the discharge of Bertha Schwarz's daily duties. It is a good enough representation of every day, as she began it, with these spoiled wild-cats. There was nothing in their mother that they respected, and they had no habit of obedience. But they referred to her ten times as often as children do who have the habits of obedience and of respect. Bertha began with amazement, soon passed through the stages of terror and home-sickness, and finally succeeded, in a certain fashion, in obtaining much more influence than father or mother ever had. Whether this did much good, either to herself or to the children, she was not wholly sure.

On this particular morning, for instance, she had shamed some and encouraged others into something like ardor, and had really succeeded in interesting

Adelaide in the geography, which Adelaide had been carefully trained " to hate," in the methods of Bertha's predecessors.

" Your big map the same as my little one? Why, Miss Schwarz, I am sure the little one is big enough for me. I never shall read all the names on it. I hate map-questions."

" I am quite sure, Addie, that one day you will be asking your father to buy you a bigger map than mine."

" I never shall ask him to buy me any book but a story-book as long as I live and breathe. I mean to tease him for a story-book to-day. Clem Saunders told me of a beautiful book her brother brought her from Buffalo."

" But now, Addie, we must study the geography. If you never know your geography, you will never know how to go to Buffalo."

" Ho ! sha'n't I? I shall just tell William to take my trunks down to the lake, and then I shall make him drive me down to the boat ; and I shall go on board, and I shall say to old Mr. Plumptre that I must have the very best state-room he has got ; and he will let me have it, because pa got him his place in the line ; and I shall have a beautiful time all the way ; and when we get there, old Mr. Plumptre will come and find up all my things, and will get a carriage for me, and I shall ride up to Gussie Flinders's. You shall go, too, Miss Schwarz. You will like it ever so much better than that horrid stage. I don't see why pa wanted to come that way."

Bertha had not advanced matters much by her suggestion of Buffalo. It was clear enough that the little goose had already learned that there were other methods for achieving what she wanted than the imperial road of learning. Yet Bertha began again.

" Don't you remember Trenton ? "

" Of course I do. Didn't we have great fun there? Don't you ever tell, Miss Schwarz, as long as you live and breathe ; but while ma and pa and you were sitting

on the piazza, after tea, with that old Dutchman and
his wife, Ferd and Lotty and I went down to the stream
again; and we began throwing rocks, and then we
made boats; and then Ferd took off his boots, and
Lotty and I pulled off our shoes, and we sat on the
rocks and paddled in the water with our feet, and Lotty's shoe got all wet; and we had such fun. Wouldn't
ma scold if she knew it. You won't tell, Miss Schwarz,
will you?"

Bertha did not commit herself in reply to this amiable entreaty, but held on to Trenton, resolved to get
her geography lesson started if she could.

"How do you suppose we ever got to Trenton?"

"I suppose — I don't know — I suppose pa bought a
ticket to Trenton from Saratoga."

"No."

"I suppose he told the railroad man that ma wanted
to go there. I know Mrs. Flinders told ma she must
go there, — that was the way ma knew about it. O
Miss Schwarz! you never saw anybody like Mrs. Flinders."

"No matter about Mrs. Flinders. That was not the
way we got to Trenton. The way was this: After
Mrs. Flinders had been talking to your mother at the
United States, your father took out this very map that
I have got here, and he looked for Saratoga, and for
Utica, and for Trenton, and Trenton Falls; and he
found them all four, and he showed them to me. He
knew we could go to Utica by the railroad. He did not
know, and none of us knew, whether we were to go to
Trenton when we went to Trenton Falls. He found out
by this map; and he showed me and your mother. I
suppose he did not show you because you hate map-
questions, and those were map-questions."

"I do not see any of them on my map," said Adelaide. There is no greater minor comfort to a snubbed
child at school, than the power to say, "It is not in my
book."

"No; Utica is on your map, but neither of the

Trentons are. Saratoga is, — there is Saratoga. Now see if you can find Utica."

" Rome — Attica — Painted Post, what a funny name — Utica, here's Utica. That's where Ferd upset the custard ; oh, how mad he was ! "

" Well, no matter about Ferd. What we want is Trenton and Trenton Falls."

" They are not in my book, that's certain. What's the use of having such a book ? "

" Not much," said Bertha. " It is only meant for little children. Suppose you look on your father's map. Bring that cushion here and sit down by me. There is Saratoga, here is the railroad." —

" Railroad on a map ? "

" Yes, on a real map, — on a large map."

" Why ! Look here, Ferd ; here is Ballston, and here is the lake, — don't you know, where we got the pond-lillies. Ferd, come here ; here is Glenn's Falls, where we saw the cave where Natty Bumpo hid and the two girls, — don't you know, Miss Schwarz ? we read it that night. Ferd, see here ! here is every single place we went to from Saratoga."

" Don't call Ferd, he is learning his verbs."

" And here is the canal ; oh, dear ! do you remember those children with the geese ? Here is the railroad, — it says ' Saratoga and Schenectady Railroad,' just as it did on the great card in the hall of the United States. Then we got out at Schenectady, you know. That's where we bought oranges of the blind man. Then we got into the other railroad, and went — and went to — Albany ! No, we did not go to Albany. We had been to Albany before. The map is wrong."

" Try the other way."

" Other way ? " said the girl, really bright enough, and interested now. " Oh, yes ! here is Little Falls, where I bought the diamonds. Here is Utica — Herkimer — Russia. I did not know Russia was near Utica, — somehow I thought Russia was in France. Russia, Trenton — Trenton — here is Trenton — and here is Trenton Falls, and here is the road. Yes ; there is one

road, and there is one. How nice it is to have the
roads down! Why are they not on my map?"

"Your map is too small, you goose," said Ferd, re-
laxing from his industry.

"Well, I don't care; I mean to make pa buy me
just such a map as this, and I mean to write down the
towns we stopped at as we came on."

So she unfolded the whole map of New York on the
floor; and before Miss Addie knew it she had learned
all the "map-questions" of the day, and many more
than even the bold book-maker had ventured to suggest.
Bertha was not displeased with her own success in al-
luring to the side of order the scholar who had most
influence on the rest of the crew; and she was able to
give some personal attention to Master Ferd's verb,
while the school-room assumed an air of quiet which
was as unusual as it was unexpected. But, in a minute
more, the door was flung open, and Mrs. Rosenstein
dashed in, arrayed for conquest.

"No more stupid books to-day," cried she. "Come,
my pet; come, Addie; come, Miss Schwarz; the day
is so fine that I am going to take you all to ride! Put
away that horrid old map, Adelaide, and never let me
see you on the floor again!"

"May I go, ma?" screamed Ferd.

"Oh, no! I can't take you; boys are such a plague."

"I want to go!" persisted Ferd.

"Of course you want to. Aren't you satisfied with
your holiday, that you must be teasing to go to ride?
Go and play with the other boys."

Ferd persisted that the other boys were all at school,
all but Ted Morris, and it was only yesterday he had
been told never to play with Ted Morris again as long
as he lived.

"Then go to that dirty, vulgar Ted Morris's for this
once. But don't come home with your clothes all covered with clay again, and don't ever repeat one word
you hear Ted Morris say."

So Ferd won his victory, which he followed up by

teasing for money to buy powder with, and went on his triumphant way.

Bertha asked Mrs. Rosenstein to let Ferd have her seat in the carriage. She would really have been glad to have the time at home, and she said so. But madame said no, and took all pleasure from the ride at the same time by giving a reason.

"The ride would be nothing without you," she said; "and you must not wear that dowdy old travelling-bonnet, you must have your new hat, and must look your prettiest, for I am going to call at Mrs. Rounds's, and there is no saying who we shall see there, my pretty Bertha."

There was a certain Carl Rounds, a fine, manly fellow, who liked Bertha, and whom Bertha liked; and Mrs. Rosenstein had a way of making her life miserable by showing her off in such fashion as this to him. So they took the ride. We have no need to follow it. It all turned out much as you might have expected. Mrs. Rosenstein had expected to meet some people whom she did not meet. Mrs. Rounds was not at home, really; but Mrs. Rosenstein chose to pretend that she was refused to her. The two girls quarrelled when they sat on opposite seats, and they quarrelled when they were on the same seat. "Ma" steadily scolded, and they were as steadily impudent. Poor Bertha got it on all hands; and the last words Mrs. Rosenstein said to her, as they all ran up stairs to get ready for a late and cold dinner, were these:

"If you knew your place, Miss Schwarz, you would not speak till you were spoken to, nor give your advice till it was asked for;" because poor Bertha, having been bidden point-blank to decide whether Charlotte or Adelaide was to blame in the ninety-ninth battle-royal of the hour, had pronounced a decision which happened to traverse the mood their mother was in at the moment she heard it uttered. Such was a fair enough specimen of Bertha's life with the pupils intrusted to her care.

If she could only have been left alone, she used to

say to herself, — for she never intrusted her griefs to
her father or mother, — if she could only have been
left alone with the children, to make the best of them
that she knew how, she would not complain. But this
pestering interference, this blowing hot and cold, just
when she saw her crystal forming so that there ought
to be no blowing from the outside at all, — that was a
grievance indeed! Ah! my dear Bertha, you will find
before you have got through, that what you are complaining of is not Mrs. Rosenstein's school-room, it is
human life. To do one's duty would be easy in the
comparison, if, as one does it, he were not always pestered on the right and on the left by the fools who want
to help, the fools who want to advise, the fools who
want to ask why, and the fools who want to hinder.
Indeed, that is a wise remark of Henry Kingsley, that
when the Devil wishes to arrest any good work, and
has failed to do so by the agency of people of intelligence, his next step is always to enlist the unconscious
service of a fool.

But Bertha had plenty of pluck. She had gone into
this matter with her eyes open, and she was not going
to cry " Enough," or to go out of it, till she had fairly
wrought through what she had started on. She had
made her bed, and she was willing to lie in it; though
there were more burrs between the sheets than she liked,
and also more rose-leaves on the pillows. Whether she
liked Mrs. Rosenstein's flatteries or her scolding least,
Bertha hardly knew. On the whole, she thought she
would rather take her chance with the burrs than the
rose-leaves.

Mr. Rosenstein, who was even lavish in all his family
expenses, had made the most generous arrangements for
Bertha's quarterly wages, and they were most promptly
paid to her. Whether he were as lavish or generous
in his business, Bertha did not know. What his business was she really did not know. There was an office
on the main street, and they sometimes stopped there
in driving. Sometimes a Jewish-looking traveller appeared at dinner or at tea; sometimes one spent the

night at the house. On such occasions Mr. Rosenstein's meals were even shorter than usual; and there would be close conclave in a little end room, which was honored by the name of the library, because there was a bookcase with a few bound volumes of "Graham's Magazine" there. At times, with very little previous announcement, Mr. Rosenstein would be away on business. No one ever knew for how long he would be gone, so he always returned as unexpectedly as he went. Bertha was always sorry to have him go; for though he had but little to say or do, when he was at home, — tired indeed, and rather thoughtful, perhaps anxious, — still he was fond of the children, and they were fond of him; he knew how to keep his wife in order, and she was afraid of him, so that the interior regimen of the house went on much better and more happily than it did in his absence. Occasionally, on what Bertha called his bright days, he would ask her to play to him. He was almost what might be called a connoisseur in music, very fond of it, — had his own tastes, and knew what they were, and really entered with spirit and interest into what Bertha was so glad to play.

Quite independent of the regular allowance which came to her from Mr. Rosenstein, with which indeed at no moment had his wife anything to do, were the presents of dress and jewelry which that lady took the whim sometimes to give to her. This made a business which was to the last degree annoying to Bertha, on every account, and in a thousand ways. In the first place she noticed that once, when she took care to thank Mr. Rosenstein as well as his wife for a showy dress that had been sent home to her, he was evidently surprised, and, as Bertha felt sure, annoyed. In the second place, she found very soon, that on any turn of ill humor, — and such turns came in quite as often as other tides do, — the last shawl-pin or the last bon-bon which Mrs. Rosenstein had given Bertha, was sure to be called up in impertinent retrospect of bounties rendered. Bertha kept all these things by themselves; for she really thought that there might come such a tem-

pest some day that she might want to return them
all in one heap of obligation discharged, even upon
the head of the giver.

It has seemed best to resume in this way the method
of Bertha's Milwaukie life, that we may throw a little
light on the spirit with which the several parties concerned went into the business of Mrs. Rosenstein's great
triennial party, which came off late in the spring, after
Bertha found herself entangled in this web-work of
falsehood, petty intrigue, ignorance, and folly.

Milwaukie was even then, as it is now, a centre of
accomplished and agreeable society. People of rare
culture came there early in its existence. Something
in the mere beauty of its situation, attracted, by a law
of natural selection, some noble families among the
throng of those who, in passing westward, happened to
land in its harbor; the enterprise and success of its
founders, gave life and cheerfulness to the whole,— the
freshness of all Western life had an opportunity to
show itself, — and a mixture singularly happy, of different races of men, gave to mutual intercourse a
charm which old and established communities cannot
know. Into the midst of such society, which was not in
the least pretentious or reserved in its ways, Mrs. Rosenstein flung herself; and either thought, or pretended she
thought, that swagger and presumption, diamonds and
paste, showy dress and more showy dancing, were
going either to astonish or to charm. She acted as if,
in the unselfish, unpretending, high-toned social order
of the little town, a foolish, false, petulant woman like
herself would be received as an article of elegance, and
in some sort feared and courted, as she had been taught
by very foolish novels, that ladies of fashion were
feared and courted in London and in Paris. The
assumption and the ambition were to the last degree
absurd in a wide-awake, honest Western town, which
did not count twelve years from its log-cabins, nor
number in all fifteen thousand people. But absurdity
never put any limit to any of Mrs. Rosenstein's
schemes.

All through the winter, therefore, to Bertha's dismay, to the amusement of people of sense, to the amazement of everybody, Mrs. Rosenstein was talking about the party she was going to give. In the midst of sociables and hops and cotillion parties and old-fashioned tea-fights, she would be heard talking about her ball. The young men made a joke of it, the girls tore to pieces the programme of it in their private talks, the judicious grieved to see anybody, no matter who, make herself such a fool. None the less did Mrs. Rosenstein blow her own own trumpet. And, because time is pitiless, at last the party came.

No, I am not to describe the various pretensions or the various pieces of solid sense which went to its composition. Not even as accomplished a fool as the hostess could make of such a party a failure. For, of a town of the size Milwaukie was then, the glory is, that it has better opportunities for social intercourse than it will ever have again. It is large enough, and not too large. Whoever is bright or agreeable, or well informed, whoever pleases in society, for whatever reason, comes forward and is known, — especially if you have that perfect institution for mutual acquaintance and introduction, the public school. If Mrs. Rosenstein had meant to be exclusive, she could not have been. She could not have drawn her line, like Miss Austen's hero, so as to include as gentlefolks only those who rode in gigs. She could not have drawn it, like Mrs. Sherman's servant, so as to include only those who drank wine and swore. She could not draw it anywhere in the fresh freedom of the new-born city. To give her her due, she did not want to draw it anywhere. Her house was large, her garden was pretty, almost the only garden in the town indeed, and the more people she could get together the better. She was by no means particular.

Our only business with the party is with Bertha's ups and downs in it; nor can we give all of these. If the full fortunes of a young girl at her first party were fairly written out from the beginning to the end, as she might relate them to her dearest bosom friend, they would fill the three-volume novel of antiquity to the last page.

As to dress, hardly a paragraph. Yet dress cost Bertha terrible anxiety. Should she wear the frock Mrs. Rosenstein had given her only three months before, which had never made but one appearance? Of course, she would have worn it, had she not been absolutely sure, from something Mr. Rosenstein had looked and not said, that the dress had been the cause of a regular quarrel between himself and madame. Should she wear some pearl ornaments which Mrs. Rosenstein had pressed on her on her birthday? She hated the ornaments for themselves, for they were by no means in her style. Yet not to wear them was of course marked; and, if she did not wear the frock, ought she not wear the jewels? Lastly, were the jewels jewels? or were they of that hocus make which, or the suspicion of which, vitiated nearly everything in the Rosenstein establishment?

"It is so hard," said poor Bertha to herself. "If I only knew what was right, I would do it, pinch as it might." She had never read "The New Timon," but she had read. her Bible; and though she did not believe that

> "He can't be wrong who but denies himself,"

she did know, that, if she set herself quite in the background, her chance of deciding right would be better. "First, then," she said, "I will not wear the silk dress; for I know Mrs. Rosenstein ought not have given it. I will wear the ornaments, because I am not quite sure whether I hate them because they look like fury, or because she gave them to me. No matter how I look; but it is matter that I shall not bring one more bone of contention into the party." So she laid everything out, sure to be ready to dress, and then went to help Charlotte, Theresa, and Adelaide in their preparations.

She did not come to either of them before she was

needed. Charlotte was in tears on the floor. Adelaide was raging up and down her room in hopeless
deshabille. It needed all Bertha's tact to soothe the
one and to comprehend the other. Charlotte, childlike, was brought to terms soonest. Adelaide was
fairly enraged at a palpable injustice of her mother,
who, having given her a beautiful set of pearls when
they were last in New York, on which Adelaide had
relied for her *toilette,* had coolly come in just before to
say she believed she would wear them herself, and had
carried them away. Adelaide declared she would not
stand it, and that she would not go to the party at all.
With her Bertha had to labor indeed. Nor would she
have succeeded, but that a divine inspiration sent her
across to her own room from whence she returned with
the pearls — were they from Serendib, were they from
Rome, Bertha asked not — which Mrs. Rosenstein had
given to her. She begged Adelaide to wear them, argued to her that they were more becoming to her,
scolded her, coaxed her, proved to her at last, that, if
she wore them, everybody would be satisfied, and all
would be well. And then she dressed Adelaide's hair
with them herself. And whether they were pearls or
were Roman imitations, no one would suspect them in
Miss Rosenstein's costume. With the governess it
might have been another thing.

Then Bertha dressed Charlotte. The first carriage
was already at the door ; but she flew back, Cinderella
that she was, and had so many fairies at her command
that she was soon ready to run down herself. Really
there had come only a few of those desperate people who
always come so early that it is impossible for them to
enjoy anything. Still, Mrs. Rosenstein had a chance
to look disapproval upon Bertha, and to say, " Always
a little behind time, my dear," which was an out-and-
out lie. But Mr. Rosenstein was cordial, and looked
pleased, as anybody might, who saw such a fresh,
cheerful, unconscious girl, all ready to be happy.

For Bertha had been used, when there was a hop or
a dance, to be chained to the music-stool, and to ham-

8

mer out waltzes and polkas and quadrilles for the
others. Or, if some saint came to relieve her, it always
happened that this saint was better trained in the music of the spheres than in that of human harmony and
melody, so that Bertha went almost crazy, as she
danced, to hear such ruin of time and tune. But to-
night there was a clever little band, such as Milwaukie
could produce more easily than most cities thrice
its size, and Bertha was to be foot-free if anybody
chose to dance with her.

If! to be sure. What an unnecessary affectation
was that, Bertha! Here were young Gilmore and
Fiske, Harry Burton and William Wallace, Carl
Rounds, of course, and I know not how many other
nice boys, and young men who would not like to hear
me call them boys, only too eager to get promise of the
first dance, or the second, or the third. Yes; and for
a brilliant hour our pretty Bertha forgot the burden she
had carried all day, and forgot there would be any burden
to-morrow, in the simple and pure joy of dancing to
music well-nigh perfect for its purpose, with partners
who were started into some life, though they were all
Americans, by the genuine enjoyment and enthusiasm
of this unspoiled German girl. Once she ran out of
the room to catch Ferdinand and to fix his neck-tie.
Once she caught Theresa, who was retiring in a sulk
because something had gone amiss, and restored sun-
shine there. But these were only ripples on the stream.
For the hour the stream flowed with pure and complete
enjoyment, which she was too true and too young even
to wonder at or to analyze.

At last there came a waltz. There had been no
waltzing before. And for this waltz Bertha had engaged herself to Carl Rounds. She confessed to herself that she did it with terror, as well she might. She
liked Carl Rounds; she liked to talk with him, and was
always glad to meet him. But it did not follow that he
could waltz, far less that he could waltz well. And
Bertha, with her old country memories, dreaded the
idea of a battle-royal on the floor, till he should be

gradually persuaded that they had waltzed enough, so
that she might stop with decency. And this had been
her experience thus far in life, in American waltzing.
If only it could have been a quadrille with Carl Rounds,
and a waltz with William Wallace, for whom she did
not care a straw! But one cannot have everything,
Bertha! No! The moment came. The band struck
up a ravishing Strauss. Mrs. Rosenstein sailed in with
a moustached man. Remember that in those days a
moustache was a rarity. Then came Carl Rounds.
" This is my dance, I think, Miss Schwarz."

Yes, it was; and Bertha looked up and smiled, nor
let him know how she dreaded the experiment. Nor
need she. An instant more, and she knew she was a
fool. Carl Rounds waltzed as well as she did, — as well
as he rowed or as he skated or as he talked. How did
it happen? I'm sure I don't know how it happened.
Only it did happen. And the music was more ravishing and more — and Bertha even forgot she was a fool,
and was able completely to enter into the spirit of the
whole. I do not say that she forgot where she was.
But she did not remember — Bertha did not often remember — that other people were looking on.

I have done a good deal of looking on while waltzing
was in progress. I have noted three varieties of waltz-
ers. 1. Those to whom the business is a hard and
painful necessity, to which they were preordained and
commanded, and which must be fulfilled. About nineteen out of twenty of the waltzing couples I have seen,
served their generation in this variety of service, sad,
serious, and sorry, but brave. 2. There are those to
whom the dance is a fine art, who enter upon it as
artists, glad to carry out perfectly a system or inven-
tion, which, because it is existing in society, it is well
for them to sustain absolutely well. These people do
not have the agonized look of the first class; they are
pleased with themselves, which is something, and they
are worth study, as illustrating one more form of harmony cast in action. The third variety — mostly Germans by nationality — are people who are thoroughly

happy, unconscious, and at ease as they dance. They dance as the thistle-down floats, which we boys used to call a zephyr. When you see their unconsciousness and really childish simplicity in the matter, it is hard to frown at waltzing, and to say it is all wrong. Such a couple were Bertha and Carl Rounds. You may go to a hundred balls to grand-dukes and not see such another.

Bertha stopped at last, not because such dancing tired her, but because Carl Rounds himself told her that everybody else had stopped, and she was ashamed to go on. She stopped and rested on his arm, and took him to task for letting her go on so long; and he said, of course, that he had no reason for arresting her, when a smart tap from Mrs. Rosenstein called her to turn round.

"That will do for one night, Miss Schwarz; you have danced quite as much as is at all proper!"

And poor Bertha was left to think she had disgraced herself. While the truth was, that Mrs. Rosenstein, who valued herself greatly on her waltzing, was mad with jealousy at a pretty girl's success, and did not care how she put her down. Something in her eye was worse than anything in her voice. Bertha thought she had made an enemy forever. And she was not far wrong.

Carl Rounds was mad enough to have struck the old woman, as he called her, the next morning. But the usages of society forbade. Bertha had to refuse herself to Harry Burton when his dance came, — that made him mad also. Carl had to dance with the Crehore, as the boys called her; that made him more mad, and Bertha ran up to her room to have a cry.

But she did not have it. I believe it was as simple a thing as a pair of scissors that had been her mother's, that saved her. She saw them on her dressing-table, and remembered why she was in that house at all, and asked a Power stronger than herself to carry her through, and ran down again, almost happy. They were going in to supper. Bertha was about to follow the train without escort, when Carl Rounds came up.

"May I hand you to supper?" he said. And on the stairs: "I took the liberty to make your peace with Burton. Would you be kind enough to speak to him when you can?" And then: "Shall I give you water-ice, or vanilla?" And when he returned from the table, he was leading a young gentleman to her.

"May I introduce to you a friend of mine, Miss Schwarz, who is quite a stranger here? this is Mr. Jasper Rising."

Bertha did not need to be told that. But Jasper did not catch her name, and for an instant could not fix her, could not remember where he had seen her. She enjoyed his uneasy self-questioning for a moment, and then laughed and said, in German: "I am sorry you forget me, Mr. Rising, — could you bring me another glass of water?"

"Oh! is it you?" said Jasper. And they laughed heartily.

CHAPTER XII.

TALK AT A PARTY.

WHY!" said Carl Rounds, in real surprise, "I thought you knew no one in Milwaukie!"

"I thought so too," said Jasper; "and I told you so. I certainly did not know Miss Schwarz was here. I left her " —

"In the biggest baskot-shop I ever saw, or Mr. Rising either," said Bertha, interrupting him and laughing. "That is where he thinks we met last. O Mr. Rounds! we could make you laugh very heartily, if we told you of our journey, But all I need tell you now is, that Mr. Rising rendered me and my mother and my poor little brother very essential service those days."

"Not more," said Jasper, "than you rendered me." For Jasper had, more than once, run back in memory over the exceeding wretchedness of that sultry afternoon, and the relief from it which had come as soon as his life was twisted in with some other life. But he did not choose to follow back that thread; and he parried Bertha's compliment by asking after her brother, and how the broken leg was. This started them on another line of talk; and Carl Rounds, seeing his Detroit friend was really interested, and, indeed, his Milwaukie friend no less so, left them to their mutual discoveries, gentleman as he was; nor lessened the pleasure he had given to each by trying either to share it or to watch it. So Jasper and Bertha, each being a simple and unaffected person, fell at once into the most natural talk in the world; and, after Bertha had eaten her ice, they left the supper-table to follow this talk out in the cooler air of the partly deserted dancing-rooms.

"I hardly think so," said Bertha, as she took her seat on the sofa to which he led her, — he sitting in a little chair at its side, — "I hardly think so. Certainly, the people I am most fond of — well, my aunt and my mother — seem to say just the right thing at the right moment, without ever having thought anything about it before. Just the wise word, or the bright joke, or the true answer, comes to their lips; and all poor stupid I can do is to sit and wonder how they possibly can know so much or talk so well. I don't wonder that all children think their fathers and mothers know everything."

"I am sure I don't," said Jasper. "I always thought my uncle knew everything; and, indeed, I think so now. But I guess it was partly because he put me so wholly at my ease. We used to say of one of the professors, when I was in college, that when you called upon him he made you feel as if you were the best fellow in the world; and so you felt that he was the next best."

"How nice that must have been! I know such people; but I am not going to own that I over-estimate my mother and my aunt. It was the aunt you took me to, the basket-day. Oh, I was dreadfully afraid of her then, for I had never seen her! But she is very lovely." — This more thoughtfully.

Jasper longed to say he thought that very likely, if the aunt were anything like her niece. Probably he would have said so eight centuries ago. I observe that in such language Lisuartes spoke to Onoloria. But it was not eight centuries ago. It was about twenty-five years ago. And Jasper, not being a fool, strangled his compliment.

"I dare say you are right," said he. "I will grant that the aunt, whom I do not know, and the mother, whom I do know, if you remember, both know a great deal more even than you and I do. But don't you see they ought to? they have been knocked about a great deal more. You and I have been to school, — that's all. We have studied a few books. These other peo-

ple, who are so nice and do know so much, have studied
people and cities and nations; they have seen mountains and oceans; they have talked with ever so many
people worth talking to; and they have tried experi-
ments, and succeeded sometimes, and failed sometimes.
I am glad I am not forty; but I should have a great
satisfaction in getting at the prompt, decisive wisdom
of forty."

Bertha enjoyed his enthusiasm, understanding very
perfectly what he meant. When she had heard Wallace at the piano-forte, brave, direct, thorough, from
the beginning to the end, her own performance seemed
to her in the comparison spongy, muffled, and sloppy;
and she had almost said she would never touch the keys
again. Now, in Jasper's eulogy on the " prompt, decisive wisdom of forty," — which word to both of them
meant age just less than Methuselah's, — Bertha recognized her own delight in Wallace's vigorous playing.
Yet, she said, she did not believe that the sense of
power came merely because people had travelled, had
seen oceans and continents, and men and women. She
also knew people of forty, who were very stupid and
very spongy, yet they kept going over the world.
There were such people at her father's and her uncle's,
— "and here," she was going to say. But she stopped.

" I dare say," said Jasper, who was in first-rate spirits now; long enough it was since he had found himself
talking with an unaffected woman, who was willing to
tell the truth even in the tones of her voice. " I dare
say. I suppose they had seen all these things without
seeing them. I suppose they had not any imagination;
if they had not, why, of course they could not see them.
Perhaps they never indulged in day-dreaming."

" Do you mean to say that you do, Mr. Rising?"

" You look so frightened," said he, laughing again,
" that I am afraid to confess it. But murder will out.
I do sometimes desert my carriage-shop for a castle in
the air. I am a carriage-builder, Miss Schwarz."

" But, — really, — do you know I have always supposed, — I have tried to persuade me that I must not build castles in the air. I sup wrong."

"Right or wrong," said Jasper, heartily, " you need not tell me you have never done it; for you have; and what is more, you like it, Miss Schwarz, I am sure."

" To tell you the whole truth, I do," said Bertha, pretending to laugh this time, but really a little uneasy; for they had come now on the verge of what was a question of conscience to her, regarding which she could not afford to joke, because she was not certain. Jasper was too sensitive and too sympathetic not to catch in an instant the drift, both of her thought and feeling. He dropped his voice, and wholly changed from the tone of half-banter, to say : " Of course, everything in excess is wrong. The word *too* means wrong, whether we say too much or too little. But God could never have given us this power of withdrawing from persecution, misery, loneliness, suffering, into a world of life and brightness, if we were not to use it on occasion. Why ! you have only to take the very case we spoke of, — of the experience people get in advance, so that they shall come to some new experience as if they had seen it a thousand times, — you have only to take that case to see how an air-castle may prepare you for very stern emergency."

Bertha was pleased with his confidence in her good sense, pleased enough to lose her shyness now ; and she said :

" Do you remember Wordsworth,—

'Who, in the heat of conflict, keeps the law
In calmness made, and sees what he foresaw?' "

And then she was frightened with herself, for fear she had said something pretentious. But she need not have been afraid. Jasper was as much in earnest as she ; and he plunged on, with quotations, and stories, recollections of his own and experiences of other people, to tell her the good which he had found in some of his air-castles.

"In some of them!" said Bertha. "I do not believe your college professors thanked you for building them in recitation-time, as you say you did."

"Ah!" said he, laughing again, "as to that, they had to take their chance. It was their business to make the Greek or the Latin entertaining. If they did not, the fault was not mine. And so, as soon as I had translated my ten lines, I was a freeman again, and might travel where I chose, — hunting deer in Virginia, crossing ice-floes with Parry, or laying out my ornamental grounds at home. I guess it did me as much good as hearing the other fellows in their blunders."

But it will never do to try to jot down the corners or trace along the long straight courses of these two young folks' talk, in this happy hour when they discovered each other. After all, it was not what they said, so much as the way in which they said it, which gave to that little talk in a room at first deserted, and afterwards gradually filling with company, a charm of its own, which made them both recall it, again and again, for years upon years after. It is to be remembered first, what lonely lives they had both been leading, — lonely as to real comparison of experience with people of sympathy, courage, intelligence, and culture. It is to be remembered, again, that each regarded the other as being a stranger, who was entitled to a certain cordiality of manner which might not have been awarded to one to the place or manor born. Each, therefore, went rather more than half-way. It is to be remembered, once more, that, as they talked, each of them once and again recalled the thought of the other, as of a benefactor, a person who had done essential service when service was rare indeed. Most of all, and beneath all, it is to be remembered, that, in the Eternal Order, these two people were two whose lives harmonized essentially, absolutely, and completely with each other, — who were thus meant for each other and

for nobody else ; and this corner of Mrs. Rosenstein's
ball-room was the place, and the moment when her supper was ended was the time, when they were first to find
out something of each other. The talk was too good
to last forever. Of course the interruptions of space
and time came in. Burton came along with that nice,
sweet Windermere girl ; and Bertha had to stop them
both, and to introduce Jasper to Miss Windermere, so
that she might herself make a chance to say : "I was
very sorry to lose my dance, Mr. Burton, but I was
under orders. If I were bold enough, I should say,
perhaps we might have it at some other time." This
was a great deal for Bertha to say ; but she knew that
Carl Rounds had told Burton the whole story, and that
Burton was a good fellow and no fool. Then Charlotte
Rosenstein came running up, her cheeks all aglow, and
her garb all awry, and Bertha had to put the pretty
silk trail in order. No, Jasper ! nothing can be welded
upon this bit of broken talk ! Take it home with you,
and make the best of it. Remember every word she
said, and every flush of conscious or unconscious color
that rushed over her cheek when she had the least difficulty in expressing herself. Remember the courage
of her eyes, as she looked you full in the face,
when you tried to explain your notion ; remember the
depth eternal into which you could look in them as she
listened with surprise, if you spoke of something which
she had thought was one of her own discoveries, but
which she found now you had thought out as well as
she ; remember how the long eyelash fairly dropped on
her cheek, when she looked down again, afraid lest she
had said too much, either in quoting Wordsworth, or in
owning to some great enjoyment or some great sorrow.
Take all this home with you, Jasper ; repeat it and re-
imagine it to yourself, again and again and again.
Keep it all, forever, for one of the treasures of your
life. But you cannot have any more to-night. The
party is in full blast again. You must dance with
somebody, — Adelaide Rosenstein or Miss Windermere.

Go find yourself a partner. And leave Bertha here; her other partners will come to try to persuade her to break her resolution and to waltz again; and these other girls will come and sit on the sofa beside her. You cannot take your nice first talk and weld upon it anything more!

CHAPTER XIII.

FAINT, YET PURSUING.

MEANWHILE our friend Oscar was left in charge of the carriage-factory in Detroit, or, boy-fashion, supposed he was. Mr. Dundas or Mr. Buffum would have been amazed had they known the weight of the responsibility which rested on his shoulders as soon as his " master" was gone. The loyalty of his allegiance to Jasper was no greater in his absence than in his presence. But, so soon as he started on his little tour westward from Detroit, the boy conceived that the time had come for him to watch over every interest for which his " master," as he called him, could have cared, were he at home.

It had always been a matter of grief to Oscar that the carriage-shop should be left at night unguarded. Once and again he had asked Jasper whether it would not be better to have a watchman there, or at the least, to let the apprentices take turns in sleeping there. Nothing could have proved his loyalty in a more pathetic way than this ; for, if there were any special joy in Oscar's life, it was in the golden hour of all, when he and Jasper were in their own room, before going to bed, — when the concert or lecture or caucus, or other evening occupation, was over, which had called Jasper away, — when he threw himself on the outside of his bed, and talked with the eager boy about the day's work, or read to him may be from the last Dickens, or let Oscar read slowly to him, that he might help him both about his reading and his English. When the clock struck ten, Jasper would rouse up, and begin to undress. But they made long talk while the undressing went on ; and it might be eleven before the boy was well asleep on his side the room, and his "master" on the other. For Oscar to offer, of his own accord, to give up this special luxury, that he might sleep in a little room in the varnishing-shed, was thorough proof of his devotion. As such, Jasper accepted it. But he never listened for a moment to the proposal. Not that in those days there was a very efficient street-patrol in Detroit, but that the customs of the place were simple, and no one had as yet found much need of night-watchmen.

No sooner was Jasper gone, however, than Oscar renewed his proposals, making them this time to Mr. Dundas, the partner with whom he had most to do. " You no know, Mr. Dundas, — I mean you do not know, what many kind bad men, loaf men, you say, go come, come go, up down, down up all the street, every street, yes, in Detroit every night ; yes, Mr. Dundas. You no know, because you have night home to live in ; pleasant home, pretty home, nice home with fire, home with lamp, home with wife. You no go come, — I mean you have not known how to go come up street, down street, all night, all evening, yes. Sleep in old cask, sleep in old pig-shed, sleep on deck of steamboat, yes, when all night watch go down in forehatch and run away. Great many men go up street, down street ; yes, all loaf men, drink men, smoke men, swear men, steal men. Loaf man, smoke man, smoke old twisted long-nine ; can't smoke him all, all too bad to smoke ; man want talk, want swear, want fight, he throw away old long-nine all on fire, Mr. Dundas. Old long-nine he go right in straw in our yard, where that boy Jem unpack the castings ; no sweep straw away ; wind blow, wind blow, straw burn, barrel burn, clapboard burn, varnish room burn, all one great night fire ; no engine, no Mr. Jasper, no nobody ; — all new carriages burn up, all counting-room burn up ; Mr. Jasper come home, and say, 'Dundas,—Buffum — Oscar,' he say, — ' what for, where gone all wagons, all carriage ?' Yes, Mr. Dundas, that what he say. Now, Mr. Dundas, I sleep little cubby room, varnish-shed ; yes, Mr. Dundas, I sleep

there. I smell old long-nine, I smell straw; Yes, Mr.
Dundas, I smell everything. I jump up bed, — one little dipper water, Mr. Dundas, — old long-nine, he, yes,
all wet, straw all wet; no fire, wagon safe, carriage
safe, all safe. O Mr. Dundas! let me sleep varnish-
shed?"

But Dundas did not see it. Perhaps he thought
that if Oscar slept there, all the boys would have rights
there. Perhaps he thought he would rather take the
chance of the wandering long-nine once in a while,
than the certainty, more or less approximate, of four
boys playing all fours at their will in the varnish-room ;
and Mr. Dundas laughed at Oscar's fears, and refused
the coveted permission.

So far was he right, that the long-nine accident did
not happen, and the carriage factory did not burn
down.

But none the less did Oscar keep an eagle eye on the
shop. He had keys to open the outer doors with. And
at midnight every night the boy walked down there, and
went in and went the rounds to be sure that all was as
it should be. Not that any one knew this, till he told
it afterwards to Jasper. It was the only satisfaction
he could take, and it helped him through his master's
absence.

The very afternoon, as it happened, of Mrs. Rosenstein's ball, poor Oscar, also, had been entrapped into
a party of pleasure. No! dear Lily, — or other kind
reader, — you need not be afraid that he was lured
away by bad boys or worse men to drink or to gamble.
It was a very modest party of pleasure, and one I hope
you might have joined in, had you then been alive.
There were three nice young women, who lived in the
same boarding-house with Oscar and Jasper, with
whom the young men had grown to be more intimate
than with any of the others of the boarders, from the
accident, I believe, that they all went to church together. Two of them were sisters ; and another, a
school-mistress she, came from the same town in Maine
as they. As the winter closed, Oscar had made a great

point of teaching them all to skate, as he said his sisters and mother did on the fiords at home. Excepting
on the North River, I think skating was then almost
wholly unknown to American women, and at first these
three girls thought it among the impossibilities. But
Jasper, with his tales of Schuylers and De Windts and
Roosevelts, in New York, and his talk of Dutch canals,
and Oscar, in his pleasant broken English and his
really earnest boyish persuasion, had overcome all
their prejudices; and many a time they had all gone
down together, to a bend there is in the river, some
little distance below the heart of the city, where, after
a while, the young people of course found the exercise
as possible and pleasant in Michigan as in Holland.
The skating had gone with the ice; but the girls, or
young ladies, as you choose to call them, had not forgotten the pretty manly courtesy with which Oscar had
managed to make everything pleasant and easy in their
skating practice; and now that they saw him chafing
and restless under his friend's absence, they concerted
to make a little pleasure-party which might take him
out from himself, for at least one afternoon.

So they told him that the spring was opening so
early, that they believed they could find some of the
earliest spring flowers in a bosky place they were wont
to go to, not so very far from the old skating-grounds,
and that they were going to try their luck on this particular afternoon, and would not he join them? Oscar
was glad to say yes. "I fond of flowers, Mees Delia;
my dear mother glad of flowers too; my sister Gretchen
fond of flowers too; yes, all glad of flowers, — pretty
blue spring flower, little veilchen, Mees Delia, close
next snow-water at home, yes, Mees Delia, close
next the snow." He begged leave to go away from
work early, left old Dan to shut up the factory, and in
his best rig was ready to escort the young people at
four o'clock.

Mr. Buffum had heard of the party, and had taken
them all by surprise by driving out so as to intercept
them, in the great job-wagon of the factory, on which

he had improvised a new cross-seat. He took them all
on board, so that they were all saved their walk out,
and had the longer time for their exploration; and a
merry afternoon, not unsuccessful in its foraging, they
made of it, after he left them to its fortunes. With
more moss than flowers, but still with no poor show of
maple-blossoms, willow-catkins, violets, and other triumphs of spring, they came out near the high-road to a
little copse of willows they had been aiming at, on their
return; and then "Mees Delia" triumphantly produced
from the concealed parcel at the bottom of her basket,
enough buttered biscuits and dried beef to answer for
an unexpected picnic supper. They were just tired
enough to sit down, and under the lee of the great wil-
low pollards it seemed warm enough for them to dare
do so. Oscar gayly took his own water cup and Mary
Frazer's, and went down to the road to bring some
water from a trough they had noticed there.

As he came to the trough he noticed that the three
ill-looking men who were standing smoking, by the
door of the wretched blacksmith-shop close by, were
talking in the loud, bickering tone of men who had
drunk more than was good for them; and in a moment
more it was clear enough that they were talking German. The words that caught Oscar's ear were a stupid,
mulish exclamation:

"Nimm alle drei, nimm alle drei; lass kein stehen."

"Take all three, take all three; do not leave any."

"Take three, lose all," replied one of the others,
as sententiously, but with less liquor in his tone and
senses.

To Oscar's ear the language was almost as familiar
as his own. But the men were careless of his presence,
as he filled the mugs; and the man most drunk of the
three repeated stolidly, "Take all three, take all three,
— one for you, one for you, one for me and my brown
mare."

When Oscar saw that it was for a mare that something was to be taken, his curiosity was just enough
roused to make him loiter a moment, and rinse out a

9

mug at the trough, not supposing for an instant that he was listening to secrets.

"You take three," said the brain possessor, "and you wake the whole street. Three wagons make a —— rattle in a still night. Take one, with the two mares, and you shall be in Toledo before morning."

Oscar did not dare wait a moment longer. With his two full mugs he returned to the simple picnic, and tried to take his part in its hospitalities heartily. But he could not come to the unconsciousness and ease with which Jasper the same evening talked to Bertha. Oscar all this fortnight had a heavy responsibility at heart, and this about mares and wagons frightened him. He tried to conceal this from his companions, and perhaps he succeeded. They still had their long walk before them. But the weather was quite too cool for long lounging at their little supper, and they were soon briskly walking into town.

Oscar went fairly home with them, and made his good-byes in his pleasant, frank way. "Yes, Mees Delia, we have what you say — yes, we have truly nice time, also especially when we get what you say wet moss, fresh moss, not wet moss, — yes,. yes, Mees Delia, we shall go another summer day." And he was gone.

Back to the shop he went, as quickly as he might. Into the shop he went, and, of course almost, the three newly-finished top-wagons which he went to find were there, just as he had left them. But how long would they be there? Who should he tell his fears to? Old Dan was a new-comer, and Oscar did not know where he lived. There was one of the hands only a few blocks off, but Oscar did not like him. He was a German, and to the boy's excited fancy might be an accomplice of the men he was afraid of. Of course Oscar ought to have gone to the police-station. But he had never recovered from his terrors, in seeing the handcuffed man carried away by the strong arm of law, — he had the dislike of government and its officials which most people have who are educated on the eastern side of the Atlantic, from Mr. Herbert Spencer downward. For an hour the boy lay in ambush in the counting-room; then he went down into the yard, and busied himself about the wagons for half an hour. Then he worked for an hour in barricading the gate of the yard with the nearest logs he could draw up, and with a drag-chain which he brought from the shed. It was nearly eleven now. The street was quiet, the boy had done all he could do, and the reaction had come on him. Perhaps he was all wrong.

Anyway, if he were right, ought he not have told Mr. Dundas or Mr. Buffum? Of course he would have told Jasper in a moment.

Poor Oscar, who knew he could have done right had this been a Norwegian problem, was not so certain here. But he looked up the street and down the street; he locked the counting-room door behind him, and ran, at his very best, to Mr. Buffum's house. He went there because it was nearest, though he did not like him as well as he did Mr. Dundas.

He pulled at the bell, perhaps too loudly.

Mrs. Buffum, herself, came to the door, frightened too. But, to Oscar's dismay, it proved that her husband was not yet at home, — was at a lodge-meeting. Could Oscar, perhaps, go to the lodge?

No, Oscar could not go to the lodge. He had very vague and very exaggerated ideas as to the institution of Freemasonary; and, fearless as he was, he knew that now time was his greatest need. He explained in his broken way what his fears were to Mrs. Buffum.

"I work in the shop — you shop, you husband's shop. To-day I hear three German blackguard speak German. They say, 'Take three, no leave two.' Other one say, 'Take one, leave two.' They want to take three new top-buggy. Yes, three new top-buggy. Tell Mr. Buffum, he come quick — real quick, to shop; three men want take three nice new top-buggy. Yes. Good-by."

And he was gone, leaving Mrs. Buffum more alarmed

than ever she was in her life, and wondering when the lodge would break up that evening.

And for Oscar, there was nothing left but to scud on, more than a mile, to Dundas's house. Why had he not gone there first of all? Perhaps his three blackguards were now storming his entrenchments. Should he not go back and see? Not he. What he had begun on, he would put through. Short way he made of the still streets as he sped to Dundas's. This house was dark. A loud ring again, and another; and then the window opened, and to Oscar's happy eyes Mr. Dundas's head appeared.

" O Mr. Dundas ! " gasped the breathless boy, " come down to shop. Come quick ; come now."

" What's the matter, Oscar? There's no fire?"

" No fire, Mr. Dundas. No, no fire. Three German loafer — three, Mr. Dundas ; yes, three, want to bring three mares, Mr. Dundas ; yes, three mares, and steal our new top-buggies, — three new top-buggies. Come quick, Mr. Dundas ! "

Dundas knew the boy was no fool. He slammed his window down, and in less than a minute was at the door, half covered with his clothes, to let him in. Oscar briefly told his story. Dundas's first thought was that the boy's anxiety had deceived him. Still he bade him return as quickly as he could, taking the city jail on his way, where he could certainly find an officer ; and Dundas wrote a line on the back of the firm's card, as a voucher for the boy. He told Oscar he would follow as soon as he was dressed. And again poor Oscar tried his speed in the silent streets, loath indeed to lose so much distance as his run to the police head-quarterters required.

To give them their due, there was little red tape there. The moment Oscar told his story, the captain nodded with understanding, and at once named the more intelligent of Oscar's three Germans by his slang name ; at least, he hazarded a guess. " Hamburg Mike again," said he in a half-aloud. " Run down, boy, as quick as you can," said he ; " though nobody can tell

whether it is not all moonshine. As like as not they
are at the Central Stables or at Wild & Thurston's. I
only wonder all the horses and all the carriages in
Detroit are not stole once a month. I'll have two men
there as quick as you can get there!"

Poor Oscar sped again; tired, but not flagging,
"faint, yet pursuing." Streets still as ever, till he
turned his last corner but one. Did he not hear the
rapid rattle of wheels? Down into the long avenue
which but just now was so silent. It is dark as Egypt,
— only a cloudy sky, — but the wretched boy's ear does
not deceive him. The sharp, hard rat-tat-tat of the
hoofs and the wheels in the long distance is only too
clear. Will he never come to the shop? Yes, he is
here at last; and in the darkness it is still easy enough
to make out that there has been little pains about locks
and keys. The whole great gate is dragged out of the
way. One of the rotten posts has been easily enough
sawed off; and all Oscar's barricade and chain as easily
pulled into the street; and the "three new top-buggy,
alle drei" are "*alle verloren, gegangen*, all gone."
There is only on the still air, the slight rat-a-tat to tell
which way they sped.

A minute was enough for Oscar to light a lantern
and see that all was gone. As he turned into the street
again, Mr. Dundas came down, and in an instant took
in the situation. Not because he saw much use in it,
but because he wanted to do something, he joined Oscar in the unequal pursuit. They could hear the two
officers approaching, and they called to them to follow.
All sound of rattling was over, however, and in a
minute poor Mr. Dundas refused to run. To Oscar's
quick blood, the slow pace he took was a misery and an
indignity; but it gave the officers a chance to join.
Oscar in advance, they all pressed on.

Nor in vain!

Five minutes brought them to a corner whence they
looked down riverward to see moving lights, and
though there was no rattle, to hear talking and shout-

ing. Even Dundas could trot again now, and in a moment they joined what was already a noisy throng.

One "top-buggy," with a panting, startled horse, was secure in the grasp of a newly-awakened wharf-laborer. One top-buggy was prostrate, making ko-tou on the street, because it had no forewheels. The third, a little in advance, was in the same position,

The three "blackguards" had taken this narrow street with success; but, as the leading horse dashed over a deep gutter which crossed it, the king-bolt had given away, the horse had sprung forward with the front wheels, and the shock had been so sudden, that, by the reins, he had drawn "Hamburg Mike" heavily forward on the stones. He lay on the sidewalk, wholly without sense, as Dundas and Oscar came up.

Oscar's drunken friend was the next in order. He had turned from the wreck sharply, and swung against the curb-stone. Exactly the same accident happened to him. But he was so far forewarned, that, as his horse went off with wheels and reins, he himself abandoned the wreck, and of his own volition, vanished into the darkness.

The third driver had tried to turn short round. But his horse had probably balked and refused. For some reason he also had left his prize and was gone.

The crash had roused a drinking-party in a neighboring bar-room, and their oaths and wonderments had wakened the nearest sleepers. With different lights, and in different costumes, a motley assembly was examining the wreck, a few of the more humane trying what could be done with the senseless man.

Dundas stood by one of the broken carriages, trying to lift it enough to see how it had fallen.

"Well, Dundas," said an officer, "I did not know your carriages smashed up the first time they went over a gutter."

Dundas was a little sore in the midst of triumph.

"Nor I either," said he; "and I don't see through it now."

"See here! Mr. Dundas," said Oscar, with his face in

a light blaze. " See here. I show you through it." And as the officer and Dundas lifted, Oscar stooped down, and pulled out a broken plug of pine-wood from the wreck. " I took out all three ; yes, all three king-bolt. I took out all three ; I put in three wooden pegs. Yes, three wooden pegs. Yes. Pegs not last long. No."

The bright boy had had the wit to remember, that, if the wagons were dismantled in the yards, there might be time enough while he was gone, to put one, at least, in running order. But, leaving them as he did, he led his three enemies into the lure he meant. And the wagons gave way, just where repairs were not easy.

" Good for you, Oscar ! You've saved Mr. Jasper's carriages."

Dundas knew that Jasper's name would please the boy more than any word of praise that he could think of.

As they crossed to the throng who were bending over the senseless German, —

" You can put up your brandy," said the doctor, who had stripped the man's chest, and was feeling at his heart. " Put up your brandy. He will never taste liquor again."

CHAPTER XIV.

IIE AND SIIE.

IT seemed worth while to tell this story of poor Oscar's recovery of the wagons, because the whole transaction marked a stage in the dear fellow's life. They all had· been fond of him, in the shop, before. But, after this bit cf presence of mind and gallantry, everybody respected him ; and, in such a place, there are a dozen little promotions possible, by which the general favor can be shown to an apprentice. Jasper was at home again before long ; and he took more than one way and time to thank Oscar for his spirit, and to let the grateful fellow feel, what it had always been hard for him to understand, that all the gratitude was not to be on the one side.

I will not say but we might follow along the Ups and Downs of the shop, its rivalry with other shops, the successes of its work in quarters which gave new customers, and the gradual confidence which Buffum, Dundas, and Jasper, the three members of the firm, grew to have in each other. Nor will I say, but, in a master's hands, the mere details of whiffle-trees, and patent axles, and enamelled cloth, and neat's oil, might not furnish out a romance as interesting as the tale of the tournament at Ashby de la Zouch. Given the master, I think it would. The firm was a good firm. Ideality, realism, caution, and daring, were well intermingled ; and all the three men were men of truth and honor. Of course they grumbled sometimes at each other ; they sometimes secretly wished, even for hours, that they had never seen each other. But none the less was it,

in truth, a good firm ; and lucky was it for them all,
that they were united in it.

But it is not the business of this story to follow out
only one of the shorter phases of Jasper's life, or of
Oscar's. And I must ask the reader to imagine for
himself, on the hints which have been given, the hopes
and fears, successes and drawbacks, of these young
manufacturers in what was still a young city ; though
its date as a frontier post ran back so far. For Jasper
himself, life had its dark sides, of course ; but it had
its bright sides in much larger proportion. Seeing he
was healthy, honest, faithful, and brave, that was of
course true. Oscar was a great comfort, — indeed, he
was a great blessing ; for it was due to Oscar that there
was no danger that Jasper should be too much alone.
Except for this, that danger would have come in. For
Jasper was proud. And he had not forgotten, in his
more recent experience of a kind of prosperity, that
there had been days when he had walked about these
same streets, driven from door to door, without anybody's caring whether he lived or died. So he could
not naturally drop into the society of the town, which
opened before him. I do not doubt that he was wrong
in this. His truer theory of life would be, to let by-
gones go as by-gones, and to make the utmost out of to-
day, meeting rather more than half-way such people as
met him. But Jasper was not a saint. He remembered
those odious calls here and there when he was looking
for something to " turn up " ; and he could not bring
himself to meet those same people again, pretending
that he liked them or respected them.

So it would have been apt to happen, that he would
have dropped back, of evenings, into a habit of sitting
late to read ; he would have taken up again the " Sar-
tor Resartus," the " Menzel's German Literature," the
scraps from Cousin and Jouffroy, which had been the
rage when he left Cambridge. He would have made an
Index Rerum out of these books, and would gradually
have persuaded himself that he was a truly remarkable
literary man, sadly unappreciated, and that Detroit was

a very boorish and unsympathetic place, into which no
man of culture or intelligence should ever be sent;
while the truth would have been, that Mr. Jasper Rising, bachelor of arts, was growing to be a very boorish
and unsympathetic man, not bearing his own part in
the social system to which he belonged. From this
delusion and folly Oscar saved him.

They took long walks together. For twenty minutes,
as they began these walks, Jasper drilled him on his
English, determined, that, as the boy became a man, he
should speak without foreign accent. He made sedulous
study of the anatomy of the vocal organs, and of the
analysis of sound, and drilled the boy on careful system, and with wonderful results. Oscar called this
twenty minutes, " going to school." This school would
bring them outside of the pig-pens and shanties of the
outskirts; and then they could enjoy summer, autumn,
or winter, as it might be. Jasper would lecture, and
Oscar would listen, learnedly and eagerly, of whatever
might be before them. The youngster who has lately
graduated knows a little about botany, a little about
farming, a little about the clouds and the weather, a
little about the shape of the snow-flakes, a little about
the forming of the ice on the streams: he knows a little
about everything. Very good. That is what he was
sent to his college for, — to lay a foundation on which,
when the time came, he might build such edifice as the
good God might order. And so Jasper was prepared,
sufficiently well, to hold forth to Oscar on this or that
or another thesis; and Oscar listened with delight to
all. Meanwhile something would remind him of home,
of fiord or of ice-floe, or of " spring beauties " there, or
of scaling the mountains. And when he found tongue,
Jasper would let him run on to his heart's content,
either in the Norwegian, which fell so pleasantly from
his lips when he was really at ease, or in his English,
which was always racy, and with every month grew
more and more pure.

Sometimes these walks gave place either to rides or
long trials of new wagons, when there was something

new to be tested. But, after all, they liked their walks the most. For they were both young, near the age of omnipotence, and in walking they had least care.

Swimming was, for two months of the year, better even than walking, perhaps. Swimming was a mania with Jasper; and it proved that it was a habit with Oscar from a period so early that he could not remember when he could not swim. So soon as Mr. Dundas found out, as he said, how crazy they both were about it, he admitted them to the secret, that, a little way up the river, he had certain well-defined and undivided rights of suzerainty, which entitled him to permit them to carry up to an old barn near the shore an old sea-chest, of which Oscar had renewed hinges and lock, and which Jasper then stored with Bent's crackers, and a Dutch cheese, while in the off-cut, of Oscar's cabinet-making, he laid in a dozen crash towels. Dear Lily, I am sorry to confess that they were not hemmed; but of some sexes one weakness is an inability to hem rapidly. The rights of suzerainty extended down the beach; so that when Jasper chose, he and Oscar could run down from the shop to the river, take a boat and row up to Flinders's, as this place was called, strip in the shade of the barn, and, to take the delicious vernacular of New England in its sweet simplicity, could " go into water."

Ah! those were the really glorious days for Oscar! They undressed slowly; they swam forever, — if it had been heaven they would not have enjoyed it more; unwillingly they came back to shore when Jasper gave the word. They ran races in the costume of the Olympian games upon the beach. They lay in the sun, and let the life from the light soak into their skin and flesh and bones. They slowly resumed the baser disguises of fallen man; and then they took the skiff, and let her, if she would, drift down to the scenes of dirt and work and barter. But there was no other time when they so discussed all realities in heaven above or earth beneath, or in the waters under the earth; nor ever, as Oscar thought, did life seem so free as when they thus got away from their harness, away from houses, away from roads, even away from work, and away from men.

These young men had less than most young men have to do with other people in the world; but they were all in all to each other.

Meanwhile Jasper's relations with the little college circle, where we first met him, fell off, he scarcely knew how. He was annoyed that it was so. But there was no reason why he should be annoyed. Letters were fewer and fewer on both sides; and, when they wrote, they found out, to their sorrow, that they had nothing to say. For Jasper himself, his life did not satisfy him, but it did not dissatisfy him. He certainly had not yet persuaded himself that he had been sent into the world only to make better carriages in Detroit than had been made there before. But, on the other hand, it was clear that making carriages then and there was the duty next his hand just then, and that it was the only place which he had just then to stand in, in the subduing of the world. And Jasper had sense enough to make out that he had not been put into the world for any mere personal purpose, but as a child of God, to whom God had intrusted a part of this business of world-subduing. Jasper knew, in his heart, that he should have liked the world much better if it had needed him as chairman of a leading committee in Congress. But there, unfortunately, the Constitution of the country said that no man should enter, even the House of Representatives, till he was twenty-five years old; and, if it had not said so, no constituency had shown any desire to return him. He knew in his heart that he should have liked the world much better, if it had needed him where it needed the young Napoleon, encouraging a faltering column at the Bridge of Lodi, or carrying an army over an impossible route to pounce on a half-defended valley. But nobody had summoned him to any such duty. He had, on the other hand, shaken his head at the Mexican war, when he refused the proposals of the wagon-contractor. He could understand very well that it would be pleasanter to work

as Charles Dickens was working at that moment, every
one of whose monthly parts Jasper and Oscar were
buying at the moment when they appeared, and de-
vouring eagerly. But just here Jasper was aware that he
could not write the " Curiosity Shop " if he tried ;· and
he even doubted whether, if he could, there were any
publisher who would take the risk of sending óut his
chapters to the world. Even at four and twenty he had
thus found that he had his limitations. And, so as the
business of carriage-building was open, he stuck to that
with all his zeal. He saw that it was training Oscar
admirably. He saw that it was raising the standard
of honor, and indeed of life, of every man engaged in
the factory. He looked forward to larger relations
into which it might bring them all with the business of
the North-west. And it made of him an efficient and
vital part of the God-made order of the civilization of
his time. So far so good. And so Jasper solaced
himself, when he reflected, that, though he had lived
long enough to be a Master of Arts, he was not yet a
Henry Clay, a Napoleon, or a Dickens. Yet, for all
this, he did not mean to be a carriage-builder all his
life.

Now, my dear Lily, if you are quite outraged because all this " excursion," as the Germans call it, does
not seem to you to help the story on at all, I am very
sorry. For really, it does help it a great deal. I know
what you wanted. You wanted, that, just as soon as
Jasper had had that nice talk with Bertha, he should
go home to his hotel, and write her just the most beautiful note that ever was written, and send it round to
her ; and walk anxiously on the lake-side for an hour,
and then receive from her, at the hands of a lovely
child, a moss rose-bud. Then you wanted him to fly
to Bertha, and fold her in his arms, and press one kiss
on her lips, and then to have them married, and have
this story done, and another story begun.

Dear Lily, I am truly sorry for you ; but, if this did
not happen, how can you and I make it happen ? Jas-

per did not see Bertha for a year after the party, and
more, nor hear one word from her. And a sad enough
business it was when he did hear. I do not say but he
thought of her very often during those fifteen months.
Yes, Lily, he did think of her; and I believe even
Bertha thought of him, if you will let me say so.
Sometimes when he was taking a long walk alone,
building some of his air-castles, he found that Bertha
was with him, and that he was very eagerly telling her
what were his grandest plans, and his most ambitious.
Once and again, when he was going through tea-fights
which good Mrs. Buffum got up, for the pure and simple purpose of making him better acquainted with some
very poky nieces she had staying with her, as Jasper
talked his hardest with Miss Melinda and Miss Frances
Maria, dragging up subjects which they had slain, and
galvanizing them, and making them skip and dance
again, only to see these horrid girls slaughter them once
more; once and again, I say, did he remember Bertha's
pleasant sympathetic listening, her unaffected reply,
her confession of ignorance if she were ignorant, or
her flash of intelligence the instant she comprehended.
When, to make himself understood at all, he had to
toil painfully through a sentence even to the hard knock
at the end of the last word, and Miss Melinda sim-
pered, and said sentimentally: "I always thought so";
and then when she showed a moment after that she
had not the slightest idea of what he had been saying
or explaining, he would recall Bertha's quick intelligence, cutting him short when he had but just begun,
so that they seemed to crowd half the best thought
and memory of their life into that golden hour of Mrs.
Rosenstein's supper-room and parlor. But through
that summer, and until the next was nearly ended,
they did not meet face to face again.

"Did not meet face to face!" says Miss Melinda,—
who at this moment is reading this chapter, without
recognizing herself, and as for Jasper, she long since
forgot him,—"Why it is only on this very page that

it says 'Bertha was with him' as he walked. How careless these people that write the stories are!"

And Bertha?

Bertha had what the vernacular of our country calls "a horrid time!"

Once and again it seemed impossible for her to bear the petty tyrannies and the great tyrannies of Mrs. Rosenstein. Sometimes it seemed as if Mrs. Rosenstein were fairly crazy: indeed, on a generous interpretation of that word, she was "beside herself." With the children Bertha could cope; although, as has been said, she lacked so often the help she had a right to look for. Mr. Rosenstein would be away, and his wife would interfere just where she ought not. But the children were very fond of Bertha, and she was very fond of them. And, as month passed after month, it was clear enough, even to her self-condemning disposition, that they were improving. The school-room, so called, was no longer a chaos, and they were not seeking for any excuse to shirk their lessons. All of them were bright; and, to Bertha's great pleasure, each one developed a special taste, which she could encourage and direct, and by which she could quicken a reasonable self-respect and pride.

It was, indeed, in the line of the very accomplishments which Bertha had used as her best allies, that she and Mrs. Rosenstein came to their worst battle-royal. Charlotte had, one morning, taken great pains with her French and arithmetic lessons, that she might be entitled to "paint" for an hour. The girl had really an eye for color; and Bertha, who knew a little of the rudimentary work of water-color drawing, had interested her intensely in its pretty processes. Charlotte had cleared away the school-books, brought out the drawing-table, set up the little table easel which Mr. Carl Rounds had given to her, and was just mixing the grays for her clouds, when a servant came in to say that Mrs. Rosenstein wanted her to go to ride with her ; Mrs. Rosenstein was going to make calls.

Poor Charlotte! She was not under any such restraint, but that she burst out into a fit of rage not unlike one of her mother's. "It is too bad! It is too bad! That's just what always happens. It's a shame!" and so on.

Bertha soothed her, so far as there was any soothing, talked to her as to a reasonable being sometimes, and sometimes as to a petted child, and at last brought her to considerations, partly of duty, partly of that miserable policy by which these four children were ruined, to go down to her mother, and to ask her leave to stay at home and draw. Poor Bertha gave this advice, as the very best which she could give, in the temper the child was then in ; and she knew as well as she could know anything, that the presence of Charlotte in the carriage was only a whim of the last moment.

Nor did Charlotte fail in tact or in duty, in presenting her request. She did not show any temper ; that had blown over in the first gale. She ran up to her mother pleasantly, caught both her hands and kissed her, and then said eagerly and confidently, " Oh, pray, mamma, let me stay at home now! I am in the midst of a nice surprise for you, and I do want to get it done before Saturday."

But Mrs. Rosenstein had been thoroughly crossed. "Surprise! surprise! I hate surprises. What is your surprise?"

"Oh! you must not know, mamma. Saturday, you shall know. No: to-morrow you shall know, if I may only stay at home all this morning. Mayn't I stay at home, mamma?"

"Tell me what you are doing, you disobedient child!" This was poor Lotty's only answer.

" Why, mamma," said the poor thing, crying, " of course I will tell, if you want me to. It is only the picture I was painting, — I was copying it from a picture Miss Bertha has. And I was painting it for a surprise for you."

" And so it is Miss Schwarz who steps in between
me and my children, and decides who shall stay at
home, and who shall not stay. I will tell Miss Schwarz
what I think of that." This was the answer to Charlotte's confession. And Mrs. Rosenstein sent Christina
up stairs to bid Miss Schwarz come down. The moment Bertha entered she was assailed with, —

" So, Miss Schwarz, there is a new mistress in this
house, I understand. It seems there is some one here
who wants to come between me and my children. I
suppose I am to thank you that I may have the carriage to go and ride myself. Would you not prefer, Miss
Schwarz, to take it this morning, and have me stay at
home? As for this disobedient girl, I will see what
shall be done to her. I will thank you, Miss Schwarz,
to interfere no longer with her, or with any of the children. I have had quite enough of this impudence. I
will not bear it."

By this time Charlotte was sobbing on the sofa.
Bertha, utterly astonished, was not so much upset, but,
at the first, the absurdity of the whole impressed her as
much as the rudeness and injustice. But of this tran-
sient amusement she showed no sign ; she even screwed
herself up to saying cheerfully :

" Dear Mrs. Rosenstein, there is some mistake. Nobody wants to interfere. Pray, what do you mean?"

" No! nobody wants to interfere. Oh, no! nobody!
Yet poor me is the only person in the house who is a
slave to every one ; and my poor children, one by one,
are stolen from me. Julia was the first, then I lost the
boys, and now my own Charlotte turns on her mother.
And it is for Miss Schwarz to say whether she shall go
out with her own mother, or stay at home, — Miss
Schwarz, whom I picked out of the gutter. And if
you please, Miss Schwarz, may I dine at home to-
day?"

" Mamma! Mamma!" shrieked Charlotte; and
Bertha turned to leave the room.

" No, Miss Schwarz, you shall not run away from
me," said the wild creature. " You shall hear me out

10

this time. I'll give you a bit of my mind, if I never speak again. I will not have this interference and impudence. I will not have such goings on, under my own eyes, with my own children. I will be the mistress of my own family." And so, — as is the law of passion, which has its laws as entirely as gravitation has, — she wrought herself up, from point to point, till she said what she had not the least idea of saying when she began, and, indeed, had never seriously thought of saying. " I thought I had hired a servant : it seems, I did hire a mistress. I was tired of her long ago ; and, if she is as tired of her place as I am of seeing her in it, she will not stay long. The sooner she goes the better."

"Mamma! Mamma!" shrieked poor Charlotte again, dismayed at seeing the storm she had brought on.

" I agree with you wholly," said Bertha ; " the sooner the better. Now, I am sure, there is no reason why I should stay longer."

So Bertha went up stairs ; and, though she had often been terribly angry with Mrs. Rosenstein, this time she was not angry ; nay, she was even glad that the end had come, almost without a word, indeed without any premeditation, of hers. She was sorry to go without saying good-by to Mr. Rosenstein ; but for the rest, she could bury all thought of the insult in the joy of going home, and that she was going home without having given up herself, that it was no thought or plan of hers.

So she packed her possessions, leaving in the bureau drawers the several gifts, costly and mean, with which in sunny days Mrs. Rosenstein had oppressed her. She did not go down to dinner, but Christina saw that she did not suffer. Bertha was a prime favorite with Christina, as with everybody else in the household, except its mistress.

The packing was interrupted, once and again, by visits from the girls and the boys, now together, now alone, and always in tears before the visits were well finished, even if the young folks came in with some pretence of firmness. Sometimes Bertha sent them away, sometimes they went away, because they were ashamed to cry in her room. She knew that a boat would touch at the pier on its way northward early the next morning; and she had bidden Christina make sure of a wagoner and a carriage to take her trunks and herself to meet it. A sad afternoon for her, for the children were indeed in earnest, and she found it hard to comfort them, when she needed comfort herself all the time.

But just as she had squeezed into the top of the trunk the last obdurate parcel of shoes, and felt she had so earned her right to undress, even if there were little chance of sleeping, there came an unexpected tap at her door. She threw it open herself; and Mr. Rosenstein came in, whom she had supposed a thousand miles away. He looked worried, and, after he had given her his hand, sat down on the trunk she had just closed, as if he did not know how to begin.

"I hope I am in time. I cannot tell you how annoyed I am, how provoked I am. Of course, if I had been here, this would never have been. Of course — you see — well, Miss Schwarz, I know there is no apology. I know Mrs. Rosenstein must have talked, — well, like a fool, I suppose. But she can make, and shall make, any apology you require. No! please do not speak — let me speak. If you please, you must see that the one chance these children have for this world, or for any world, is with you. You must see, that, if you leave them, they can never have such a chance again. Charlotte says you have been crying. Their mother has been crying all day long, they tell me, ever since this cursed outbreak. No! please let me speak. I do not want to persuade; but, if you could see that there was any duty in the case, I know you would stay here. Is it possible for me to show you that you have a duty to these children? At least, I can show you that you will render an inestimable service to me."

Bertha looked up this time; and, when she looked

up, she saw that Julia was in the room also, her eyes
red with tears, resting on her father's shoulder as he
spoke.   As Bertha looked up, this poor child, who was
to be left to the whims of such a wild-cat as Bertha was
leaving, looked on her, to implore her.   And she, too,
found words to say, "Pray stay!"

And Bertha staid.

CHAPTER XV.

BERTHA STAID.

BERTHA staid.

And from this time her life with these wild children, and their half-crazy mother, with its occasional glimpses of poor, worn, sad-looking Mr. Rosenstein, had new elements, and began to partake of ups and downs quite as wayward as those of anybody else in this story.

When she first went to Milwaukie, whatever the roughness of the machinery of Mr. Rosenstein's household, there was no lack of that useful oil on which social machinery runs most easily, known as money when it is spoken of without a metaphor. The children asked for money, and got more than they asked. Mr. Rosenstein gave money open-handed, for house-keeping and for the expenses of dress, without being asked; and had only to be approached with any demand, however outrageous or absurd, by his wife or any other member of the family, to answer it lavishly and immediately. It used to be said of Deacon Miles, that his only fault was that he never could tell what a woman should have to do with a five-dollar bill. Mr. Rosenstein had many faults, but this was not hidden among them. People of Mrs. Rosenstein's type are apt to think that anything conceivable is gained if they only have plenty of money. Alack and alas! I remember poor Mary, who married on that supposition, and found in three days that she had a sulky, selfish, silent brute in her house, who had only wanted to marry her because he could thus spite the dozen adorers who were dying to marry her, whom she had placed there by her own consent, and kept there by her own solemn vow and promise, and that from year's end to year's end, and from life's end to life's end. Every cup was to be soured by what he chose to put into it, and every breath she drew to have a choking twitch, because this creature was there! Poor Mary! There was plenty of money! But, if she ever smiled again, I never saw it.

Bertha had found out, if she needed to learn it, that many things besides oil were needed to make the Rosenstein machinery run easily; and this we have sufficiently explained to the reader. But now even the supply of oil became unsteady. Sometimes there would be a great rush of oil, pouring itself all over the machinery. But sometimes the wheels would creak and groan, and get very hot on the bearings, because no oil was to be had. Or, speaking in the fashion of the street, sometimes Mr. Rosenstein was flush, and sometimes he was very, very dry. There would be dreadful borrowings from child to child, from child to mother; borrowings even from Bertha to pay such trifles as an express fee, all so many evidences that the supplies had been stopped. And from these, and many other tokens, Bertha knew that Mr. Rosenstein's business must be sadly disarranged.

She knew too little of business herself to make any guess which she could hold to for a week at a time, as to what his occupation was. Such secrecy she had never dreamed of, as was observed by common consent about it. · She wondered sometimes that she could go on as she did, with French verbs, and German exercises, and the latitude of Cape Walsingham, and the population of Pekin, just as if she were the most commonplace governess in the world; when, in fact, she was living in an atmosphere of secrets which was worthy of the Inquisition itself. One day her indignation passed all bounds. She had heard great altercation down stairs, which was then hushed, so that Bertha went on with her writing. In a few minutes more there was a knock at her own door. It was Mr. Rosenstein who knocked, pale with rage. "Miss Schwarz, the person with me is a United States officer, who holds what is called a search-warrant, and affects that he has the right to go into every room in this house with it. I have permitted him to go into my wife's and mine, rather than make a row. Would you be kind enough to let him see how much tobacco you have in your bureau drawers?" This was said with a profound sneer. It did not, however, annihilate the officer, who stepped forward and opened the drawers, ransacked them pretty thoroughly indeed, and then, with a rather clumsy apology, said to Bertha that he was sorry to have annoyed her,— he was only doing his duty. His eye fell on Bertha's travelling trunk which stood in her closet, of which the door was open.

"Please, Miss Bertha, give him the keys of your trunk," said Mr. Rosenstein. "You see he is not satisfied."

"He can examine the trunk," said Bertha, proud as a queen and savage as a lioness; "but there is nothing in it, nor has been, these six months. It is not locked, sir. Do your duty." This with a sublime sneer.

The officer was no fool. He knew innocence when he saw it, apologized in his fashion again, and went his way.

As Bertha was going to bed that evening, one of those whims crossed her, in which women take pleasure, of altering the arrangements of their sleeping-rooms. Perhaps the incident of the officer had made her think that the trunk should not have been in sight. She would ask Christina to take it up stairs, and she should have more room in her closet. She tried to draw it out into the room, but did so only with great difficulty. The trunk was so heavy the weight surprised her; she loosened the straps, and found, to her new amazement, that the trunk was locked. Had she locked it herself? She never locked it; she would have sworn it was not locked: she remembered how fiercely she had told the officer it was not locked. She found the key in a moment, unlocked the trunk, opened it with difficulty, so heavy was the upper half of it, and then found that both top and bottom were fully crowded home with specimen cards of English cutlery of every variety. Knives, scissors, surgical implements, table furniture, — things that Bertha had never heard of nor dreamed of were there. But only one of each kind!

Poor Bertha! this was the trunk she had so bravely defied the officer to examine.

What did it all mean? How could it be that Mr. Rosenstein was a receiver of stolen goods? and what ought she do? Should she go and find the officer, and tell what she had found? It seemed cruel that she should have to denounce any one in whose house she was living. Should she demand an explanation from Mr. Rosenstein? should she insist on leaving a house where there could be such mysteries? Poor Bertha! She got into bed feeling that she should never sleep again.

In fact, she was asleep in fifteen minutes. But the next morning, of course, all her cares returned. She determined to take one card of the knives from the trunk, and carry them down to Mr. Rosenstein, and demand an explanation.

She opened the trunk, and there was nothing there!

Bertha went down stairs, puzzled and provoked. Of one thing she was sure, she would have an immediate explanation. But, of course, when she found them all at the breakfast-table, as, to her surprise, she did, she did not rush in with a carving-knife, and cry, "Explain! explain!" She sat down and let Mr. Rosenstein offer her everything, and give her a spoonful of omelette. Of course she could not have an explanation then. As it happened, she had not eaten her breakfast before he was called to the door on business. No sort of allusion was made by anybody to the officer or the search-warrant. Bertha loitered down stairs, before she joined the children in the school-room. But on inquiry, it proved Mr. Rosenstein had gone out. And he did not return for more than a week. So for that week Bertha had to live without an explanation.

When Mr. Rosenstein did come home, it was not Bertha who sought an explanation from him ; it was he who came to make one to her.

It was, however, a minimum of an explanation. Simply and sadly, — with sadness, indeed, which commanded all Bertha's sympathy, — he told her that he found his establishment was much more expensive than he could maintain. His business had not been successful ; he had determined to sell his house and furniture, and remove his family to New Orleans, where his partner lived. He was very sorry, after Miss Schwarz had staid purely at his request, to break his engagement with her. But he must do so. They were all to break up so suddenly, that he must notify her at once of his new plans. He supposed she would like to go to her father's at once ; and, if she wished, he would take her passage in the boat of the next day for Detroit. He would make up her salary to the end of the year. And, fairly with tears in his eyes, this incomprehensible man thanked her again and again for her kindness to the children, and said she had given them the only chance in life they had had since they were born.

Could Bertha possibly ask for an explanation then ?

She never did ask for one, and she never got one. The real explanation was, that Mr. Rosenstein was a very important link in a very large combination of smugglers ; who, by arrangements which need not be described here, were systematically defrauding the revenue on an enormous scale.

CHAPTER XVI.

NUMBER 47.

A S Jasper came down to the shop a little late one day, Mr. Buffum met him, and said, with an anxious look, " I am very glad you have come : would you as lief see these Peoria people? I think my breakfast does not agree with me. I have a sort of faint feeling, and I had rather keep out of the sun."

Of course Jasper went over the drying-shop with the Peoria people, and got their orders.

When he came back into the office, he found Mr. Buffum, to his amazement, lying at full length upon a wretched apology for a sofa they had in the counting-room. Such a thing Jasper had never seen before. He was distressed, of course, and came to his friend eagerly to serve him. He was more distressed as poor Buffum turned languidly round to look at him. There was the same anxious look that he had half an hour before, and his features seemed strangely sunken. " Oh ! " said he, faintly, to Jasper, " I am glad you have come back ; I lay down here for a minute, because I am in no condition to do anything. I have a strange weight at my stomach." Jasper was more alarmed by the manifest look of anxiety on his face, than by what he said. He sent Oscar at once for Mr. Dundas, who was in the carpenter-shop ; bade one of the boys put a horse into an easy rockaway, which stood in the yard, and then he and Dundas easily prevailed on poor Buffum to go home. Dundas slipped on his coat, and drove ; and Oscar sat in the carriage, that Mr. Buffum might rest on his shoulder, for he seemed hardly able to sit upon the seat.

Neither of them returned till noon. " I never saw such a change in a man in my life," said Dundas. " We could hardly get him to bed, — his poor wife and I. And now, if you were to go in and see him, Rising, you would not know who it was, his whole face has fallen in so, and his expression is so changed."

" Did he know you when you left him? "

" Oh, yes ! he is wholly conscious, but he is in terrible pain." And as Mr. Dundas said this, he passed through into the inner office, giving Jasper a sign with his eyelids, as he passed, that he wished him to do the same.

Jasper followed him, and closed the door, that Oscar and the other workmen, who were clustering about him, need not hear what he said.

" Is it cholera? " said he to Mr. Dundas.

" Not a doubt of it," was the sad reply. " He has already the most agonizing cramps. It is terrible to see any one in such pain ; and poor Buffum has been so tender and gentle all the time. Did you not notice that blue margin round his eyes? Well, after we got him to bed, his eyes flashed with a brilliancy I never saw before, and this corpse-like blue was horrible. The doctor is there now, with his camphors and laudanums and brandies, but I could not see that they made a hair's-breadth of difference. I told Oscar to bring me back, because I knew you would be anxious. I will send him now with a message to my wife, and then I have told Mrs. Buffum that I will spend the afternoon and night with her." Here Dundas dropped his voice. " You see, if he gets no relief, he will not be alive in the morning ; and people are so frightened that she will find it hard to get any one to stay with her."

The truth was, that the Asiatic cholera had been making the second of its terrible incursions of the present century. Everybody in Detroit had been watching, wondering, and expecting it ; but there had been no certain case till this. Dundas had not wanted

to give unnecessary alarm, and so had made his story
to his partner private.

But little use was there in secrecy, or hope to maintain it. His prognostic regarding Mr. Buffum was only
too true. The attack was tremendous in its celerity.
Jasper stopped at the house as he went home at night,
to offer any service, and went up into the poor patient's
room. He did this, not only to be of any relief he
might to him, but to encourage the rest, if he could, by
showing that he had no fear of contagion. Mr. Buffum
answered him when he was spoken to, but Dundas had
been quite right in saying that Jasper would not have
known him. Features, color, expression, the whole
face was wholly changed. Even his voice was unnatural, so that there was nothing left to be recognized;
and to see a man of Buffum's strength so utterly prostrate, utterly without muscular power of any sort, in so
few hours since they had seen him standing and moving, was the greatest mystery of all. There was
nothing Jasper could do, but to try to say something
hopeful to the poor wife; and then he bade Oscar
drive him home.

At the shop, the next day, he met the announcement
that it was all over with his poor partner. He had not
lived till daybreak. There were some faint turns,
Dundas said, which seemed almost a relief after the
suffering they had seen; and for himself, he confessed
that all treatment had been so powerless, that he had
felt a strange relief when he saw death creeping on,
and knew that his poor friend had some relief from his
agony. He only came round to give Jasper this news,
and then went home to undress and sleep, if he might.
Meanwhile, Jasper learned that two of the men were
down, either from the disease or from fear. The next
day two or three more were absent; but it was thought
by the one or two who remained that they were not
sick, but had fled the city. Of work, indeed, there
was little enough to be done in these sultry August
days. Jasper only kept up the forms of work, that the
men's minds might be turned on something beside

" premonitories," of which every one was talking. He occupied himself, as did all men of intelligence and public spirit, in making proper arrangements for the poor emigrants, who landed from every steamer bound up the lakes, and in the depressed state of their constitutions were just so much food for the disease. Three or four temporary hospitals were opened for their treatment; and bodies of volunteer nurses, of both sexes, came to the relief and assistance of the physicians.

The next Monday, when Jasper and Oscar came to the shop, after a Sunday which had been consecrated to hospital service, he was distressed to find a note from Mr. Dundas, saying that he himself was not well. It was nothing, the note said; but he thought it best to be prudent. Jasper called Oscar in, to bid him put the horse to a wagon; but as the boy entered, he perceived in an instant, and with a sinking heart, that his step dragged, and that something was the matter with him. Jasper framed a longer sentence than he had meant, that he might get a full look at Oscar's eyes; and there, too certainly, were the blue circles around them, which he had learned to know so well.

" Just sit here for a minute, Oscar," said he, without saying a word more to alarm the boy. " I will be back in a moment; lie back on the sofa; you look tired." And Oscar did so, amazed at himself, first that he was tired; and next that he made no protest against his master's order. He knew, as well as Jasper knew, that it was very strange that he should consent to lie down in that room.

In two minutes Jasper had two horses in two carriages. Sadly enough, the thought flashed across his mind, that the one in which he sat was one of those which Oscar had saved to the firm while he was in Milwaukie. He lifted Oscar gently into the same rockaway in which they had carried Buffum away for the last time. One of the workmen held him, and another drove the horse, as they went, all three, to the hospital where Oscar and Jasper had both been on duty all the day before. Jasper himself then swung to the gates, and bolted them within. There was not a man left in the shops or in the paint-rooms. He passed through the deserted counting-house, and locked the door; unfastened his horse, mounted the wagon, and drove as fast as he could to his surviving partner's.

The old story again! Dundas was in bed by this time. His voice was changed, though he did not know it; his natural color gone, and his eyes sunken. Still his courage held. "You need not have come round to see me, Rising, though it is very kind in you." Then, after a pause, of which he was hardly conscious, "I shall be all right to-morrow." Then another pause, and one effort more: "Anything at the shop you want to ask about?" But Jasper said cheerfully that they should do very well at the shop; that he must not concern himself, drew Mrs. Dundas aside, to say that he would try to be back before the day was over; and then, as soon as he might, followed to the hospital, to which he had directed the men to take poor Oscar.

An old warehouse by the river-side, which, in the earlier days of Detroit, had been some sort of government storehouse, Jasper thought, and in later days seemed to have been put to any or no use, as anybody or nobody might wish,—this was the temporary hospital. They might not have done better, had they built one on purpose. It was close by the river, so that they were sure of as good air as could be had anywhere. It had no windows originally; and, for the present purposes, very large windows had been cut,—which were, in fact, so many barn-doors,—and gave to all the rooms the most ample ventilation. A loft, some fifteen feet above the first floor, had always existed over about half the building. No effort had been made to enlarge this; but a convenient stairway had been built, by which there was easy access to it. There were, therefore, two wards to the improvised hospital; one down stairs, occupying the whole floor, and one up stairs, of half the size. When the authorities took possession of this building, there were some rotten sails in it, which had been carried out and made into tents on the river-side. All its other contents had been carried away, and the whole interior doubly white-washed, — floors, ceilings, and all, under an impression which widely prevailed, and which had, probably, some foundation in truth, that there was virtue in the clean-liness of new lime on walls.

In four regular lines, which extended the whole length of the building, were the rows of neat pine bed-steads, which had been put together on a simple pat-tern, for the emergency, and were also neat and sweet. There were, as one would guess at a glance, about twenty beds in each of the four rows; half of them had never been occupied. The Marseilles quilts, which had been taken from the supplies of some steamer, covered them nicely, and gave even a cheerful aspect to the sad place. An unpainted chair stood at the head of each bed, on one side, and a little unpainted table of white pine on the other.

Jasper arrived at the hospital within an hour after Oscar and the other party had come there. Jasper stopped a moment at the little office, which was a sep-arate, ten-foot building, on the outside.

"What do you think of my poor boy, doctor?" he said, finding that one of the gentlemen on duty had returned for a moment to the office.

"O Rising! is it you?" said Dr. Wirt, looking up for a moment. "I am sorry to say, there is no doubt it is a real attack. Indeed, he looked badly when he stopped here this morning with your message, and I tried to persuade him then not to go any farther. But I might as well have spoken to the wind. You had told him to meet you at your shop, he said; and it was very clear that he would have gone on and met you, if he had died. We have got him to bed. I have been giving him hot teas, just as we were ordering yes-terday; and he is not, as yet, in any pain. You will be of more use to him than we shall be."

"I wish I thought so," said Jasper, as they passed

into the building together. " How many new cases
have you?"

" Well, I believe we have eight, counting Oscar,
since you left yesterday. But, per contra, we have
only lost two. It is the best night for a week. I do
not think we can say it is the treatment. But it does
seem as if the violence of the attacks were less as the
number increases. Certainly, our proportion here is
better. Do you know what Sabine says?"

No, Jasper did not know; and, as he said this, they
came to No. 47. Oscar was No. 47 from this time,
and by No. 47 Jasper took his seat. He acquainted
himself in a few minutes with what had been done, by
the nurse whom he found on duty; and then he assumed his charge of Nos. 46, 47 and 48. This was
service which both he and Oscar had been rendering at
intervals now for three or four days.

" It is that my head aches, dear master, as I did not
know my head could ache. And I do not hear very
well what Dr. Wirt says to me, and what this nurse-
man — man-nurse, what you call him? — wants to say.
But now you have come, my dear master, your poor
boy will be well soon — well soon." And then he sunk
into the silence which was so much more natural than
continued speech, in this terrible prostration.

As Jasper sat, as he varied the treatment according
to the doctor's direction under the constant change of
symptoms, he persuaded himself, once or twice, that
this was not going to be a severe attack; once or twice,
again, that it was one of unusual severity. And he
learned, thus, what he had not known before, that a
nurse may be too much interested in a patient to see
symptoms and treatment with a perfectly unbiassed eye.
The time passed rapidly. Jasper was not discouraged,
when, at four, Dr. Wirt came round, and confirmed
Jasper's feeling that Oscar was not sinking since two.
He had certainly held his ground.

" If you will send me in some one to take these three
beds," said Jasper, " I will get myself some dinner,
and go round and see how Dundas is."

"Dinner!" said the doctor. "Are you mad, to have put off your dinner a minute beyond the usual time? Do you suppose we can do without you?" And he ordered another nurse to the spot, and sent Jasper out of the building.

Jasper got his dinner, and drove to Mr. Dundas's, but did not get an encouraging bulletin. He let Mrs. Dundas give him a cup of tea, and then went back to Oscar. As he approached the bed, he saw one of the lady nurses was on duty, between 46 and 47.

Jasper passed in between 45 and 46, and said, "I will relieve you now, madam."

The nurse turned to thank him, and he saw that it was Bertha.

11

CHAPTER XVII.

A FRESH WATER VOYAGE.

BERTHA'S parting from the Rosensteins had been a hard business, — hard to her and hard to them. Mrs. Rosenstein was in tears or in sulks from the moment she heard of it; angry and sorry by turns: nor could any one have supposed that there had ever been moments when she had pretended that she wanted to turn poor Bertha away. The children were real mourners. Bertha loved them, they loved her. She had, indeed, lifted them to the knowledge of what real love is; nor would it be too much to say, that, in their intercourse with her, they forgot for the first time the teasing and the intriguing habits to which they had been used from childhood, even in their relations with each other.

Bertha was to return East, from Milwaukie, by steamboat. The boat left Chicago on its northward course in the morning; and, from the higher windows of the house, the children were on the lookout to announce when its smoke appeared, and when, therefore, their dear Miss Schwarz would be torn away. At last the signal came. It was certain that this chimney and this smoke were the real chimney and the real smoke. Mrs. Rosenstein had ordered out the carriage, to give all dignity to Bertha's departure. All the children were to go to the steamer with her. Mr. Rosenstein, however, had not appeared, and they had been forced to drive without him.

Bertha had private reasons for regretting his absence; and her regret was only partially relieved, when, just as the carriage came to the door, Pix, as the children called the office-boy, came up with this note from Mr. Rosenstein, explaining his absence : —

TUESDAY, P.M.

DEAR MISS SCHWARZ, — I am very sorry not to say "good-by." I am also very much annoyed, because, from the absence of the cashier at this moment, I cannot send you your money. I enclose forty dollars, and on your arrival at Detroit you will find my check for the balance, which your friends there will readily cash for you.

Wishing you a pleasant journey, my dear Miss Schwarz, I am,

Very truly yours,

A. ROSENSTEIN.

Forty dollars was, in fact, enclosed. But Bertha knew then, that forty dollars might not carry her back to Boston ; and she was sorry to cut loose from her base wholly dependent on a letter to be received on the way. However, there was nothing to be done. She kissed Mrs. Rosenstein for the last time, and departed.

For one, I never thank the enterprising railroad companies, which, by carrying their rival lines across Michigan, have robbed us of the old delight of the voyage through Lakes Michigan and Huron, which used to come in in such charming relief between Detroit and Milwaukie. Bertha was sorry to leave her pupils, but she was very glad to be going home. She had met life for the first time on her own responsibility. And she had done what she set out to do. She did not know it, but in her first battle she had come off conqueror.

A battle, as defined by a distinguished commander of men, is a scene of wild disorder, where you think everything goes wrong. But under its excitement, he says, time passes very quickly. You find perhaps, after a few hours, which seem not many minutes, that more things have gone wrong on the other side than on yours. And then, to your amazement, you know that you are victorious.

This was exactly what had happened with Bertha

Schwarz. She had undertaken to hold a certain post, where she had been stationed for an indefinite length of time. A very hard post it had proved to be. Once and again it seemed as if she must beat a retreat, and march off as she could, colors flying or colors trailed. And at last, without any act of hers, she was told that she was relieved from this " Castle Dangerous " to which she had pledged herself; and, while she was in fact gaining everything she would have gained by retreat, she was not retreating, but everybody was surrounding her with tenderness, and grieving for her departure. Yes : Bertha had had her first tussle with life, and had come off victor.

And now there was this delicious summer voyage before her to rest in. She had soon arranged her pretty state-room, opened the windows for the best draught, and then found herself sitting in the shade on deck, pretending to read, but really dreaming of home, as the boat dashed along on her voyage to Mackinac, and the big, fleecy clouds which made mountains above the horizon slowly drifted by on the clear blue. It is the poetry of travelling : and it is a sad pity there is so little left of it. The boat stopped once and again, for passengers, for freight, and for wood. The weather was calm, — so calm that Bertha felt no sea-sickness. She could read if she cared to read, — she could draw the outlines of the cumulus if she cared to draw. Best of all, she could sit and watch the clouds, or at night the stars, with the happy consciousness that she was not obliged to do one thing or the other. She might be as lazy as she pleased, and in her laziness she was stealing no one's money or time. She might dream of the future, she might remember the past ; and there was no fear that the charming reverie would be broken by, " Where is Miss Schwarz ? " or, " O, Miss Schwarz ! the book is wrong. I am sure it is wrong."

There are some little islands called the Manito Islands, near the north of Lake Michigan ; and at one of these the boat touched for wood. The captain came, and told Bertha that they would be detained there an hour, if she

liked to walk; and that he should give all the passengers ample warning when they must return, if only they
would be careful to listen for the bell. Bertha gladly
joined quite a large walking-party, and they went on
shore. How strange that anybody should want to live
on this little island! And yet, clearly enough, the
people that lived there were very like the people who
lived elsewhere. Nay, Bertha was conscious, as possibly we all are, of a certain interior sense of delight
which must accrue were one monarch of all he surveys.
True, I observe that all islanders quit their principal-
ities when they can. Even Robinson Crusoe, with Friday;
even Peter Wilkins, Masterman Ready, the French
cabin-boy, all that redoubtable company, with the single
memorable exception of the Swiss Family, have, at an
instant's call, abandoned happy home, goats, wheat-
fields, pipkins, bows and arrows, grottos, cocoa-nuts,
melons, turtles, eggs, and savages, and everything else
they had to make them comfortable, and, from insular
independence and security, have returned to continental
laws, tenures, and dangers, — to living on wages, and
working at other people's direction. None the less, in
our dreams of creature bliss, do we all wish, like Sancho-
Panza, and Gov. Steuben, that we were lords of islands.

The walking party fared inland, began collecting
flowers, looked in at one log-cabin and another, and
came almost immediately on one, the smallest of the
group, which was evidently the school-house, so voluble
and loud was the storm of treble enunciation which
came pouring from the open door. Bertha, from professional interest, and one or two of the other passengers, stopped and went in.

A slight, pretty girl, who did not seem to be more
than seventeen years old herself, came forward to meet
them. She offered the only chair, her own; bade two
of the bigger boys rise, that their bench might serve for
the visitors, and, with shyness undisguised and undisguisable, thanked them for coming to see her school.
" I do not have many visitors," she said. The children,
meanwhile, did not affect to continue their studies, but

dropped their books upon their knees, and contemplated the dress of the strangers, and their every movement, with undissembled curiosity.

It was not long before the other passengers had seen all they wanted to see ; where, in fact, there was nothing to see but what they had seen a thousand times before. They bade good-by. But Bertha was drawn to the young school-mistress, by a certain likeness in their positions ; and, while the others walked on, she staid behind to question her as to her experience.

There was hardly any story to tell. The little mistress was not native to the island : she had come thither, a few weeks ago, from Manitowoc, a little lumber settlement on the main land ; hearing, from the mate of a schooner, that they wanted a teacher here. Yes, she was lonely sometimes ; but she found all the people were kind to her, though they did not know much about books. They knew enough to know that the children must learn to read them,· and that, the sooner they learned the better She thought the last teacher must have been careless, some of the children were so much behindhand. "But then," said she prettily, "I am afraid the next one will say the same of me. For really, I know so little myself, that I am ashamed to pretend to teach them."

Now, Bertha had said this to herself ten thousand times, and she knew she had. She had said it, in these very words, in the last letter she wrote home ; and she knew she had. But, for all that, the moment she heard this sister in the craft say so, Bertha, as in duty bound, took upon herself the part of comforter, and bravely said, " Why, you know more than they do. You know that *a b* spells ab ; and that is more than some of them know. You know that seven times seven is forty-nine. That is much more than these little boys know, I am sure. That is the way I comfort myself. For I am a ' school-marm ' too."

" Are you ? " said the shy girl ; and her heart opened at once to Bertha. " But you have had some chance to learn. And I, — I have only had the school at Manito-woe ; and I did have father and mother ! " and her large blue eyes were full of tears.

" Yes," said Bertha ; " I have had good teachers ; and many a time in the last year have I wondered why I was such a fool as to let them slip by me, without my learning more from them. Only give me another chance, and you shall see ! " And they both laughed, so as to make the school-children wonder. " But let me tell you one secret, that my uncle told me. It was a story. He told me that a great French professor fell sick ; and his son, who was a very young man, had to go and take his classes in astronomy. Now, the young man did not know near so much as his father. But the scholars liked him a great deal better. And somebody asked him how this happened. The young man laughed, and said, ' It must be because I am only three lessons in advance of the scholars.' You see, he knew what their troubles and trials were.

" It is as my father says, — his ladder had the rungs nearer together. If that is all they want, mine are close enough together." And the shy girl laughed, as if again quite at ease, and as if she had known Bertha always. For this was Bertha's way. Had these been the days of street-cars, Bertha would always have had the confidence of all the women in a car before they came to Union Place or to the City Hall.

Bertha asked the little school-mistress what she had to read. " Oh ! " said she, " that is the hardest of all. The people take a few newspapers ; but they are full of politics. You do not know how much I know about the county elections in the State. I brought all my books with me, and I read them, and read them, till I know them by heart. Did you ever read the life of Henry Martyn ? I have one volume of the large edition of that. Then I have Dwight's Sermons, and a volume of Flint's Letters : they were at the house I boarded at, and some other books."

Bertha was amazed at the poor child's cheerfulness. She knew, in her heart, that she should have died with such a library. Her first impulse was to say, " Let me

give you some books." But she knew that was not
best; and, as the words formed themselves, she said
the right thing, and not the wrong. "Would you not
like to borrow some books of me? I have a good many
in my trunk, which I shall not need all the way home."

How that child's face brightened! But how she said
it was impossible! Then how Bertha explained, that,
when she had finished the books, she could send them
to Milwaukie. Then the school-mistress confessed that
her uncle, the mate of the schooner, often touched at
Milwaukie, and would do anything for her. Then it
proved that school was nearly done; and the mistress
dismissed the scholars, nothing loath, a little early, and
walked quickly with Bertha to the landing. The two
girls rushed on board, nodded to the mate, who was
directing the business of the wood, and learned from
him that they had still nearly half an hour before the
boat would sail. Half an hour was a long time, indeed; and Bertha and Ruth entered Bertha's state-
room joyously, and in a moment more had her large
trunk open, and its contents scattered on all the two
beds. How Ruth's eyes watered, and how her face
glowed, as she saw Bertha's treasures!

And Bertha, she was so full with the delight that she
knew her treasures would give, that she was willing to
part with almost all of them. Not from all. There
were two or three of these books, and those the most
worn of all, which had been partners of too many sor-
rows and too many joys; they had been wet with too
many tears, and they had too many pencil-marks, records of old sympathy and appreciation, for Bertha to
be willing to part, even for a day, from them. But the
two girls turned them all over. They talked and they
questioned and they answered. Bertha offered more
than Ruth would take. And, after all, Bertha had to
judge, not Ruth, — as how should she? Bertha brought
together, on the chair where they had spread the newspaper, her two-volume Tennyson, Miss Austen's "Em-
ma," Mrs. Follen's Selections from Fénelon, the "Elements of Perspective," which happened to have strayed

in from the school-books, in which Ruth showed a curious interest ; an odd volume of Lockhart's Scott ; Lowell's little first volume, "A Year's Life," and a volume of Uhland's poems. Ruth said she had one or two German children, and she "might as well" learn German that winter from some of the mothers. Bertha felt all the grotesque oddity of the collection. Ruth felt as if it were a bag of diamonds. Bertha looked at it, and said, "I must put in something more. Oh, here it is ! take my 'Christian Year.'" And she put into the top of the parcel the miniature volume, and said to Ruth, "Now, that one is a keepsake from me. Do not send that back when you send the others."

"Bang ! bang ! bang ! bang !" said the bell up stairs ; and hastily the girls folded the newspaper round their treasures, and tied up a sorry-looking parcel. They kissed each other, and kissed each other, as if they had known each other a hundred years ; and Bertha led Ruth to the gangway, and bade her good-by.

The sun was yet two hours high, and they started again on their way to Mackinac.

The last morning of the voyage, Bertha found herself sleepless ; for her, an unusual experience. So soon as it was light, she rose and dressed herself, put on her cloak, and went on deck, that she might be sure to see the sun rise. The deck was wet with the fog, and the lake was white with it ; so that the steamer pushed on as through a cloud. But Bertha was well shod ; and though she found it too chilly to sit still, — indeed, there was no bench or other seat dry enough for her to sit upon, — she walked bravely up and down and across the boat, and warmed herself by exercise.

As she walked forward on one of these excursions, — for the boat was so large that they almost deserved that name, — she observed that below her, on the forward deck, there was a group of men speaking in subdued whispers ; and among them, in a moment, she made out the captain and the first mate, whom she already knew well. A moment more, and the captain threw up his hand, as a signal to the man in the wheel-house above him, close by where Bertha was standing. Bertha heard his bell strike, as a signal to the engineer. The engine stopped, and the boat lost way slowly. The captain beckoned to some one between decks, below where Bertha stood. All this passed without a word spoken aloud, and her curiosity was excited more and more. In a moment, six of the deck-hands came forward together, bearing on three handspikes, of which they grasped both ends, a coarse wooden box, which they laid upon the gang-way plank. Bertha had already observed that this lay on the deck, as if for a landing, though there was no land in sight; and that the low plank bulwark of the forward deck was down, as if some one were to come on board or to land. One or two deck-passengers, who seemed to be of the poorest class of emigrants, — men who had been disappointed in Chicago and were going back to Detroit, followed the little procession of the bearers. From the manner of them all, Bertha had no doubt that this was a coffin she was looking down upon.

The whole group, as it gathered below her, was perhaps a dozen men, all rough men in their look and apparel. As the boat at last lost head-way entirely, the mate nodded again to the captain : the captain removed his cap, and said, "Will you take off your hats, while we bury the dead?" The men 'around instantly and respectfully obeyed. Two of them lifted the inner end of the gang-way plank as high as they could, and as quickly. The coffin shot suddenly off into the lake. It had been weighted sufficiently, — it sank beneath the surface, — a few rough bubbles rose and broke, and then the little waves beat against the steamer's side as they did before. Two deck hands, without being bidden, replaced the movable piece of the boat's low bulwark; the captain waved his hand to the pilot, the pilot touched his bell for the engineer, the engine panted and snorted, the walking-beam began to move and the paddles to turn, the boat was in motion, and the funeral was over.

Bertha, as it happened, had never seen any funeral service before. The complete respect and simple reverence of these rough sailors in the presence of death, made her think that the most stately ceremonial would hardly express more.

As she resumed her walk up and down on the promenade-deck, she met the captain.

"I saw you looking at our funeral," he said. "I hope it did not shock you. We sailors are a rough set, perhaps. But I could not carry this body into Detroit."

"I was not shocked," said Bertha. "I was greatly moved by the sympathy and respectful bearing of the men. But who was this? Were there no friends? Could you not have left him at Detroit, and why?"

The captain told her that this was a poor homeless fellow who had come on board at Chicago to beg a passage, which had been given him. But the day before, too late to leave him at Mackinac, he had suddenly been taken sick; and there could be no doubt to any one who had ever seen Asiatic cholera, but that that was his disease. "Now, you know, Miss Schwarz, that, so far, they have no cholera at Detroit; and they would not thank me to bring them a case from the westward. I thought the fairest thing I could do for them, anxious as they are, was to bury the poor fellow in the lake. It is as near to heaven as on land, as brave old Gilbert said."

And Bertha asked if he had no fear about his other passengers.

No. None thus far. As she knew, he had but few deck-passengers, though on his last voyage West he carried two hundred. "We do not carry near so many the other way." And then the courteous captain expressed again the hope which he had expressed before, that Bertha would go with him all the way to Buffalo. Bertha was herself not certain. She would gladly go to Boston as quickly as she might. But, at her aunt's request, she had written to Mrs. Emlen, in Detroit, to say that she would visit her for a day or two in her

return eastward.   Mr. Rosenstein's arrangements about
money now compelled her, at least, to go to Mrs. Emlen to find his letter there.   She did not dare attempt
the journey to Boston, with its chances of interruption,
with what was left of her forty dollars.   So she told
the friendly captain that she could not decide whether
to go on with him or not, until she had seen her friends ;
and he told her that his boat would remain at Detroit
for the better part of the day, before passing into the
lower lakes, and that she might have that period for
her decision.   Before they parted, he gave her a hint
which she was perfectly willing to act upon, — that she
had better say nothing to the other passengers of the
impromptu funeral service she had seen.   To speak of
it would do no good, and it might make them anxious.
As soon as they came into the river, he would tell them
the whole story, and they could decide whether to go
on with him or no.   "For myself," said he, "I have
seen cholera too often, and know too well how little any
man knows of it, to be more afraid of it in one place
than in another.   I shall do my duty by this boat,
which the owners have intrusted to me.   And for the
rest, the good God will care."

Bertha said nothing, but looked him full in the face,
and gave him her hand with a frankness which showed
him that she trusted him.   And, from that moment,
she would rather have made all her voyage with this
captain, although she saw the risk of a cholera-tainted
vessel.   Bertha also had lived long enough to learn to
believe in men more than in things.

Nothing was said at breakfast, to show any alarm
among the passengers.   The captain's secret had not
yet found its way so far as the occupants of the first
cabin.   But, as the morning passed, as Bertha sat reading in the saloon, she noticed that a gentleman, who
was playing euchre not far off, was summoned to his
state-room.   After a few minutes he returned again,
and came to Bertha herself, directly, to ask her if she
would see his wife, who was taken suddenly ill.   Bertha had made their acquaintance on the voyage ; and

they had very kindly shielded her, as they could, from the discomforts of loneliness. She went at once to the poor lady's room, — I had almost said her cell, — and saw in an instant that she was very ill. Not that she complained much; but she said, " O Miss Schwarz, I am so weak! I don't know what ails me. What do you think can be the matter with me?"

Her face had a pale, sunken, earthy look, so that Bertha even wondered if she should have known her. But what alarmed her most, as the poor lady looked at her with an expression of anxiety rather than pain, was that bluish margin round the eyes, of which she had read the description so often, that it would have told her the whole story, had she not known that one man had already died of cholera on that vessel since midnight. She sent Mr. Umberhine at once to the boat's kitchen for hot water. She brought her own little stores of medicines from her state-room, and overhauled the sick lady's. So soon as it was known that anybody was ill, she had a heterogeneous mass of bottles thrust upon her by all the different passengers, from the pure laudanum of the "thorough" school, round to the lobelia and cayenne pepper of the come-outers. If Bertha had administered in turn from each of the phials which she took and thanked for, and arranged out of the sight of her hardly conscious patient, her practice would have been as intelligible, and perhaps as efficacious, as most of the cholera practice of that day. As it was, she hardly ventured on the physician's field. She knew what peppermint was, and that she dared to administer. Two or three times Mr. Umberhine took the responsibility of laudanum. But, for the most part, all they could do was to try to keep their patient warm, to follow the symptoms as best they could, and to hope for a favorable turn.

Before dinner-time had come, they were not alone in their anxieties. Everybody on board the boat knew that they had cholera as a fellow-passenger.

Two other ladies, a little child, and one of the gentlemen in the first cabin, were sick in their state-rooms;

and it was whispered that that fine first mate, with whom Bertha had had many a good walk in the early morning and late in the evening, was dying in his room forward. There was nothing for it but to look at the declining sun, and to pray that evening would come ; for by sunset they would arrive at the city.

Sunset came. They arrived at the city. And nobody was dead. There was so much to be thankful for. The good captain was relieved from at least one anxiety the moment he landed. He called the shore-clerk on one side, in a whisper told him that he had cholera on board, and asked whether there were any port-regulations which would hinder his landing his passengers. But before he was done, the man told him that poor Detroit was cholera-stricken already; and that five cases, more or less, would neither make nor relieve alarm. They determined, in their hurried council, to land the passengers who were well as soon as might be, and then to run the boat to a landing lower down the river, whence the sick passengers could be transferred more easily to the hospital. This determination was at once announced to the passengers of both grades. The captain also told them that he should defer his after voyage to Buffalo, at least till the boat could be cleaned and fumigated. They had no choice, therefore, but to go at once on shore.

Bertha staid with her suffering friend. But by this time she was certain that the paroxysms of the disease were not so acute as before ; and her sleep, due to the laudanum perhaps, was sufficient to relieve her, in a measure, from pain. When the boat had run down to the hospital landing, and when the careful hospital attendants were ready with their litter to carry the poor lady to her bed, she was in one of these drowsy, unconscious turns ; and it seemed as if they made the transfer without her knowledge, and without new pain.

When they saw her lying tranquilly in a civilized bed, with a-nice Quaker nurse directing every little accessory for comfort, Bertha felt a sense of relief, almost as if the disease was already conquered. Mr.

Umberhine, for his part, took her by both hands, the tears flowing unchecked down his cheeks, and said, "I can never thank you enough, Miss Schwarz. But you must not stay here to be thanked. You have been breathing this atmosphere of contagion too long. What can I do for you now, and where can I send you?"

Bertha saw that there was nothing for which she was needed now; and she told Mr. Umberhine, that, if he would find a carriage for her, she would go to her friend Mrs. Emlen's.

She said her "friend Mrs. Emlen's." But she had been painfully conscious, all the afternoon, that Mrs. Emlen would not know her from Eve or from Adah or from Zillah, except by costume. Nor was it quite clear to Bertha's mind that Mrs. Emlen would welcome, with the utmost cordiality, a strange girl, who would have to confess, in the first moment, that she had just come from an infected vessel, and that she had been all day long hanging over a cholera patient. But, after thinking it all over, Bertha determined to try the adventure, as the old romancers say. It was doing as she would be done by. That she was sure of. If she were living in Boston, and Mrs. Emlen came to her and said she was Aunt Mary's friend, she would welcome her gladly, though she came at midnight, and came after nursing forty cholera patients. At any rate, she must go to the Emlens' to get Mr. Rosenstein's letter. For, indeed, until she received that, she had hardly a right to go anywhere. Bertha was sorry now that, even at the last moment, she had not ordered her trunks back from the boat at Milwaukie, and waited for the boat of Saturday. She saw now that she should not have started on her journey without the money.

Mr. Umberhine was long in returning with the carriage. It was after nine o'clock before he came. Even then there was a good deal of doubt of where they were to go to. Bertha was quite sure of the address, — of the name, and of the street. But the driver of

the carriage was quite sure, that, if she had the name
right, the street was wrong, — that nobody named
Emlen lived on that street; indeed, there were but
three houses there. As for Mr. William Emlen, the
driver knew him as well as he knew his own father.
Indeed, he hardly knew any one else. You would
have thought the happiest hours of his life were spent
in going to Mr. William Emlen's house, and in taking
Mr. William Emlen's children to ride. Before such
pertinacity Bertha gave way, though the man had to
confess that his Mr. William Emlen lived far from the
place hers lived. Mr. Umberhine faintly offered to go
with her on this night quest. But this she would not
hear of. She told him to stay with his wife, and she
would be sure to see them early in the morning.

So they rode and rode and rode, nearly half an hour,
as it seemed to Bertha. At last they came to a handsome house, evidently quite on the outskirts of the city.
To Bertha's relief it was lighted. She had been afraid
they would all be in bed. She rang, and announced
herself at the door, and awaited somewhat nervously
her welcome.

She was not asked in, but was left standing in the
hall. That was a bad omen. In a moment Mrs.
Emlyn came herself, an elderly lady, tall, dried up,
and decidedly forbidding. Poor Bertha worked through
her explanation as best she could, trying not to apologize, and especially not to cry. But, before she was
half through, the old lady condescended to set all right
by explaining, in a very magnificent manner, that it
was all a mistake: that she was Mrs. Robert Emlyn,
and that this was Mr. Robert Emlyn's house ; and that
they spelt their name " lyn," and not " len." As for
Mr. William Emlen, who spelt his name " len," she believed he was a very respectable person ; indeed, she
was sure he was ; but he was no relation of theirs.
She believed he lived in Avery Street ; indeed, she was
sure he did ; which was just what Bertha had been sure
of in the beginning. So poor Bertha had sunk the
better part of an hour, and had gained nothing. She

tried to keep in her tears, bade the stiff old lady good evening, took care not to apologize or to thank her, there being nothing to thank her for, and did not abuse the crestfallen coachman. For Bertha's grandfather had taught her never to quarrel with a porter.

Back again in the dark night, retracing more than half the way which they had come. Here is Avery Street at last, and here at last is the house! But it is dark as midnight. What a pity! They must have gone to bed; and no wonder, for it is long after ten. With some hesitation Bertha rings. No answer. She rings again. No answer from the house, but a man's voice hails her from the opposite side of the street.

" Who are you trying to find?"

" Mr. William Emlen. Is this his house?"

" Yes: that's his house, but the house is shut up; the family went to Rochester about a month ago."

Nothing for it, but to bid the coachman drive to the nearest hotel.

At the nearest hotel, Bertha observed that the attentive porter whispered to the coachman before he opened the carriage-door. Then the coachman found some difficulty in opening it; and before the door was opened the attentive hotel-clerk was on the sidewalk, and asked if it was true that the lady had come from the " Henry Clay." Bertha said she had. The attentive clerk was very sorry, but he had heard that the " Clay " had some cholera cases on board. Bertha said she certainly had. The attentive clerk said he was still more sorry, but his regular boarders would certainly not permit him to receive any passengers from the " Clay." Perhaps the lady had some friends in town; or perhaps she could spend the night on board the boat; indeed, there could be no difficulty in her spending it there.

This time Bertha was angry. But she said nothing to the attentive clerk. She only bade the coachman take her back to the boat's regular landing. No, my poor dove, no! No rest here for the sole of your foot! The ark you left is gone! There are the lights of the boat out in the stream, where the captain has taken

12

her, and has anchored, for the best breeze he knows how to find.

"Then take me back to the hospital," said Bertha. "There is one person in the world who will be glad to see me, and she is there."

So poor Bertha spent that night at the hospital. So it was that the next day she volunteered for duty as a nurse; and so it was, as evening drew near, that she was sitting between 46 and 47, when Jasper Rising said to her, "I will relieve you now, madam."

CHAPTER XVIII.

THE HEAVEN ON THE EARTH.

FROM the moment when Jasper found that poor Oscar also had broken down, he had, for the first time, despaired. Not that he would, in any formal way, have owned this to himself; far less to any one else. Still, he despaired. The stake was so precious that he dared not play the game, and he knew he should not play it well. For he had become endeared to this waif, whom the flood had thrown at his feet when he was himself poorest of men, with a tenderness which only those can conceive who have, at any moment in life, been absolutely lonely. In a thousand ways, little or great, as you may choose to call them, Oscar, who called himself Jasper's man Friday, had become an essential part of this poor, lonely Robinson's life. And now Oscar's life was threatened too. Jasper, who had kept a cheerful face before, kept that now. But his face was a lie. He had had a cheerful heart before, and that was now hopeless. Even when he had gone to Mr. Buffum's house, or to Mr. Dundas's, he had had a braver feeling. There he could see the wealth of ministration. There was all the lavishness of home nursing, which retains every energy of the household for the service of the sick, changes stones into bread almost, and water into wine, by its miracles of devotion; and, when one sees that, it is very hard to feel that victory can be refused to forces so resolute. But when Jasper saw his poor boy lying on bed No. 47, under its plain white coverlet, with nothing at his side but the regulation table and the regulation chair, and, more than all, when the doctor had sent him away from that bed, Jasper, in his heart, despaired.

One element in the despair, and an element which he did acknowledge to himself, was, that he had no woman to bring to the rescue. Most men, from early training and habit, hate sickness, know nothing of it, despise themselves when they are sick, and under-estimate their own powers in a sick-room. For the same reason they over-estimate the resources which woman certainly can bring there. If they can once turn a competent woman in on the case, men feel as if the victory was already won : as Barbarossa knew he should have the heron the moment he had slipped his falcon. The element of despair, therefore, which Jasper did understand, was, that he had no woman whom he could bring into the fight. He would not send for his aunt. He thought he had no right to expose her to danger. He knew Mrs. Dundas well enough to have been willing to take his poor boy to her. But Mrs. Dundas had other care now. And as Jasper went down that night to the hospital, it was with the wretched feeling that the crisis was as good as over, and that the turn would be against him : that he must try to do, in his clumsy man fashion, what needed, through and through, the most exquisite womanly instincts : that he could not for love, certainly not for money, command these in the exigency. This was one reason — and Jasper had many — why, in one word, he despaired.

It was with that feeling that he came to No. 47, and saw Bertha sitting between it and 46. "I will relieve you now, madam," he said ; and Bertha turned round.

"Are you here?" said Jasper, and then it was all but aloud that he added, — what passed distinctly through his heart and mind,— "then all will be well."

May it be confessed, in the secrecy of these pages, that an emotion or a thought not wholly dissimilar passed through Bertha's mind? Bertha had been dissatisfied with herself. The self-congratulation of the first exit from Milwaukie had gone. Four or five days only had been enough to show her that she was not

steering her boat very steadily nor very wisely. Yes:
it had been very fine to be rid of the persecutions of
Mrs. Rosenstein. Nay, it had been a rest not to have
the questions of the children to answer. But to be
foot-loose in a strange city, without a roof to one's head,
— that was not fine. To be seven hundred miles from
home, with hardly money enough to go there, — that
was not fine. To be one of a hundred passengers from
a cholera-tainted vessel, of whom six or eight were
already dead or dying, to be this in a strange town,
where no one of her friends knew that she was, — that
was not fine. To receive word that it was not determined when the steamer would go forward to Buffalo,
— that was not fine. Bertha was addressing herself to
her new duty with such energy as she could ; but she
could not resist the feeling that she was, for all human
companionship, utterly alone. And just then Mr. Rising walked up to the other side of No. 47 ; and when
he said, "Are you here?" Bertha could hardly keep
herself from saying aloud, — what, perhaps, she might
have said without criticism, — "Then all will be well."
In the secrecy of these pages, it may be confessed that
the thought passed, distinctly yet gladly, through her
mind.

And was it sympathy, or do you choose, my dear
Buchner, to say it was mechanism, that, when Jasper
had, with real surprise and with eyes that flashed with
delight, shaken hands with Bertha across the narrow
bed ; when he had nodded in answer to her unspoken
intimation that the boy seemed to be asleep, as he sat
in the regulation chair, and looked down to see if that
chalky face seemed quite as anxious as when he left the
bed-side, was it sympathy, or mechanism, or accident,
that Oscar threw his head back, and smiled with his
exquisite smile, and without opening his eyes, just adjusted his head on a cooler part of the pillow, and said
aloud, with his pretty foreign accent, "Oh! are you
here? then all will be well." Then the boy did go to
sleep. A sleep which seemed so natural, whose breathing was so quiet, and in which he lay so easily, that it

was hard to think it was laudanum, and only laudanum. They sat, still as death, watching the boy, till Jasper could bear the silence no longer ; and he rose from his seat, and, with the absolute silence of a determined man's firm step, walked across the ward, and beckoned Bertha to follow him. She came as noiselessly as he, and joined him at the window.

"It is such a relief to find you here, Miss Schwarz ! I came down the hill wishing, and I may say praying, that God would send a woman here."

"I am sure I am glad I am here," said Bertha, wondering as she spoke whether any man could know how glad a separated woman is to find herself again in a home where she is needed, and can take her turn.

"But you do not know," said Jasper, eagerly, "you cannot know, what this boy is to me. And how do you find him? Do you think he has failed this afternoon?"

"Failed !" said Bertha, this time with surprise. "Certainly, not failed." And Jasper blessed her as she said so. "You know," said she, "or rather you do not know, that I know nothing of this disease. I never saw it, I hardly ever thought of it, till yesterday morning. But I have been here now, with these eight beds, since half-past four. I cannot think there is any failure. He has lain perfectly gently, has asked for nothing, and has seemed free from distress, certainly for two hours. He has not spoken till just now."

Two hours of quiet, if it were as quiet as this, clearly not the quiet of collapse, which Jasper knew only too well, this was something. He was too good a nurse to run and ask the doctor how much it meant ; but he was tempted to take the boy's words as an oracle, and to accept Bertha's cheerful statement as prophecy as well, and believe that all would be well.

Then he told her, as far as he could in the hurried whispered talk of twilight there, who Oscar was, and what he was to him. His eyes fairly filled with tears and ran over, as he tried to make her understand this, by a little history, and even by one or two details, which, without his meaning it, showed what he was to

Oscar. And as he wasted just one word perhaps, or stepped just one hair beyond what was wholly necessary in telling her how lonely he had been without Oscar, and how like death to him the thought of being without him again, poor Bertha, fresh from her memories of the last twenty-four hours, could not help arresting him by saying, " You need not describe loneliness to me."

Of course, they did not stand there chattering. She went back to her regular charge, passing quietly from bed to bed of the eight intrusted to her, and sitting by each patient long enough to get that specific and distinct notion of each individual case which is invaluable to the physician, and on which, indeed, the whole struggle depends. Jasper, also, had reported for duty ; and once and again, as the night went by, he went his rounds. But the most of the night he spent by No. 47, watching each change, and answering as he best could every entreaty of his boy.

Not a long night, either. I think Jasper could tell us to-day each turn it took as the hours went by, of the varying fortunes, the ups and downs of every bed from 39 to 47, between the late sunset and the early sunrise of that hot July night. Most distinct of all, however, was this, that there was no cramp-turn for poor 47 ; sleep scarcely broken ; and, more and more clearly, sleep nature-given and not opium-bought. Jasper himself looked like another man, to say nothing of his patient, when at sunrise the doctor came round. And Bertha, oh, how pretty she was in her little hospital cap ! she was fairly lovely in her glad sympathy.

No : there was no doubt so far. Of course there might be a relapse, and by this time they knew, all three, what a relapse was. But clearly this had been one of those cases where this mysterious disease stopped as suddenly as it began. The handsome, kindly doctor said all this with as much feeling and tenderness as Jasper himself could have asked, and seemed not the least happy of the three. Indeed, it had been a good night through the hospital. God Almightly only knew what, but something had happened ; everything seemed better to-day. " We have some good angel here," said the doctor reverently, as he went on to No. 48, who heard every syllable, and was better because he heard.

And for poor Oscar, there was no relapse. No. There were days on days, indeed, before he was done with it, weeks on weeks of abject weakness incomprehensible to him, who, till now, had known nothing but the sheer omnipotence of sixteen, seventeen, and eighteen years. First, that he might not be up and about ; second, that he could not, if they would let him ; these were two incomprehensible mysteries. Jasper reasoned and directed, tried to amuse him, and sometimes, perforce, had to threaten him with the doctor, and to lay down the law. But Bertha, she could manage him fifty times better than Jasper. How it happened she did not know. She laughed about it herself. For she was a very young matron, not a day older than Oscar, if one may guess. But all the authority of every mother, aunt, grandmother or school-mistress of them all had fallen, like some heavy mantle-piece, on Bertha's head ; and what she bade Oscar do he did ; and what she bade him shun he shunned. The wisest, jolliest, most ingenious and most gentle little nurse you ever knew.

" I don't like to have them walk," said the doctor. " I am half of that German's mind, that the original human being got on his hind legs a little before he was ready ; or better, if you please, that the human being of to-day does not recline enough. As my wide-awake classmate, Sargent, says, — how I wish he were here ! — ' Let us preserve the horizontal attitude.' I don't like to have them walk ; if you could get down one of your easy rockaways, Mr. Rising, the boy. is so eager to see something besides the river and the opposite shore, we might indulge him."

" Why not row ? " said Jasper.

" Oh, well ! exactly, if you think you can hunt up a boatman : nothing could be better. Let Miss Schwarz tumble some rugs or pillows into a boat, and he can keep the horizontal. The sun won't hurt him, if you shade his head. Sun does people good. Miss Schwarz, go with them, and do not let Mr. Rising give the boy a sunstroke, nor get one himself, either."

Wise doctor! kind doctor! How far-seeing these men are who prescribe not only for their patients, but for the families; yes, and for the nurses also.

Easy enough, of course, for Jasper to find the boat, so long disused; to empty her from the water which had kept her from leaking; to paddle her down to the quay, where poor Oscar was so tired of sitting the whole afternoon. Then what a Cydnus-barge they made of her, with their hair-pillows and wraps, their rugs and blankets! Then how gently Jasper lifted Oscar in, and what a deft arrangement which made an umbrella awning over him and Bertha too, as she sat in the stern, and guarded her patient from any turn of sun or splash of water. And how happy Jasper, as he dipped his oars and slowly pulled the boat up to the old bathing-place again.

"This is too good!" said Oscar. "This is the heaven on the earth."

"You love the water?" asked Bertha.

"Is it that I love the water? yes; every one loves the water; but it is that we always take the boat when there is no care. When there is no customer who cannot be suit: man wants wagon to weigh nothing at all, but must have strong steel axles, that shall not bend one hair, all the same: when there is no screw loose in the workshop; lazy dog, English, beer-drinking-dog, say he come and finish job, and no come; go off on spree, never come at all. When it is all right and all smooth, then Master Robinson he take the canoe, I take the paddle. I man Friday, Miss Schwarz; and we come go up the river here, and we swim. O Miss Schwarz! this is the heaven on the earth. All will be well now."

Bertha and Jasper both remembered the oracle of that first night by No. 47. She caught his eye, and he hers; and each smiled a happy smile. Then the boy ran on in his simple talk about the things he saw:

every warehouse, every hulk of a canal-boat or stranded steamer laid up for repairs, had a story for him, or suggested some pleasant memory. Jasper was in no hurry. It seemed the heaven on the earth for him. And a lovely invalid's tour it was along the cool river, with that soft, fragrance-laden south wind blowing over them, till they came to the familiar landing, and Jasper and Oscar saw the little out-door comforts of their summer bathing-place unmolested by the marauding Norsemen, nomads of the shore.

"Here he will be perfectly happy," said Jasper, as he made the boat fast.

"Perfectly happy he has been for an hour past," said Bertha, smiling. Then she and Jasper together made a throne, which was a sort of bed of justice for the boy, on the shady side of the little shanty. There was enough dry, sweet hay to give it substance; there were wraps enough in the boat to cover it, had it been for five boys. And then Jasper, in triumph, took his man Friday in his arms, carried him across the gravel, and enthroned him.

"Now you are king," said Bertha, "and you must tell us what to do. I will not give you any orders till we are back again at the hospital, if you are only good, and do what I choose without being ordered."

And she laughed. Oscar laughed too. "I will order you by-by," said he. "Now I only order both of you rest you. He rest because he rowed. You rest because you sit up so stiff, hold fan, hold rudder. Oscar rest too." And almost as he spoke, his head dropped, with his bright smile on his lips, back on the pillow she had placed against the door-post, and in a minute the dear fellow was sweetly asleep: the excitement of the little voyage had so far told on him. Bertha threw the light shawl she had over him, and turned to Jasper.

"What a blessing to be able to give him this air-bath! I mean to be a nurse or a doctor all my life, and to found a hospital on the basis of the open air. We will call it the air-cure."

"What a mercy and blessing," said Jasper, "to be in health, especially after what you and I have seen! I believe it has all been meant for a lesson to me. Do you know, my uncle always said I was hard on sick people? He said I was very tolerant to bad people. If a drunken dog killed one of his cows, or smashed a horse-rake, I always had an excuse for him, he said. It was the man's first offence, or he had temptations we did not know of. And he said I was very lenient to fools and blunderers. I always said God made them so, and that they must distress themselves much more than they did us. But when any of the workmen said he could not stand the day out in mowing, or sent word that he had the shakes and could not come to the lumber-yard, I had no mercy on him, my uncle said. It was not quite true, but I am afraid there was something in it. I have never been sick one minute in life, and I do hate a shirk."

"Then you are hard, Mr. Rising," said Bertha bravely, her spirit rebelling as Jasper thus intimated that people could like to be sick, or could shirk from the love of shirking. "You are hard, and you must take your poor Oscar for your tutor. Oh, dear! I have seen men as strong as he, and as strong as you, who would have given, — what would they not have given for one week of life unembittered? and they could not buy it. Oh, no! you must thank God for what you have, and be all the kinder to the rest of us."

And, as she spoke, Jasper registered his vow, that, so far at least, he would obey her. He was a little confused; but he rallied enough to say, "Why do we not enjoy more, when God gives us everything to enjoy? To sit here, as I sit now, in perfect health, yes, and perfect happiness; even to feel this air moving on my skin, to see that white cloud round its surfaces so lazily on that perfect blue, to smell these roses and this hay, as the wind draws over us, why," — and he laughed when he said it, — "to have my mouth taste sweet, and to know I should drink a glass of water if

you gave it to me, yet not to be thirsty; that I should
eat a cracker if it lay here, yet not to be hungry; not
to be sleepy, but to know I could sleep in two seconds
if I lay down, as that boy does; and while I am talking to you, and while I am smelling the roses, and
seeing the sky, and feeling the breeze, to be hearing
this brown thrush whistle, — to know all along that if
need were I could walk thirty miles before midnight,
and yet to know that no need does call, — is it not
glory enough and blessing enough to live? Yet we
choose not to think so. As poor Oliver did, we are
asking for something more."

Jasper was stimulated to say all this because he was
perfectly happy. Perhaps the last and sweetest point
to his happiness had been that Bertha had found fault
with him. It is an exquisite thing to be blamed or
criticised by one you believe in, or love, if the criticism
seem to reveal a degree of interest in you that you have
not been certain of before. He was a little startled,
however, when he found he had said so much. It was
not the least in his fashion to do so. And he even ran
back over his rhapsody, afraid that he had made a fool
of himself. But Bertha said, and he had never known
her find so much trouble with her English, —

"I think, — I do not know, — I shall not make myself clear. I think we do not more often take these
delights as we do now, — I am sure I do just as you do,
but not always, not often perhaps, — because we want
to know how we can make others share in them. You
and I, to-day, know it was for him we planned them;
not for us. It would not have been nice to you, to
bring up the pillows alone, and make the throne alone,
and go to sleep on it alone. You and I have done our
work. I do not mean that we have earned our play.
I hate all that earning. It is so dirty, so mean, I
mean. Oh! I wish I could speak English. Should
you know, should you understand if I spoke German?
This is what I mean : this must all happen, it must not
be made on purpose."

"The good Father must give it to us, and we must not try to cut it and shape it for ourselves," said Jasper reverently.

"Yes: that is it," said Bertha, and this time she spoke in German; and she was silent then, and her eyes filled with tears.

Filled with tears; and she enjoyed the exquisite satisfaction which a true woman or a true man feels, when another true woman or true man bravely breaks the spell which in matters sacred keeps us parted from each other. No wonder, indeed, that we will not scatter the precious pearls of life broadcast. No! And therefore, when reticent man or reticent woman ventures to speak to you on the thing most precious, you are sure that that man or that woman holds you and prizes you among the sacred few!

And so the hour passed by. Sometimes they talked, but now as if they had known each other from the beginning of eternity. Sometimes they sat silent. That was because they were perfectly sure, each, that silence was better than speech, then, — each that the other understood that silence was better than speech; so that silence was, as it is so often, the best communion. At last Oscar turned and started.

"Have I been asleep?" said he. "What a lazy man Friday! But I have had a beautiful nap," he cried, sitting up and rubbing his eyes. "Ah, yes: all will be well now."

They laughed with him and at him, and with each other and at each other. Jasper laughed and talked with the *abandon* of one who had been living through the very happiest hour of his life, and knew he had. This I know, for he told me so. Bertha has never told me so; but, all the same, I believe she had the same consciousness at heart. Jasper took his boy lightly, and carried him to the boat again. Oscar declared he could do anything, and was permitted to do nothing. Again he lay' in the stern : again Bertha fanned him and screened him; again Jasper pulled both oars, and slowly, but only too fast, they came back, oh, how happy, all of them, to the musty, fusty, ungainly old sail-loft, which was to all of them, now, the happiest, noblest, and sweetest of homes.

CHAPTER XIX.

A CARD CASTLE.

THAT night Jasper thought over everything. He did not sleep a wink, not he. How clear, right through, the hand of Providence; and that Providence so kind, which had brought him and this queen of his life together, this woman of all women, this pure, true, brave, lovely girl. And how false to himself, and to her, and to the good God, if he did not tell her this; tell her that his life would be wretchedness without her, but that with her there was nothing he could not dare, nay, nothing that he could not do. Did she care for him? He did not know; but it would be easy to find out. Did she care for any one else? He did not know; only if she did he should die. This was sure, he was man enough to take care of her her life through, to screen her from every storm, to lift her when she needed lifting, to comfort her when she was troubled, and to love her always. Nay, his life, and what people called his fortunes, were enough established for him to offer her a home. It should be — he knew were it should be — on a lovely piece of land Dundas owned, just above the boat-house. Oh, what a home it should be, if she could only think that such loyalty and devotion as he could offer her made life with him worth living! Would she think so?

Well, he could see.

Jasper was no such mean tradesman, that he would offer nothing unless he was sure of everything. He would not disgrace himself in his own eyes by dawdling and waiting, trying to surprise Bertha by this trick or that innuendo, into an avowal he was not man enough to ask for. She might know, all the world might know if it chose, that with his heart of hearts he loved her. Then if she could give him nothing back, why, that was his misfortune. None the less should she have a woman's right to say yes or no; and she should have the fair honor, in her own memory afterwards, to know that she herself, in her own loveliness and truth and purity, commanded the allegiance and reverence of this one honest man. He would tell her so.

He would tell her so that very afternoon. They could take Oscar to the bathing-house again. They could sit in the shade again. And there, in the sinking of the afternoon sun, he would tell her the whole of his life and of his hope; and there she might say whether he was to be a prince among men, or whether his whole life was a blunder, and was to be thrown away.

All this Jasper determined.

The first place where he saw Bertha in the hospital day, was always the mess-table of the nurses. The moment he saw her, he saw she was pale, and that she seemed excited. Had she slept no better than he? She said not a word at breakfast, she who was generally the life of their little circle. After breakfast, even before they had their orders from the doctor, she called him. Could he come out on the beach?

"See here, Mr. Rising," as soon as they were alone; "I have my letter."

"From Mr. Rosenstein?" For no letter from that rascal had ever come.

"Oh, no!" said Bertha; "not from him, nor ever shall; but from my mother. See, will you read this page?"

And she gave it to him, forgetting that it was in the German character which so few students of that time in this country read easily. Jasper tried, and had to say:

"You know I do not make out your handschrift well."

"Oh! I forgot; but it seemed as if I could not read it. I am so foolish. It is all so strange. I wish things would not happen. But I am not quite a fool;" and, sitting on a low post, as Jasper stood beside her, she read:

"I had sealed the letter, when your father came in. What do you think has happened? He had letters from every one, from your Uncle Fritz, from the pastor, from Marie and Ernestine, oh, so many letters! Bertha, my child, your Uncle Wilhelm, who was lost, long, long ago, has been found; or rather, he has died, so we know where he was lost. It was in Singapore, my dear Bertha; he was very, very rich. The pastor says, to whom the Indian letter came, that his fortune was six hundred thousand dollars; and he made a will, which is in the English courts, and your father is the heir. The pastor writes, and Uncle Fritz writes, that we must all go home. I do not know, but you must come here as soon as you can: your father encloses twenty dollars, as I said before. I hope it is enough for you, for none of the six hundred thousand has come. Always your poor old mother."

Bertha's face was running tears, — tears of clear excitement. "Do you wonder I am a fool?" said she. "I ought to be so glad, and I believe I am not glad at all."

Jasper knew some one else who was not glad at all. But he gulped down, — why did he gulp down? — the words with which he almost said so. With determined effort he said slowly, instead:

"But you will be glad. This is everything to your mother, everything to Wil., everything to your father. God grant it be everything to you!"

But with that cold blast, his own card castle fell.

13

CHAPTER XX.

PROVING IDENTITY.

JASPER'S card-castle fell.
It was, perhaps, his own fault that it fell. If Bertha Schwarz was what he felt, believed, and knew by the highest knowledge, that she was, the mere accident that her father had inherited six hundred thousand dollars had nothing whatever to do with Jasper's relations to her, nor with what Jasper was going to say to her. If she were not that Bertha Schwarz that he believed and knew her to be, the sooner he found out his mistake about her the better, no matter how hard the process which undeceived him. In sad and lonely days which followed, Jasper had time enough to think out and set in order this alternative; but he did not think it out in time. He did not say, when Bertha translated to him her letter, "Dear Miss Schwarz, that is a matter of very little consequence compared with what I have to say. Will you come and walk on the pier with me?" That would have been the truth; but Jasper did not say so.

At this moment, indeed, he made one of the great mistakes in his life by keeping silence. And as he thought of it afterwards, and repented of it bitterly, he was afraid that it was a mistake which came from reading artificial novels, and seeing artificial plays; for he had done just as the paper hero has to do. He had refrained from telling Bertha how he loved her, from the stupid fear that she would think he was mercenary and mean. Now, if he had been mercenary and mean, this would have been a sign of his better nature, that he was afraid of being thought so; but as he was not, as there was nothing mean in his enthusiastic love of this womanly girl, why, he had simply acted very foolishly in permitting the death of an old man in Singapore, or its neighborhood, to have anything to do with what he said to her in Detroit, or anywhere.

Let the American boy or girl remember that it is not safe to take the illustrations in English or French novels for the guidance of our simple American life.

For Bertha, dear child, let us not ask her how she felt all that day, or how she explained Jasper's absence of mind, only relieved by his eager care for her comfort on her lonely journey home. The hurried preparations were made at last. Jasper succeeded in making the heiress borrow from him twenty-five dollars more, lest she should be stranded penniless again on her journey to Boston ; and poor Bertha started, all " sole-alone " again, on a long bit of travel, far more fatiguing, not to say adventurous, than it is now.

Arrived at home, she found everything in excitement ; and, aside from the enthusiasm that welcomed her, everybody in the little house probably felt some satisfaction, that, in their counsels, there would now be somebody with a head as clear as Bertha's and a hand as firm as hers. Little enough experience had she, poor child ! but she was not dreamy and wholly unpractical, as her father was ; she was not so wholly domestic as to be afraid of the sea, afraid of travel, afraid of speaking above her breath, as her dear mother was. If there were a letter to be written, Bertha knew how to " face her perplexity," so far as to write it ; and, if there were a vice-consul to be seen, Bertha knew that the best way to get him out of the way was to see him. Such knowledge as this, dear Lily, and the prompt acting on such knowledge, is what gives power and character to what is called the man or woman of business ; and it was, undoubtedly, an advantage that a person appeared in the household who had such habits of meeting the daily perplexities of preparing for a voyage, even though that person were an inexperienced girl, only eighteen years old.

Aunt Mary had been summoned on from Orange, and Bertha found her doing her best as main-spring and balance-wheel together ; a combination which in human affairs is not infrequent. Aunt Mary was pacifying and encouraging, proving that this was possible, and that was impossible, as might be necessary in the strange new complications. Kaufmann Baum had not been able to come on, — "busiest season of the year," he said unconsciously ; not knowing that he had said the same of every season of the year since his sister lived in Boston : but he had acted on a general principle which had never failed him in life ; nor, in my experience of a half-century, have I ever known it fail anybody. Reduced to practice, it amounts to this : that, if you cannot in person discharge a duty, there are few exigencies which a "draft on New York" will not fill, if it only be sufficiently large. Kaufmann Baum had implicit confidence in his wife ; so he sent her to get his brother-in-law off to Hamburg : he had confidence almost implicit in a "draft on New York ; " so he gave her a draft for a thousand dollars, with directions to use it according to her discretion. Nor was his confidence in either instrumentality a misplaced one. Aunt Mary appeared on the scene with all the Vermont ability to put things through ; and the preparations for Mr. Schwarz's voyage to Hamburg were well forward when Bertha reached the little home.

Queer enough it was to Bertha to find how narrow and how crooked the streets in Boston seemed to her, after her experience of Detroit and Milwaukie ; but in a minute more, when the carriage stopped at the little house, sixteen feet in front at the outside, and when Bertha surprised them all so happily in the narrow passage, — for they had not expected her before Saturday ; and when she kissed them all, over and over again ; and when Aunt Mary then slipped out and surprised her in turn ; and when Bertha was fairly sitting on a little footstool at her mother's feet, and had her dear hand in hers, — she was the happiest girl in the whole world ; and she felt as if the little, crowded parlor was the most charming place in the whole world. It was not till the next morning, when she and Rosebud were setting the breakfast table, and she felt how dreadfully crowded everything was, and how close that hot September air was, — it was not till then, that, with an over-sensitive conscientiousness, Bertha began to rebuke herself that she should have had the nice large rooms of the Rosenstein house in Milwaukie, while her dear mother was here, confined in this little old house in this narrow street in the very heart of Boston. Dear Bertha, was not the gorgeous Rosenstein palace a very hell? and, as you rest in this home of love after all your loneliness, is it not a very heaven?

And now Aunt Mary gently put Bertha at the fore. And Bertha saw the consuls and vice-consuls, and Bertha made all the arrangements for the winter's house-keeping, and Bertha consulted with her mother whether they should or should not move to better surroundings. No: Margaret Schwarz would not move. She had been very happy in the little house, and she would not leave it till they all were together at home again. You see, it had been settled in two seconds, — settled long before Bertha came home, — that she must go to Hamburg with her father. Dear, dreamy, unpretending Max Schwarz, — how would he ever identify himself, or satisfy notaries or prothonotaries or chancellors or other officials, alone? He would turn back with the pilot before he lost sight of America, if he ever started alone. Some one must go with him ; and of course that some one was to be Bertha.

So Margaret Schwarz, with Carl and Wilhelm, now a capable half-Yankee boy, and little Rosebud, were left in the little tenement, to work out their own salvation, while Bertha and her father sailed for Liverpool. Comfortable and regular packets to Hamburg were still unknown.

Poor Schwarz himself was wretchedly sea-sick. Bertha escaped more easily. It was a delicious month, that September ; and the ship's deck was so steady, that the little children ran their locomotive toys back

and forth across the deck without knowing that it
trembled. How could poor papa feel the motion so
much when there was so little to feel! Bertha was a
little lonely without him at first; but she found to her
joy in the cabin, a splendid Broadwood grand piano, in
tune much better than sea-going pianos are wont to
boast. She found that nobody else seemed disposed to
use this, and the "gentlemanly captain" begged her
to make the best of it. Bertha was only too glad to do
so. At the hospital, of course, she had had no instrument. At the Rosensteins, she had played or had not
played as the whims of madame dicated, excepting in
the occasional intervals when Rosenstein himself was
at home. To sit there in the airy saloon, to know that
she worried nobody, to open her little travelling *reper-
toire* of some of her father's favorites and her own, and
hour by hour to call into companionship her dear old
Mozart and Gluck,— this was luxury. Or sometimes
it would be a theme from Bach, and often and often it
would be Beethoven whom she summoned; sometimes
Palestrina, sometimes Weber or Schubert; and, best
of all, and choicest of all, she would call on Mendelssohn. It was one companion or the other of them, as
met her mood the best; and this was all absolute joy
to Bertha. Of course, she did not often play there,
unless at very exceptional hours, without a little audience from the passengers. But Bertha soon satisfied
herself, first of all, that no one else wanted the piano;
second, that she bored no one; third, that, with one
exception, there was not one person in this audience
who knew anything of music. She found out that she
really had it in her power to give them pleasure while
she pleased herself; and so, having put herself at her
ease, she made the saloon her home.

Are you disappointed that she did not spend the time
in contemplating the immensity of the ocean? Why,
the ocean, from a steamer's deck, in a calm passage,
seems neither immense nor sublime. It is a round
wafer, all you see of it, of a dull gray color; and all
you can work up of emotion about it is indignation that

it looks so small. When there is a stiff sea running, go forward as far as they will let you and look forward, and you may have a better chance. For Bertha, she took her constitutional walks twice or thrice a day; she sat a good deal with her father; but, when he drove her away, she summoned her companions as she sat at the piano in the saloon.

The one person who knew anything about music was a bright, intelligent English physician, a young man of seven and twenty, returning with his mother, who looked delicate, from Toronto to her home. Their name was Farquhar. From the first day that Bertha found her way to the piano he was there also, unless some particular crisis in poor Mrs. Farquhar's state-room kept him at her side; and, as soon as Mrs. Farquhar rallied sufficiently from her sea-sickness, the doctor would bring her into the saloon, as soon as the notes of the piano could be heard. He knew enough to know, not only that Bertha played good music, and played it well, but that this was the music of an enthusiast, who had the divine genius which discovers genius, interprets genius, and makes genius live again, immortal, indeed, while kindred genius is its interpreter. It was not long, of course, before, what with turning over the leaves of music, what with bringing up his own music from his own state-room, what with Mrs. Farquhar's asking Bertha to play this or that to her, the free-masonry of music had made good friends of all three. In a few days more, poor Mr. Schwarz was able to crawl up stairs. Bertha introduced him to Dr. Farquhar, and he to his mother. Then they took their constitutional walks together up and down the deck, fifty-six turns to the mile, and four miles every day. Mr. Schwarz even tried to bring his violin into the saloon; but that was quite too much for his poor, weak head, and he gave it up. But all this ocean business was an old story to the doctor. He had no swimming head, and, at the suggestion of the violin, he produced his flute; and Mr. Schwarz lay on one sofa, and Mrs.

Farquhar on another, while Bertha and the doctor played duets together.

The society of these cultivated and truly charming people made the voyage very short to Bertha; and they all were very intimate. When the evenings were chilly, if the sky was clear, the brisk evening walk with her arm in her father's, Dr. Farquhar accompanying her on the other side, was thoroughly satisfactory. He had served, he said, — she did not then know in what service, — in all parts of the world. There was nowhere he had not been, there was nothing he had not read; nay, it seemed to Bertha that there was hardly any one he had not seen. She was in the first enthusiasm for Tennyson. Dr. Farquhar knew the poems by heart; could and did repeat "Locksley Hall" from end to end; and when, one day, Bertha expressed some curiosity about Tennyson's personal appearance, he answered the question. Not that he knew him, but he had seen him once and again at Cambridge, when, as it happened, each of them was on a visit there. All young America was then enthusiastic about Queen Victoria: the coronation of a girl of eighteen, so few years before, had been too romantic an incident, and her bearing had been too sweet and noble not to create enthusiasm, particularly among the young. Well, Dr. Farquhar did not pretend to have been presented at court, or to have thrown his cloak over a muddy hole for the queen to walk on; but, as it happened, in his boyhood he had lived in the Isle of Wight, near the home of the princess and her mother; he had seen her riding to and fro on her donkey, when she was a girl; he had once or twice been at children's parties, where multitudes of the neighbors' children had been summoned to meet her; and in a pleasant way he told boy anecdotes of her girlhood, as, through such key-holes, he had seen it. Little glimpses are such things of a great world; but to Bertha it was the beginning of one of the great luxuries of life, — the making real in imagination what has been only a matter of books and record. Of course, their musical enthusiasm swept all three away

in such talking and walking. Dr. Farquhar was the
only one of the three who had seen Mendelssohn, whom
they all three so loved. He had once heard him play.
He had been at the grand opera in almost every city
of Europe ; and had a faculty of making them see with
his eyes, if he could not make them hear with his ears,
as he described the enthusiasm which welcomed one
and another master or *prima donna* of the time. A
loyal, true-hearted gentleman, of the best training
England could give, of an experience which had taken
him into every quarter of the globe, modest and manly,
he had everything to tell which should interest a girl
like Bertha, standing just on the edge of the world,
wondering as to its mysteries, and knowing it, as yet,
only from books, and so little from men and women.

Nor did Max Schwarz make any contemptible appearance in this trio, when it was a trio, or in the quartette,
when it became a quartette. He was a great reader, as
well as a musician to fanaticism. His criticism in music
was such as a man like Farquhar respected through and
through. Farquhar saw at once that here was a master,
while he was only a performer. Yet the doctor knew
enough of music, as well in its history as in the best
performances of the time, to appreciate and enjoy his
new companion's criticism and analysis ; and Bertha
would be proud indeed of her father, when the word
came to him, as they walked, and he either ran back to
show the worth and value of some of the men now half-
forgotten, or when he boldly looked forward and proph-
esied the steps which would surely come ; which, as he
said, the world was ready for ; that step which in
twenty years more has been taken so firmly, — so that
we talk as simply as we do of " the music of the future."
Bertha hardly knew whether she enjoyed the talk most
when Dr. Farquhar lectured to her, as he would say,
or when her father lectured to him ; but Dr. Farquhar
knew perfectly well that he enjoyed it most, when, by
guile which she did not suspect, he had won Bertha
herself round to talking. One day, by a turn in the
talk, she found herself describing her strange hospital

adventure to Mrs. Farquhar ; one day it was the curious
Norwegian emigration in Wisconsin, which she was telling him about ; one day she made them all scream as
she described her infant class in the Sunday-school at
Milwaukie, — one Swedish girl, one Norwegian, one
French, one Low German, one High, and one Irish boy.
Whatever the subject was, Dr. Farquhar, and, for that
matter, Mrs. Farquhar, was equally pleased. Dear,
unconscious Bertha ! When they did tempt her to tell
of her little experiences, which seemed to her so small
in comparison with the talk about queens and poets and
masters, she was so full of life and humor, she was so
unaffected and brave, she showed her true self, without
knowing that she showed herself, so completely, that
Dr. Farquhar and his mother were both charmed with
her. To Mrs. Farquhar, an invalid who hated to be
an invalid, there was a particular comfort in Bertha's
friendly and even tender little cares, after they became
so intimate that she could offer them.

So it was, that, by the time they landed in England,
England was by no means the country of strangers
Bertha and her father had feared it would be. Had
they not these two loyal friends here? Bertha had no
more care of her father, nor he of her, in landing, than
if they had had a suite of forty couriers. Dr. Farquhar, without any fuss, provided for everything ; and
they all went together to the London train. Arrived
in London, Mrs. Farquhar made a thousand apologies
that she could not take them to her house, poor Bertha
feeling all the time that she should be frightened to
death if they went there ; but the doctor arranged still,
as if Max Schwarz had been his father, and took them
to very comfortable lodgings, where, in this dead season,
they found rooms, as he knew they would, with a friend
of his, a nice Scotch widow, where, for their stay in
London, they would be made quite at home. Then he
parted from them, renewing the promises which his
mother had made at the station, that they would both
come round the next day.

For Bertha and her father had no little business to

do in London. It had been explained in the letters from Singapore that the public administrator at that place, an officer appointed by the English government, was the person with whom the correspondence about Bertha's uncle must eventually be conducted. The verifications of personality would be more simply made if English magistrates had a hand in it; and the lawyers consulted, both in Hamburg and in Boston, had advised a stay in London long enough to make the proper depositions there, and, if necessary, to place the whole matter in the hands of English counsel. For Max Schwarz was resolute in refusing to go to Singapore, even for forty fortunes ; and Bertha was sure that no sort of result would follow his going, even if he assented to so vast an enterprise. So father and daughter had been fortified with letters of introduction to the right lawyers and men of business ; and Bertha, when she left Boston, had pretended to be very brave about all she had to do in the great city. "It would be just like a novel," she said. At heart, she was frightened to death about it all ; for she knew very well how little her father was fitted for the enterprise in hand : but this was only one instance more of the courage with which she "faced her perplexities," to borrow for the second time that admirable phrase of the Bishop of Burlington.

But now ! Why, going to bankers, and officers of probates, and making depositions, was all easier than going a-maying, or stringing lilac necklaces. Here was Dr. Farquhar with a cab every morning. Every visit to the city or to the lawyers, was like a pleasant excursion to the scene of something in Shakespeare or Scott or Dickens ; and the banker or the lawyer or the notary came in almost as part of the exhibition. The doctor prepared himself with such powerful notes of introduction, or was so respected for the love people had for his father or his uncle or his grandfather, that they all seemed, Bertha said, passionately determined to bring her father's money in their own arms to Boston. Never did business pass so pleasantly, even though the days were more than she expected when she came to London.

And the afternoons and evenings were only more charming. Mrs. Farquhar taught Bertha, that if they had been the people of fashion, such as she read of in novels, they would all say London was a desert; but as they were not such people the least bit in the world; as they lived happily in "the wilds of Bloomsbury," not two blocks, as Bertha found, from her own lodgings, — why London was to them the pleasant home which more than ten years had now endeared, and which she had left only two years since that she might join her son in Toronto, for the period in which he was stationed there. It seemed his father had died, now nearly three years gone by. Horace had now resigned, and was going to establish himself in practice in London, evidently with great advantages; living, so happily for his mother, in the old home, which was now so dear, from associations of pleasure and of pain alike. His married sisters had been putting the house in order for the returning wanderers; and Mrs. Farquhar really seemed another person in the joy of her return home. For the afternoons and evenings, then, she was ready to plan all the possible parties of pleasure, and to carry them out with energy and tact that were astonishing for one so frail. There was an excursion to Hampton Court, managed on a legal holiday, when no banker nor notary of them all would attend to any business, Horace said, — Hampton Court, which to the American not travel-spoiled is such a marvel: there was Windsor, and then beautiful visits in Kent, within striking distance. But Horace and his mother found, and were amazed to find, — what they would have found with any nice American girl, — that to Bertha, while everything was delightful, London and its revelations were the most delightful of all. They found that she had at her tongue's end questions about its local history that they had never thought of. She stopped to see St. Anne's, and went out of her way to find St. John's, that she might tell Rosebud she had heard all the bells

that rang out the fate of "London Bridge;" she
dragged Mrs. Farquhar to St. Paul's to attend service
there; and on the other Sunday to Westminster Abbey:
two feats which, as Mrs. Farquhar told her, she had
never performed before. Bertha told her she must be
grateful that she did not propose to go upon the monument. Never was a visitor more delighted, and never
were hosts more thoughful and hospitable.

But it had to come to an end. Max Schwarz was at
last completely identified, and the last power of attorney
was signed, and every document that could be thought
of, which could supply the place of personal presence,
was sealed and delivered. The last day came. They
were to take the packet for Hamburg the very next day.
Horace engaged their passages in advance, and came
in triumph with some magnificent bunches of black
Hamburg grapes, which the boat had brought over in
her last passage, when he came to give them the number of their state-rooms. "These are the first fruits,"
he said, as he gave them to Bertha.

Then Bertha asked him if he would do her one last
favor. To tell the truth, she asked it in too bungling
a way only because they had been loading her so with
favors, and she and her father had taken so much of
Dr. Farquhar's time, that it seemed graceless to ask
for more; but, in rather a bungling way, she explained,
that, as it happened, she had not seen any good bookseller's: she said "book-store." She had tried once
or twice with her father, but was sure they had not
gone to the right place. "Now, what I want, Dr.
Farquhar, is this: I want, while I am here, to buy some
really pleasant books for that nice girl I told you of,
who kept the lonely school on the Manito Island. It
will please her to know that I remembered her as much
as it pleases me to remember her here. And, if you
will go with me to the right place, I shall be ever so
much obliged to you."

Horace was delighted, really delighted, at a proposal
of something where he could be of real service, and
connect himself with one of her personal plans or fan-

cies.   All the more was he pleased, when, rather blun-
dering again, Bertha asked him if he were willing to
look at her list.   He could certainly help her about
editions of which she knew nothing.   Would he also
help her by adding anything that she had not thought
of, because she did not know enough?   This was only
a hurried list that she had made all herself.   Aunt
Mary had promised to help her; but, at the last moment, there had been no time.

Well, it was a queer list: probably not so bad a one,
after all; for, as one young girl made it for another,
she had some method of judging which the wisest professor of them all would not have had.   There was
more poetry than prose; beside the more familiar English poets, there were Faber's poems, of which Bertha
was very fond, and Montgomery's hymns; and she did
not know that she could not buy Jones Very's Sonnets
in London, so she had put that down.   The list gave
Horace Farquhar a chance to tell her of some of the
books which had been most to him.   He put in Jeremy
Taylor and Thomas à Kempis.   He asked her if she
did not know Herbert's poems and Vaughan's; and
found these were new to her.   He made his own present to the Manito school-mistress in a copy of Owen
Feltham, all full of his own pencil-marks; and so they
started very happily, after a nice talk on all sorts of
books and authors, for a book-shop at the West End.

I think Horace Farquhar had intrigued a little that
his mother should not accompany them, as Bertha had
expected, and as had been at first proposed.   There
had been some gallery that they were to see at the
same time; but, at the last moment, he brought a line
from Mrs. Farquhar saying she must give up the gallery, and would come round in the evening to say good-
by.   So Bertha, who was all ready for a brisk walk,
was just starting with Horace alone, to his entire satisfaction, when her father roused up from the Hamburg
newspaper he was reading, and asked if it would trouble
the doctor too much to let him join them, and show
him how and where he could best buy some little pres-

ents he wanted to take over to Lauenburg to his little cousins there, — presents which, in fact, in his dreamy way, he had till this moment forgotten. Horace could only assent, of course. Never, till that moment, had Mr. Schwarz been in the way. How impossible it was to tell him he was in the way now! There was nothing for it but to make the best of the unintentional addition to the party. How Horace wished he had brought his mother!

It was a very pleasant expedition, that is true, though it was not all Horace Farquhar wanted it to be. It was charming to Bertha to be in this embarrassment of riches of the beautiful London book-shop: it was more charming to see her so charmed. The list grew and grew; but Horace's judgment was good, and Bertha's taste was simple. When it was well-nigh complete, he said, "I know why you have put in no novels or other stories. You think she will get those anyway; and yet it seems to me, when I think over books, almost ungrateful not to recognize the good novels have done to me."

"I have been thinking of that very same thing," said Bertha. "If I ever were tempted to tell a lie, this 'Helen' would rise up and save me;" and she put her hand on Miss Edgeworth's "Helen."

Horace fairly started. "Why, that is one of my sacred seven!" said he; "the seven novels that have helped make my character;" and he was so serious that Bertha looked at him with all the earnestness of her deep gray eyes, as she asked what the others were. "Robinson Crusoe is one," said Horace. "I pity the man who is not more a man for that, — there is the loyalty of friendship, and trust in the providence of God; then there are one or two of Miss Austen's novels which have done me more good than most sermons have; there is Dickens's 'Christmas Carol,' and the 'Chimes,' which we were speaking of; and the seventh on my sacred shelf of the novels of character is Miss Martineau's 'Deerbrook.'"

" I know them all but that," said Bertha. "That is a book I never saw."

" Can you bring me 'Deerbrook,' by Miss Martineau?" said Horace Farquhar to the attendant. And while they waited, Bertha said :

" What is the lesson that ' Deerbrook ' teaches?"

Horace was startled by the question : he even hesitated before he replied ; but then he said firmly, " It is the lesson that no man should ever be tempted, even in the noblest effort of self-sacrifice, to marry a woman even the noblest, if he does not love her. And the other lesson follows : that he should let no advice of friends, no false etiquettes or social entanglements, prevent him from telling the woman whom he does love with all his heart what she is to him, and what he could be to her ; " and his eyes filled with tears, so tremendous was his excitement.

" Doctor," said Max Schwarz, "look at this. Can this be a misprint? Here is your new man, in his ' Survey of the Sixteenth Century,' says Palestrina was born in 1679. Then he was only fifteen years old when he died." And good Mr. Schwarz laughed heartily, little thinking what a jar the false date was to Horace. But there was no more chance for other talk. The seven novels were added to the box, the strange direction to Milwaukie given, and they all went to the toy-shop, to buy travel-presents for the cousins-German.

Nor in the walk home, nor in an evening visit afterwards, could Horace get another moment alone with Bertha. Not that she avoided it, — she was too unconscious ; but there were tradesmen coming in with parcels, there were German friends of Mr. Schwarz coming to say good-by ; and all that Dr. Farquhar could do was to leave this note in Bertha's hand as he bade her good-night.

WEDNESDAY EVENING.

My Dear Miss Bertha, — The fates have been against me to-day, or I could have said what I wanted to say, and what I shall write so clumsily. I wish I

could hope that it does not surprise you. I wish
I could think that you knew, that you had seen already, how you are everything to me, and how much I
could be to you if you would let me. You know me so
little, it is so short a time since we met, that I have not
dared till now to tell you how bright and true all my
life would be, if I could persuade you to share it, and
how wretched and dark the fore-look is to me, if you
say I must live it alone. I have not dared to say this
till now ; and now I do not dare to let you leave us
without saying it. I know how much I stake on my
venture, stranger as you must think me ; but it seems
to me as if we had known each other for our lives long.

Pray see me in the morning, and let me tell you this.
See my dear mother, who knows all I write, and hopes
with my own hope. Ask her if I cannot make your
home happy, if you will let me ; but do not answer
this note yet, if you have only to say that four weeks
ago we were strangers. Four months or four years
hence, if you choose, you shall know me better. But
four months hence, or four years hence, I cannot be
yours more truly and sacredly than I am this day.

Always, most truly yours,

HORACE FARQUHAR.

"Oh, dear ! " said Bertha to herself, as the note fell
from her hand. She had kissed her father good-night,
and had taken it, quite unconsciously, to read in her
own room.

14

CHAPTER XXI.

THE TWO MANITOS.

A ND Jasper?

Not for the first time in life, he " faced his perplexities," as he found himself with Oscar alone, after they had looked their last on Bertha at her departure. And perhaps Oscar made himself even dearer than ever to Jasper because he pined after Bertha so manifestly. Oscar was a boy, Jasper said to himself: he was not strong, and he was not afraid nor ashamed to show how much he missed her. Jasper was not a boy: he had not nearly died in cholera, and he knew that Bertha was the light of his life. He had these three reasons, good or bad, for not showing the same outspoken sorrow in her departure which Oscar showed.

But everybody was willing to say that the hospital life was wholly changed. The onslaught of the epidemic had been over long ago. They were but closing up their affairs, and began to look in the face the time when they should no longer be patients and nurses, but men and women in the usual cares and joys of life. Still all that staff felt, even the least demonstrative of them, that they, who had gone through the valley of that shadow together, who side by side had looked Death in the face, and with their very best patience had fought him as they met him, would bear a relation to each other more close than this world often knows. Bertha's departure seemed to break the circle; and now one by one followed fast. If Oscar had only been stronger, and had shown more power of standing alone, Jasper would have been among the first to desert, after she had gone.

" You had better send him away," said the doctor ;
" or, better yet, take him away. You need the change
almost as much as he does. If you had not been made
of iron, you would have gone under long ago. Why
not go down to the sea?" said the doctor, after a
minute's pause, craftily and skilfully ; for the doctor
saw many things, and cured many diseases where he
was not consulted. " Why not go to Boston, and take
him to the sea? The boy is a Viking's son : give him a
salt bath, and he will be well. It serves us all right,
this hole of horrors," said the doctor, looking round,
" because we ever did leave the sniff of the sea, and the
salt of the air, which the good God gave us when we
were born."

Crafty doctor, skilful doctor, kind doctor! who had
guessed something how matters stood with Jasper, —
would fain help, if only he knew how, and so con-
structed this sudden admiration for the sea and sea-
bathing. It was a temptation to poor Jasper ; but he
was on his mettle now, and he would not yield. No
seashore for him that summer ! He had the factory to
re-create, if it could be re-created. And he doubted if
he could send Oscar away alone.

But Oscar must go somewhere, — that was clear
enough, — if he was to renew the vigor of his life.
Jasper sent him, for a few days, to the country home
where his aunt was ; and the experiment worked well,
Jasper having persuaded the boy that it was quite necessary to him that he should go. Then he cast round
for some other expedition which should give him more
responsibility, and the good of bracing air. The old
mission-house at Mackinaw occurred to him as a place
where Oscar could range at large, and return a little
toward that savage life in which is health and strength.
Turning this over to construct an excuse, — for the boy
would never go for his own sake, or as a recruiting invalid, — the very happiest presented itself: nay, it did
Jasper almost as much good as his patient.

There returned, all unexpectedly, from the friend in
Milwaukie to whom it had been intrusted, a small box

of books, which, even in Detroit, Bertha had found time and means to bring together to send to her little friend, the school-mistress; of whose interests, as we have seen, she was mindful even in the distractions of London. The doctor, the Detroit doctor, had contributed to the box; Jasper and Oscar had contributed; Oscar had nailed it up with his very best carpentry; and it had been sent across to a business correspondent of Buffum, Rising, & Dundas, at Milwaukie. This correspondent now returned it, wisely or unwisely, saying that he could find no such person as the uncle to whom it had been addressed.

Such a memorial was it of Bertha at a time when Jasper was most heart-sick, and Oscar most in need of a mission!

Jasper made of the box even more than it deserved. He told Oscar that they must try more direct means. He must go to Mackinaw, and make inquiries there. If necessary, he must go on to the Great Manito Island and the Little Manito Island, and find which one had the school upon it. He must not hurry when he was once there, but stay till he was sure he was well enough to go to work in the shop. If he could find anybody whom he could trust to get out some spokes or some whiffle-trees, he might make a contract for them also. Thus commissioned, he sent the boy away, well pleased if, by one expedition, he could please "his master," and please Bertha.

Poor fellow! he had no fondness for the lake. Once and again he had gone on it with his father, as he, poor man! was pursuing one and another of the will-o'-the-wisps which were leading him to his ruin. Oscar's associations with steamboats were all connected with his father's eager excitements and bitter disappointments. The earlier associations were "first-class" associations,— of saloons and state-rooms. Then the later associations were "second-class,"— of herding on the forward deck with emigrants and horses, as his father's means grew less and less, and he had to economize more and more as they travelled. And now Jasper had

charged him to secure his own comfort, and not to regard, in comparison with it, the expense of his journey.
Jasper had taken pains to engage the best state-room
on the steamer. And the young man, on his first journey alone, found himself receiving attentions from
clerk, captain, and the rest, which, as he painfully re-
marked, his father never knew.

But Oscar did not live in the past, nor indulge in
long griefs. He accepted the hospitalities and the introductions which came through "the gentlemanly
clerk's" courtesies; and, before the voyage had advanced far, was a favorite with all the young people
among his fellow-travellers.

The old mission-house at Mackinaw stood, in those
days, a curious reminder of the zeal with which the
Church had done its best, and not in vain, for the Indians of the frontier. This was at about the time when
missionaries were going westward in search of new
worlds to conquer; and Oscar found little enough of
preaching, or the machineries of conversion. But none
the less was he in a new world. The Indian squaw, or
her husband or child, appeared here much more often,
in what Oscar could imagine the native costume, than
in the streets of Detroit, and with less of the expression of wretchedness which he was used to there. And
as Oscar waited for some boat which would be likely to
touch at the Manitos, — having left his own boat, which
had freight for the Sault, — he was once and again
solicited and advised by people whom we should now
call drummers in an humble way, who chose to suppose
that he was accredited with funds unlimited from some
Eastern house for the purchase of furs. To the Mack-
inawese, as to most Americans of the frontier, it was
impossible to suppose that any man had come to their
country with no notion but to see the country, and to
change his air. The American of the frontier, wherever he lives, generally supposes that the stranger
within his gates has come intending to buy a city, and
to lay out lots for sale. But in Oscar's case, it was
clear that he was indifferent to landings, or surveyors'

lines, or reservations. The next hypothesis, therefore, was, that he had come to buy furs; and as an agent for fur-dealers, evidently with little experience, but probably with untold resources in silver and gold, was he entertained by the young gentlemen who introduced themselves to him at the hotel.

But on the second day, as Oscar, greatly to his own amusement, was playing off the agents of one dealer against those of another, he lighted by accident on the skipper of a little lumber-schooner, who, as it proved, had in old times sailed for Mr. Hughitt, Jasper's uncle. This man had run into Mackinaw because he had come short of tobacco; and, having supplied himself with that commodity, was just getting under weigh again, when Oscar, with the magic of youth, discovered him, discovered that he was an old friend of Jasper's, that he was bound up the lake, and that he was only too glad to drop him at the Great Manito. To the astonishment, therefore, of Mr. Fergus Mac Tavish, who supposed that, when Mr. Oscar had once seen his last winter's beaver, he would be sure to buy at twice their value, Oscar was seen by the whole population to pay his modest bill, and to walk down with Capt. Zadock to the lake, to go on board the "Susan," and to depart from the embraces of all Mackinaw without so much as buying a single mink-skin.

So far so good for Oscar. He has passed the first station-house in the enchanted journey of life, and he has not made a fool of himself so far.

Whether his next station were so fortunate may be doubted. It is for the reader to see and to decide. Jasper had never known — if, indeed, Bertha had ever known — whether the pretty school-mistress were on the Great Manito or the Little Manito Island. Indeed, it was by rather a broad generalization that they had inferred that she was on any Manito at all. Jasper had fully explained to Oscar his uncertainty in this regard; and that, because he was uncertain, he could not give the little book-box to the clerk of any Milwaukie steamboat, with directions to leave it at the Manito landing.

Oscar knew perfectly well that his first commission was to decide between the respective Manitos, and not to deliver his freight, till, by personal intercourse, he had verified the school-mistress. Oscar knew no better way than to begin with the Manitos, and bravely follow them through. There might be more than two, for aught he knew; but none the less would he make personal examination.

"It is personal presence," as Jasper always taught him, "that moves the world."

When he confided to Capt. Zadock these views, and the general character of his commission, as the great mainsail of the schooner filled, and they left the mission-house, the fort, the light-house, and their country's flag, behind them, Capt. Zadock had no doubts whatever.

"Oh, sartin! it's the Big Manito. They can't have no school at the Little Manito, nor at any of them other places. But the Big Manito, — yes: sartin it is there. Why, I remember that school! Sis Fortin, old Zeb Fortin's daughter, taught school there when I first landed there."

Oscar asked when that was.

Oh! that — that was nine years ago. Sis Fortin afterwards married, — married a poor stick, anyway. He ran away from the "Gazelle," — the "Gazelle" was a steamboat which Oscar must remember: the same that took fire and burned at Windsor in the winter after Ned Hapgood ran away from her, and married Sis Fortin.

No: Oscar did not remember the "Gazelle." None the less, however, did he accept these views of the skipper as the best information he was likely to get, and determined to land at the Big Manito, as the skipper advised, not to say directed him. This matter well settled, they could both lie back comfortably on the deck, not asking for other couch than the rough boards of the deck-load; and, while Capt. Zadock smoked with new zest after his temporary abstinence, Oscar pumped him for stories of the old days at Duquesne, — of Mr.

Hughitt, and, most of all, of Jasper's boyhood. There was a little interruption when Capt. Zadock's wife announced that supper was ready : but in the captain's long yarns the evening passed quickly ; and it was late before Oscar turned in, expecting that they should make a landing at the Big Manito early the next morning.

Earlier, it proved, than anybody expected. Before four, Capt. Zadock summoned him ; and Oscar found in a moment that the "Susan" was running off on her very best tack, at a speed he had never given her any credit for. Truth was, the wind was blowing almost a gale ; but it happened to be so far favorable to Capt. Zadock's views, that he had thus far refused to shorten sail, although Mackey, the mate, had once or twice suggested it, and although the breeze was so stiff that Capt. Zadock had chosen not to go below. Under the stars, he pointed out to Oscar the line of the Big Manito as they approached it ; and told him, that, with this fresh wind, he believed he would only lie by enough to drop him, and that he would not come to an anchor, as there had been some proposal of doing the night before. Accordingly, he ran as close as he could to the landing where the steamers were used to take wood on board, — made a short tack there ; and, as the "Susan" went about, Oscar dropped his box of books and his valise into her only boat. Mackey and he rowed to shore : he landed, and bade good-by with a parting hail ; and so found himself, before light in the morning, at the end of a crazy plank-wharf, on an island all but desolate, with his welcome to win from the aborigines, of whatever race or disposition they might happen to be.

The boy pleased himself, as he walked up and down waiting for daylight, by remembering his favorite conceit that he was Jasper's man Friday. Only this time it was not Robinson, but Friday, who was watching for the savages, and exploring the island. He had no fear that his luggage and his precious box would be stolen, and walked up the roadway to reconnoitre the scattered houses which made the only village, trying to make out the school-house, and to plan out his campaign of the morning.

An hour more, and the little settlement showed signs of waking. As soon as Oscar satisfied himself that the household nearest the water was well in action, after allowing a good half hour from the time the smoke began to curl from the chimney, he boldly climbed the rail-fence which separated the cabin from the roadway, knocked at the door, and pushed his prearranged question:

"Can you tell me if Miss Ruth Cottam lives on the island? I believe she keeps the school."

"Ruth Cottam? Ruth Cottam?"—this was the immediate answer of the old lady whom he addressed— "I don't know. Jabez! Jabez!"—the last to some boy too lazy to appear just yet,—"what's the teacher's name?"

"Doan know."

This was Jabez's unsatisfactory reply.

"Amelia Ann! Amelia Ann! what's the teacher's name?"

No answer.

"Jabez! Jabez! ask Amelia Ann what's the teacher's name."

Amelia, upon this, appeared, such toilet as she was accustomed to make being but half completed, but with some curiosity to know what contingency had started the unexpected question. Gradually this curiosity gave way so far, that she was able in a measure to devote herself to the answer; and the answer was, that the teacher was Miss Coop,—an answer for which Oscar was not prepared, and from which he attempted without success to dissuade her. It was Miss Coop, she said, and never had been anything else: she was Gershom Coop's sister, and had "taught school" on the island now for three years. Oscar tried in vain to elicit some memories of Miss Schwarz's visit to the school, but with no success. The boat often touched at the island; and, while they are wooding up, the folks often walked up to the school. Amelia Ann dared say that the particular people Oscar knew did walk up, or she dared say they did not walk up : it was quite evident that she had her memory sufficiently under control to make it recollect anything that was desirable. It was equally evident that the value of its oracles was all the less from this ease with which the pythoness could evoke, could utter, or could refuse them. The only thing certain about these oracles was, that the teacher's name was Miss Coop. Oscar put a few questions, from which to learn whether "Miss," in the language of the Manitos, indicated maiden life or married. From the answer to these, it appeared that Miss Coop must have lived many years, or what Amelia Ann called many, in a maiden state. Oscar had not been foolishly reticent, and early in the interview had explained who he was, how, and why, he came there ; and, indeed, had briefly anticipated the questions by which his own would otherwise have been parried, — acting on Dr. Franklin's very admirable rule for such circumstances. Jabez had joined the group before long ; and then Jabez's father and his uncle, and a tribe of Gershoms and Elizabeth Sarahs and Sauls and Phebe Marias, making a family of eight or nine children, and more elders than Oscar could well place on so short an interview. All parties offered advice and suggestions, but practically all advice amounted to this : that he should take his breakfast where he was, and then, guided by Saul, should go and find Gershom Coop's house. Gershom could tell him where "Miss Coop" was, and she could tell him, if anybody could, of Ruth Cottam ; and this was done. Oscar ate such a breakfast as he had long forgotten. He declined the molasses which was proffered for "sweetning" to his tea ; he boldly engaged the saleratus bread with the omnipotence of youth, but came off somewhat discomfited. He would not appear grand, however ; and he tried the salt pork with more success. He flattered himself that his want of appetite had not been observed, when the queen of the table, by way of adding honor to it, bade Phebe Maria the younger climb to the top

of the closet which served as pantry, and bring down
a plate she would find there. Amid a rapturous chorus
of applause from the youngsters, Phebe Maria rapidly
ascended from shelf to shelf, and returned more rapidly
with some cold huckleberry cake, which had been pre-
served with care, as all parties knew, for some state
occasion ; and poor Oscar found, that, by his courtesy
all round, he had made an impression so agreeable that
madam's heart was softened, and the meal was to be
made a feast in his honor. With such zeal as the compliment could arouse, he gave himself to his new duty,
and engaged the cake. He was well-seconded by the
children ; and, as this last relay was exhausted, one
and another pushed back the blocks and stools upon
which they were sitting, and proclaimed that they were
" done." So Oscar was set free to visit Gershom
Coop's.

Saul led him to the cabin, chattering all the way.
The school, as Oscar had already learned, was closed,
after a short summer term of a few weeks. The boy
showed him the little school-house, — a small, neat
enough log-cabin, — and they loitered a minute to look
in. Arrived at Gershom's, they did not find him, but
did find a hard-featured, dried-up woman, tall as Meg
Merrilies, and, as Oscar afterwards said, as old, who
was setting out her milk-pans on a sunny shelf outside
the cabin.

" Teacher," cried Saul, in some terror, " here's a
man's got some books for you ! "

Miss Coop looked down contemptuous upon Oscar,
but softened more than he had thought possible, as she
asked him to come in. The introduction was a misfortune. Oscar was, of course, convinced at once that
Miss Coop was not Ruth Cottam. He explained, as
best he might, who he was, and who he was not. He
told, as best he could, of Miss Schwarz's visit at the
school-house. He was firm, beyond persuasion, in the
statement that it was Ruth Cottam he was in search of.
And he need not have been alarmed. It very soon appeared, that, though Miss Coop wanted her rights, that

was all she wanted. She wanted quite as much that other people should have theirs. Nay, to his amazement, Oscar observed, or thought he did, that books had no particular charm for her. She dropped the remark that the children had enough books, all except "Introductions to the Seventh National"; and Oscar had early explained that he had no such "Introductions." She had tried to persuade him for a moment that he was a book-peddler, and could sell his wares to anybody he chose. But Oscar had, of course, rejected this hypothesis of his duty and destiny. Arrived at this point, he asked meekly if there were no other school on the island.

Oh, no! There was no other school: there never would be. It was "as much as ever" they kept up this.

And she was quite sure that Miss Ruth Cottam had made no visit here this summer?

Of course she was. Not so many people on the island that another teacher should come, and she not know it. And, as this answer came, Oscar detected an insinuation which implied danger to the "teacher" who should thus come prospecting on what, with all her scorn of it, she regarded as her own reservation. All this time, be it observed, the conversation went forward as if he were some guilty party, whose sins she had discovered, and was discovering, by cross-examination. In tone, and almost in gesture, in a certain snap of the eye which Saul evidently dreaded, Miss Coop cross-questioned Oscar with a determination which fairly made him wonder whether he were a detected criminal. But, as he had no sins to confess, he confessed none. Fairly puzzled, however, he dropped the phrase, half-aloud. "If there were any school on either of the other islands?"

"And who said there was no school on the other islands?" demanded Miss Coop loftily.·

"Why, Capt. Zadock said so," said Oscar, surprised.

"Capt. Zadock had better mind his own business. What does he know about school-keeping? If he knew

enough to keep his sloop from going ashore on the ' two
pigs,' it would be better for him. Capt. Zadock talks
a good deal more than's good for him."

Clearly there was some prejudice regnant against
Capt. Zadock ; and it had reacted on Oscar, as one of
his passengers. But, as soon as Miss Coop thus relieved herself, she pointed out the other Manito, and
was willing to explain that a school had lately been
established there. She did not know who kept it, but
she did know that Capt. Fortin came over before Thanksgiving last year to talk with her about it. She did
not doubt they had started the school then. Indeed,
" come to think of it," she was sure that Jerushy Whitney had told her that all her children were at the school
all winter.

Why in the world could she not have said all this
before? This was Oscar's wonder. Poor Oscar, he
will find that problem a hard one to solve, as he goes
through life : why third-rate people, when they do know
anything which is of any use, hold it back with such
resolute stupidity or stupid resolution?

" I must go to the little Manito," said he. " I am
very much obliged to you, Miss Coop."

And Miss Coop, in her rough way, bade him good-by,
and returned to scouring her tins, with the distinct feeling that she had rebuked to the face one who deserved some blame. That is a way with such people.
Poor Oscar went his way, hardly conscious that he had
given such a glow of self-satisfaction to the old terma-
gant for the day.

What he was planning for was another voyage. Man
Friday must see what was on these blue islands in the
offing. There was no friendly lumber-man this time.
There was much trudging from wood-lot to beach, and
from beach to barn, and from barn to cabin, to see who
could take him across ; for Oscar would not wait — not
a day. This scheme failed, and that ; but the boy was
determined ; and as the breeze gathered, after a sultry
noon, he found himself in what these people called a
batteau, which means a flat-boat, not unlike the dory

of the Eastern fisherman, with Jabez Good to bring the
boat back, and with the box and valise, which he had
guarded so faithfully, put in for ballast. The wind rose
as the young fellows pushed off, and Jabez satisfied
himself that he could carry sail enough to make time
nearly as good as they would do with their oars. Oscar
satisfied himself, after a minute, that Jabez understood
his business ; and so they escaped the necessity, which at
noon they had both admitted, of rowing across under a
hot sun from island to island. The line of the smaller
island lifted, the dark blue changed into shades of
green ; and, before the sun went down, they found themselves picking out a place for a landing. They could
have gone round to the steamboat wharf. But it was
clear that that would cost two or three extra tacks ;
and the young men determined to beach the boat on a
white beach which was full in sight as they drew near.

A sort of natural landing offered itself. A white
pine had fallen seaward long ago, from the little bluff
which rose above the shore ; and, with its roots still
tangled as they grew, stretched its gray, half-rotten
branches out into the lake. Jabez ran the skiff up to
the side of this trunk ; and Oscar, taking her painter
in his hand, swung himself lightly on the log, and
picked his way carefully among its rotten branches to
the shore.

A group of bare-legged children had witnessed the
approach, and came screaming and chattering down the
shore as Oscar stepped along. They were followed by
a young woman, too young to be their mother, who
might have been an older sister. Oscar found he had
rather more on his hands than he had expected, as the
rope tangled itself pertinaciously among one and
another outstretched branch of his little tree-bridge.
He stepped back and forth : he could not spring back
into the boat, or he would gladly have done so. He
was on the point of bidding Jabez put off and make
his landing alone, when this girl called out pleasantly,
" Throw the painter to me." And Oscar did so ; she
standing well clear of the old pine, that it might not be

tangled again. She caught it with a handy grasp, ran along, and up the beach with it, all the children shouting and helping ; and Jabez was landed, dry-footed, too, before Master Oscar had stepped through, over, and among the rotten branches of the pine, and came, laughing, up to the merry party.

"You are a better sailor than I," he said, as he thanked this pretty longshoreman. "I made a poor landing ; and now, perhaps, you can tell me what I come from the other island to ask, — whether there is a school on this island, and who the mistress is."

Oscar had made such a botch with his tree-trunk and his tangled rope, that his "lady of the lake" was a great deal more at ease than she would have been had his coming been more dignified. The children were in a gale ; and she was not far from it herself. So, when he spoke in his half-puzzled, half-joking way, she answered in just the same mood and tone. "School? Yes : there is, or was ; and I am the school-ma'am."

"She's a real good school-ma'am, too," said little barefoot the youngest. "She lets us have lots of fun." And then little barefoot subsided, frightened with her own audacity.

"Are you really Miss Ruth Cottam?" said Oscar, amazed and amused that his Odyssey had ended so suddenly.

" I am really Miss Ruth Cottam, and nobody else," said the pretty Manitoan ; "but, pray, who are you?" And she laughed heartily, and so did Oscar, and so did Jabez.

"Why," said Oscar, " I am what they called an expressman. You remember Miss Bertha Schwarz? I have brought you a box of books from her." And he showed her her name on the box, as it lay in the boat.

"Dear Miss Schwarz ! how kind she is to remember me. I knew she remembered me. She said she should send these books ; and I knew it was a mistake that they had not come before. It is just like her to send them. And — and I am sure, sir," said Ruth, beginning now to feel shy, and that she ought to have felt shy before, "I am sure, sir, I am very much obliged to you : you have taken so much pains." And then a terror came over Ruth, that perhaps she ought to pay him for bringing the books. He said he was an expressman ; and through the newspapers the meaning of that word had dawned on her. This terror was horrible to sustain. But she choked it down with the resolution that if he wanted any money he might ask for it : she would die before she said anything about it. And, meanwhile, Oscar was casting about to find what his next turn was to be. Fortunately for both of them, there was a duty next his hand, still, of the carnal or material kind.

"Jabez, how are we to get this box to Miss Cottam's house ? "

Jabez proposed slinging it by its rope-handles to the oars, and carrying it between them. But Ruth knew better than that. She bade them both leave boat and box and valise where they were : led them through the wood-road by which she and the children had come to the water ; sent up "into the lot" for old man Kreuzer ; and, when he appealed, sent him with his ox-team round by the beach ; and, meanwhile, herself, in an easy and charming hospitality, made the young men at home on the shady side of the cabin. Before old Kreuzer had come up, Ruth had a little table, with a white cloth and three tea-cups upon it, standing on the broad, flat stone in front of the door, and had her welcome cup of tea, and her matchless half-loaf, and her pretty pat of butter, and her dish of raspberry-jam, upon the same.

Oscar, meanwhile, was telling the story of Bertha Schwarz's life from the moment when she and Ruth Cottam parted on the steamboat. Of the cholera on the boat, and of Bertha's disappointment at Detroit, he had to tell : then how fortunate that disappointment was for him ; for he insisted upon it, that, but for her care, and Mr. Jasper's, he should have died, — which view was probably the true one. Then how lovely she was to everybody, and how she was the life of the whole hospital, and how they hated to have her go away. Then why she left because she was an heiress; and how Mr. Jasper said they should never see her again.

Who Mr. Jasper was, who constantly appeared in Oscar's story, Ruth did not know; but she thought, not unwisely, that if she waited long enough she should learn. Oscar went on with his story, with much more detail than would have been needful, or than he would have dreamed of had he not a listener so sympathetic, and, shall we say? so pretty, and so graceful in her attention and attentions. For Ruth Cottam was on her own heather now. Had two gentlemen come to visit her in her school-room, where she was not sure of herself, she would have been frightened out of her senses; or had she been in Detroit, among the grand people she had never seen, she could not have said a word for herself. But her guests were people who had rendered her a real kindness and an essential service. She would and could direct the hospitalities of her cousin's house in welcoming them; and she had determination enough to put her quite at ease as she did so. Better than this, here was news of this bright, lovely Miss Schwarz, whom she had blessed every day since they parted.

Oscar made her laugh most heartily as he described Miss Coop, and told how that lady had scolded him and frightened him. Miss Coop had never heard of Ruth Cottam; but many was the tale of Miss Coop which one and another islander had brought to Ruth's ears, — all of them, alas! reflecting a certain acidity and ferocity. Oscar's half-unconscious imitation of her severity of manner revealed no novelty. Ruth said she thanked him all the more for her books, now she knew through what perils he had passed to bring them.

And so they finished the tea, though they drew it out so long. The children gathered round the door-step listening to the talk; and Oscar began to feel a terrible heart-sinking, like that of Bruce when he thought he was at the head of the Nile. Poor boy! he had no more worlds to conquer. Here was the box, and here

15

was the owner. And must he, therefore, turn round and go away, when she was so charming, and he would be so glad to tell her stories of Miss Schwarz as long as she would listen? Might he pretend that his health required him to stay? How long ought expressmen to stay when they brought boxes? Jabez was restless. Jabez had said but little ; but he intimated now that the wind would lull after sunset. Did Oscar mean to go back, or not? Ruth could not say anything. She knew there was not much on the Little Manito to interest people.

Poor Oscar ! What should he do? Go back as he came? or could he find any reason for staying on the Little Manito, and letting Jabez return alone?

CHAPTER XXII.

HARD WOOD LUMBER.

JABEZ urged again his suggestion that the wind would die away as the sun went down. And then, speaking by a sudden inspiration, Oscar answered, " I think it will ; and you had better take the boat back now. I shall not go with you. Mr. Rising wants me to buy some spokes and some seasoned ash ; and I shall see if I cannot find it here." And he turned to Ruth, as innocently as if she had been a lumber-merchant sticking planks in his yard, and asked her if she thought any of the people on the island had ever cut and shaved spokes for carriage-builders.

That will do, Oscar. With that decision and readiness your chances for this world's successes are not bad. Jabez, you may go. The reader may imagine Jabez departing, and will not be troubled to attend to him again.

Ruth was not uninformed about spokes or ash-timber. At Manitowoc, which is a settlement on the mainland, her uncles had once and again taken orders for seasoned wood for wheelwrights and carriage-builders. And Ruth simply launched out into details of what the island could and could not do ; as to which the reader of these lines need not be instructed. For the more important detail, it was evident that Oscar must wait until her cousin came home.

And he waited. And, from spokes and ashen whiffle-trees, the conversation drifted round again not unnaturally to his little voyage in the boat ; to his bigger voyage in " The Susan ; " to bigger voyages yet in one and another steamer ; and to the biggest voyage of all,

from Hamburg to New York, when he was only a boy.
And so he came to tell of fiords and mountain-climbing
in his own home; of wild, exciting skating-parties in
winter, which he could just remember; and, again, how
once, when he first went away from his own home, his
uncle took him up, far up, on the northern coast, and,
night and morning, they saw sunrise and sunset at the
same time. How he made friends with the little troops
of Laplanders, he told; and how one of them gave him
a reindeer for his own, and how wretched he was with
the present. He made Ruth and the listening children,
who had quite outstaid their bed-time, laugh heartily
with this misadventure.

Not that all this narrative of the lively boy was one
steady lecture or unbroken yarn. Quick and almost
dramatic as he was in the vigor and animation with
which he presented to her again the scenes he had passed
through, he startled Ruth, who was sometimes so shy
and quiet, into an animation and freedom which afterwards surprised herself; and, without knowing it, she
was capping stories with him, and trumping the leading
tales in his narratives. For a demure little school-mistress on a Manito she had had her share of adventure
too. Poor child! she remembered neither father nor
mother; and when Oscar once, without pausing, hurried
by an allusion to his mother's death, as if he could not
trust himself to speak of it, her great eyes brimmed
full of tears, without her saying one word, but not without his knowing the sympathy. Her voyages had been
lake-voyages and canal-voyages, and one long voyage
on the Mississippi. But she had, with one and another
uncle and aunt, and as she was forwarded by one aunt
and another to some third aunt or fourth uncle, made
many weird and queer expeditions through the forest.
She had slept in wagons, and under wagons, and under
tents, and at open camp-fires. And Oscar soon noted,
that, in the midst of her undisguised curiosity as to the
manner of life in detail which people led at such great
centres as Milwaukie and Detroit, to her the cabin in
which they were at the Little Manito, which, even to

him, was primitive in its simplicity, seemed an advance
in comfort on much of the home-life that she had been
used to. She understood its full capacities, and knew
how to make the best of them.

And tales of camp-life, and of slow emigrant journeys
over corduroy-roads, or mere lumber-roads, over on the
mainland, led to talk about the forests and forest growth,
and the prairies and prairie wonders. Each of these
two had been thrown in childhood much on themselves
for their childish amusements. And it would be hard
to tell which of the two knew most, or talked with most
glee, of the way in which they had hunted bird, beast,
and butterfly; of the tramps they had made for berries
and nuts, and varieties of barks and roots savory to the
tooth of childhood, and of other triumphs of a gypsy
career. And it seemed as if there were nothing that
either had done which the other had not done. When
Oscar, with infinite detail and infinite fun, told of a
certain trap, which, day by day, he had watched in his
determination to catch a particular flying-squirrel when
he was only a child, Ruth Cottam fairly started, and
she said, "Are you a witch? That is exactly the story
I was going to tell to you."

It was then that she noticed how late it was; and
that, under the pretext of amusing the children by telling them stories, they had been really rehearsing, each
to other, their own biographies. "Short exhortations"
and short farewells sent the children up the ladder by
which they climbed to bed; and once more Oscar
alluded to his remaining business on the island, and
they wondered when her cousin would return.

At the moment, his tall, stout figure darkened the
light space left in the sky between the trees; and in a
minute more he had joined them. He gave Oscar a
cordial welcome; whispered a minute with Ruth as to
the best way to find the young man lodging for the
night; and, having solved this question, proposed to
him that they should go together to the next cabin,
where he knew the widow Mulligan would be glad to
entertain him. "We are rough folks here," he said;

"but we will make you as comfortable as we can. You'd better come over here for your breakfast, and then we can talk about the spokes. Did you say you wanted ash for fills?" And so Oscar left romance and beauty and youth, and retired, talking of the strength and seasoning which time gives to timber.

It is not the place of this story to go into the detail of the market for hard wood in the forests of Michigan and Wisconsin. We may pass by the success and the failure of Oscar's negotiations for spokes and for thills, only remarking that they were not futile.

The widow Mulligan gave Oscar a cordial welcome, and a shake-down on the floor, and a heavy comforter with which to keep himself warm. Youth, and the fatigue and adventure of his varied day, did the rest; and an unbroken sleep of eight hours parted Oscar's first and second visits to Shadrach Turner's cabin. No! not one dream. Not one vision of pretty Ruth Cottam. It was as if she had no brown hair, no long eyelashes, no dark-blue eyes deep set, no puzzled smile, no rounded cheek, at once pink and brown: it was as if Oscar had not thought her face, as she listened to him, the most charming revelation of possible beauty. He covered himself with the coverlet that was given him. In his mother's language he said the prayer his mother taught him, "Vor Fader," to the end: and then in a moment the gates were closed on him, till, as the sun rose, the widow Mulligan's cock-a-loo-loo welcomed the day, and Oscar sprang up to consciousness; to the cold water which he drew for himself by her long well-sweep from her well; to life, and to the joy of life. For Oscar was young and brave and true, and knew how to live his utmost in to-day.

Shadrach Turner had bidden him come to breakfast; and to breakfast where Ruth presided, I am afraid Oscar would have gone even had he not been bidden. And Ruth gave him a welcome so pretty! It was impossible not to contrast it with his experience of the morning before at Abner Good's. I think Ruth had slept well too. She never told me. But they were all young and

all happy, and the log-cabins gave little chance for car-
bonic acid. So I think Ruth slept well. And how was
she dressed? Dear Lily, I shall not say. Only
this I know, — that, on the beach, the ... ...
had caught her the day before just as she was; which
means just as she happened to be after she had cleaned
up after dinner, and then taken the little children, as by
promise long before exacted, through the Burkes' wood-
road to the shore. For my part, then or now, I would
as gladly see Ruth at any moment just as she was, as
with any decorations which her little trunk then, or her
upper bureau drawer now, might provide. But Ruth
was not quite of my mind; nay, perhaps is not at this
moment. And when the widow Mulligan's bird of
morning cried cock-a-loo-loo, and so challenged Shadrach Turner's to cry cock-a-doodle-doo, they had not
wakened Ruth. They had found her just tying up her
bonny brown hair with her bonny blue ribbon; just
turning to judge the work of Hiram and 'Lonzo, who
had been starting her fire, and of Cecilia Susan, who
was setting the table, this time in-doors. In a moment
more Ruth was in full line of battle, as with these un-
subsidized allies, her faithful liegemen and damsel, she
" got breakfast; " and, probably because she was mistress of the position, she was wholly at ease when
Master Oscar appeared; though she blushed, as I believe
she always did when she spoke to anybody, and wondered whether she ought or ought not to give him her
hand.

" The boys are too early for me," said Oscar. " Mrs.
Mulligan let me draw her water, and I brought Mrs.
Good one of her buckets full yesterday: but I see you
want no extra watermen here."

No; the boys declared that all that Ruth wanted done
they could and would do. Titus, in an aside which was
at once sheepish and proud, told Oscar that they washed
the dishes.

" They are real good boys," said Ruth proudly; " and
they have got a real good sister too," she added carefully, in her determination that Cecilia should not be

pained. " There never was a home where there was less
quarrelling and more work, and more good times too, I
believe, Hiram."

And Hiram said rather clumsily that it was so; and
could not be repressed when he chose to add that it
was all because Ruth had come to take care of them.
All this time he went on in the preparation, which she
supervised rather than conducted, for breakfast. And
to this mutual admiration Shadrach Turner entered,
coming in with Kreuzer from the humble slab-barn
where they had been pitching down the breakfast for
the cattle, and preparing for them their substitute for
hot coffee. Turner with his voice, and Kreuzer silently,
bade the young man good-morning; and they sat down
to breakfast, and to the renewed discussion of whiffle-
trees, thills, and spokes, of ash and hickory; and not
only of the qualities of the wood, but of the qualities
of the men who, it was supposed, could furnish it.
Once and again Turner appealed to Ruth in this talk,
as if, in her dealings with school-committee-men and
fathers, she might have taken the measure of some of
the new-comers on the South Point, as he had had no
opportunity to do; and Oscar found, that, in her
rambles with the children, Ruth knew the various high-
ways and by-ways of the island quite as well as her
cousin did.

Oscar was not new to log-cabin life. But he had, in
person, seen it only in the old Norwegian forms, as his
father, and his father's friends, transferred them from
the Old World to the New. The Norwegian at home
lives in wooden houses as does the American settler.
His log-cabin in Norway looks to the eye unaccustomed
to it, exactly like the log-cabin of a Western pioneer.
Once and again, in the broken life of his boyhood, Oscar
had made his home in such a cabin. But there were
details that were new to Oscar. As he turned to Ruth
to hear some story by which she illustrated the character
of an old fisherman at the South Point, he saw that
Master Titus's eyes were growing round with satisfaction; and in a moment more he saw the reason, which

had been screened from him till now. He knew that Cecilia was busy at the fire behind him ; but he had not heeded the sound there. The enlargement of Titus's eyes was some signal that her preparations were ended. In a moment more, there fell before Oscar's astonished gaze something upon the empty platter before him, which he saw was what in Detroit they called a flapjack. With a ready and skilful hand, Cecilia had whirled this from her griddle with such precision that it flew through the air, over his head, upon the dish which lay ready for it. With all Oscar's *savoir faire*, which seemed, indeed, to come naturally to him, he found it difficult not to start at the suddenness of the fall. The children, and the rest, however, all took it as matter of course. Another followed, and another. They were removed to one and another plate almost as rapidly as they fell. A rapid consumption of this manna from heaven, as, when it fell, it seemed to Oscar, reinforced by the presence of wild raspberry, which is one of the native dishes of these regions, and the maple-sugar, which takes the place of all other sugar, closed the morning meal.

Then followed a day which Oscar always looked back upon as a day of singular and blessed good fortune. Turner gave him all the information he could about men with whom it was well to discuss hard wood. But Turner himself could give nothing more. He must use every hour of the day with a party of men who were at work in repairs on the steamboat-wharf ; and the boat down the lake from Chicago and Milwaukie was due that afternoon. Before she came, the wharf must be ready. The boats, as has been already said, were then accustomed to stop for wood at the island. But Turner intimated to Ruth, very readily, that all Oscar would need was guidance to one and another of the outlying points of the island, where he could see one and another of those men of whom he had been telling. For means of communication, the island had little to boast ; but such as there was was placed at Oscar's disposal : and so it was that he spent most of that Sep-

tember day threading the woodlands of the Little
Manito, with this young girl for a guide, yesterday
such a stranger, and to-day one of the oldest and nearest of his friends.

There was resemblance enough in their history to
compel each to sympathize with the other, as, indeed,
each understood the other when words were only half
spoken. Each of them, though each was so young, had
seen a mother die, and a father. Each of them, almost
from childhood, had been without a fixed home. Each
of them had known what it was to gnaw very close to
the bone. And, again, each of them was now in com-
parative comfort, in what each thought luxury, under
the care and protection of a loyal, manly friend. And
then appeared the inevitable distinction. Oscar's ambition, though it hardly expressed itself in words, was
the wish, if only he might work it out, that he might
be independent in fortune and position, so that he could
take care of Mr. Jasper, and keep Mr. Jasper from anxiety, and save Mr. Jasper from the necessity of work
which he thought wore on him. The boy had found
out already that Jasper had not the native instinct for
money-making. But Ruth, though she hardly dropped
a word of this, was, as clearly, glad to be under Shadrach Turner's wing; glad she could help his children;
glad she had him to turn to when the Committee was
unreasonable; glad she was not what Oscar called independent in the world. Of these similarities and contrasts they said next to nothing; nay, they thought
nothing at all. They talked about what was round
them, — about the men Oscar dealt with, or their children; about the varieties in the shrubs and trees of the
forest; for both of them were pure Aryans, and as keen
as Indians in their quest of leaf, berry, and lichen.
Oscar paraded before Ruth some of the marvels of
Jasper's botanical lore. Ruth told Oscar of mysteries
in fibre and cell which she had learned from Sacs and
Foxes and Chippewas, — mysteries which had never
got themselves written down in Master Jasper's learning. Ah me! what a happy day it was! How soon —

all too soon — did the long shadows come again ! The spokes were ordered ; the whiffle-trees were ordered : but he had found nothing fit for thills. The last excuse for staying had been pumped dry : and poor Oscar stood on the finished wharf with the faithful little valise, and the umbrella which Ruth had mended ; with a group of the children and their friends ; with Shadrach Turner and with Ruth herself.

The steamboat rounded into the little cove ; and hands only too quick, from island and from boat, here wheeled, and there threw, the wood upon her decks. It was all done too soon. The boys scrambled on board with Oscar's modest luggage, and he bade his friends good-by.

" I shall write to you, if you will let me," said he.

" Oh, certainly ! " said Ruth ; and the long eyelashes fell on her cheek again as she looked down. This was the last word. " All aboard ! " said Capt. Peleg ; and Oscar hurried across the gang-plank, which was withdrawn in a moment, and the boat swung off from shore. He kissed his hand : Ruth waved hers ; and this was all.

CHAPTER XXIII.

SHALL WE GO ON?

JASPER was sorry to see Oscar back so soon : but he could not but see that his little voyages, his adventures, such as they were, his success in all he had attempted, had done the boy good ; had lifted him out of the rut, the routine, of convalescence ; and had given to him the start which the careful and wise doctor had sought for. Oscar "told his times," — told them in detail sufficiently precise to satisfy even Jasper's demands. Jasper was well pleased to hear of dear old Capt. Zadock, and that Oscar had arranged that he should come and see them at the factory. The name, and the stories tied to it, waked up slumbering wishes of his that they might both go back to Duquesne, and start again the enterprises which had given way before the ruthless fire, and the more ruthless "smart man of business."

But Jasper had other ravages to repair besides those of Duquesne. The carriage-shop had been closed now for nearly three months. Both his partners were dead, — the two men whose knowledge of the business had given to their work much of its reputation. Every workman whom they had employed had left Detroit. Actually, as Oscar stood with him in the counting-room, he and Jasper were the only two representatives left in that city of that busy throng, who so little while ago had been at work, within sight or sound. In this wreck what was Jasper to do? Was he to build up another carriage-factory out of nothing? That reminded him too much of Theo Brown's old *bon-mot*, about women's beginning of stockings. Theo said, " They made be-

lieve once round, and then knit into that." Even the
rent of the premises expired in October. Such orders
as they had, fewer it seemed than usual, they had had
to turn over to firms in other cities, because they could
not pretend to execute them. Fortunately there were
almost no debts, — nothing but what would be paid at
maturity by the funds which Jasper was daily collecting
from their own customers as they settled their accounts
with him. On the other hand, however, the smart men
of business, who were looking out for Mrs. Dundas's
rights and Mrs. Buffum's, were asking what arrangements he was making for paying over their shares in
the firm, which, as the reader knows, had but just entered on its existence. Not a very simple nor a very
agreeable outlook for Jasper.

He did what in such a crash it is wise to do : he re-
verted to first principles. How came he to be a carriage-builder at all? Answer : He had had this opportunity to train Oscar to independence ; and he had used
it. He had found, at the same time, that he and Buffum
and Dundas could each of them lend a hand to the other ;
and he had taken that opportunity. It was clear enough
to him, that by honest work, and loyal following-up of
opportunities, he and they had made a business, which,
if he could hold to it five years more with the same advantages, would open before him everything he wanted.
He would be subduing the world in an honorable place.
That is the first thing a man should ask. He would
see Oscar succeeding ; he would be in a position to support a family, if, alas ! he had one to support, which
was now impossible ; and he could do by the Public,
by the State and Church, by the People, what to State
and Church, which is to say, to the People, each man
owes. All this the young man saw. But the five
years had not passed, and the opportunity was gone.

Jasper's decision was probably wise. Wise or foolish, it was this : He would not attempt single-handed
to carry the enterprise forward which had needed the
best work of all three of them. Ordinarily he hated
partnerships with that aversion with which most men

of strong individuality regard them. But he determined, that if he could find, with reasonable inquiry, some man who would replace Dundas in his constructive ability, and should have some measure of the admirable good sense of that man, — some man, that is, who would not be afraid to work, and to lead other workmen, and who knew enough to command their respect as he did so, — if he could find such a man who would be his partner, he would go on. Or if he could find any man who wanted to trust ten or twenty thousand dollars in a partnership with Jasper, himself being a sleeping partner, so that Jasper might with some confidence reorganize his own establishment, with a responsible foreman at the head of each department, — with such a partner he would go on. But if neither of these men appeared, on reasonable inquiry, he would take it for granted that the decision of a wise Providence was against his going farther in the art, craft, and mystery of carriage-building. This decision of Jasper's was probably wise. Wise or foolish, as has been said, it was that on which he acted ; and, when Oscar returned, he found Jasper awaiting the results of his first efforts in carrying it forward.

Jasper had written first to a man named Croffut, whom he had seen at Cleveland, who was, in a small way, carrying on the carriage-building business there. He had proposed to him that he should remove his little establishment to Detroit, and that they should form a new firm together, to take advantage of the well-established reputation of Buffum, Rising, & Dundas. He was awaiting Croffut's decision as to this proposal. He was also awaiting a letter from Asaph Ferguson, his old class-mate and crony. Jasper believed in friendship : he was right there. He believed in the advice of friends, whether it encouraged or discouraged ; and he believed three men could pull out from a hole in the ice better than one : he was right there again. He therefore wrote a long letter to Ferguson, in which he told the story of the success of his carriage-building, and of its crisis in the cholera ; showed him how he must begin all over again ; and told him of his two plans. In one of the plans, he said he had made this proposal to Croffut. Suppose this failed, did Asaph think that any of the old set would like to enter into carriage-building in the West to the tune of ten or twenty thousand dollars, if he, Jasper, took the enter-prise in charge?

To these letters Jasper was awaiting answers when Oscar came home with his tidings. Oscar and he daily opened the shops. Jasper hired one or two workmen, and mended a smashed buggy when one was brought in, and took care of other job-work. He confirmed Oscar's Manito bargains ; but he made no other con-tracts for stock.

Ferguson's letter had ten times as far to go as Crof-fut's. That was not the reason it came sooner ; but it did come sooner. The reason it came sooner was, that Ferguson, having fifty letters to write every day, wrote them ; while Croffut, having one to write every month, put it off. Ferguson's letter savored of the old times.

NEW YORK, SEPT. 29.

DEAR BOY, — I have your letter ; have read it care-fully, and understand it. The thing seems reasonable. I cannot help you ; but I think I know who can.

Still, it requires lots of talk and arrangement ; and it would be worth everything if you could meet my man. Can you not come on here at once, and see me and him? I say at once, because I sail for Europe on or about the fifteenth in this tangled affair about the hemp invoices. Unless you can come, I do not see how I can do anything.

Come !

As always, yours,

ASAPH FERGUSON.

This looked well. Of course it was not certain. But Jasper told Oscar that he thought he should go. He waited a day or two for Croffut's answer still. If Crof-fut were willing to go on, he had rather have a working partner than a sleeping one ; but, if Croffut were not willing to go on, he should go and see Ferguson. Jasper explained everything to Oscar in all their affairs. It did him good, indeed, to see if his notions on any subject were definite enough to be stated in sentences, with nominative cases, governing verbs, and verbs obeying submissively.

Three days he waited, and no answer came. On the fourth day he went as far as Cleveland, and saw Croffut. Croffut had written his letter that morning, and was going to take it to the post-office as he went home that night. He had written to say that he could not see his way clear to move to Detroit ; and Jasper found that his opinions were definite, and he could not move him.

The same night there arrived at Detroit this letter from Asaph :—

NEW YORK, OCT. 2.

DEAR JASPER, — Come at once, if at all. I sail on the tenth. I have seen the Chinaman, and I think it will go well ; but he wants to see you, and I want you to see him.

In haste, always yours,
ASAPH FERGUSON.

This letter Oscar opened. In those days, however, the telegraph was not working between Detroit and Cleveland ; and Oscar could only hope Jasper would go on.

Jasper did go on ; not as he would have gone now, — leaving Cleveland one day, to be in New York the next, — but by a system which men then thought rapid, but which we think slow and cumbrous, — steamboat here, trains there, no very close connections anywhere. None the less, travelling night and day, did Jasper arrive in New York in time to find that Asaph had left that morning for. Boston. He had left word that Mr. Rising .was to be told that he would be back on the eighth, and could attend to their business before sailing. And so Jasper, at the critical moment of his life, when time

was of the greatest consequence to him, or seemed so
to him, was left to kick his heels, wholly without occupation, and almost without friends, in one of the great
cities of the world. He did find up a few of the old
class; or, rather, he found where their offices were
when the last directory was issued. But they had all
moved since, and no one knew where they had moved
to. He called on Mrs. Van Braam, whom he remembered as Rose Cornell at Cambridge: she was in the
country. He went to the theatre every night, and tried
to be amused. But never did Jasper know as he knew
now that a day is made up of twenty-four hours, and
that each hour is made of sixty very slow minutes.

At last, Asaph Ferguson came home. The hemp
business was involved, — terribly involved. Would
Jasper go to Russia with him? There was quite enough
for both of them to do. Ah me! when Jasper remembered who was in Hamburg, or as near it as Lauenburg,
here was a strain. But he said No. And, in all the
anxiety and worry of the preparations for a departure
which might cover years, Asaph never one moment forgot. He saw the rather sensitive friend whom he had
sounded about the investment in carriage-building. He
went with Jasper to see him by appointment; but, when
they arrived, Mr. Williams was engaged, — was very
much engaged. Would Mr. Rising name a time when
Mr. Williams could see him the next day? Of course
Jasper said one time was like another for him. Mr.
Williams was sensitive, and was particular. He would
not put Mr. Rising to any trouble: he would call on
him at his lodgings. And Jasper, seeing that he was
in earnest in his punctilio, named nine o'clock on the
morning of the tenth as the time when he would receive
him at the hotel.

"That is settled," said Asaph as they left. "He is
fussy; but he likes you: I could see that in a moment.
He will give you the capital. Pay him ten per cent. a
year on it when you are prospered, and tell him the
truth when you are not prospered, and he will ask nothing more. A queer man, but true."

16 .

Still, when nine o'clock approached the next day, Jasper was a little more nervous than he liked to be. Just before nine he went to the office of his hotel to say, that, if Mr. Williams called to see him, he should be found in the smaller sitting-room.

"Yes, sir," said the indifferent potentate, who seemed to have left an old Russian barony that day to amuse himself for half an hour with playing at clerk in an inn.

Jasper was not wholly pleased with the indifference displayed, and loitered a moment. "Mr. Williams is an elderly man, — gray-haired, — not very strong. Let one of the boys show him into the small sitting-room."

"Yes, sir," as before, with such indifference as I believe barons do not show.

And Jasper retired to his small parlor.

Precisely at nine, Mr. Williams's carriage stopped at the hotel entrance; and, with his rather halting step, he came up the hall, his card in hand.

"Will you send this to Mr. Rising of Detroit, — Mr. Jasper Rising?"

The disguised baron looked his unconcealed amazement that any such proposal should be made to him. He turned to an array of strips of paper at his side, and said, "Mr. Rising is not here: he left before light this morning."

"I think you are mistaken," said the courtly invalid. "I have an appointment with Mr. Rising at nine."

"No mistake, sir; no mistake of ours. John, take that basket up to 134. Patrick, say that 77's carriage is waiting. Michael, take these cards to 410."

Mr. Williams waited. "Please send to Mr. Rising's room. I think he is expecting me."

"I tell you Mr. Rising has left the house," said the baron in anger, before which even Mr. Williams did not think it proper to stand. He walked through the reading-room, looked into the larger parlors, did not know of the smaller room where Jasper was sitting nervous, and went back to his carriage, annoyed, and gradually provoked, by the young man's inattention to business.

Jasper waited a full hour. He knew Mr. Williams's health was delicate, and he kept saying to himself that beggars should not be choosers. The last half of this hour he spent in the great hall of the hotel, where, if he had been wise, he would have spent the whole of it. Once and again he asked if no one had inquired for him. But by this time another nobleman was behind the counter, who told him that no one had called. At ten, Jasper left word in writing that he had gone to Mr. Williams's office. Arrived there, he found he had come and gone : in fact, he had gone to the steamship to bid Asaph farewell, — where Jasper did not dare follow him. Jasper rushed back to the hotel. A gentleman had called, and had left no name. " Was he gray-haired and delicate?" No : he had red hair, and weighed three hundred pounds. Jasper again waited till one, not daring to desert his post. He went down again to Mr. Williams's office ; but that gentleman had returned to his country-seat in Jersey, not quite well.

Jasper called at that office for some successive days in vain. Finally he wrote a short note, explaining that he was disappointed in missing any meeting, and asking for another interview. But some cloud had come over the invalid's mind. This was the answer : —

" Mr. Nathan Williams has Mr. Rising's note of the 13th. Mr. Williams will not trouble Mr. Rising farther. He has determined not to make any investments in the West at present."

CHAPTER XXIV.

HOME AGAIN.

BERTHA sailed down the river on the Hamburg packet; and her father tried to quicken her interest in the Tower, the Observatory at Greenwich, the forests of masts, the colliers, the fishermen, and the rest: but poor Bertha, with her best effort, could not pretend to a great deal, and at last persuaded her father to join some German compatriots, who were on the deck, and to let her go below and lie down. Lie down, — that was easy enough. Sleep or forget, — that was impossible. Had she done anything wrong? Had she in any way made this kind, good Dr. Farquhar think she liked him otherwise than as she did? She did like him. She liked him extremely, and his dear, dear mother. Why did not she love him as he loved her, and as he wanted her to love him? Was there one element in any girl's ideal of a man which he did not have, and have in large measure? He was accomplished; he was modest; he was unselfish and brave; he was good; he was kind to his mother; he was religious, she knew that; he was not pretentious; he was eminently entertaining, and made you know your own best qualities; and he was never instructive, never dictatorial, never prosy. Had she ever, when she was a school-girl, dreamed of a more heroic hero, or of an offer of marriage which embodied more which was desirable, or even delightful? And yet, to the very end of her fingers, and in the bottom of her heart, she was sorry that this noble fellow had made to her this offer, and was cross-questioning herself as to whether she had done anything in the matter which she ought not to have done, or whether she had left undone anything that she ought to have done. She had, too, to face the further question, — which the reader has answered for her, perhaps, but which she had not answered for herself. Why did she set aside so summarily this proposal so manly, offering to her a home so attractive? Because she did not love him, — that was plain enough. But how did she know so perfectly well that she did not love him? All he asked for was a chance to make her love him, a chance to show her, man-fashion, what manner of man he was, and whether he were not worth loving. Then, you see, came questions that Bertha did not like to face. And I am not sure that she did face them all. She did not pretend that it was her passion for home that made her renounce London. She knew perfectly well that she liked London better than Boston ; and she knew it was very likely that she would spend years of life away from home : that was her destiny, as it was the destiny of any governess. No : poor, dear child, she would not answer her question to herself ; but, as she lay there in that musty, snuffy berth, the only intervals of quiet thought were those in which there came back old happy pictures, — how Mr. Rising took care of her and her mother in the great basket-stores ; how she waltzed with Mr. Rising in Milwaukie ; how she blessed God for finding a home and a duty for her in the hospital at Detroit ; and of that lovely sail upon the river the last day when she was there. Such pictures came up ; and, for the minute, it rested her to look upon them in the close berth of the fetid state-room. And then she would shudder to recollect that she must not be looking back on such things ; she must think how she would answer Dr. Farquhar's manly letter : and, oh, dear ! she must be facing her perplexities again : in two days more she must be landing their luggage, without any Dr. Farquhar now, and must be taking care of dear, dreamy father ; must be finding her way to Lauenburg as best she might ; and, all the time, he must not know what a weight it was she was carrying at her heart.

Poor Bertha! Is the whole world, then, a stage; and has she nothing to do in it but to be acting a part?

A rough, tumbling passage. Fog and head-winds, — lying to in a gale, because we are afraid to run on in those narrow seas. But the worst comes to an end at last; and Bertha is landed again in her own land: and of all the people in Hamburg there is not one who feels so thoroughly a stranger as does she. Her poor father himself did not feel much more at home. Since she left home, the great fire had ravaged Hamburg terribly; and the rebuilding had changed it in just the regions he knew best. As it happened, also, the particular Friedrichs and Wilhelms whom he meant to see and confer with were out of town, or had moved their habitats, so that he could not easily find them. It mattered the less, because the steamer had landed in the morning; and father and daughter both were determined to go up to Lauenburg without a moment of unnecessary delay in the great city.

Yet here was one of the fancies in the mind of the returned exile which Bertha had to submit to, — not unwillingly indeed. He was most eager to surprise them all in Lauenburg, which was not difficult in fact, as no one knew by what packet they would leave London. To surprise them, of course, he must go up as promptly as he might: it is some ten miles (of ours) from Hamburg to Lauenburg; and every peasant he had recognized in the market that morning would be retailing at night the news that Max Schwarz and his daughter had come home. On the other hand, he could not bear to go home by any way than the way he left home. He had come down the Elbe on one of the Oberlander boats; and he wanted to take Bertha back the same way. No man should say he was purse-proud because he had come home a nabob. He and his had bidden good-by to the little town as they stepped across from the quay into the boat; and there, please God, he would welcome the little town again. Now, an Oberlander boat does not go up the Elbe so swiftly or so easily as she comes down. But Bertha had known, since the voyage from America began, that her father's heart was set on this modest return to his home; and she was well pleased to find that, with a little delay, his wishes could be met: she was more pleased, when, with bag and baggage, they were safely on board the queer craft, and, with a fresh, favorable breeze, were speeding home, — as they began to call it once more, — up the current of the noble river: she was most pleased when they arrived.

Nobody at the landing whom they knew. That was forlorn and queer. They came to the house through streets which were perfectly familiar to Bertha, but which now looked absurdly short and small. At the door of the house, some sort of wandering piper, or neighborhood musician, was whistling away on his rude clarinet: barefoot he stood, with his boots hanging over his back for uses more important than travel in the village-streets. Eager in front of him were a cloud of little folks, some of whom Bertha knew must be cousins, — two little girls hardly big enough to be intrusted with a baby-sister, — and on a bench by the door Bertha's own grandmother, and a little boy resting on her arm, almost as his own puppy was resting on him. In the door-way, and behind the garden-fence, but leaning over it, were the father and mother of the family, — her mother's brother and his wife. All parties were so much amused by the delight with which the three little girls listened to the piper, that no one, not even the children, observed the approach of the American relations.

Bertha's father pushed her forward, loitering just behind in the humor of the occasion. And Bertha, who remembered her grandmother perfectly, touched her slightly, so as to call her attention, and said in English, "I beg your pardon, but can you tell me where Friedrich Baum lives?" She knew that the old lady understood a little English, and was proud to have that recognized. Her grandmother looked up, saw the tall girl clad in her Boston travelling-dress, and shaded with her Boston parasol, but did not miss the resem-

blance to her own Thekla, which always affected Kaufmann Baum. "My God, my Thekla!" she cried at
first in German, and then in English was beginning to
beg pardon, when Uncle Friedrich himself turned
round from the little shop-door, and Bertha's aunt,
who was looking over the garden-fence, — and, of
course, they saw Schwarz himself, just hanging back
though he was. Now, seven years had not changed
him, — no, not by a hair, and I had almost said not by
a rag. He had a gift of consulting old-country tailors,
and Margaret had a gift of making for him old-country
shirts; and the two gifts resulted in his costume being
exactly the same as it was when he left home. Bertha
at nineteen was very different from what she had been
at twelve; but Schwarz was unchanged. With one
loud cry, they welcomed him; and with the same
moment Bertha was in her grandmother's embrace,
and well-nigh smothered by her kisses.

No, I must not stop to tell you, as I fain would, of
that night's jubilations. At another time, perhaps, we
will tell of that, but not now. The trunks came, and
were unpacked. The travel-presents from London and
the travel-presents from Boston were divided. Bertha
had birch-bark canoes and Indian moccasons from Niagara for them, — to encourage their notions that all
America was in the sway of savages. Nor did she tell
them that the moccasons were made by the gross at works
at Patterson in New Jersey. It would be a pity to
break the spell! Maple-sugar she had for the little
ones. Something there was for every one, — the children whom she had never seen, and grandmamma
whom she so well remembered. A jubilant évening,
and they went early to bed; for, as Max Schwarz said,
in the new importance which he tried to assume sometimes, "We have grave business to occupy us to-morrow." Why did Friedrich Baum, and why did the
good grandmother, look a little uneasy when he said so?

To-morrow showed. They had the old-time breakfast, as Max's mother herself would have served it for
his father in the old days, — only the very best china

was on the table, and the tankard which, as Bertha knew very well, only came down on state-occasions. And, when breakfast was finished, Max Schwarz pushed back his chair, and said with that same pretence that he was a man of business, —

"Now for the pastor! I will go first to tell the pastor I am here; and then I will go across to the old home, and see my sister Marie!"

Then, and not till then, did Friedrich Baum gather courage, and explained what had happened only on Sunday. The pastor, when they came to church, had sent word that he wished he, Friedrich, would stay till after the service; and he had staid. Then the pastor had taken him, Friedrich, into the vestry, — as he always did when there was anything about which he wanted to consult him, — and had taken out a letter which had come the night before. It was an East-Indian letter, and had on it the same stamps with the first letter, — the letter that told of Moritz Schwarz's death. And this letter was written by the same lawyer that wrote that letter. And this letter was to say, that, in the week before it was written, there had appeared at Singapore a man named William Schwarz, who said he was son of Moritz Schwarz, and that he had two brothers also, who were Moritz Schwarz's sons. This William Schwarz said, that Moritz Schwarz married at Calcutta, and that he had the marriage certificate; and in fact he produced it. He produced, also, the certificate of his own birth and baptism, and those of his brothers. And the letter ended by saying that his claim to the estate of the late Moritz Schwarz would be properly examined in the court at Singapore, and that the pastor might be assured that justice would be done to all parties. As Messrs. Jellaby & Jellaby had communicated with the pastor before, they had thought it proper to communicate with him again; and they had the honor to be his most obedient and most humble servants. This letter the pastor had translated to Friedrich Baum; and Friedrich's mother had since seen it, and had satisfied herself that the pastor had translated it correctly.

It must be confessed that this news, probable as it was, came at the first on Max Schwarz with an element of relief rather than regret. He knew very well, that as a master of music, occasionally buying or selling a few sheets of printed music, he was filling very decently his place in life. He was by no means certain how decently or how well he should fill the position of the master of six hundred thousand dollars which he had never earned. For Bertha, it must be confessed, that she was still so young, that she, at the first moment, looked simply at the queerness, not to say the absurdity, of the whole position. The solemnity and quaintness of her uncle Friedrich's announcement; the asseveration of her grandmother, that, whatever else was wrong, the English was correctly translated; the fear of her aunt that Max would be terribly overwhelmed, or that Bertha would be terribly disappointed, — all these, joined to the sense that she and her father had both been on a wild-goose chase, and at the end had not even clutched a feather, made Bertha much more disposed to laugh than to cry. After a moment, she looked uneasily at her father; and in the same instant he looked uneasily at her.

" Dear father ! " " Dear Bertha ! " that was all ; and, in true German demonstrative affection, they flung themselves into each other's arms. Then Bertha assured her father that she should not be distressed — no, not the least bit in the world, — if the whole vision of their untold wealth vanished like a dream of the night. And her father called God to witness, most seriously and reverently, that it was only for the children that he cared for it, or thought of it ; that Margaret did not care ; and that surely he did not care. Friedrich Baum could not bear to see a million good thalers so coolly disposed of, as if they had been an old dish-clout. He interrupted the sentiment by his protestations of his convictions that the William Schwarz was a liar and a cheat ; that he was in league with Jellaby & Jellaby ;

and that they were in a league with him : nay, he went
so far as to imply that the English courts were no better than they should be ; and that, not till justice was .
administered in Singapore as it was administered in
the southern provinces of Denmark, or in the free city
of Hamburg, and by the same forms, would he, Friedrich Baum, believe that this William Schwarz was anything but the vilest of impostors. In these views, I
must confess, his mother seconded him, who had lived
long enough in this world to know that ten dollars
would buy more bread and butter than one, and that a
hundred thousand would buy much more than ten.

But they could not, both of them together, move the
even balance of Max's soul. All he would say was,
" We will go to the pastor." And to the pastor he and
Friedrich and Bertha went accordingly. Of course the
pastor had nothing to tell but what he had already
told. Here was the letter from Jellaby & Jellaby.
It seemed, on the one hand, clear enough, that, if they
were believed when they wrote their first letter, there
were just the same reason for believing them when they
wrote their second. In the next place, it was clear
enough, that, if a fortune of six hundred thousand dollars were lying round loose, waiting for a claimant, it
was not unnatural that in all the islands of the East a
claimant should appear. In the third place, it was
known and conceded that the Schwarz who had died
was an " ugly" and cross Schwarz ; that he left home,
almost before any one could recollect, in a fit of anger ;
and that he had never directly communicated with any
of the family. This had been known and conceded all
along. It was therefore clear that he might have had
ten wives, and buried them all, and that information
would not have reached Lauenburg of any one even of
bereavements so distressing. The pastor was sympathetic ; but even a sympathetic pastor cannot, by his
unaided good wishes, kill three nephews on the other
side of the world : far less can he cancel their past existence when they have been in operation twenty years
and more.

Evidently enough there was nothing for it but to wait. The proper affidavits had been sent from London; the proper commissions had been given to trustworthy people in the East. Nothing else could be done, unless, as Friedrich Baum frantically suggested, Max Schwarz himself went out to Singapore to confront the impostor-nephews. This Max pointedly refused to do, as he had refused from the beginning. First, he would not go to the Indies on any account: second, he did not know that these men were impostors. Bertha was perfectly well aware that her father's presence in Singapore would not in the least help the business forward; so she did not favor the plan. Friedrich then hinted pretty broadly that his presence in Singapore, particularly if he appeared suddenly in the office of Jellaby & Jellaby, would confound those conspirators. But nobody seconded the suggestion which he made, implying his readiness to undertake the voyage. The only duty that was clear, was to wait, — communicating, of course, with the counsel in London.

It became, therefore, Bertha's somewhat difficult duty to write a letter to her lover, as soon as she came home that morning, which should say two things, on two very different subjects. First, with all tenderness, she was to tell him why she could not take the priceless gift he offered her. Second, she was to ask him to see the counsel in London, and put in their hands some explanation of the new phase which the Singapore inheritance seemed to have taken. That is to say, her father was urging her to do this, as they walked slowly home; and poor Bertha was so used to doing what everybody else told her to do, or asked her to do, or wanted her to do, that for the moment she supposed that this was really necessary.

But then, she found herself in her little room in the attic, with her portfolio on her knees, as is the custom of her sex. Then she had had one good fit of crying, — yes, and then — let me say it reverently — she put her head on her hand, and waited a minute, listening if the Good Father had anything to say to her; and then, in so many words, she asked Him to help her through. Then she opened her portfolio, and looked on the paper a minute, and wrote this letter, which she then read over, and, without one minute for reconsideration, sent by little Fritz to the little post-office :

LAUENBURG, OCT. 30.

MY DEAR Dr. FARQUHAR, — Ever since I received your note, so kind as it is, I have been distressed with one thought : I have been afraid that I have misled you without once meaning to. But if you knew what a relief your mother's kindness — yes, and yours — to a poor, frightened girl, away from home, was from the beginning, I think I know you would pardon me. Of course I now know that I should have said or done something : I should have been more guarded. I know it now, when it is too late to know it. If I had known it then, I should have spared you great pain, — and myself as much, dear Dr. Farquhar, I do assure you.

But I never dreamed of this. Do me the justice to know that I never dreamed of this. Do not think — no, I know you do not think that I would willingly cause a moment's pain to you who have been so kind and so generous to my dear father.

What you ask for is simply impossible. What distresses me is, that I did not know or see or think in time to save you from the pain of asking. The books say, — those very books that we were talking of so merrily on Thursday, — oh, dear ! it seems a year ago, — the books say, that every woman can put every man on his guard, and save him this suffering. Dear Dr. Farquhar, it is not so. I know you will believe me that I would most gladly save any suffering to you and yours.

When she had come thus far, Bertha drew a black line all across the paper, and went on.

The will-o'-wisp that led us here has gone off to his own bogs again ; and I think he will stay there. I hope my dear father will get off his letters to London to-day to explain to " the counsel " the overthrow of our castle. But I find it impossible to say that I am sorry we came. Dear Dr. Farquhar, I should be false to myself, if, even in this letter, I did not say, that I shall always remember your kindness and your mother's among the choice blessings of my life.

Pray give my love to her, — pray ask her to forgive me ; and believe me

Your grateful friend,

BERTHA SCHWARZ.

Then Bertha went down to her father. He knew she had sent a letter away, and he supposed that all was done which was to be done. And she found him in the back of the little shop rummaging among some old sheet-music, — which was just where he had left it, — and disinterring this sonata and that symphony with the joy of a child let loose upon an old closet of forgotten playthings. Bertha had to recall him to himself and to his dreams of fortune, and to explain to him that he, and not she, must write the fatal letter to the counsel. Alas! I fear that Max would gladly have sold all that birthright for a mess of pottage ; that if Bertha would have let him open his violin case, which had now come up from the pier, and just play for her a few passages which he had hummed to her once and again on their voyage, or just explain to her the true rendering of the Sonata X, or just give her a hint of what Mozart meant in the *adagio* in the Apollo, — if Bertha would have only consented to this, I am afraid that he would have let the counsel go perish, and the inheritance itself sink in the sea. But Bertha was as the nether millstone in her hard-heartedness. She dragged him away from his beloved closet, and dictated long letters to the counsel, and set him to copying Jellaby & Jellaby's new letter ; while she made another copy for the family at home, and, in one word, converted the day to business. Bertha was quite sure that there was nothing else to do but to face the perplexities, and drive this matter through.

Nor is it necessary that this story should linger for

me to describe in much detail the Ups and Downs of the Singapore correspondence. The overland mail from India was not then what it is now; but before long the letters on each side began to be answers of those which had been sent before. The English counsel had correspondents high in office and high in reputation in the East, in whom they had implicit confidence. These correspondents had been early propitiated — so to speak prejudiced, if you please — in the interest of Max as the rightful heir of the Schwarz who was deceased. The London counsel could suggest nothing better than waiting till these very distinguished correspondents could be heard from. They were heard from sooner than could be expected. Even in the East, such a fortune as this of the late Schwarz attracts some attention, when nobody seems to own it, and when it is going a-begging. And the moment they had been retained in the matter, they remembered it daily; and, as soon as the putative William Schwarz appeared, the distinguished correspondents, without waiting special orders, examined his credentials. They examined him before his face, and they examined much more behind his back. They sent to distinguished and very reliable private correspondents of theirs in Sydney and in Melbourne, who would doubtless, by early mails, inform them of the real history of the putative William.

After all this communication there was more waiting. More letters came from Jellaby & Jellaby. Very clearly they were convinced of the genuineness of the putative William, or were retained to say they were. More waiting still; and then began to appear copies of letters from the confidential and highly-trustworthy Australian correspondents of the highly-trustworthy and confidential Indian correspondents of our London counsel: and all these letters seemed to indicate that the three Schwarzes whom William Schwarz represented were genuine Schwarzes, — born in great poverty, and deserted by their father, who was well remembered as an " ugly," cross, sulky, passionate German, who spoke very bad English, and left Australia and these three children twenty-five years ago. Next there began to arrive a wholly independent set of documents from Australia direct to our English counsel. They had written to their own very reliable and confidential friends in those colonies, so soon as Pastor Merck's letter, copied by Max Schwarz, had come to hand. The answers they received direct were therefore wholly independent of those which came from India. Poor Bertha found the tears running from her eyes as she read them. It was the story of a poor German widow — as she thought herself, and was thought — fighting sickness in wretched poverty, as she dragged along a miserable life with these fatherless boys. There were copies of letters from clergymen and churchwardens and charitable ladies, who had befriended her. And at last she had died. And then the boys had been cared for, as often boys are in new communities. They had fought their way along, — a good deal mixed up with horses and stables, — not a bad set, it seemed from the letters, — and as all parties agreed, not men who would willingly press a claim in which they did not themselves believe.

Bertha, by this time, gave up the whole thing as the will-o'-wisp indeed, which at the beginning she had called it. Her father took curiously little interest in these details. Once and again he said that he wanted nothing which belonged to another. Once and again he tried to recollect something pleasant about the brother whose whole behavior seemed to have been so worthless; and once and again he failed. As for the whole community at Lauenburg, which was regularly informed, week by week, of the progress of the nego-tiation, its opinion was distinct, that the East-Indian Schwarz was the most worthless emigrant who ever left that town ; that, if he had children, they were not born in wedlock ; that, if Max and Bertha were cheated out of their inheritance by any who belonged, or affected to belong, to him, this was only the last and lowest of his worthless deeds. In all this criticism, it was steadily forgotten that the million thalers in question was the result, at the least, of his parsimony, if not of his industry, thrift, and enterprise.

And Dr. Farquhar?

No, he did not give it up so.

First of all, he put himself into daily communication with the London counsel, — nay, he had professional friends, and old army friends, and friends in the government in Sydney; and he started an independent series of confidential inquiries among reliable persons about the antipodean Schwarzes. Really, in those days, the origin of the Schwarz family must have been the principal subject of conversation in the best circles of Australia. And every time he heard anything from the counsel, and every time he heard anything from the antipodes, the brave doctor, hoping against hope, made it an excuse for writing to Bertha another letter. Poor Bertha! she answered some of them, and some of them she did not answer. She did the best she knew how to do when every letter came, and bound herself by no unyielding policy.

Here is one of his letters:

Horace Farquhar to Bertha Schwarz.

LONDON, FEB. 11.

DEAR MISS BERTHA, — The Australian steamer is in; and I have letters from Mr. Hutchings, — the Methodist minister of whom I think I wrote you, — and from Col. Clapham, under whose command I served a winter in Toronto. Col. Clapham's letter contains nothing which will interest you, though he promises in his next something decisive. I enclose Mr. Hutchings's letter; he seems to be an honest, well-meaning creature, who has evidently done his best, but as evidently misunderstands the object of my inquiries; for I was at least comparatively indifferent whether this poor Sara Schwarz had experienced religion in his method before her death or no. But I would have given a good deal for any adequate account of her husband's personal appearance, and still more of his origin; and this I do not receive.

17

Believe me, it is to me the greatest pleasure — indeed, Miss Bertha, it is my only pleasure — to collect and forward these scraps for you, — always with the hope that they may in some way be of use to you or to your excellent father. I can understand very well what a wretched business such suspense as yours must be. I wish, with all my heart, that the matter may be decided for you soon, — one way or another. Let it be decided any way you wish, — if only you could be free to care less for odious business-details, and to enjoy your home again.

For me, — I do not ask again for more than you permit; at least, I do not ask it now. You shall not say that you are friendless, even if your friends cannot serve you. Nor must you say that you are left to work out these problems alone, while a dozen of the best men in England are doing their best that you shall have your rights. Believe me, they shall be urged up to this by another, who is not one of the best men in England, but who is, and who will be,

Yours, and only yours,

HORACE FARQUHAR.

"This will never do," said poor Bertha. "Yet what in the world can I do about it?" And then she turned to the other letter which came by the same mail:

Jasper Rising to Bertha Schwarz.

NEW YORK, JAN. 30.

DEAR MISS BERTHA, — You were kind enough to say I might write to you when you left us: and I did write to tell the result of Oscar's quest for Ruth Cottam. Since that time my life has strangely changed; and I venture to write again, that I may tell you that Detroit is no longer my home, and may never be again.

The cholera broke up all business there, — mine, perhaps, most of all. My partners both died, you know: my best workmen were all scattered. I made one and another effort to reëstablish myself: but, both in my search for men and in the other search for money, I was disappointed ; and I could not but doubt whether Providence really meant that I should be a carriage-builder. Circumstances brought me here once, and then again. I believe all rivers, however small, in the end flow into the sea. My prime object in ever going into carriage-building was to make a thorough mechanic of dear Oscar. I found an admirable opening for him here, in one of the best shops in the country ; and, really, because he came, I have come as well. He is at work, and happy. I am waiting for work, and am therefore miserable.

Meanwhile, I hear from your uncle, — on whom I called yesterday,— that there seems to be some cloud over the brilliant prospect which opened before your father when you left us all in the hospital. I need not say how sorry I shall be if he is disappointed ; how wrong it will be if any sharper gets possession of a property which is rightly his. And yet, for some of us, there would be a compensation in any news of which the issue should be your return to America. I hope you have some associations with us more agreeable than a year spent with smugglers, or a month in hospital. And, whenever you do return, I can assure you that there are two old friends who will be ready with the warmest welcome.

For one, I have always wished that the Mr. Schwarz who lived in Singapore had lived a thousand years. I have no association with him, but that he called you away from Detroit, and from your patients. I wish him and his no harm ; but I do not see why, from his spice-islands, he need be interfering with the happiness of me and Oscar.

Whenever you have gone as far as is necessary at the call of his ghost, we hope you will return to America. I say " we " ; for in this wish I am joined by Oscar. I beg you to count me, in any event, as

Yours very truly, — yours always,
JASPER RISING.

I do not myself think that Jasper wrote as good letters as Horace Farquhar ; but I am not sorry that he wrote when he did. Bertha knew enough to read under the seal of that letter. That letter taught her that what she had guessed was true. She knew now that Jasper hated her uncle's fortune, and that it had worked him woe. For her part, Bertha had hated it from the beginning.

CHAPTER XXV.

TEN DAYS LATER.

IT became evident to Jasper Rising that his carriage-building days in Detroit were over. Nay, he was not certain but that his carriage-building days were over. In trying to solve the problem he had in hand, he thought much more of Oscar's position than he thought of his own ; that, indeed, was Jasper's way. From the beginning the carriage-building enterprise had seemed to him to promise well for the boy, and it was clear that the decision had been a good one as far as Oscar was concerned. Now, as we have seen, Jasper had been thwarted at last in every direction in which his good fortune or his enterprise had favored him before. On the other hand, in the city of New York itself, as he went into one and another of the great factories, where he was not displeased to find his name already known, he found two or three admirable openings for carrying further Oscar's education in the line which he had entered upon. Foremen of shops in New York were very glad to engage one such man, ten such men, who meant to earn promotion, and had as good sponsors as Jasper. It was clear enough that New York offered Oscar just now, more than Detroit could offer him. For Jasper himself, Detroit offered nothing. In truth, New York offered little to him. But there was one and another " nibble " in New York which was tempting ; New York is always tempting to young men. One and another of the carriage-builders whom Jasper talked with, were glad, in a vague way, to suggest that there would be some change in their arrangements in which there might be an opening for him. And thus it

happened, to shorten the story of more than one journey back and fourth, of much questioning and cross-
questioning, terrible anxiety and low spirits in proportion, as the autumn and winter drifted by, Jasper sold
all the remaining stock in hand of the late thriving firm
of Buffum, Dundas & Rising; and with Oscar's little
patrimony considerably increased, and his own earnings enlarged in the same proportion, Jasper bade
Detroit good-by, and in early spring came to the great
metropolis, as so many other young men do every day
of every year, to seek his fortune, without full knowledge in what line that fortune was to be found.

All along appeared the magnificent superiority of
Oscar's position. Oscar had the beginning of a handicraft, which is to say, the beginning of independence.
The more delicate the handicraft the more certain the
independence, and Oscar was already no inferior craftsman. To him the large shops, the division of labor,
the thoroughness of work, were all a luxury. The foreman under whom he worked at first, saw the genius of
the boy, and took to him. Who did not take to Oscar?
So this man, Klous, let Oscar have this and that and
another chance to try the different work-rooms in turn,
training himself now on one branch of his duty and now
on the other. He had, therefore, what in mechanic
work is the greatest compensation of all,—he had
variety of occupation. He did not have to do the
same thing for a year of life, which, whether it be in
keeping school, in canning oysters, or in paving streets,
is the only hardship worth complaining of. Oscar
throve with Lowndes & Karrigan, and was only angry
with himself that he was so happy while his poor
master was so ill at ease.

Jasper would not brood. He kept his eyes open,
right and left, and was as willing to take hold of whatever might offer, as he was the day he took to car-
cleaning. But he declared that nobody wanted him to
scrub railway carriages. Meanwhile he ran about a
little. He visited Boston and Cambridge again, for the
first time since he left college. Cambridge was sadly

dull. There was hardly any one who remembered Jasper there. And, instead of being at the top of the walk, — going and coming in the college yard as if no man knew the law of the instrument quite as well as he, — he found himself now almost sneaking along the paths, deprecating the inquiring looks of freshman and sophomore, who, as he met them, seemed to ask themselves, and almost to ask him, why men of his age thought it worth while to continue in this world.

Jasper treated himself to a visit at the house of Mrs. Schwarz, to inquire after Bertha. But the visit was unsatisfactory. Mrs. Schwarz was afraid of him, as she was of most persons in this world. She did not remember much about him, — the experience of her first day at New York had been swept out of her mind by the rapid changes of events since then, — and in the hurry and worry of Bertha's departure for Germany, she had not understood much about Detroit, or the relations of Bertha and Jasper there. Nor, indeed, could she have told much about Bertha's fortunes if she would. The letters only told that they were well, they were very well, but when they would return Mrs. Schwarz did not know. So this was all Master Jasper got for his expedition to Boston. Had he repented that he had not said one word more to Bertha before she left Detroit? Ah! who shall tell what does or does not weave itself in with the hopes and the memories, the fears or the doubts of eager youth, — touched as Jasper had been touched? But if he expected to pick up any stitch which he had dropped in past life, by making this visit to Boston now, he was sadly disappointed. He spoke German much better than he did when he took Mrs. Schwarz and Bertha to the great basket-store. And Mrs. Schwarz spoke English better than she did then. But she did not understand him very well. He did not understand her very well. She was afraid he was an agent of the lost nephews, trying to entrap her simplicity. He did not dare tell her that if the fortune could be blown sky-high by an explosion of saltpetre in Singapore, he should be the happiest of men.

And so, like the Sultan of Serendib, he returned as sad as he came.

Poor Jasper! he had pretended even to himself, that he had gone to Boston and to Cambridge for the sake of seeing how the old places looked, and shaking hands with Kenney and any of the rest of the old set. Transparent delusion! Kenney was in Washington in charge of a patent case. Jasper did not find one of the old set for whom he cared one straw. And the real object of his enterprise, which he had not ventured to confide in form even to himself, was this visit to Mrs. Schwarz, which turned out so wretchedly.

New York is a university in itself, if only man or woman go there resolved to learn, and knowing how to study. If this story were not hurrying to its close, so that every line of it is precious space, I would here and now devote three or four chapters to notes from Jasper's memoirs illustrative of this position. But we must let them go. Perhaps at some time he will himself send them to " OLD AND NEW " : — " Passages from the Diary of a Retired Carriage-Builder." In those days they had no Cooper Institute, and the Astor was in its infancy. But there were the Mercantile and the Society Libraries, and Jasper soon made friends with dear, kind Dr. Cogswell, who gave him the luxury indescribable of ranging through the undigested collections which he had begun in Bond Street. For the rest, a University is not made only or chiefly by its libraries. Jasper was in the churches, in the courts, at the medical college, always tolerant of loafers and visitors. He had friends at the Union Seminary ; he knew all the better men at work on the press, which, for all its boasting of to-day, had quite as competent men engaged in its duties then as it has ever had. Jasper wanted to learn and knew how to study, and so New York was for him a University.

In this university he and Oscar lived, of course, as chums. They had hired two little rooms in the fifth story of a tall warehouse on the Third Avenue. It was then thought to be very far up-town, being in fact between 14th and 20th Streets. The young fellows made their own breakfast; they dined down town almost as frugally as Franklin in his apprenticeship, though Jasper would not live without meat, and could not live without oysters. Still they lived frugally, for all this violation of Franklin's rule ; and every evening they were together, just as in the old happy evenings at Detroit, — Jasper teaching and talking and Oscar listening, each of them relishing the evening, whether it was at home, or whether they were rowing, or whether they were following up one of the clews of acquaintanceship which open in as hospitable a town as New York to two such youngsters ; but always together, and, because they were together, always enjoying life. Of which university life we shall learn the detail when we get the "Diary of a Carriage-Builder."

May opened upon them cheerily. And in May an adventure happened to the two young fellows, where Jasper advanced his fortunes one step, by the inevitable success which waits on doing the duty that comes next one's hand. They had an off day at the carriage-shop, repairs in the engine-room or something, and Jasper and Oscar made a day of it, with young Mr. Karrigan, who was a junior partner in the firm. Karrigan had more than once joined Jasper in a sail in the bay, and on this occasion he asked him to give him his advice about a boat he had a fancy to buy, — the "Meg Merrilies," — which was owned by a friend of his, who was tired of her. Mr. Karrigan himself knew nothing of boating, but thought he should like to own a boat, and that in that case he should learn. Jasper, from the old Duquesne days, and Oscar, from the old blood of the Fiords, were skilled boatmen.

A long, jolly, and adventurous day they had of it, — of which, as before, the "Carriage-Builder's Diary" will give us the detail. Four or five of them in all, — well off soundings, and most of them used to hard work on week-days. But of that day this page tells nothing till its close. Jasper had put down the little "Meg's" helm, very unwillingly, to return to smoke and dust and noise and rush, when, as he threw his eye seaward, he saw that a Liverpool packet, which for half an hour they had been watching, had changed her course, and was on another tack, as if the wind with her had come round so far as to compel her to beat in. Jasper's practised eye caught the change of purpose of her pilot, and he cried to Karrigan, "She will not come up to-night. Let us run down to meet her." And, without waiting to consult, he went about again and ran down to the stranger. Nobody asked him why; nobody cared; they were young and they were happy, and no one wanted to go home. The "Meg Merrilies" ran off smartly before the wind, and in a very few minutes she swept up under the stranger's quarter.

"Do you go up to-night?" cried Jasper to the mate of the vessel, whom he saw standing on the rail with his hand on the shrouds. And the mate answered sharply, "Not to-night, with this wind. Will you give us a tow?" And they all laughed.

The "Meg" was falling aft, as the "Clyde" pushed slowly forward, and Jasper hailed again. "How many days' passage?"

"Twenty-four from the light," cried the mate; but he did not ask the news, for he had a pilot already.

"Twenty-four days!" said Jasper, surprised. "Heave us some papers, then! We are from the 'Journal of Commerce.'"

But the mate, sick of the conference, put his thumb to his nose, as if to indicate that our young friends did not look like newsmen, and walked indifferently away. The "Clyde" still forged forward, the "Meg Merrilies" drifted aft still, and the interview would have ended, but that a lady who had watched it all from the upper deck, ran into the saloon, was out in a moment, ran aft on the deck, — and, to the astonishment of the young men, cried, —

"Mr. Rising, Mr. Rising, here!" And with a firm hand, she threw — one, two, three, folded newspapers down. Karrigan caught one, one fell on the ballast, the third fell in the water. Oscar, all in the spirit of the adventure, went in after it, and, in a moment more, had it in his hand, and, all screaming with laughter, they hauled him in over the " Meg's " stern. The " Clyde " still worked on her way, the " Meg's " sails took the breeze again, and they were parted. Jasper waved his hand to his unknown friend, but the sun was against him, and he could not see her face. He had his papers, and he held to the purpose with which he asked for them.

To do justice to the mate of the " Clyde," if he had known, what he learned five minutes after, that the " Great Western," the steamer which in those days brought the English news to America on nearly every voyage she made, had not arrived, having had probably to put back by some accident, he would not have been quite so testy about papers. Jasper knew — as every other man in the city, who kept any run of affairs, knew — that New York was again thirty days behind the news of Liverpool, just as if they had been living in ante-steamer days. It was just a recollection of this which had made him bear down on the " Clyde," and, when he found how short her passage had been, ask the officer for papers.

The moment he knew that the " Clyde " had news only twenty-four days old, Jasper asked for papers. And his unknown friend had answered that wish, so that now he had only to beat the " Clyde," and he could relieve the news-famished city. The " Clyde " soon proved no rival to the " Meg," however. Each kept on her course, the " Meg," as it happened, saving all the breeze there was, and the " Clyde " creeping out of it. Before an hour, the " Clyde " was becalmed in a fog in the lower harbor, and Jasper and the " Meg " were at Staten Island.

They dried Oscar's well-earned " Times " carefully on the little quarter of the " Meg Merrilies." It proved that their prizes were the " Liverpool Mercury " of April 29th, the "London Times" of the 28th, and a " Hamburger Correspondent " of the 26th. They could not have asked for better pickings. Now, if no " Her-

ald." boat or " Courier" boat ran against the " Clyde"
in her fog-bank, the " Journal of Commerce" should
electrify the world next day.

Jasper risked nothing. He left Oscar and the others
to bring up the " Meg " from Staten Island. He took
the 9 o'clock ferry-boat himself, and came up to the city
in her. He ran up to the editor's room of the " Journal," produced his prizes, and was received with all the
honors.

" It is like the old days," said the young man in
charge. " We have not run in news in this fashion
since the year one. Have you looked at the papers,
Mr. Rising? What is there?"

And while Jasper told in brief what Lord Melbourne
had said, and what the Chartists were doing, the head
of the composing-room had come down in answer to
Mr. Hale's message. " We have ten days later news,
exclusive, Mr. Faust. See that no boy, no cat, and no
dog leaves the office before the mail edition is in the
bags. We shall need five full columns. It is like old
times, Mr. Faust."

Mr. Faust smiled intelligently, and expressed his satisfaction. And, though many men and boys came into
the " Journal " office that night, no one of them was
permitted to come near the compositor's room or the
press-room, unless to stay till daylight in those sacred
precincts. These three precious papers were the only
papers of like purport on this continent. And what
there was in them, down to trials before magistrates in
London, appeared before an admiring world in the
" Journal of Commerce" of the next morning.

" Ten days later from England."

" Consols fall one-half per cent!"

" Change of Ministry in France."

And every man connected with the press the next
morning was gossiping about the stroke of divination
by which the " Journal " had triumphed, and " No other
paper had the news."

Jasper found Oscar in bed as he went home after two
o'clock in the morning, after his first night's observation

of editorial duty. The boy waked and rubbed himself, welcomed his master cordially, and sprang out of bed. "Mr. Jasper," said he, "did you see her? Do you know who the lady was?"

"Not I," said Jasper.

"I thought you not know," said Oscar, who, when he was excited, sometimes lost his grammar. "Still, I thought you not know her. Why, Mr. Jasper, she was Miss Bertha! I saw her as I see you. I saw her before she run get the paper. I saw her when she jump on seat and throw paper over. Yes, Mr. Jasper, it was Miss Bertha."

It was Bertha! And he had been fool enough to be watching the mate all the time! Bertha, of course! That was the reason they had this Hamburg newspaper. Bertha on board the "Clyde"! How could he have failed to know her voice? "Mr. Rising! Mr. Rising!" Well, there was one comfort! The "Clyde" could not get up in the fog till to-morrow!

No indeed! And at five the next morning, Mr. Jasper Rising was on the alert. Oscar, to his great grief, could not join him, but none the less did Oscar send the heartiest, I might almost say the tenderest, messages to Miss Bertha. Jasper was at the Battery before six, — he had found his boat and his boatmen, — and in an hour or so more, he had found the "Clyde," and was on board.

His first interview was with Bertha's father, the one member of the family whom he had never seen. Jasper found it difficult to explain who he was to poor Mr. Schwarz, nor indeed was it very necessary that he should explain very minutely. Enough to say that he was a friend of his daughter's, and had come to welcome them, and to render any help he could in their landing. Bertha was engaged, for the moment, in the last cares of state-room life, and her father did not so much as go to call her. Jasper had to nurse his impatience as he could, by entertaining Mr. Schwarz with accounts of his visit to Boston, on which he looked back with more satisfaction than he had done only yes-

terday. It enabled him to give to poor homesick Mr.
Schwarz the very latest advices from his wife and his
children. Poor Max Schwarz! He did not ask many
questions about human life, but he did permit himself
to wonder why this Mr. Jasper Rising took so much interest in him and his family. The last person they
saw in the Mersey was Dr. Horace Farquhar, to whom
it had been impossible to say "No" to, but he would
come down the river in the tug and say the last good-
byes. And now in America, the first person he meets
is not Kaufmann Baum, as he supposed it might be,
but a young man who seems to know his wife and
children as intimate friends, of whom poor dazed Max
Schwarz does not remember to have heard a word.

But Jasper could not talk forever of Mrs. Schwarz,
and the interview began to drag, when, from the companion door, emerged Bertha, — not for an instant sus-
pecting whom she was to see. Dear Bertha! Yes!
there is no doubt of it for an instant, — her flush and
her look are of undisguisable pleasure. With perfect
frankness she approached Jasper, and gave him both
hands, and told him how glad she was to see him, while
he was stumbling over his own satisfaction at her
return. "I knew it was you, though I did not recognize Oscar till he went into the water — so like himself.
And how is he? I have thought of him so often, and
told my little German cousins so many stories about
him, and Detroit, and everything in America."

The sentence dragged a little perhaps, for now was
coming in the natural shyness, and the suspicion that
she might have been talking too fast took its turn.
And Jasper took the chance to tell her of the wonder
she had wrought by her happy toss of the papers. He
made her laugh very thoroughly as he described the
news-boys' salutations as he came down Broadway.
Little they thought, he said, who was the heroine of the
occasion! And then he abused his own stupidity that
he had not recognized her at once, and confessed to her
that it was to Oscar that he owed the pleasure of this
interview. Here Mr. Schwarz got in a word edgewise,

and reminded Jasper that Bertha would be glad to hear
something of her mother. And again the fortunate fellow began on that tale, and again nursed to the very
utmost every bit of family information he had extorted
from Mrs. Schwarz, and concealed the inexplicable reticency in which she had seemed so unwilling to tell him
more. Yes, Jasper made out a good deal of news for
people who had had none for six weeks. He could tell
of Kaufmann Baum and of Aunt Mary. He had been
out to visit them not long before. And what perhaps
pleased him most was that Bertha was evidently so glad
to hear of Oscar's fortunes in New York. Yes! and
Jasper thought she listened with a real sympathy, — he
knew she did, poor fellow, as he told her of the re-
verses of his fortunes.

Tell me, Jasper, why do you talk to the heiress so
bravely and so intimately now, when not a year ago
you failed to tell her that she was queen of your life,
simply because she was rich and you were poor?

Ah! Jasper cannot tell us, excepting this, that he
knows now what a fool he was then. And he will
never again let the highest pile of counters in the world
keep him from the woman who holds in her hand the
thread of his destiny, — the woman who would be the
same to him if she and hers were beggars. Would he
not be proud and glad to fold in his arms and to shelter her from every storm, and watch over and care for
as if she were a princess, even if they all stood before
him houseless and penniless? Jasper has learned wisdom now, and he will not make that blunder again!

And so the "Clyde" works her way up the bay.
Yes, Jasper is of use as the customs men appear, and
when at last the landing is made, Kaufmann Baum fortunately is not here, as how should he be? Bertha's
letters, naming the ship in which they sail, are in the
"Great Western," and she, as we know, has been
driven back to Bristol. No, it is for Jasper, lucky boy,
to see the luggage divided, — some sent to the Norwich boat, and some to the American House, where he
has elected to take them. It is for Jasper to worry

through the inspection, and finally to bring them to the hotel. Then it is Jasper who brings Kaufmann Baum, wondering and apologetic, to meet them, — "So sorry to have missed them. No idea they were on the 'Clyde.' Busiest day in the year, and had not seen any one." And Kaufmann Baum, in the presence of a stranger, will not ask anything about the last turns of the Singapore correspondence.

But Max Schwarz himself, simple as childhood, has no objection to publishing the whole story of his inheritance in the "Correspondent" or the "Allgemeine Zeitung." The first moment the voluble and apologetic Kaufmann will give him, he blurts right out in German with the whole truth.

"Think only, my Kaufmann, that our bachelor brother should have married in Sydney and have three boys, who are now men, to him so fortunately and so silently born. To think, Kaufmann, that we should for no purpose the two oceans have crossed over, and that we should your thousand dollars at the same time especially to no purpose moreover have expended. But, Kaufmann, there is no little part of the thousand dollars yet to your account remaining, and if we prosper — as we shall — it can and shall moreover especially in the speedy future be, part by part, to you repaid."

Kaufmann tried in vain to stop him, especially when the thousand dollars were alluded to. Jasper saw that Kaufmann was troubled by his presence, and walked to the bell-rope and pulled it, and then looked anxiously out of the window. All the same did he find it impossible not to take in every word of Schwarz's harangue. What exquisite pleasure did every word of it give the poor fellow! What more could to-day offer him? To find what he had not dared hope, — that Bertha was — what she had always been!

The waiter answered the bell, — and in a great fuss Jasper made about ice-water and biscuits and Neuchatel cheese, in asking Baum's advice about the cheese, and making Schwarz laugh at the waiter's ignorance, — Jasper succeeded in carrying out the wish of Bertha's uncle, and shutting off revelations which he found injudicious. Then Mr. Baum hurried himself off, to see if it were not possible to bring Aunt Mary over to see them before the Boston boat left, and Jasper was left with them alone again.

But of course he could not stay forever! How he wished he could! But he had finished off every excuse. He had told everything he had to tell. The boldest imagination could not pretend that Bertha wanted to walk in Broadway. On the other hand, the boldest lover could hardly offer his hand and fortune to Bertha in the ladies' parlor of the American House, in presence of her father. Sir Charles Grandison did such things on his knees, in the presence of twenty people, — but Young America is too bashful. So, having given every order that could be thought of for the comfort of his charge, Jasper dragged himself away, only promising to call again in the afternoon to go with them to the boat for Norwich. He remembered the good luck which the Norwich line had brought him.

He was no more certain of his future than he was the morning when he waked in Detroit, determined to offer to Bertha everything a man can offer. Nay, he was not so certain. Then he could offer her a home, he was in an established position, with a small income reasonably certain, or he thought he was. Now he was nowhere, and had nothing to offer, but hope which was eternal, and himself. But Jasper knew, at heart, that this was something to offer.

> " Perhaps then first he understood
> *Himself*, how wondrously endued."

He walked on air, as he went down Broadway. Where could he kill what was left of the day, till it would do to call again with escort for the boat. Or would he not perhaps go to Boston with them?

He went first to the office of the " Journal of Commerce" to congratulate on the " 'Ten Days Later from England.''

18

"Can you wait a minute, Mr. Rising?"

Wait, certainly he could. All poor Mr. Rising had to do just then was to "occupy the time," and it was a comfort to know that that was what any one else wanted him to do.

"Our Mr. Macomber wanted to see you, if you came in."

So Jasper waited. He asked for what was left of the Hamburg "Correspondent," and amused himself with its queer advertisements. He read through a prospectus of the Missouri Iron Mountain Railroad, and wondered whether in that direction might not be the opening for his destiny. He waited and wondered, and was just leaving, lest he should seem perfectly worthless to all the gentlemen in the office, when Mr. Macomber appeared.

Mr. Macomber took him into his private room, and showed him some correspondence which he had had with some gentlemen in New Altona, who were interested in the "Gazette," a newspaper published there. The old editor had just now gone into a coal speculation in Western Virginia, and the paper was publishing itself, as newspapers sometimes will when they have been running for some years. But the proprietors needed better charge of it than this, and they had sent to Mr. Macomber to ask him if they could not find him some man of some newspaper experience, who would take hold and edit their paper for them. "Some one who has some snap to him and some sense, if such a man can be found." This was the order. How often, alas, is that order vainly given! But it had seemed to Mr. Macomber, the night before, as Jasper Rising sat translating German, that he would "fill the order." And he had asked Jasper to wait, that he might ask him if he would like the position.

"I know nothing of printing, practically," said Jasper, a good deal amazed.

"I do not see that that is necessary. They have a very good foreman there. I sent him myself, from our own office, a man named Schaffer."

"I have never been regularly connected with any journal," said Jasper, regretting for the first time that he had declined to be one of seventeen editors of "Harvardiana."

"I do not see that that is of any consequence," said Mr. Macomber, who liked his man, and was determined to serve one who had served him.

"Take time to think of it, Mr. Rising. They offer fifteen hundred dollars a year, and a quarter of the profits. If you like the place, you will own the New Altona 'Gazette' before you are five years older. Good-morning, Mr. Rising. John, tell Mr. Flanders, the roller-man, I can see him now."

And Jasper retired, wondering yet once more to see the springs which move the world. Bertha Schwarz had given to him the place to stand in which now he would offer to her!

No! Jasper. It is not Bertha who gives it to you. It is "Jasper" who gives it to "Mr. Rising." The man who always does the duty that comes next his hand, finds that the world needs his help as much as he needs to help the world.

CHAPTER XXVI.

THE HEROINES OF SCOTLAND.

IT was the end of a sultry, muggy day in June. The general work of the shop was done ; and the greater body of the hands had gone home rejoicing in the length of the day after work was done. But Oscar, who was at this time compassing the mysteries of the paint-shop, had a particular matter on hand which had been intrusted to him ; and he staid long after the others, smoothing with pumice-stone the last coat of paint which had been laid on preparatory to the final coat of varnish, which was to be so perfect, that it might serve for the mirror of the bride for whom the carriage was ordered. Hot with the exercise involved in the pumice-work, stripped to his shirt, and with his face streaked in dark brown lines by the dust of the dry paint which he had been rubbing down, Oscar ran down to the counting-room to be sure to catch Mr. Lowndes before he left to go up town.

He was but just in time. Mr. Lowndes was standing with his hat on, and his hand on the little bar which separated the office from the rest of a long ware-room. His manner was the determined manner of a tired man resolved to be civil, though at heart he is desperately cross. Oscar saw that he was speaking to a woman, and stepped back himself, that he might not appear to interrupt the interview. Women were not frequent visitors in the carriage-shop. He did not attend, therefore (he tried not to attend) ; and he did not catch the last words which Mr. Lowndes addressed to the stranger.

"It is impossible for me to subscribe," that gentleman said : " that is the reason why I will not take your time by looking at the book. I know I shall not subscribe : you would know it too, if you knew how many portfolios and how many books have been brought here this week by agents, There was no kindness, madam, in the man who set you on this duty."

" I found that out long ago," said the young woman whom he addressed. " But I have begun, and I must go through. Good-evening, sir." And her voice broke a little as she said " good-evening," and turned away.

Oscar had stepped back upon the stairway ; and at this instant he returned, — just in time to catch the words, " Good-evening, sir," and to note this breaking of the voice. The poor girl was ready to cry.

Mr. Lowndes did not notice it, and turned away, almost impatiently, to the window, that she might go, and that he might be done with her. She crossed the shop to go out by the outer door, which was opposite Oscar's ; mistook the door, though it stood open ; and passed instead into a passage which went across to the leather-room.

Oscar sprang forward. " You have missed the way, madam." She half turned to thank him. But by this time the poor girl's face was covered with tears, which she did not wish to show, so that she only half turned, and almost awkwardly slid into the doorway which he indicated. This time, however, there was something in her movements which attracted Oscar's attention. He sprang forward himself, so as to see her face fully as she turned to go down the stairs.

There was no mistake. The crying girl was Ruth Cottam !

" Miss Ruth, Miss Ruth ! is it you?" he cried ; and he sprang across the entry-way to detain her, and all but offered her his chocolate-colored hand.

Ruth turned, amazed, as well she might. If her tears had not blinded her, she might well be excused, that in that face — grimy with the sweat of Oscar's brow, for the last six hours ground in with fine powder of vandyke brown reduced by pumice to impalpable dust — she did not recognize the speaker. The moisture of his eyes had left two circles perfectly white in the muddy mixture. For the rest, in the several wrinkles or dimples caused by the play of muscles, the coloring-matter had hardened somewhat, and was darkest. Between these two extremes the young man's face wore every shade of brown, from a dark yellow, through chocolate, into what seemed black. His hair was mostly hidden by a square paper cap, once of the color of brown paper, now of such various tints as the exigencies of carriage-painting, or the whims of fellow-workmen in their leisure hours, had contributed. A shirt, once of blue linen stripe, now bore colors more various and more festive than Joseph's; and a like effect, suggestive of a kaleidoscope, had been wrought in upon the overall hempen pantaloons which he wore. Ruth did not recognize Oscar; and no wonder. So far as personal aspect went, there was little to remind her of the companion of the happy October day, when together he and she went from point to point on the Little Manito, pricing lumber, and talking wood-craft. But, be he who he might, he knew her name was Ruth; and it was a long, long time since any one had called her by that name. Certainly Oscar never had; only, poor boy, he had thought that name, and written that name, many, many times as the winter had gone by. He had read it in his Bible till he could repeat the pretty pastoral there; and it was far more natural to him in this unexpected exigency to cry out "Miss Ruth," than it would be "Miss Cottam." All the more quickly, of course, Ruth turned, and with all the more surprise.

"You do not know me; you do not remember me. I am"—

"Yes," said Ruth, smiling this time, even though her cheeks were wet with those tell-tale tears, "I do know you: I know your voice. I did not know you till you spoke."

"I am so glad to see you!" said Oscar, saying first what he thought deepest, and not hinting at his surprise. "Could you wait one minute at the foot of the stairs, till I can do my errand with Mr. Lowndes?" And Ruth said she would wait. And she waited.

The errand was only to tell Mr. Lowndes on what day he might be sure that the new phaeton should be finished which Mr. Hilliard was to give to Miss Clarissa Folger for a wedding present. Oscar had satisfied himself on this point; and on this point he reported. Mr. Lowndes thanked him, — thanked him for staying, to be sure, and to tell him; and then said kindly, "Now go home, my boy; never let me hear of you as in the shop till midnight again;" and they both laughed, for Oscar knew what he meant. Oscar said he would lock the outer doors; and Mr. Lowndes went down, brushing by Ruth Cottam quite unconsciously as she stood waiting in the doorway.

Oscar followed close upon him. "Wait a few minutes more, Miss Ruth, pray do, till I can be fit to walk with you; and then I will go with you wherever you will go."

And Ruth said he should find her on the sidewalk; and he, poor fellow, rushed back to his ablutions and his toilet. There was every temptation to make them short; there was every temptation to make them careful. One must not keep Ruth waiting; one must not join her, looking as if he were Red Jacket or Black Hog. Oscar did his quickest and his best together, thinking all the time of the words that he had just spoken, and remembering, "Where thou goest, I will go; where thou stayest, I will stay." Would Ruth ever say to him what he had just now said so gladly to her? Dear Oscar! And yet he had never seen Ruth Cottam but in that visit of twenty-four hours on her island. Did Ferdinand see Miranda longer upon hers? And Oscar had twice written to Ruth, and had had two short little answers from her, which, as he ran down the stairway, lay against his heart in a choice letter-case he had bought for them. "Where thou goest, Ruth, I will go; where thou stayest, I will stay." Only this he did not dare to say aloud. He locked the outer door: he looked

up the street, down the street; there was Ruth Cottam
walking slowly, and waiting as she had promised him.
She came up to him gladly, and took frankly and without reserve the hand which he offered to her.

"I must beg your pardon," stammered Oscar, who
was fairly out of breath, "for asking you so coolly to
wait in the street for me. But it was such a surprise
to see you, and such a pleasure!" he added very shyly.

"You are very kind, Mr. Esmark," said Ruth. "I
was very glad to see — any friend," she said after a moment; "and I am sure I may call you a friend. Indeed, Mr. Esmark," she said, with a moment's hesitation
again, "I need some one's advice sadly; and to see any
one I had ever seen before, in this terrible loneliness,
which makes me shudder now, — that is of itself a
pleasure." Poor Ruth's voice faltered again; and she
almost broke down.

"Do not try to talk if you are tired," said Oscar
shyly again; only anxious to relieve trouble which he
only partly understood. "Do not try to walk if you
are tired. Shall I not stop a stage? Where are you
going?"

"I am going — or I suppose I am going — to this
place," said Ruth, taking from the book in her hand a
soiled and broken printed card, which showed that Mrs.
Sproul kept a "fashionable boarding-house" in Varick
Street. "I am going there, unless I can find some
place which I like better;" and the poor child looked
up jealously toward the sun, to see how much of daylight was left to her tired feet before she must give up
the wretched liberty she had enjoyed since she left Mrs.
Sproul's fashionable boarding-house that morning.

Again Oscar saw that he had said the wrong thing;
that is, that he had given pain where he had not meant
to. But Oscar was no fool, by which I mean he let his
instincts guide him when his judgment was at fault for
want of information; and he said boldly:

"You are in trouble, Miss Ruth. Have you no
friends here? How long are you here? I wish you
would let me help you if I can." He was almost

tempted to say, "advise you." And how he wished
that his "master" was not at New Altona. For, for ten
days past, Jasper had been pressing his arrangements
for carrying forward " The Gazette."

" I am in trouble, Mr. Esmark; and as for friends,
you are the only friend I have this side of Cold Water.
I have made a mistake in coming here; and the best
thing I can do now is to go away. But I cannot do that,
so far as I can see, till, till — I can sell some copies
of this picture-book." And she looked with an air of
utter contempt on the portfolio which she carried, in
which were her specimens of

"THE HEROINES OF SCOTLAND,"

A SERIES OF

EXQUISITE LINE ENGRAVINGS,

BY

THE FIRST MASTERS.

To be published by subscription only.

NEW YORK: SCHMIDT AND PUSGRABER.

" Why what are you doing, Miss Ruth? Are you
selling books on subscription? "

Then Ruth explained to him at some length, as was
necessary if she explained at all, that, at the end of
the winter term, she had determined that she would
come to the East to some good school, and spend six
solid months in study before she undertook to teach
again. Her uncle had brought her in his schooner to
Detroit; and, with such economy as she found possible,
she had wrought her way to Albany, having been attracted by a lying advertisement, which by ill luck she
had seen in a stray number of " The Ladies' Monitor,"
which offered all the advantages of all universities, at
the flourishing collegiate Institute at Bellmont, in the
beautiful village of Stitchkill, on the North River. Ladies could be received at any time, could study anything; and the charges would be only a hundred and
eighty dollars a year, of which a considerable part

could be earned by the students in various handiworks
of pencil, needle, and pen ; which handiworks were to
be taught to them and explained at length when they
arrived. Poor Ruth must be pardoned. There was
nobody in the Great or Little Manito who knew any
better than she. She believed it because it was printed
in " The Ladies' Monitor," and from her hard-earned
wages she had spent near twenty dollars before she
arrived at the landing at Stitchkill. An unpromising
place was Stichkill. But a little inquiry satisfied her
that an unpromising place might stand one step higher
than a promising place like Bellmont ; for the promises
of Bellmont had been scattered on the forty-eight winds
of heaven. The institute had been sold by the sheriff
three months before. Ruth told this story in brief to
Oscar, as they walked, and more briefly told how she
had then gone, first to Albany, next to Hudson, next
to Nyack, and, last of all, had come to New York, still
thinking that there must be somewhere some academy
for young ladies, where her waning purse might provide
for her at least a half-year's schooling, and still disappointed.

"Mr. Esmark, you have no idea how fast money
goes when you are frightened, — how frightfully fast it
goes ! Every porter, every cabman, every hotel-keeper,
has seemed to me to take more from me than the one
before." Ruth had written to her uncle : she would
have been wiser to go to him. But she could not believe,
now she was here, that it was not best for her to stay
here : and that mistake, for it was a mistake, had led
to her last mistake of all, — to her selling herself as an
agent for the circulation of " The Heroines of Scotland."

She had found her way to Mrs. Sproul's by means of
an advertisement, and to Schmidt and Pusgrabber's by
means of another. These persons — Hebrew by blood,
countenance, action, and speech, according to Ruth's
description — were established in Nassau Street. They
had cross-examined her very sharply, because, they said,
it was necessary to employ only ladies of the first re-

spectability ; and, having found out her little history, they had extorted from her all the rest of her money, except four or five dollars, as a deposit ; which, they said, was invariably paid by agents who could not give a good city reference, as security for cost of outfit and honesty in accounting. And then, providing her with the usual " outfit," they had sent the delicate, innocent girl out into the streets of the worst city in America, on the most forlorn business of the age, and in the very worst place for succeeding in it. It is no wonder she had not obtained a single subscriber ; the only wonder is, that even her steady courage had not failed her in an hour, instead of carrying her through that whole inexpressible day of impertinences and disappointments.

Ruth Cottam was not in the habit of throwing herself upon the help of others. She had paddled her own canoe too long, and in waters too rapid, to shrink from the responsibility of her own blunders. But after a wearing and disappointing day in early June, when she had hardly heard a voice all day but her own as she pointed out the beauties of the " Heroines of Scotland," and the replies, now harsh, and now gentle, of those with whom she dealt, there was no wonder if Ruth Cottam did feel a sensation of exquisite relief to find herself side by side with some person who had seen her before, and knew something about her. If she were run over by an omnibus now, there would at least be some one to write West to her uncle, and tell him that she was dead. Such was the cheerful reflection Ruth made as Oscar carefully piloted her across a street, and she felt the contrast between his protection and the necessity of running the gauntlet alone, as she had done so often. Then Oscar was so wildly sympathetic ! His English was not sufficient for his wrath, when, in their talk, the sins or the peccadilloes of one or another innkeeper or school-keeper came forward in Ruth's story. Here was some one who did not think she was a fool, who did not wonder even as much as she did herself, now she had learned ten days' worth of the craft and subtlety of the world. Nay, it was not a little thing that Oscar insisted on taking the dead weight of "The Heroines of Scotland." After a little demur, Ruth permitted him ; and the relief from that drag was beyond account. When he joined her in the street, Ruth had hardly dried her tears from her last disappointment. As she told, briefly as might be, her little story, the tears, to her rage, would break forth again and again. But the young fellow had the very instinct of tenderness ; and it gave him tact which a diplomatist might have been proud of. Without knowing that he soothed her, he soothed her ; and she, without knowing that she was soothed, was soothed. Before they had walked ten squares, Ruth was laughing ; before they had walked twenty, she felt herself really rested ; and, when they arrived at the unsatisfactory boarding-house, she was fairly cheerful, brave, and strong again, — strong enough to be provoked with herself that she had broken down before.

Ruth had dropped a word intimating that she was dissatisfied with her quarters ; and Oscar had turned over, as they walked, the somewhat difficult question whether he should advise her about changing them. Failing any solution of this question, he said nothing till they approached the steps of the house, and could see that some of the " boarders " had already gathered on a modified stoop there. Then he had to speak, and spoke from impulse. " You spoke as if you disliked this place, Miss Ruth. I know the city better than you. Let me help you find a better place to-night or to-morrow ? "

But Ruth was all right again now, and brave enough to meet forty old harridans, though they were assembled in convention to overwhelm her. " To-morrow, perhaps, Mr. Esmark, I may trouble you, if there is any moment when I can see you ; but to-night I am too glad to go to bed to think of moving." Brave Ruth ! as if she knew how she was going to settle her little account with Mrs. Sproul in the morning. Oscar was eager to say that he would meet her at any time she would appoint ; and, to arrange this, passed up the steps with her, and threaded the jungle of impertinent starers

of both sexes who crowded the somewhat narrow way,
and, as Oscar thought, were none too ready to make
room. He repressed the natural desire to engage them
all, to strike their heads stoutly against each other,
and to leave them on the ground even more senseless
than they were. But to do this, might, on the whole,
embarrass Ruth more than it would help her; and
Oscar followed her, as peacefully as Una's lion would
have done, to the soup-and-onion-scented dining-room
of the hostelry, which proved to be also its reception-
hall.

"I will call in the morning, at any time you name;
and then I can introduce you to some ladies, who are
friends of mine, who can advise you about your home.
Or, as I said, we have still a long evening before us, if
you had rather go now."

Oh, no! Ruth only wanted rest now. And Ruth,
who had grown up among people who were not ashamed
of work, knew very well that Oscar Esmark ought not
to be making calls on ladies on the morning of Wednesday. She said, if he would cross over at noon from
his shop to the little book-shop she had noticed on the
corner, she would be glad then, perhaps, to advise with
him; or she would tell him if she needed any advice.

Oscar hated to go away. But there must be a last
moment. "Before I go, there is one thing more," he
said.

"And pray what is that?" said Ruth, who did not
quite make out a sort of nervous eagerness in which
Oscar was talking.

"You ought to guess," he said. "For a bookseller's
agent, you show great indifference to your business.

"Mr. Jasper Rising is very desirous to take early
impressions of 'The Heroines of Scotland,' on large
paper; and he wishes you to take his subscription for
the whole series.

"The Young Men's Christian Union wants to take
one set of the small-paper size; and Mr. Esmark, a
friend of yours, wants a set in large paper also. I will

take the copies of numbers one and two myself: I see you have them here."

" Mr. Esmark, what nonsense! You shall do no such thing," cried Ruth.

Oscar looked up with the gravity of a Norwegian bishop, affecting not to understand her. In his own language he spoke ten or twelve words, which, of course, she did not understand, as if they were entire strangers. Then he selected, with care, two large-paper sets, now pretending to set aside one or two copies as damaged. Then he picked out with equal care another set. Ruth, half amused and half provoked, continued her protest till she saw Mrs. Sproul had made a pretence to come into the room. Oscar saw this too, with the back of his head. That boy saw everything.

" I shall pay you, ma'amselle — how you call him? — I shall you make recompense en avance pour tous les series, — for all the series, ma'amselle. Pardonnez moi. Twelve dollars for the small book, je crois, I believe, ma'amselle, fifteen and fifteen for the two large book. It is, je crois, ma'amselle, forty-two dollar in all. Le voila, ma'amselle." And he forced forty-two dollars on the unwilling girl, who was not quick enough to see why this French jabber had come in. But in an instant she caught his drift, when he said very slowly, in an undertone, " Prenez, prenez, mademoiselle, la vieille chatte voit tout." And Ruth counted the money slowly, and gave him three receipts, with the precision and business of a veteran. She bade him good-evening with just the formality which her position as a book-vender, and his as a subscriber, demanded. And he carefully rolled up " The Heroines of Scotland " as if it were the most precious purchase of many years, as indeed to Oscar it was. And so they parted.

It was a valuable study to see the courtesy of Mrs. Sproul to the young lady, who had, at least, forty-two dollars in her pocket ; albeit, when she came into the room, her intention had been to warn this young woman to vacate her attic.

" Hare you not very tired, Miss Cottam? The day

is so 'ot! No, do not go up stairs till hi 'ave 'ad
ha nice dish of tea brought 'ere. Meg his bringing hit;
but these Hirish hare so slow!"

Ruth was amazed at the courtesy. It was a side of
Mrs. Sproul which she had not seen before. But Ruth
had never before received forty-two dollars when Mrs.
Sproul was standing by.

It was nearly nine o'clock the same evening, when
George Withers, the minister of the Church of Life
Eternal in New York, came home, wilted and dusty
after his tramp, ride, sail, and tramp of the afternoon.
Harlem on the north, and Staten Island on the south,
had been the range of his pastoral beat of that day.
He had compassed some twenty miles, had wrought out
two or three of the romances of daily life one step
nearer to their *dénouement*, had buried an old man, had
baptized a child, had married two emigrants, and had just
now given his deposition in a matter where his testimony
was needed in Australia. He had now washed himself,
and put on a white jacket; and his daughter Annie had
persuaded him to let her bring his tea into the study where
she was sure it was a little cooler. The large window gave
access to a narrow piazza; and the odor of the grape-
blossoms came in as they sat. Withers sipped his tea;
and Annie sat at his feet on a little cushion as he told
her the story of the day. Just then the door-bell rang.

"No rest for the wicked," groaned Withers. But
Annie started to her feet. "Dear papa, you shall
not move a step. Rest for the wicked, indeed? How
do you know it is not the gas-man or the census-man?
I understand them both a great deal better than you
do."

But, alas! Christine brought up a card. "Mr. Oscar
Esmark."

"Who in the world is Oscar Esmark, Annie?"

"Oscar Esmark, — why don't you remember? he is
that young Swede, no, Norwegian, who is in the Bible-
class. He came to our reception in April. Don't you

go near him, papa: you sit here. I will see Mr.
Esmark."

"He was very particular," said Christine; and then,
catching Annie's warning eye, she stopped abruptly.

"Well, Christine, particular about what?"

Christine could blunder, but could not lie, in her
young mistress's service, and was obliged to confess
that the gentleman was very particular that it was Dr.
Withers he wished to see.

"My dear child, he wants to ' ask papa.' "

"Nonsense, my dear father! listen to reason: you
are tired to death. Do you wish your murder to be on
this young man's conscience? 'Executed yesterday,
at the tombs, the young Norwegian who took the life
of Dr. Withers — by untimely boring.' Do you wish
anything so hard as that for a young man you never
heard of till now?"

"My dear girl, listen to reason. He has come for
some purpose. Maybe he wants to be married. Maybe
it is an occasion not so sad, — perhaps the funeral of a
child and her mother. Anyway, he wants to see me;
and I choose to see him."

"Papa, you are more unreasonable every day. I
shall see him myself, and tell him you are very ill, and
that he must call to-morrow, at nine."

"To-morrow at nine I shall be at the meeting of the
Hospital Directors. Seriously, dear child, this may be
life and death. If I did not mean to see the man, I
should have said so twenty-seven years ago, before I
was ordained, and should have taken to sign-painting
instead of preaching. Christine, show Mr. Esmark up
stairs."

And in a moment Oscar entered. If, as he waited
down stairs, he had felt himself a little embarrassed
about the counsel he was to ask of Dr. Withers, all the
more was he embarrassed when he found that he was
to ask it in the presence of Miss Annie Withers, to
whom he had been formally presented, and whose face
he remembered perfectly. Was there, perhaps, the
least shade of discomfiture as he sat down? Anyway,

George Withers, with a fine instinct, asked in a moment if Oscar wished to see him alone; and Annie started as if to retire.

"Not at all," said Oscar bravely. "Pray do not leave us, Miss Withers;" for the instant had been enough to bring to him one of Jasper's favorite mottoes, — "Tell what you have to say." On this text Jasper would learnedly descant. "If you started your true nominative," he said, "and compelled it tyrannically to govern its verb, you could say anything you wanted to." When people told Jasper that they knew what they meant, but could not express themselves, he was generally incredulous, and turned upon his heel. "Had not you better start with a nominative case?" he would say.

So Oscar, with all his real embarrassment, would not let Miss Annie Withers retire.

"There is a young lady in town, Dr. Withers, whom I knew when she was a school-mistress at the West. She is a good teacher, and a spirited, brave girl. She has drifted to New York, by mistake, I think, and is all alone here. She is staying at a boarding-house in Varick Street, which seems to me a bad place for her; but I am a stranger here, and I hardly know what to recommend myself. I am also very much a stranger to her" (and the young fellow blushed here, but pulled on bravely); "but I knew if you would advise her what to do, the advice would be right; and I knew she would very gladly take advice from you."

Dr. Withers was all this time taking the measure of Mr. Oscar Esmark mentally; and all this time the measure was more favorable and more. Oscar made no apologies, he knew the value of time. He made no unnecessary explanations. He got his subject in early in the conversation. He conquered his own bashfulness. He explained why he could not do himself that which he asked another to do. So, by the end of Oscar's little speech, Dr. Withers's heart had warmed to him, while his judgment had pronounced the young man one

19

of the most sensible people he had seen for a long time.

"Thank you, Mr. Esmond," said the doctor, whose pencil and note-book were in his hand. "Where shall I find her?"

"Oh!" said Oscar, "it is too far for you: she shall come here, or I will. Or if you are willing to introduce her, on my introduction, in any quiet place where it will not be too expensive for her, why a note from you will answer."

"I had better see her, Mr. Esmond: she will feel more at ease, and I shall understand better. Is she comfortably lodged to-night?"

Oscar explained that Miss Cottam wished to make no change of quarters till the next day. Annie Withers proposed that she should call on Miss Cottam; but to this both gentlemen demurred. "Ask Miss Cottam to call here, Mr. Esmond; perhaps she will lunch with us at one. Annie, has not Mrs. Alden room for Miss Cottam? A good many of her people must be out of town."

Annie thought so, felt sure, would write a note, and was at her desk at the moment. Oscar was on his feet to go.

"No, Mr. Esmond, let Christine bring you a cup of tea while Annie writes. You do not come to see me so often that you should hurry away."

Oscar said very frankly that he had taken too much time already.

"Not a bit of it, my dear young friend. You have done the right thing. What is the Church of Christ for, or its ministers? Now tell me about Norway, Mr. Esmond. Were you at the university?"

Oscar laughed. He had never been at any university. He was a carriage-builder, or hoped to be.

"Ah, well! I hope you will not make us ride in Norwegian carriages. It is five years since I was in Norway; and a very happy summer I spent there." And then he made Oscar feel quite at ease, and delighted him entirely by telling him of a charming interview he had with Bishop Tegner.

But the note was written. It was before the days of a reliable penny-post; and Annie Withers intrusted it to Mr. Esmark's own hand. She emphasized the last syllable of his name in the hope that her father might condescend once to call the young man rightly. And he did.

"Good-evening, Mr. Esmark. To-morrow, at one, if you please."

And Oscar retired.

"You see, Annie, the whole enterprise would have failed had I sent him away till to-morrow."

Oscar Esmark had thus, in six and a quarter minutes, won for himself, and, as it afterwards proved, for Ruth Cottam, the firm and lasting regard of one of the most accomplished men, and one of the most lovely women, in the world. He did this simply by beginning at the beginning of his story, and by going away the moment he was done. Annie Withers always remembered him afterwards as the young man who saved her father's life. Dr. Withers himself remembered him as a frank, straightforward fellow, who knew what he was about, and was true to a friend. Had Oscar staid half an hour more, merely because he found himself with two agreeable people, I cannot say what that jaded man and that anxious daughter might have thought him or called him.

And where was Mr. Jasper Rising all this time? Why did not Oscar consult with his natural patron and adviser?

CHAPTER XXVII.

YOU ARE TRYING TO SPARE ME.

JASPER RISING had been at New Altona, watching with intense interest the fortunes of "The New Altona Gazette" in that regeneration which he was supervising. The regeneration of a man or a woman is an experience over which angels weep. Lacon says, indeed, of saints newly converted, that they are like roads newly repaired. It is to be hoped that there may be an ultimate improvement; but, at the moment of repair, the traveller is apt to think that he preferred the old road to the new. This is but a cynical statement; but it marks a danger observable in all regeneration. Now, the regeneration of a newspaper is a hundred-fold more delicate and difficult than the regeneration of a man; for it probably involves the regeneration, or renewal in some form of life, of one or two hundred men, all of whom have to do something they had failed to do before. Jasper Rising had to flatter one, to coax another, to bribe another, to convince another, of these two hundred people more or less, in the hope to make "The New Altona Gazette" a journal as wakeful as he found it sleepy. Nor was his work all in vain. All parties in New Altona, and on the steamboat and railroad routes which connect with that flourishing town, found out that "The New Altona Gazette" was terribly in earnest. Each day's issue gave a fillip to the nerves of the people of New Altona, as if their ulnar nerves had been hit suddenly.

In a month of this work, that is to say in a month of teaching bricklayers how to lay brick, stove-men how to lay flues, engine-builders how to set up their

steam-engines, firemen how to make fires, and "engineers" how to make steam; a month of persuading
pressmen that they could live, even if they worked from
two to four in the morning, while they had been wont
to work from seven to nine in the evening; a month of
explaining to reporters that they were not to have opinions, but eyes and ears and pens; and of hinting to
visitors that the reason there was but one chair in the
editor's room was that nobody but the editor was to
sit down there; a month of cutting off worthless ex-
changes, of cutting down a gigantic free-list, of offend-
ing some old supporters of "The Gazette," and con-
ciliating a great many enemies of that journal, — in
this month's time, Jasper had found time and opportunity to write seven long letters to Bertha Schwarz.
And they were skilfully worded, these letters: they
made it necessary that Miss Schwarz should write at
least six letters to him. Jasper's were long letters, —
as long as could be handsomely written on the one
quarto sheet allowable under the postage of that day.
Bertha's were not so long; but they were nice letters,
— letters which made the young man very happy to
receive, and which, in the simplicity and sometimes
quaint prettiness of their expression, were very well
worth being read over and over, and kept in the pretty
letter-case which Bertha herself embroidered for him
when they were all in the Cholera Hospital together.
Life was made just endurable to Jasper Rising by these
letters, almost unendurable though the time was when
he was waiting for one of them, and wondering if it
would come. At the last, after four weeks of such endurable and unendurable life, he persuaded himself that
the new steam-engine would run for forty-eight hours,
even if he did not poke the fire; that the carriers he
had started on new routes would not carry to Belleville
the papers that were meant for Flirt-town; that Mr.
Polk would not veto the internal improvement bill before the week was over: and so he sent for Mr. Schaffer
the foreman, as the morning edition went to press, and
told him he had important business in Boston, and

should not be back till Saturday. Then he took his
scrip or carpet-bag to the station, and waited for the
passage of the night-train. The train was on time ; and
it flew along, compassing fifty miles with every hundred
minutes as the dawn crept up the sky : but to Jasper
it seemed to crawl. The mood came over him which
made him feel as if he should never arrive anywhere.
Sleeping and waking, trying to read, or trying to talk,
it was all the same. For Jasper was, and knew he
was, on the edge of the catastrophe, or crisis, of his
life. He was determined, as he had been once before,
in a great resolution. Once before he had been foiled
before the moment of crisis came ; and now he might be
so foiled again. Such is the reason, I suppose, why
the rapid rush before one comes to Niagara seems sometimes so deadly slow.

But time was with Jasper ; and at five that afternoon
he was in Boston. An hour more, and he left the
American House, and found his way to the little four-
roomed half-house which he knew so well.

Yes, even to Jasper, there could be no doubt Bertha
was glad to see him. There could be no doubt that
Mr. Schwarz remembered him, almost as soon as he
saw him. Even shy Mrs. Schwarz asked him to join
them at tea ; and Jasper was not discouraged by his
reception.

This was the same sultry day in June in which Ruth
had been trudging round in New York with " Flora
Mac Ivor " and " Rose Bradwardine " and " Mary
Queen of Scots," till she took in that hatred of their
names which she has never since got rid of. This was
the evening when the old cat saw the forty-two dollars
counted over, and when Annie Withers gave her father
the cup of tea. " On such a night as that " it was perfectly true, as Jasper said to Bertha, that it would be
cooler walking on the Common than it was in the little
parlor of Mrs. Schwarz's house, where his neighbor Carl
Blum had come in to play the flute in accompaniment
to Schwarz's violin. " On such a night as that," the
new moon, but three days old, was reflected in the bay

below Fox Hill: that bay had not yet been covered with buildings. "On such a night as that," as the moonlight trickled through the branches upon the paths, Jasper and Bertha walked slowly down the "upper mall," and Jasper said to her, —

" I want to say what I wanted to say a year ago to you, and ought to have said then. I want to say, that unless I can somehow persuade you to share my life, and let me share yours, life will be terribly hard to me to bear : indeed, it will not be worth living. Indeed, Miss Bertha, I can say that now as I could not say it then ; for I have tried it during this wretched winter, and I know " —

Then he paused a minute ; and Bertha said nothing.

" I wanted to say this," he went on, "that day when we were by the river, with Oscar. But everything was so lovely there, that I could not bear to have you say ' No ' to me. Still, the next morning, I did not dare let the day go by without saying this ; and then that dismal letter came ; and I — O Bertha ! I was such a fool that I thought I must not tell you anything because you were an heiress.

" Was not I glad, when I heard that the cousins in Australia had appeared?"

And Bertha still said nothing. They walked a hundred paces, and she said nothing. And Jasper fairly trembled in his terror. But he forced himself to say, —

" You are trying to spare me great pain."

" No, no," she faltered ; " but, Jasper, why did not you speak then?"

CHAPTER XXVIII.

THE LAST SUMMER.

AND so that vista between the elm-trees, with the glimpse of the water under the moonlight, and the long row of lamps beyond, has been to Bertha and to Jasper for twenty years, and more, the most exquisite prospect on earth — or shall I say in heaven? since there, for them, there came into the kingdom of their heaven a reality so exquisite and so sure. For my part, I never walk down that beautiful avenue without other memories, of the days when I panted between the thills of a boy's " truck," dragging behind me one or another of the two boys who knew the secrets of that avenue. Or they drew me. Or, spurning the " truck," we drove our high hoops — mine was named Lightfoot — at the speed of 5.30 down the hill. Or we lay panting on the bit of turf which some sentimental workman had cut in the shape of a heart, and which no one living now remembers, except me ; for neither of those two companions will ever tell the secrets of the Upper Mall or of the Charles-street Mall to any one on this earth now. But Jasper and Bertha were not Boston born or bred. They drove their childish hoops by the river-side in Lauenburg, or by that at Duquesne : it was only here that they began to drive them together. And so, as I say, the elms, the Gothic arch between them, the memory of the water which is now gone, and the silver of the constant moon, which shone last night on other lovers there, as it shone then on them, — these make for these two the centre of their kingdom of heaven.

You see, there was everything to tell. Jasper had

to answer Bertha's question, and tell why he did not
speak then. Bertha had to tell, not simply of carnal
things of the moment when it became sure that their
sudden riches had taken wings and were gone, but of
things much more important and much more lasting.
She had to answer Jasper's cross-questionings, and tell
whether she were glad or sorry that he wrote to her
when she was in Germany, whether she were glad or
sorry when she saw him in the boat in the harbor of
New York, — nay, whether she expected to see him,
and when and where. Then he had to explain to her
yet again, how, under that divine decree which had
steadily brought them together in ways so strange,
from the moment when he carried her poor lame
brother home, till now, it was she, and only she, who
now gave to him for life, that home and that work
which were just what he was made for, and just what
he had not dared to ask for. And both of them had to
laugh and wonder because it was so strange that she,
almost a Hamburg girl, should be tossed about the
world so long, to settle down in a new Altona. For
the real Altona in Germany is almost a part of the
real Hamburg, Lily ; and this seemed a queer bit of
predestination. So long had Bertha been tossed about
the world ! For, if you have all computed rightly, you
have seen that Bertha was by this time fully nineteen
years old, and well-nigh approaching twenty : by consequence she thought herself much older than she does
now, when a quarter-century more has gone by.

So it was — shall I confess it? — that it was after
eleven, it was nearly twelve, of that summer night,
when Jasper left Bertha at her father's house, and bade
dear misty Mr. Schwarz good-by at the door. Fortunately, Mr. Schwarz neither knew nor cared whether
it were ten at night, or four in the morning. So long
as the gaslight burned, so long could he give life to the
buried melodies in the heaps of time-stained music he
had brought from home with him, and so long was he
unconscious of time, and perfectly happy. Bertha

kissed him, told him it was time for them both to be in bed, and that was all.

But when Jasper called the next morning, as soon as it was decent to pretend that the family could have finished their breakfast, Bertha had told her mother and her father all that had happened. Dear Mrs. Schwarz, timid as always, was enough inspired by her love for Bertha, and her certainty that Bertha was always right, to break quite over bars and obstacles, and to talk with Jasper more volubly and heartily than she had ever done before. It was all in praise of her darling child; and her darling child had to go out of the room while the good mother ran on, and Jasper listened, well pleased. For the good-man of the house — in his dreamy way he told Jasper he might take his daughter, and make her happy. Jasper had not the slightest idea what would have happened in such an interview, had the father been a prosperous merchant in dry-goods, educated on slab benches in Vermont, and the mother a prosperous belle still remembering the triumphs of Ballston Spa. But none the less was he aware that there was a queer Old-World tang about the welcome that was given to him in the home where he was now to be a son; and none the less racy was it for its oddity.

Somehow it happened — he did not know how — that they were alone, he and Bertha, in the tiny dining-room. And somehow it happened — she did not know how — that she was sitting on his knee, and his arm was round her waist to keep her from falling. And so it happened, all circumstances being thus auspicious for the most careful and solid business conversations, that Jasper dashed right into the details of their married life. Bertha told him he thought it was just as if the minister were in the parlor, and her trunk were packed, and a carriage to be at the door in half an hour. And Jasper laughed, and told her, that, in fact and practice, it was just the same. Anyway, he must tell how she had allied herself to a young man who was only not a beggar; but he wanted her to understand,

so that her father and mother might understand, all
about "The New Altona Gazette" and his salary, and
his other prospects ; and what a very nice tenement
there was, quite separate from the rest of the house, in
I Street, near the corner of 17th, which they could
rent for only a hundred and twenty-five dollars, if he
applied for it at once : and would she be willing to let
him apply for it at once, and let him come on, — say
early in September, though August would be better,
and be married then, and go out to New Altona so
soon, and begin?   And Bertha laughed at this long
sentence as she had not laughed since the old Detroit
days, and told him this was the wildest nonsense in the
world, and that no such thing must be thought of.
And then she explained to him, very seriously indeed,
that because he had been pricing houses, and making
estimates, and getting himself ready generally, she had
not been doing any such thing, and that he must understand that she was all in a dream yet, and all taken
by surprise.   And so, somehow, they got talking about
the boat on the river at Detroit, and Oscar, and how
he lay asleep there on the shore, and what Jasper said
to Bertha then, and Bertha said to Jasper — Oh, dear
me !   I do not know what they did not talk about, till
there was a rattle at the door, — prolonged rather sus-
piciously, — and Bertha had just time to arrange herself decorously in a rocking-chair, and Wil. came
bounding in.   School was over, he said, and his
mother wanted to know what time they had better have
dinner.

School over !   Where could the morning have gone?
Worse than losing the whole morning, as you see
they had, was the wretched fact that Jasper must leave
for home, as he called it now, early the next morning.
Forty-eight hours, at the outside, was the longest
period for which Mr. Polk could be trusted to abstain
from a veto.   And if he should veto the bill, and New
Altona not know what to think of it, of course it would
be all up with the hopes of the tenement-house on the
corner of I Street and 17th Street.   Under these cir-

cumstances, the day not being at all warm, as they both voted, the wisest thing for thoughtful young people like them to do — seeing they had all the plans for future life to make in so few hours — seemed to be to walk up to the Common again, and see if there were not a good breeze there, and an unoccupied seat somewhere on the Upper Mall. And this they did. In their search they were successful, and, thanks to Park-street Church clock, were not much behind time when they came back to supper.

No dates were fixed in the remaining conferences of the day, if I except an understanding, not very formally made, that, of course, they would write to each other daily. But Jasper left with a determination, perfectly defined, to hire the I Street tenement; and hire it he did, and got the tenants out as soon as he could. Then he had the whole interior painted, — the doors in two colors, from a hint Oscar gave him. In fact, Oscar went up to New Altona, superintended the whole work, and did three-quarters of it with his own hands. Then Jasper went down to New York; had endless conferences with Aunt Mary, who proved an ally worthy of such crown of friendship as Orestes and Pylades won. And together they bought carpets, chairs, tables, and other belongings. Ask Mrs. Stowe and Mrs. Whitney to tell you how pretty they were, and how cheap they were at the same time. Loyal Aunt Mary! In the dog-days of August, she slaved round with Jasper from point to point, and they figured and cheapened and decided what Bertha would like best, and bought it. And Jasper flew back and forth to New Altona in second-class cars, and gave to New Altona its opinions on broad gauge and narrow gauge, on vaccination and hydrophobia and ventilation, just as if the most important subject in the world really were not, whether, in the long run, American Brussels at $1.30 were not cheaper, though it be so narrow, than three-ply at eighty-seven cents. By such loving help was the upper tenement at the corner of I Street and 17th Street fitted and furnished by the time the first of

September came. In a general way, Bertha had been consulted by letters about these things; but nobody told her how soon her advice was acted on when it came.

But, on the first of September, Jasper persuaded Dan L'Estrange, who was only too willing, to take the helm of "The New Altona Gazette" for a whole week. And Dan L'Estrange was sworn not to put her head to the wind in that time, nor in any way to be bumptious. He was to discuss domestic service, and the independence of the judiciary, and religious toleration, and the other safe subjects, and not to launch out into those forbidden themes, which, between ourselves, no man living understood as Jasper Rising — thought he did. Dan L'Estrange swore, and to his oath he held. And once more on the slow wings of the express-train Jasper sped to Boston. "Personal presence moves the world," as he had said two or three hundred times to Oscar, and perhaps seven times to the people of New Altona. And he found Bertha ten times as lovely, and as gentle, and as true, and as wise, and as simple, and as girlish, and as womanly, — ten times all he had remembered her, and all he had dreamed of her; he found her ten times dearer to him, and that he was ten times dearer to her, than ever before.

Lovely days at Nahant, with little picnics on the rocks, the children perfectly happy. Lovely days at Cambridge, where he showed her his old favorites, from folios down to Elzevirs, in the college library, and where they had their picnic under trees now long since cut down to make room for suburban cottages. One lovely day on the shore at Nantasket. One lovely day by Charles River. One lovely excursion as far as the waterfall in Malden. Children of the people, as they were all of them, they knew, as only the people know, how to live and to enjoy. And the week was one week more of heaven, if, as I suppose, heaven is all pure enjoyment, and faith unwavering, hope unflinching, and happy love.

In such days, and in the cool evenings after, which

sealed them, Jasper told Bertha that he had been sure
it would be wiser for him to be ready whenever she was
ready: so he had taken the house, and made ready the
rooms. Not that he would press her, dear girl, not for
a moment. He had waited, and he could wait, — seven
years, if she said so, or fourteen. He would never say
another word, but that the home was waiting, and the
door was open, whenever she chose to come.

And my dear Bertha! She had found that the summer was all broken. To say unsatisfactory would be
cruel, seeing she was at home, and not in Germany;
seeing she was happy, and not unhappy; seeing her
life was certain before her, and not a mist-wreath or a
dream. But she could settle to nothing, she could de-
termine on nothing, she could be nothing, while, —
while half of her being was there, and only the other
half was here. Bertha permitted herself to be persuaded, and wrote to dear Aunt Mary and Uncle Kaufmann that they might come to the wedding in the
middle of October. Nobody else would be asked. It
would be the simplest wedding that was ever heard of.
But they must come.

"Busiest season of the year," said Kaufmann Baum,
when dear Aunt Mary read him the letter. "But I
would not miss the wedding for a thousand dollars! I
liked that young fellow the first day I ever saw him.
Mary, I tell you what we will give them. You shall
go to Chickering's, and pick them out a nice piano.
Ah, me! do you remember her playing the Apollo
here?"

That same evening, Bertha and Jasper drew up to
the table with great forethought, much paper, two pen-
cils, and Waterman's catalogue of household goods, as
they did so often now. And this night they made out
the order for crockery, — what was absolutely necessary to begin upon. A pity that Miss Folger, who was
to be made Mrs. Hilliard, whose carriage Oscar was at
work upon on the hallowed and ever-to-be blessed summer evening in June, — a pity that she should not have
seen this list! It might have helped her in filling her

china closet. Here it is, Fanchon : here it is, Annie. Copy it, it may be of use to you some day.

It had been agreed between them that the table-service should be as simple as possible, and as cheap as possible, so that any money that could be saved should be spent, not in the elegancies of china, but in fine art more satisfactory. Jasper had sent, accordingly, to Wedgewood and Benvenuto for a price-list of the cheapest dinner-set which they could furnish. The list began, "One soup-tureen, round, eight inches, two dollars and a half." Jasper immediately checked this ; but Bertha stayed his hand. "Not at all," said she ; "all the soup we can eat, with Oscar's help, can be put in a large covered vegetable-dish, or at least in two."

Jasper then checked, "sauce-tureen, one dollar and a quarter." "Not at all," said Bertha. "You must be satisfied to have your sauce in a bowl."

Jasper then checked two "boats," thirty-seven cents each ; but Bertha scratched out his check, and so with "pickle" and "salad dish."

"You are the most extravagant boy," said she, "I ever" —

"Agreed to love, honor, and obey."

But Bertha permitted him to have two "plain pudding-dishes" at fifty cents each, two "vegetable-dishes" at fifty cents each, two "oval, covered," at one dollar, — "they will do for your soup," said she, — and one "round, covered."

Then she marked a third-size "dish" at eighty-eight cents, and a fifth-size at thirty-seven. She let him have six dinner-plates, six breakfast-plates, and three soup-plates ; and all these cost them a dollar and three-quarters. Then she gave him three cups and three saucers "with handles." There was a teapot and coffee-pot for sixty cents each, a sugar-bowl, cream-pot, and two other bowls, which came to a dollar and fifteen cents. The great extravagance of all was six plated teaspoons, "good," as they were marked by Wedgewood & Co., six table-spoons, also "good," six knives, and six forks. These extravagances alone cost eight dollars and one cent. And the various glass-ware cost four dollars. The mathematical reader will perceive, therefore, that the table outfit of these young people cost twenty-one dollars and eighty-six cents. At the very same moment, the new dining-set which Mr. Hilliard had sent to Miss Clarissa Folger, in preparation for their marriage, arrived at No. 571, 14th Street. The crate was opened down stairs ; and the butler carried up a few of the dishes for Miss Folger's inspection. "How pretty it is !" said she. "Mamma, see how pretty the dinner-set will be. Really, George's taste is exquisite. That will do, Michael : you can take them down."

This was all the fun Miss Folger got out of her Dresden dinner-set, for which Mr. Hilliard had paid eleven hundred and fifty dollars that morning.

"The very first winter," said Bertha, "I will paint them, piece by piece. There must be a dentist in New Altona, and he shall bake my painting with his teeth."

"With his teeth !" said Jasper, aghast.

"Child of mortality, he shall bake them in the little kiln in which he bakes molars and bicuspids. One has to be so scientific when one talks with these herren editors."

"You shall paint myrtles and roses on them."

"I shall paint no such thing. I shall paint the Rising crest and coat-of-arms, as 'The New Altona Herald's ' office shall instruct me."

CHAPTER XXIX.

MRS. MERRIAM'S.

A ND where was Oscar all this summer? "Have I not told you, dear children, that he went to New Altona, and painted the rooms there, doing more than half the work with his own hands? That was the way in which he spent the six-days' holiday which was granted to every son of Adam who earned his daily bread at Lowndes & Karrigan's.

"Do you want to know more? I will tell you, then, that, from the paint-shop, Oscar went into the leather-room; that he made himself a great favorite there with Mr. Cupplethwaite the foreman. He always made himself a favorite with everybody. He is a favorite of mine: that is the reason I call him dear Oscar so often. There, now, I have told you how Oscar Esmark spent eleven-fifteenths of his conscious hours through all this summer, — excepting Sundays. Sundays I suppose he went to church and heard Dr. Farley preach, or the ministers who 'exchanged' with him."

"Dear Mr. Hale, how can you be so provoking? You know perfectly well that we want to know about Oscar and Ruth. We do not care anything about the paint-shop or the leather-shop, or Mr. Coppergraves."

His name is not Coppergraves, dear Fanchon, and never was. His name was Cupplethwaite, as you would know if you listened more carefully. So you really want to know about Oscar and Ruth? That is curious. You want to know if Ruth Cottam came to love Oscar Esmark half as well as he came to love her. And if, when she met him in the church, or when he came to see her at Mrs. Alden's, her heart stopped beating, and

20

her brain stopped thinking, as his did, if by great good luck he saw her. Yes? Well, this is more important than the paint on Mr. Hilliard's carriage, or than the questions about the top to Mr. Stewart's droschky. It is as much more important as heaven is than earth. For this is an infinite question that you ask, and it belongs to the eternities.

Let us begin at the beginning.

The day after Ruth and Oscar walked up to Mrs. Sproul's together, and that old cat saw him count out forty-two dollars to the tired girl, Ruth met him at the little bookstore as they had appointed. And then he told her, with no little hesitation indeed, what he had to tell her, — that he had been asked to bring her to lunch at Dr. Withers's, and had said he would ask her to come. Ruth was frightened, but not so much taken aback as she would have been, had not her life been so very simple. Indeed, had it not been for "The Ladies' Monitor," and some other trash of that sort of which she had, alas! read too much, I am not sure that she would have been frightened at all. If dear old Parson Merwin at Manitowoc had known that there was a Norwegian girl who had just come to town, who wanted a home, he would have sent to her to come round to the parsonage in a minute; and she would have gone as soon as she was sent for. And Ruth would have regarded this invitation to lunch as just as simple as Parson Merwin's message, had she not read some stories about New-York life, and its etiquette, and its grandeurs, in the journals I have alluded to. The truth was, that the writers of these stories knew less of what they were writing of than Ruth Cottam did; but nobody had told her this, and it was no fault of hers that she did not know.

So Ruth did look at her walking-dress, and said frankly to Oscar, "I am hardly dressed to go visiting." But she added, with a thorough good humor, "if they wanted my clothes, they should have sent for them;" and asked Oscar anxiously if he should only go with her,

or if he could stay through the entertainment, which, to
both of them, loomed up as something rather awful.
Could he stay? Had he not lain awake an hour,
blessing the providence which gave him this certainty
of sitting with her at the same table? He had told
Mr. Lowndes that he should like to have "leave" for
the afternoon. They would have granted Oscar anything in that house, and "leave" was something that
Oscar had never asked before. Time was none too
long; and he and Bertha went to the appointment at
Dr. Withers's.

And a pretty thing it was to see Annie Withers and
Ruth Cottam together, — the simplicity of admirable
training, of great familiarity with society, and constant
intercourse with men and women, coming side by side
with the simplicity of the prairie, the log-cabin, and the
lonely island. Annie Withers could see at a glance
how pretty Ruth was, and Ruth saw at a glance how
gentle and tender Annie Withers was. Annie Withers
was perhaps six years older than Ruth in years; she
was a thousand years older in experience. She had ten
thousand ways therefore to make her feel at ease and at
home. She met her far more than half-way in entering
into acquaintanceship. She drew her out, even to tell
her experiences of travel and of lonely city life; and in
half an hour Annie told Ruth that she had thus been
learning things about New York and its ways, which
twenty years had never unfolded to her before. Without the least insincerity or flattery, she made this
stranger see that there were points in which experience
had given to her, in all her strangeness, the advantage;
and her sympathy was so tender, that Ruth knew that
they were friends.

And Dr. Withers, with that quick, nervous, penetrat-
ing way of his — he was watching Ruth while he
talked with Oscar, and again taking the measure of the
young man, and forming his judgment of the girl. Dr.
Withers at five and fifty was a good deal younger than
he had been at five and twenty. Such is one of
the pieces of good fortune of immortal beings; and so

it was, that with all that rare wealth of observation and experience, remembering what half the noblest men of his time had said to him personally, and remembering, as well, what the other half had written, Dr. Withers was, all the same, on a level in years, in quickness, in power to enjoy with Oscar; entered into his eagerness and anxiety, and learned from him, while he cautioned and advised him. And so was it, that with him, too, Oscar came very readily to be at ease and at home. This division of talk lasted for half an hour. Then, as they loitered at table, the doctor interrupted Annie bluntly, and said to Ruth that she must listen to him, made her laugh heartily at a droll story he told them all, and from that moment all four were at ease with each other. And so, in a little while, it came perfectly easy for all four to discuss plans and prospects, to propose this, to suggest that, as if they had known each other for years.

Of all which the result was, that Ruth did go to Mrs. Alden's for a day or two, as Annie Withers had suggested the night before, till she could honorably adjust her engagements with Schmidt and Pusgrabber, — a duty which a visit from Dr. Withers decidedly simplified. But, within a very few days, Mrs. Merriam, a lady who kept a pretty family school for twelve girls in Brooklyn, came over to see Ruth, talked with her — oh, a whole afternoon she talked with her — about teaching and books and schools in log-cabins, and then proposed to Ruth that she should go home with her and see how she would like to be pupil and teacher together, — to teach the little girls and learn with the bigger girls. Would she like it? Poor Ruth was wholly upset. The big tears came pouring out from her big eyes. It was the kingdom of heaven for her; yes, this was the kingdom of heaven again. Faith unswerving, hope unfaltering, and happy love, make that house also a place where the kingdom has come.

Nor was there bar nor ban there; but Mr. Esmark could come to see Miss Cottam when he would.

Oscar made his home also on the Brooklyn side, and

he did not fail to use his privilege. Summer was upon them. All the pupils, except two from the West-India Islands, went home. Ruth could not see why they left a place so wonderful in its changing beauty as Brooklyn Heights. For herself, she was at rest for the first time for many long weeks, and she was under the care of a loyal Christian woman. Ah, it was long since poor Ruth had known what it was to have a mother! The West-Indians, and this prairie-girl, and Mrs. Merriam made a strange company, — none the less charming because it was strange. In this company, on many a summer evening as they sat watching the sunset beyond the water, and on many a Sunday as they tried the various resources of a great city, Oscar was made welcome.

Thirteen-fifteenths of his waking time were given to Lowndes & Karrigan, and to the journeys which took him to their shop and back again. He did not dare to acknowledge, even to himself, that he longed to spend the remaining two-fifteenths at Mrs. Merriam's. But she was good, she was as young as ever, and she welcomed him always when he came. She made him useful to herself; and in ten thousand ways she did for Oscar what Jasper never could have done, nor any other man. And Oscar, — passionate as ever in his love for Jasper, eager to execute any commission which he received from New Altona, delighted, when he had that chance, to go to that New Sybaris, and paint rightly Bertha's new home, — still did not find the summer lonely or long. There were four weeks when Mrs. Merriam took all the girls with her to her father's home in a farm-house on the coast of Maine; which weeks Oscar found interminable. For the rest, the months were very short, and he was very happy.

When "the girls" did come back from Maine, at last, Oscar opened his heart to Mrs. Merriam. He did not call them "the girls;" but there is a tradition that Josephine Morland, that black-eyed, dashing chit from Jamaica, did say, "we four girls," when she was describing their sail through Merry Meeting Bay; and that she justified the count by declaring that Mrs.

Merriam was the youngest of the four. Oscar opened his heart to Mrs. Merriam. He talked to her as one might wish all boys would talk to their mothers; and she talked to him as it might be wished all mothers would talk to their boys. He told her how he had missed her through the four weeks; and he told her that to have Ruth away was wretchedness itself. He had fared very well, he said, before the day when Ruth came into the shop, though he thought of her every day, and prayed for her every night, long before that time. But to be with her as he was with her here, and then to have her go away, and to be terrified with thinking that some one man of the thousands whom she might see in travelling (seeing, of course, that she was the loveliest creature in the world) might want to take her for his own, and might take her for his own, — this to Oscar seemed most terrible. "Now tell me, my dear Mrs. Merriam, what I may do: what have I any right to do? I am nothing but an apprentice in a carriage-shop. I am well forward; I am earning now twelve dollars every week; and in the bank I have got something. Still I do not lie to myself, Mrs. Merriam. I am only an apprentice; and it will be two years before my contract with the firm is up, and before I am free of the world; so, if I were mad enough to think dear Ruth would care about me one speck more than about anybody else she was kind to, do you think I have any right to tell her that I love her with all my heart and soul, and to ask her to give me a chance to show her that I do?"

To show her, indeed! Dear Mrs. Merriam had had such confidences before now. She kept her countenance bravely. But, if Oscar had not been showing this to Ruth every hour since the day Ruth first came to this house, then nothing was ever shown by man to woman. Dear Mrs. Merriam, she did not laugh. She spoke to him as his mother might have done.

"Dear boy, do not mix up ten dollars a week, or ten thousand dollars a week, with what is priceless. What you offer Ruth is the priceless love of a man's heart;

and money has nothing to do with that. He is to say whether she will take it, and will give you in return the only return which can be given. For the rest, you are not old enough to marry her; and she is not old enough to marry you. If she is not willing to wait till you are old enough, she is not worthy of you. If you are not willing to wait, you are not worthy of her. If she is not willing to marry a journeyman carriage-builder whom she loves, she is not worth the having; and, in that case, you would be lucky if she said, No. If she does love you enough to wait till you can make a home for her, and then you are ever mean enough to forget that confidence of hers, — why, you are not the Oscar I take you for."

"Then I am to tell her" —

"You are to tell her the truth, — the only thing that is ever worth the telling."

The introduction here of this little interlude between Mrs. Merriam and Oscar must be pardoned by the reader. I know, only too well, that the history of this summer, whether for Oscar or for Ruth, for Bertha or for Jasper, cannot here be written. This story has now been told, if we are to bind ourselves by the promise in its second chapter ; for Jasper and Bertha henceforth are to rise on one wave when their fortune takes them up ; they are to sink in one gulf when the ship that bears them lurches down. The courses and the currents of life have at last brought them together, bound them together by the indissoluble tie, and with that bond this story is done.

October came at last. Even the kettle on the kitchen-fire, though it be filled with the coldest of water, and watched, though it be, by a surrounding circle of ten children eager for breakfast, — even this kettle, of all kettles, at last consents to boil. And, in like manner for Jasper, this summer, longest of all summers which ever ground by since the world hung on its axes, or moved in its orbit ; a summer in which from day to day he flashed or thundered or beamed, or distilled in dew, upon the publics of New Altona, of Belleville, or of Flirt-town, — even this summer, longest of all conceivable summers, at last ground by. The paint was dry and hard at the corner of I Street and 17th Street; the little store of earthenware was clean on the shelves; the stove was shining in its unused glory; the white window-shades, spotless, hung upon machinery, which, for the moment, would do what it was meant to do. Jasper confided to Mrs. Cordelier, his nearest friend in New Altona, that, if all went well, they should arrive on the evening of the 14th; and she pledged herself that the kettle should be on the stove, and the German girl in attendance, when the two arrived. And Jasper once more left the " New Altona Gazette " in the charge of his lieutenant *pro tem.* Congress had adjourned at last, and there was no fear of vetoes. And Jasper took the affirmation of Dan L'Estrange, that he would not commit the paper to free-trade, or Spiritualism, or any other heresy; that it should not say " commence" for " begin," nor " in our midst" for " among us," nor " we nibbed our pen," nor " we laughed in our sleeve." And, thus guarded, he started on the last lonely journey of his life. Once more two minutes to the mile seemed slow. But once more gib-keys held to their places, water volatilized at a temperature of 212° of Fahrenheit, as it always had done since Tubal-Cain put kettle upon fire. Once more the driving-wheels flew round as the expanding steam compelled them; and so once more, in face of Jasper's impatience, neither helped by it nor hindered, he arrived at the American House in Boston, at five in the afternoon, and was at Mr. Schwarz's before half-past five.

And the next evening, in the little German church which Mrs. Schwarz loved because it seemed to her a little like Lauenburg, Jasper and Bertha, Oscar and Ruth, Mr. and Mrs. Schwarz, Aunt Mary and Uncle Kaufmann, stood in the little chancel; and Mr. Fleischhauer married them in the dear old service of the dear old church. Jasper put a ring on Bertha's finger, and she put a ring on his. Jasper made his responses in

German ; and his memory ran back on the instant to the hot afternoon when he talked such bad college German to her in the train. And Bertha felt as if she and Jasper and the minister were the only three people in the world.

CONCLUSION.

No. The story is not quite done. The party all
went back to the little half-house, and there was a
merry evening there; for Jasper and Bertha were not
to take up their line of march until morning. Of Jasper's friends, Haliburton and Gilman were the only two
there. Both of them had come from far away to be
bridesmen at the wedding; and both of them were
already far gone in a loyal enthusiasm for Bertha,
whom they had never seen till that day, which binds
them and her together to this hour. Of bridesmaids
Ruth Cottam was one, pretty, shy, and very happy;
Bertha's sister was one; and the grown-up cousin who
came with Aunt Mary was one. A real fatherland
frolic was it all. Uncle Kaufmann led the revels, made
the speeches, sang the songs, kept every one on the
alert, and would not permit even Mrs. Schwarz to be
sad at the prospect of Bertha's departure.

Only Oscar, of the whole party, seemed ill at ease,
and anything but himself.

And what was the matter with Oscar? He had been
escort for Ruth on her journey to Boston. For three
days, he had been at Mr. Schwarz's house almost every
minute, and had seemed the gayest of the gay. Ruth
had not been unkind to him. If any two people in the
world understood each other, and were true to each
other, it was this boy and this girl. Oscar had been
all right till he came round with the carriages that were
to take them to the church. Then, in an instant, Ruth
saw that something was amiss. But she would not
ask, and she hoped no one else would notice it. Perhaps no one did notice, while the party were filling the

carriages, while they were at church, and as the merry company was crowding the little rooms. But then Jasper noticed, and Bertha noticed, that Oscar was not at ease. He showed it in forty ways; and Bertha and Jasper and Ruth all knew him too well, nay, loved him too well, not to be conscious that something had happened.

In the midst of a round of laughter which Kaufmann Baum had started by one of his droll German songs, Jasper passed into the little passage-way, and beckoned to Oscar, who, unlike himself, was standing in a corner, speaking to no one. Oscar caught the sign in a moment, and slid out of the room.

"Come up with me, Oscar: we can talk up stairs." And the young men ran up together into a little dressing-room, hardly bigger than a closet, where the gentlemen had left their hats and coats.

"What is the matter, Oscar?"

"Read this letter. No! — not read it now. Let me tell you first. I am all surprised."

And, when he was surprised, Oscar's English always showed marks of his discomposure. When he was quite at ease now, it was only marked by a slight accent. But with Jasper, of course, he could talk in his most familiar dialect.

"If I once thought, dear master, it was anything, I should have written to you. You know I should write if I thought. But I not thought. I write my letter to the man; and I forget the man, I forget the letter!"

"What letter, dear boy? What man?"

"Oh, yes! Let me tell! Last week, only last week, Monday, you know, Miss Ruth, — dear Miss Ruth! is she not just lovely this evening? — yes, dear Miss Ruth give me two books, you know, 'Martin Chuzzlewit,' for me carry back to Mercantile Library when I go up town next day. I must tell you. Yes, well, two books, I tell you; and she saw it rained when she came to door with me, — dear girl, she always comes to the door with me, — and, when she saw it rain, she ran back into dining-room, and brought out paper: this paper "— and Jasper produced a bit of an " Evening Post "—" was part of it; and she wrapped up the books and gave all to me."

" Yes, yes," said Jasper, not quite impatiently, but wishing he were with the revellers down stairs.

" Yes, yes, I know," said the boy. " I quick as ever I can, dear master : I must tell you all. I bid good-by; I took books; I go to Mercantile Library, and leave them ; and then of course, you know, I keep the paper, because dear Miss Ruth gave him to me. I would not, you know I would not, throw away what she gave to me."

" No," said Jasper, " I suppose not." He was think-ing on a little museum he had at home, of waifs and strays from Bertha.

" No, no ! I no such fool as that. I keep the paper here ; " and he pointed to his breast-pocket. " I go to shop, go to work ; come twelve o'clock, I eat my lunch, I read the paper ; come one o'clock, I fold up the paper, and on other page — see here ! See what I read ! "

And he held the folded paper to Jasper, who was interested by this time, and who read with some little difficulty in the dimly-lighted room this advertisement :

NORWAY.—Will the representatives of Michael Esmuck, late of Stav-anger, Norway, communicate with Williams & Rothe, attorneys at law, 299½ Madison Street, Chicago.

" Yes," said Jasper, " and you wrote ? "

" Yes, I wrote. I laughed ; but I wrote. I thought some old bill my father owed for clothes, for rent, for something : I glad to pay. I no mean to have my father's ghost owe any man."

" What did you say ? "

" I said my father's name was Michael Esmark, not Esmuck ; that he was from Stavanger in Norway ; and that no man named Esmuck ever lived in Stavanger, or in Norway. Then I said, if he owed any money, I would pay it. 'Send your bill,' I said."

"But you should not say that," said Jasper. "You'll have half the Jews in Illinois after you with bills."

"Time enough when they come," said Oscar. "No come now. This what come,—come to Lowndes & Karrigan : ' Mr. Oscar Esmark' (I teach them how to spell), ' care of Lowndes & Karrigan ;' and Mr. Karrigan has forwarded him to me." And the eager boy pushed the attorneys' letter into Jasper's hand.

It was a well-written lawyer's letter, as anybody who remembers Williams & Rothe will understand. It began by explaining to Mr. Esmark that the firm knew his name very well, having been looking for him for years, or for some one who bore the same surname. It' had only been by an oversight in the office of "The Evening Post," that this name had been printed Esmuck,—an oversight which, as he would find, had already been corrected ; and a copy of the Esmark advertisement was here wafered on the letter.

It went on to explain what reasons the firm had for seeking for Michael Esmark. It appeared from the records of registry of Cook County, that Michael Esmark had been at one time the purchaser of twenty acres, being one-eighth of a quarter section, in Cleaverville in that county ; and these records did not show that he had ever sold any part of the same. He appeared to have paid one tax on the property ; but, after that time, no trace of him or of his claim to it had been found. It was probable that he had sold it. If so, could Mr. Oscar Esmark inform Messrs. Williams & Rothe to whom he had sold it? If he had not sold it, would Mr. Oscar Esmark state what his intentions were regarding the property? For non-payment of taxes, one and another bit of it had been sold from time to time, and were now held by the purchasers under those sales ; but, as Mr. Oscar Esmark was doubtless aware, no title would hold under such purchases against the title of a minor who had not been properly advised of the tax or other lien on the estate. If Mr. Oscar Esmark desired to recover these parcels, as Messrs. Williams & Rothe supposed he would, in view of the present value of the property, they would be happy to communicate with him further. In any event, indeed, they would be happy to communicate with him; for the non-use of so large a tract immediately adjoining the city of Chicago — practically a part of it, indeed, as it would soon be really on the change of the city lines — was a serious inconvenience and injury to property-holders in the southern part of that city, many of whom were represented by Messrs. Williams & Rothe. At the instance of these property-holders, Messrs. Williams & Rothe had put the advertisements in the papers; one of which had fortunately attracted the attention of Mr. Oscar Esmark.

This was the substance of the letter.

"Do you remember?" said Oscar.

"Of course, I remember," said Jasper. "They are the swamp-lands I wrote about to those men at Michigan City. There was no attorney then in what is now Chicago. And you, my boy, own twenty acres of land in Southern Chicago. Why, there is many a prince in Germany who is not so fortunate. These lawyers are good fellows, too."

"You see," said Oscar, "I get the letter just now, — just as I come from American House with carriage. I would not speak then. Dear master, it is yours, — it is all yours. You say, 'I a prince.' I say, 'dear Miss Bertha a princess.'"

"Yes, my dear boy, dear Miss Bertha is a princess; but she is not a princess who shall wear borrowed feathers. The Princess of Cleaverville is a princess who has just now one white rosebud in her hair, — the same who gave to my Oscar the talisman which makes him a rich man. Oscar, dear boy, to-night's service has made us nearer than ever. Nothing could part us before; nothing can part us now. But from this night, Oscar, you will have to show whether a man of fortune — a man with a hundred thousand dollars to throw away — can live as pure, as honest, and as true as he has lived when he painted carriages, or filed on axles. I trust you, Oscar, I trust you; I was never afraid for you when you were in adversity, and I trust you quite as bravely now you are to be tempted by prosperity. But perhaps your hardest times are yet to come."

" No," said Oscar, " nothing is hard to me now. As I left the church to-night with dear Ruth, — I not call her Miss Ruth to her again, — I asked her — if I would be brave and honest and true for two years, five years, seven years, like Jacob — if she would let me call her mine.

" And she said to me, 'I am wholly yours now.'"

" And have you not told her that you have come into your fortune?"

" Dear master, the fortune is all yours."

THE END.

www.ingramcontent.com/pod-product-compliance
Lightning Source LLC
Chambersburg PA
CBHW060530030726
47498CB00004B/1138